AFTER THE END OF THE WORLD

ALSO BY JONATHAN L. HOWARD

THE LOVECRAFT SERIES
Carter & Lovecraft

THE JOHANNES CABAL SERIES
Johannes Cabal the Necromancer
Johannes Cabal the Detective
Johannes Cabal: The Fear Institute
The Brothers Cabal
The Fall of the House of Cabal

YOUNG ADULT NOVELS
Katya's World
Katya's War

AFTER THE END OF THE WORLD

JONATHAN L. HOWARD

Thomas Dunne Books
St. Martin's Press
New York

THOMAS DUNNE BOOKS.
An imprint of St. Martin's Press.

AFTER THE END OF THE WORLD. Copyright © 2017 by Jonathan L. Howard. All rights reserved. Printed in the United States of America. For information, address St. Martin's Press, 175 Fifth Avenue, New York, N.Y. 10010.

www.thomasdunnebooks.com
www.stmartins.com

Library of Congress Cataloging-in-Publication Data

Names: Howard, Jonathan L., author.
Title: After the end of the world / Jonathan L. Howard.
Description: First edition. | New York : Thomas Dunne Books/
  St. Martin's Press, [2017]
Identifiers: LCCN 2017025195 | ISBN 978-1-250-06090-7 (hardcover) |
  ISBN 978-1-4668-6666-9 (ebook)
Subjects: LCSH: Conspiracies—Fiction. | GSAFD: Alternative
  histories (Fiction) | Fantasy fiction. | Dystopias.
Classification: LCC PR6108.O928 A69 2017 | DDC 823/.92—dc23
LC record available at https://lccn.loc.gov/2017025195

Our books may be purchased in bulk for promotional, educational, or business use. Please contact your local bookseller or the Macmillan Corporate and Premium Sales Department at 1-800-221-7945, extension 5442, or by email at MacmillanSpecialMarkets@macmillan.com.

First Edition: November 2017

10 9 8 7 6 5 4 3 2 1

In memory of my mother, Enid Margaret Howard, 1929–2016.

She gave me life, and saved
it on more than one occasion.

CONTENTS

CONTENTS

AFTER THE END OF THE WORLD

Chapter I

UNTERNEHMEN SONNENUNTERGANG

Joe Stalin was never happier than on the day he died.

Friedrich-Werner Graf von der Schulenburg was suspicious of the Soviet leader's joviality that afternoon, just as he was suspicious as to the speed and ease with which the meeting with Stalin and all the rest of the 18th Politburo was agreed to and organized. He felt very sure they knew why he had requested it. It seemed likely that the Führer wanted Stalin to be in no doubt as to the very unexpected visit of Foreign Minister Ribbentrop to Moscow; why else would Schulenburg have been informed by telephone rather than an enciphered telegram? He had no doubt that the line was less than secure; indeed, it would be astonishing if agents of the NKVD or NKGB or whatever they were calling themselves that week were *not* listening in on every call made to or from the German embassy. From there to Stalin's ear via the secret service chief. That must really have made Merkulov's day, vicious dog that he was, and always eager for his master's favor.

But then, it was momentous news by any stretch of the imagination. Schulenburg had been getting a distinct sense of hostility from his government toward the Soviets, an offhandedness from the Foreign Ministry with respect to his own efforts to foster good relations. For six years he had tried to encourage the Führer to see past dogma and into the very real advantages of an alliance in the East. Stalin could see them easily enough; it was always the NSDAP's ideological distrust—loathing, almost—of Bolshevism that proved the obstacle. Briefly, Schulenburg had entertained hopes that pragmatism was prevailing in Berlin as rumors of offering a place in the Axis to the USSR grew, a logical extension to the pact settled by Ribbentrop and his Soviet counterpart Molotov. Such hopes had guttered and failed some time before, however, and Schulenburg had feared his last official act in Moscow would be to deliver a declaration of war to Molotov's desk.

Then, the telephone call. The wonderful, unexpected telephone call.

In the space of twenty minutes, Ribbentrop had tersely laid out to Schulenburg how the Führer had weighed up the situation in Eastern Europe and decided the only sensible solution was to bring the Soviet Union into the Axis, how Ribbentrop would shortly be flying to Moscow to present the offer himself, and details as to how Schulenburg was to prepare the ground. If all went to plan, an agreement could be ironed out very quickly, and then it was merely a case of arranging the signing; Goebbels would lead on that to liaise with the Soviet education authority, education and propaganda being interchangeable there. It would be a grand event, no doubt. Bands, photographers, pretty girls handing over bouquets of flowers. So much smiling.

Schulenburg was smiling. He was chatting with Molotov in the grandiose meeting room that Stalin had decided would be best suited to greeting Ribbentrop. He and the other members of the Politburo were sitting or standing in ragged groups—candidate members, underlings . . . it had become a little party, and the drink was flowing. In a pause in the conversation, Schulenburg looked at the scene before him and, unaccountably, shuddered. There was something wrong here, he was sure. He had a nebulous presentiment that refused to come into any real focus, a feeling that all was not quite how it seemed. It was a curious and unpleasant experience, a form of *déjà vu* in which one has not merely been through the present moment before, but . . . last time it was different.

Molotov was looking at him curiously. "Are you all right, my friend?" he asked.

Schulenburg looked at Molotov and realized that, to an extent, they really were friends. They had spent many hours discussing relations between their great states and discovered many commonalities in their personalities and interests. Schulenburg understood with a small shock that there was a kind regard between them, a mutual respect, even a fondness.

The presentiment niggled at him, telling him that—in all worlds—that friendship was doomed. "The time is out of joint," he said quietly to himself.

"What was that?"

Schulenburg shook his head and smiled, embarrassed. "*Ach*, just a line from Shakespeare. 'The time is out of joint.' Hamlet says it when he is thinking of the current state of affairs in Denmark. How things are not right, but may be repaired." He raised his glass and saluted Molotov with it. "May today's meeting mark the beginning of that healing and presage a golden age between my Fatherland and your Motherland."

As Molotov raised his own glass, an attaché appeared at Schulenburg's elbow. "Excellency," he whispered, "a telephone call for you. From Berlin."

"Here?" Perhaps they really did not care about confidentiality at all. They might as well transmit the conversation in clear Russian over the airwaves as expect a borrowed line in the Kremlin to be secure.

Making his excuses, he made his way to the small office that the Soviets had put aside for his use. As he'd left the meeting room, he'd seen Merkulov lifting a telephone receiver, no doubt to tell his eavesdroppers to be ready. Schulenburg pursed his lips as he picked up the handset in the office. Very well. He would have an unseen audience.

"Schulenburg."

"A moment, please."

As he waited to be connected, he briefly wondered what might be so important. Perhaps the deal was off. It had seemed too good to be true, after all. It would hardly be the first time the Führer had changed his mind as peremptorily as he had made it. He hoped that wasn't the case this time; quite apart from souring an already problematical relationship, it would be left to him to go back to the meeting room and tell Stalin and his cronies the bad news. Even a diplomat has his limits.

"Schulenburg? This is Wilhelm Ohnesorge."

Schulenburg frowned. Why was the state secretary speaking to him? One of the Führer's inner circle to be sure, but nothing to do with foreign policy. He racked his memory: Ohnesorge was responsible for the Reichspost, too; something to do with radio propaganda; some other technical interests. There was no denying that the man was a polymath, but Schulenburg could only assume he was involved with the matter at hand by dint of his friendship with the Führer. That, he supposed, should please him. Everyone wanted to be part of what was coming.

"Is everyone assembled?"

"I beg your pardon?"

"Herr Stalin and his . . . and the Politburo—are they all in attendance?"

"Yes, Minister."

"Excellent." Even over the telephone wire, Ohnesorge's nervous excitement was plain. The ambient sound over the line became muddied for a moment, as if a hand had been placed over the mouthpiece. Then Ohnesorge's voice returned clearly. "Excellent. The aeroplane . . . Ribbentrop is aboard the Führer's personal aircraft. Apparently there were some hydraulics problems and he is about fifteen minutes behind schedule. The Condor will be arriving at Khodynka Aerodrome shortly."

Schulenburg had organized the landing clearance at the nearest airfield himself through Molotov's offices, but he knew it would not be diplomatic of him to point that out, so he only said, "Yes, Minister. Everything is in place." The detail that Ribbentrop was traveling in the Führer's personal aircraft, however—the beautifully appointed Condor Fw 200 V3, designated D-2600—was new to him. They really were pulling out every stop in order to impress the Soviets.

"This is very exciting, very exciting." Ohnesorge seemed to be talking to himself. Then he said more clearly, "I have somebody who wishes to speak to you. Hold a moment, please."

Schulenburg heard a click on the line; it could have been the sound of being transferred to another telephone, or the sound of an incautious NKVD eavesdropper making his presence known. Each was equally likely.

"Schulenburg?" The voice on the telephone broke into his reverie, and momentarily startled him. That voice . . . surely not? "I wanted to speak to you personally today, Friedrich. Today, everything will change for the better, and it could not have happened without you." There was a pause, but Schulenburg knew it to be a rhetorical one. It was just as well; he had no idea what to say. "The hand of history is upon your shoulder. Can you feel it? For Germany, and for the Soviet Union, nothing will ever be the same again. I wanted to speak to you now, to thank you for all you have done. I truly do not believe this could have happened without your abilities and your excellent working relationship with Foreign Minister Molotov. The German people will honor your name throughout the coming ages."

Another pause. Schulenburg was not so sure that this one was rhetorical, but he found it difficult to speak all the same. The Führer's emotion was clear. Any lingering doubt that he had in Hitler's dedication to an alliance with the USSR was dispelled.

"Thank you, my leader," he said, fighting to control the emotion in his own voice.

"You will always be remembered."

The line went dead.

Schulenburg took a moment to steady himself. Then, filled with a confidence born of certainty, he left the office to return to the meeting. He had no doubt Merkulov would be smirking, but that didn't matter. Finally the German people would be able to turn their undivided attention to the war in the West, to affirming ties to the Japanese in the Far East, and perhaps giving more thought to the United States, dithering on the sidelines in a posture of old-maid-like isolationism. Good. With the Axis made unassailable by the addition of Soviet forces, the Americans could stay like that forever, and do so with his blessing.

At 20:14 local time, and barely an hour of sunlight left, a Focke-Wulf Condor bearing the name "Immelmann III" and the registration D-2600 approached Khodynka Aerodrome, a civilian airport less than five miles to the northwest of Red Square. All other traffic had been redirected by the Soviet authorities, and a fast car with a good driver was awaiting the Condor's landing to rush the distinguished visitor aboard directly to the Kremlin as quickly as was safely possible in the company of a senior *apparatchik* of Molotov's ministry. The Germans had insisted that no formal welcome beyond that was necessary—only that SS-Obergruppenführer Ribbentrop be taken to meet Comrade Stalin with all reasonable dispatch.

Things will always tend to go wrong when pressure is at its greatest, however, and the flight director at Khodynka was deeply relieved when the trouble turned out to be outside his control or responsibilities. D-2600 radioed the tower to ask for visual confirmation that its tail wheel had deployed correctly. Binoculars were raised to watch the aircraft as it performed a flyby; no, the rear wheel was not down and locked although the main port and starboard wheels had done so correctly.

The Luftwaffe pilot sounded pained rather than worried. "It's not my aeroplane," he told the tower. "I don't really want to upset the owner by scratching the paintwork."

This was received gleefully by the flight director and his staff, who had already identified exactly whose aeroplane it was.

"I think there's a kink in the hydraulics," the pilot reported. "I'll fly around for a few minutes and see if it sorts itself out. I don't want a bumpy landing."

Khodynka cleared D-2600 for five minutes of orbiting in an attempt to clear the problem even as the political officer was putting in a call to the Kremlin to inform his superiors of the delay and its root in inferior capitalist engineering.

Oberleutnant Hugo Trettner felt no emotion as he closed the radio link and settled himself down for a very short flight. He was a dead man in any case, and had become reconciled to the closeness of his final moment for some time. There had been the usual stages of disbelief, denial, and so forth when the specialist that the *Gruppe* medical officer had sent him to had confirmed he had cancer. Inoperable, terminal cancer. He would feel fine for a few more months, and then his strength would leave him, and the pain would start. The doctor offered his sympathies, but that was all he could offer. There was no hope, and the doctor considered it a cruelty to even suggest it.

Trettner had expected to be cashiered out of the air force—a bomber pilot with little life expectancy and who knows his time is short cannot be considered an asset in most situations—and that was how things had gone for a while. But then the Oberst had come visiting and told him that, while his death was a certainty, the manner of it was still in his hands. There was a mission, the Oberst told him in great confidentiality.

Unternehmen Sonnenuntergang.

Even the Oberst hadn't been briefed on exactly what it

involved, only that it required a good pilot used to larger aircraft, and that he be entirely expendable. The Oberst did not use exactly those words, but that was the gist of them, and he had the grace to look embarrassed as he said them.

"It is of the utmost secrecy and importance. That is all I can tell you."

It was all he needed to; the Fatherland might expect its children to shed their blood for it, but it would only ask for a volunteer for certain suicide under the most extraordinary of circumstances. Trettner did not ask for time to think. He agreed then and there.

It took another two months before everything was in place, two months during which he fretted and worried that the cancer might accelerate and make him too ill to fly before things were ready. He was certain they would have other volunteers, but feared they might be able-bodied. Better him than they. Every day he was examined, and every day the illness progressed as predicted. He would be at Death's door in six months if left alone, but Oberleutnant Trettner planned to call upon Death long before that, in his own time, by his own terms.

The Condor he flew was not Hitler's personal aircraft, simply a similar one that had been repainted and numbered to mimic it. The interior was not at all luxurious, bare metal and struts where the real D-2600 was the epitome of comfort. It would have been an unpleasant journey for his passengers, *if* he had been carrying any. Trettner, however, was the only soul aboard.

In the main body of the Condor that the Soviets believed was stuffed with Ribbentrop and a coterie of diplomats, functionaries, and bootlickers, there was only the thing that the Reich had been at such pains to hide from all its enemies, its rivals, and even its friends. The thing that would change all.

Schulenburg was at the window. The word had just come in that the Condor was suffering some minor mechanical problem and was trying to clear it before landing. He saw the unmistakable lines of the aircraft, the low sun illuminating it in fiery orange. Molotov joined him at the window and they looked at the approaching aircraft together.

Schulenburg pointed at it. "That's Ribbentrop."

Moscow was outlined in fire, the setting sun blazing the buildings in orange and deep shadow. Trettner had exhaustively examined maps and models of the city until he felt sure he could have found its heart if he had parachuted into it blindfolded. Its geography held no mysteries to him now; he knew exactly where he had to be.

And now here was Red Square. Still feeling no fear, no regrets, and wondering how that could be, Hugo Trettner lifted the cover from the button mounted by him, flicked the arming switches as he had been shown, and—almost exactly two hundred meters above the onion domes of the Kremlin—he triggered the great gray steel sphere that everyone in the know described as "the device."

At 20:19 local time on the twenty-first of June, 1941, the world entered the atomic age with the airburst detonation of a weapon yielding a blast equivalent to twenty kilotons over the center of Moscow. The fireball touched the earth, vaporizing the Kremlin to do so. Schulenburg, Molotov, Stalin, and the rest of the Politburo ceased to exist faster than the mind can process a thought. The violently superheated air snapped outward, causing an overpressure wave to propagate at twenty pounds per square inch upward. Glass splintered, the fragments traveling like bullets. Stone shattered. Concrete ruptured. Any human caught in it stood next to no chance of survival. After all, if the pressure didn't kill them, the fierce pulse of radiation that accompanied it surely would.

Five hundred rem of radiation bathed the area out to perhaps a mile, enforced by a million, million tiny motes of uranium borne away from the casing of the device. The scientists who had built it had known this would happen, and, indeed, had been ordered to make it happen. It wasn't enough that the heart of Moscow be cut out, but the land must be salted in the newest, most modern way to make it a wasteland for years to come.

The pressure wave carried on outward, carrying the killing dust, still powerful enough to bring down buildings a mile and a half from the detonation site, crushing, burning, and poisoning any Muscovites there. Even where the pressure dropped to merely a howling gale, it carried a heat that would cause third-degree burns to anyone it touched.

An estimated forty thousand died in the initial detonation with three times that many injured. The death toll had barely begun to climb.

No one understood what had happened. The German visit was known only to a few, and most of them died in the explosion. The only ones who might have been able to give a reasonable clue that D-2600 had somehow exploded like a small star and decapitated the Soviet Union in a burning moment were the flight direction staff at Khodynka Aerodrome, and they had no opportunity to talk to anyone who mattered before it all became far too late. As the country flailed without comprehension or leadership, in the West the massive armed force assembled by the Third Reich for Operation Barbarossa started to pour eastward. With the 18th Politburo eradicated to a man, any likely successors were already dead thanks to Stalin's murderous paranoia, and the Russian people terrified into hopeless dismay by the inexplicable events and rumors of what had occurred and might happen again, the defense of the country was sporadic and feeble.

Years, decades, generations later, the newsreels survive. Heroic Wehrmacht troops streaming across undefended kilometers of Russian countryside, while unopposed Messerschmitt Bf 109s of the Luftwaffe soar overhead to hunt and strafe isolated pockets of the Red Army. Leningrad, fallen. Stalingrad, fallen. The

Ukraine, the Baltic states, falling one after another under German control.

The human cost was hidden from the watching world. The inhuman cost was hidden from almost everyone.

Chapter 2

THE UNFOLDED WORLD

The flags snapped and flickered in the stiff breeze coming in from the Atlantic. There were many flags, each with their own poles, ranged across the ornamental lawns before the hulking assembly building, muscular and massive in red stone. These were not the flags of every nation, but the vast majority. Daniel Carter and Emily Lovecraft sat upon a bench, eating an *al fresco* lunch, and never quite able to stop staring at one flag in particular.

Lovecraft took a sip of coffee from a polystyrene cup and watched the crisp red, white, and black of the swastika wave over New York.

"Well, fuck," she said. It summed up the feelings of them both exactly.

They had known things were going to be different, but the degrees and types of difference had taken them by surprise. They had not expected the Nazis to still be around post 1945, for example. Yet there they were, large as life and twice as unwanted, taking senior roles in the United Nations. Except it wasn't the United Nations. It was the League of Nations. Not the toothless League of history, which is to say, Carter and Lovecraft's history, the *folded* history. Apparently the institution had undergone reforms after the contention over Poland had come to an abrupt halt with the vaporization of Moscow that signaled the beginning of Operation Barbarossa, the Third Reich's entirely successful invasion of the USSR.

As footage of the mushroom cloud that ended the reign of Stalin made its way around the world, the USA abruptly became very quiet about the evils of the Nazis even as the British feverishly evacuated London, convinced it was the next target.

The bombshell when it fell, however, was not atomic. With potential global domination within their grasp, Germany instead pointed to the conquered swathes of Russia forming a Greater Germania, called it sufficient *Lebensraum*, and gave up the war in the West. No A-bomb fell upon London, or anywhere else. Instead, the Nazis sued for peace, and they offered excellent terms. The occupied countries of Europe were handed back to their governments, the exceptions being the territories ceded by Germany in the Treaty of Versailles and taken back by force in 1940, which were now held by them for perpetuity.

The West pretended not to notice that Poland had essentially ceased to exist or that Czechoslovakia's situation was scarcely any safer, and agreed.

Up in Arkham, which used to be Providence, but had been Arkham before that, Carter and Lovecraft hadn't opened the bookshop they co-owned for a week while they pored through books and scoured the Internet. So much was different, and so much was the same. There was a Cold War of sorts, but with the Third Reich instead of the Soviet Union, and it had fizzled out by the early fifties. The Nazis were being so damn *reasonable*, and after all, Hitler's flavor of Fascism was always joined at the hip with capitalism in general and corporatism in particular. It's hard to stay mad when there's money to be made.

"How can everyone be so cool with the Nazis?" Carter had asked. "What about the Holocaust? They can't have been given a free pass for that, can they?"

For her answer, Lovecraft passed him an atlas and told him to look up Israel in the index. He did, and found it listed, which was a relief. But then he went to the page indicated, and found himself looking at a map of the southern half of the continent of Africa. In the corner was an inset of Madagascar; the north of the island down to the nineteenth parallel was labeled "Israel."

He'd looked at Lovecraft, speechless.

"Yeah," she'd said.

In this world, the Nazis had enacted their plan to dump their Jews and other undesirables on Madagascar, now a German holding after the fall of France. It was a difficult transition for the refugees, but this Israel was much larger than the Middle Eastern version, and it was rich, verdant land. Policed by the Gestapo until 1955, it had been given full independence in return for favored trading partner status. In this world, the Jewish people might not have loved the Nazis, but nor did they hate them with much enthusiasm.

So, no Holocaust.

Though . . . there *had* been a holocaust, but it had been in the East, and the victims were Bolsheviks, Communists, and other degenerates the West couldn't get excited about.

The weird thing was that Carter and Lovecraft had both known it. They had lived in the Folded World consciously, and the Unfolded World by association. They were people with two histories sitting one upon the other, and with a little shift of focus that became easier every time they practiced it, they could read this one or that.

It being considered freakish to hate the Nazis for something they absolutely would have done if things had been just a little bit different, though—that was difficult. Here, the Third Reich was not a touchstone of evil. Here, the Final Solution had involved burning Russian corpses on pyres of *Das Kapital*. But Stalin had been slaughtering his own people long before the Germans dropped an atomic bomb in his lap, went the argument, so what were a few more after that? And look how stable the world was now, with Greater Germania in the West and the Imperial Japanese territories in the East. Who could find fault in such a wonderful world?

"How's your coffee?" Carter asked Lovecraft.

She looked ruminatively into her cup. Then she emptied it out onto the grass and tossed the cup into a garbage can. "Like Himmler pissed in it. Let's go."

Detective Martin Harrelson sometimes took his badge and ID out just to stare at where it said "City of Arkham Police Department" where once it had said "City of Providence." He was a member of a very exclusive club of, as far as he knew, three members who could recall Providence. To everyone else, the place was Arkham and had always been Arkham, sitting upon the Miskatonic River close by where it emptied through a mess of islands and bays into the North Atlantic. The area had been ground zero for changes caused by the unfolding of the world; Lovecraft said that was because it had been the same when things were folded in the first place. Arkham was back, the physical geography of the coast had changed, and now there were new towns in the area he'd never heard of before but that had—still according to Lovecraft—always been there. Kingsport. Innsmouth. There was some tiny place on the turnpike to the west called Dunwich that nobody in the department had one good word for. The word they did use more often than not was "inbred." They used that word a lot about Dunwich, and some about Innsmouth, too.

Harrelson didn't like the word "inbred"; it reminded him of the Waite family in Providence, as was. He worked hard to forget all about the Waites if he could manage it at all. At least this dumb-ass version of the real world was helping him out with that. The little corner of Providence that had held the Waites—and everything they represented, like a diseased sac containing putrescent blood—had gone. The little lick of land sticking into a backwater of the Providence River called Waite's Bill and containing the few houses of Waite Street, every one of them owned by a Waite, was now just an even smaller lick of land sticking into a backwater. It was fenced off, and a fading sign said something about an "exciting riverside development" that had never happened.

He'd kind of known it even before he'd driven down there to check, which was freaky, but everything was freaky these days. There were Nazis on the moon. An actual Nazi moon base. And a Nazi space station orbiting the Earth.

The first man in space had been a Nazi. The first man on the moon had been a Nazi. Nobody knew who the fuck Neil Armstrong was. That steamed Harrelson, who'd always admired Armstrong's quiet heroism.

Living in the Unfolded World meant he couldn't get drunk in company, because God only knew what might slip out. *Yeah, the Cold War was all about the USSR. Remember when the Berlin Wall came down?* That was crazy talk now. He'd got drunk by himself a couple of times, but he didn't like where that was headed, so now he only drank with people who understood. All two of them, and he wasn't sure if he liked them that much, either.

The details were vague, but he kind of had the idea this was Carter's fault, though Lovecraft said things would be a bunch worse if it hadn't been for him. How worse? Well, just as bad, really, in terms of the day-to-day. But there would be no hope to put things back as they were if Carter hadn't done something they were real vague about, so that was something, wasn't it?

It was obvious Lovecraft and Carter did not have the first fucking idea how to make everything go back as it was so, yeah, that was just peachy keen and grounds for bubbling optimism for sure.

It was all he had, though, and he'd take that pinch of hope and work to put things back how they should be. Neil Armstrong deserved it.

He put away his badge, looked at the computer screen on his desk at Arkham Central, read some of the crime reports, and sighed. Folded or not, the world contained some real assholes.

The following day, Emily Lovecraft was back in Providence. No . . . back in *Arkham*. It still took an effort to use the name even after the months they had spent living in this world, which was different in gross and subtle ways. It was still easy to be depressed and angry that the Nazis were still around and that nobody understood *why* this was a thing to be depressed and angry about. What was more insidious, however, was how politics and attitudes had slid over a few notches to accommodate this new world order.

For one thing, it was like twenty years of social progress had gone up in smoke. Antisemitism was reflexive and commonplace. The great shaming that the Holocaust had caused in the Folded World was not a thing here, the mirror of a prejudice taken to its logical conclusion; she routinely heard "kike," "yid," "heeb," "hymie," even "half-dick." They were liars, they were cheats, they were rats in human form, they should get a ticket to Israel and take their stink with them.

Things hadn't improved elsewhere, either. The "N" word had gone back to being plain old "nigger" again, and she heard it way too many times a day. What was weird about it was that it was so often said without obvious rancor or intention to hurt; standing in the aisles at the local store, she'd overheard a nice old lady she'd sold a book to the previous day recommend the bookshop to a friend, but she concluded the recommendation with "the nigger behind the counter really knows what she's talking about." Lovecraft had to walk out, sit down in the park, and breathe deeply for a while. The irony that this sort of shit had at least been widely understood to be offensive in the Folded World, the product of her own famously racist ancestor, was not lost on her, but that didn't make matters any better.

The store itself was not so very different from its folded version, at least internally. Externally, it was of the same architectural style as the rest of the street: an American brand of collegiate Gothic mixed with the remnants of an older colonial Gothic that lent veracity to the cityscape as a whole. Arkham was a city that valued its history and there were any number of building regulations to maintain that past, to the extent where it had a distinct "Old Town" surrounded by an architecturally more anodyne "New Town."

Carter & Lovecraft, the bookstore, was well inside Old Town, making it one of the few things about the new situation that pleased her. She had, she realized, always loved the description of Arkham in the stories of her great-great-uncle: the streets described as "ancient" in the 1920s, the gambrel roofs, the sense that somebody had torn up pieces of seventeenth-century Europe, glued them together in fanciful forms, and dumped the resulting gallimaufry onto an unsuspecting America.

It was like nothing she'd ever seen before—not fanciful or whimsical, but a functioning town that happened to look like it had escaped from the set Hammer movies had used to represent everywhere from Cornwall to Transylvania. Chains and franchises were strictly limited here by local ordinance; she had found a Starbucks wedged fearfully into a low-ceilinged building with minimal signage, as if it were afraid of being discovered. The whole of Old Town felt bohemian, not least because it looked kind of Bohemian in the geographical sense.

The store was on the northwestern corner of Church and Parsonage, a pleasant enough location on the southern side of the Miskatonic. There was a nice little park across the way, and it was close enough to the college precinct that she got a lot of student traffic. Her smile was still a little strained when she saw so many of them come in wearing Miskatonic University shirts, but she was beginning to get used to it.

"Get used to it." The human capacity to accept the extraordinary and adjust to it had proved vital. She still had too many moments when she wanted to deny the reality around her, would give almost anything to only have to worry about Islamist extremism instead of, say, *fucking Nazi Germany* as, far and away, the greatest world power ever seen.

It was everywhere, not helped by the Nazis being, in the eyes of many Americans, okay guys who weren't maybe so great on the democracy thing, but who were capitalists to the bone. Almost all of the largest corporations had their HQs in Berlin. Ford was now a subsidiary of Volkswagen. Smith & Wesson was a marque of Mauser. She knew Carter now regarded his Glock with disdain; the *Anschluss* of 1938 had never been revoked here and Austria and Germany were still conjoined. Carrying an Austrian weapon was therefore pretty much the same as carrying a German one, and that meant some of his money had gone to the German treasury as tax. He was looking into replacing it with a Colt, which was loudly and proudly still an American company. They only produced one decent pistol in his opinion, however: a modernized version of the M1911 .45 ACP, which seemed a little too much of a hand cannon for his taste. He hadn't taken the jump yet, just grumbling about the Glock at random moments.

He kept his grumbling to a minimum; it was considered weird to see the Reich as malevolent. The USA and the Nazis had been the best of pals since the fifties, after all. Sure, the French had militarized their border to high hell, and the British still hadn't forgiven Hitler for stripping them of their empire (as if it wasn't falling to pieces anyway) and leaving them as a margin note in history, but that was their perspective. History, after all, belongs to winners, the smart money loves winners, and Wall Street loves what the smart money loves. It occurred to Lovecraft that if, in the Folded World, Stalin had attempted to dominate the West financially, it would have been far more effective than putting all that money into tanks and missiles.

At least running the store was still pretty much the same as it ever was. The Internet was still the Internet except for a few small changes in how it came to be and in the common sites everyone knew. It had been almost as big a surprise as learning that Hitler died in 1971 as it had been to boot up the store's computer and discover that the standard, popular browser was Netscape. "You're really not in Kansas anymore, girl," she'd said to herself, looking at a high-definition letter-N icon behind which stars twinkled and swooped.

The phone rang. With the small sense of impending doom she suffered every time the Unfolded imposed upon her in any way, no matter how small, she answered it.

"Carter & Lovecraft Books, academic, secondhand, and antiquarian. Can I help you?"

"Ah, yes." A man's voice, unsure. Somebody who didn't like using the phone. This was going to be hard work. She heard noise on the line as the handset at the other end was juggled, a piece of paper unfolded. "I'm . . ." More paper noises. "I'm looking for a book."

A pause. *Oh, good*, thought Lovecraft. *A customer who believes I'm telepathic. Those are the best.*

Still, it was generally wise not to taunt the customer. Not at first, anyway.

"Which book would that be?"

"It's . . . Just a moment, I've got it written down." More crackling noises. When he'd taken as long to open a piece of paper as it would have taken her to make an origami swan from it while wearing mittens, he finally said, "It's a German book. Do you stock German books?"

She shot a dirty glance at the political memoirs section, which had become even more expendable in her view thanks to the addition of several editions of *Mein Kampf*. "Yes, sir, we stock some German books, and we have good connections over there." They did, as well. The store's address book contained far more European contacts than it ever used to.

"Oh? Oh, that's good. I don't think it's in print in the U.S.

Maybe not even in Germany. It's called *Unaussprechlichen Kulten*."
There was some mumbling as he subvocalized other pronuncia-
tions, reading from the paper. "Yeah, I'm pretty sure that's right.
Did that sound right to you?"

Lovecraft raised an eyebrow. "Yeah. I've heard of it. Robert E.
Howard, right?"

"Uh, no. Some German guy, I guess. Friedrich Wilhelm von
Junzt, it says here." He pronounced it with an English *J* rather
than a Teutonic *Y* sound. "No mention of anyone called 'Howard.' Maybe he's the translator? Sounds English."

Lovecraft cradled the handset against her shoulder and typed
into the proprietary book database the unfolded version of her
had subscribed to. "Let me see, sir. Just checking if I can locate
any copies for you. May I ask what the book is for? It's kind of
obscure."

"For? Well . . . research. I'm reading comparative anthropol-
ogy at MiskU and just came across a reference to it. It looked
useful."

Useful, thought Lovecraft. *That's one way of—* She paused,
staring at the screen. The search had brought up several copies
across the world that were available for sale. Her eye settled on a
flash alongside one of them.

"Hello?"

Lovecraft blinked and said, "Uh, sorry. The computer is acting up. Look, can I take your details? I'll see what I can find and
get back to you within a day. Is that okay?"

She scribbled down his name and number, finished the call,
and put down the phone in a distracted way, the flash on the
screen drawing her eye back to it with mesmeric power.

VENDOR: CARTER & LOVECRAFT, ARKHAM, RI, US

She looked at the safe. She hadn't really had much cause to
go through it since the unfolding except for the usual business
of putting in and taking out the cash box. The bottom section
behind its battered black steel door had been empty except for
old accounts. She looked at the bulky, ancient safe for a long

minute. Then, spurred by a desire to put the impossible back into abeyance, she quickly unlocked the safe and opened the lower section. There were ledgers there, but on their edges, not stacked. They were standing like books because most of the space was taken up by a stack of black file boxes. They looked more threatening than any file box had a right to.

She realized she'd put her hand over her mouth in an expression of horror, a deep foreboding of what she might find. First, however, she went and locked the door, turning the sign to *Closed*. Then she returned to her place behind the counter, took out the topmost box, and placed it on the surface. As cautiously as opening the case of an armed bomb, she lifted the lid.

Inside was a bulky book wrapped in bubble wrap with a few silica gel bags lying alongside it to keep down the humidity in the box. She removed the book from the box, placed it on the countertop, and stared at it. It couldn't be. It simply couldn't be. *Unaussprechlichen Kulten* was a fictional book. Robert E. Howard, the creator of Conan and Solomon Kane, invented it as a detail in a short story. Even if she accepted everything about the Unfolded World, about how Arkham and the Miskatonic were real, that didn't mean everything else in H. P. Lovecraft's stories and the others it inspired had to be real, too.

Lovecraft realized that she was trembling. Almost outside of her volition, she took up the paper-knife she kept under the counter and slit the lengths of tape holding the bubble wrap in place. Then, with a few short, nervous flicks of the knife's tip, she exposed the book.

The knife fell from her hand and she sat down heavily on the stool.

The book was not *Unaussprechlichen Kulten*.

Instead, in battered silver leaf on the badly stained cover— its red leather darkened with age—she read the single word . . .

Necronomicon.

Chapter 3

THE LAWMAN

Dan Carter was in hot pursuit.

Just as the client had suggested, he had been in the right place at the right time and seen the transaction going down. It would have been nice to just stroll over and arrest the guys, but he was no longer a cop. Yes, he still had the power of citizen's arrest, and they were clearly guilty as hell—he'd been taking pictures the whole time, after all—but he wasn't being paid enough to take a risk with his personal safety.

The contact took off in a white van (Carter had already photographed it and made a written note of the license plate just to be on the safe side), leaving Kuzkin behind. Carter was just taking a beautiful picture of Kuzkin counting the damn money in the middle of the parking lot like an idiot when the idiot looked straight at him and freaked out.

If Kuzkin vanished into the city, he would be almost untraceable, the client would *not* be happy, and Carter's payment would suffer. Carter grunted with displeasure as he set off in pursuit, hitting the still swinging door from the parking area back into the hotel.

Kuzkin had seen too many movies where people get chased through hotels, obviously; the corridor came out into the building's third story and almost the first thing he did was push over a maid's cart and the maid with it. In the wide corridor it presented no sort of barrier at all. Kuzkin disappeared around the corner as Carter ran past the cart and the maid, who was swearing with great venom and imagination at the fugitive. "Kick his ass!" she shouted at Carter as he sped by. "Kick that punk's teeth in!"

Before the chase began, that would have seemed disproportionate to Carter, but that was before Kuzkin decided he was going to be an idiot. Now a few well-placed kicks when he caught up with the moron were starting to look pretty good in a cathartic kind of way.

The hotel was not one of New York's grand old ladies, but a nineties build intended more for business and conventions. The reception area was reasonably large, but bland, and having a pursuit across it was probably the most action it had seen in months. Kuzkin, living up to expectations, did not head for the foyer door and out into the street to lose himself in the crowd like an intelligent human being. No. Kuzkin headed for the restaurant.

"You have to be kidding me," Carter muttered under his breath. As he followed the target into the room, empty but for a couple of staff at that time of day, he saw Kuzkin half-hurdle the bar, butt surf it for a couple of yards, drop onto the other side, and run through the *Staff Only* door behind it. Carter did not bother following him, but headed for the double doors that led directly into the kitchen.

Kuzkin was halfway to the rear exit, pushing trolleys over behind him in a cacophony of clanging metal and crashing plates, blissfully sure that Carter was as foolish as him and following directly on his tail. When Carter suddenly appeared in his path and tackled him to the floor, the look of astonishment on his face was a joy to behold.

"What the fuck is this?" demanded a sous chef, seeing Carter roll Kuzkin on his face and put a flex cuff on him.

"Get the duty manager down here," said Carter.

"It was just sheets, man!" whined Kuzkin, his voice blurred from the floor tiles hard against his face. "Sheets and towels! Fuck! Those cuffs hurt!"

Carter sat on him, panting with exertion. "Yeah, crime of the century. Why'd you have to run? Idiot."

"Fuck you!"

"Yeah, and fuck you, too, Moriarty." Carter settled down to await the arrival of management and the police.

It all went pretty much as expected after that. The duty manager turned up and blamed Carter for Kuzkin's running and the damage he'd caused without actually saying as much. Then the police arrived and found the whole scenario mildly amusing, especially the sight of a decorated former NYPD detective foiling a clandestine bedding theft conspiracy of the most desperate kind. He accompanied Kuzkin to the precinct, but nobody seemed really keen to take his statement, and he was sitting around for forty minutes before they remembered he was there. Then the statement, then another twenty minutes when Kuzkin said he wanted Carter charged with assault, but then Carter said, fine, maybe we should ask the maid he pushed over whether she wants to press charges as well, at which point Kuzkin went off the idea.

Two hours later, and all the more irritated since he'd discovered that a seam had torn in his jacket when he'd tackled Kuzkin, Carter returned to his office in Red Hook. Just for once he really wanted to do the PI thing: drag a bottle of bourbon out of his filing cabinet, pour himself a stiff shot, and drink it while he looked out on the naked city from his office window. Alas, his filing cabinet contained files and stationery, and all he could muster was a can of Sprite from the little cooler in the corner. He consoled himself that at least he could drink it while looking out at the naked city from his office window.

In reality, three things went through his mind as he stood there. Firstly, he made a mental note to go to the old-school tailor a block over and see about getting the seam fixed. The world seemed to have a lot more old-school businesses than it used to, so that was a plus. The second thing was he toyed with the idea of getting a bottle of bourbon for the office, but then decided not to because it would be pretentious and, anyway, he wasn't that big a fan of bourbon. He'd drink it, but he preferred Scotch. Thirdly, and not for the first time since things had changed, he marveled that the sun now shone into his office directly.

Before, there had been a row of tenements across the way that stopped the sun from ever shining upon the small building that contained several rental offices including his own. The only time he had ever seen the sun enter had been during a brief fugue, a waking dream, while talking to a client. In the Folded World, the client wanted evidence of her husband's adultery so she could divorce him. In the fugue, she had wanted Carter to kill him. Carter remembered he didn't seem to have a problem with that in the dream. He could deal with that thought because the sun was shining into the office in a way it never could, so it was all a phantasm and nothing to do with reality. Yet now it shone into the office exactly as it had done in the vision. Did that mean that, in the Unfolded World, he'd calmly taken the pistol in the plastic bag she'd given him and used it to commit murder? Maybe the truth was in his files. So far he'd avoided looking.

He realized the can was empty, turned away from the window, and froze. He was no longer alone.

Carter had not heard the door open or close, had not heard the chair creak as it was occupied, but now there was somebody sitting there, smiling pleasantly at him.

"Mr. Weston," said Carter slowly. "You startled me."

Mr. Henry Weston, attorney at law, senior partner and sole owner of the law firm of Weston Edmunds, seemed unperturbed that he had done so. "Your door was unlocked," he said, unnecessarily.

He looked very nearly identical to how he had first appeared to Carter some months before, five six, 120 pounds, neat dark hair that was almost unnervingly perfect without the slightest change since that last meeting. The only element that was different was the three-piece suit he wore, and even this was still obviously bespoke and expensive despite its unadventurous color and cut. Then he had appeared in Carter's office in much the same way, like a genie from a very quiet lamp, and told Carter that he had inherited a property in Providence.

"So nice to see you again, Mr. Carter. How interesting that our paths should cross again."

Carter walked back to his desk and shook Weston's hand, though Weston did not rise to do so. Once again it felt to Carter that he was shaking the hand of a showroom dummy. Weston's grip was warm, dry, but felt too firm. When one shakes a hand, there is always the intimation of bone within the flesh, the skeleton within the skin. That intimation was missing with Weston.

Carter sat down behind his desk, mentally noting yet again that he really wanted to change the chair for one with wheels. This one didn't have them, and it irritated him for a reason that he couldn't quite isolate.

Weston looked at Carter brightly across the desktop, like a man waiting for a chess opponent to make a move. The silence endured for several seconds until Carter realized that it was only bothering him, so he broke it.

"I wasn't expecting to ever see you again, Mr. Weston. Is anything the matter?"

"Yes. Something is the matter, and that is why I am here." Weston's smile didn't waver. If anything, it brightened, as if he were teaching an ungifted child to play that game of chess and they had made a legitimate move rather than chewing on a bishop. His expression changed to one of concerned curiosity. "But first I must ask, how are you enjoying your inheritance? I'm afraid I was consumed with curiosity—that's only human, after all—and did a little investigating of my own after I parted from you last time. The property is a bookstore, I understand? How wonderful! I am a great admirer of books. I have several. Perhaps I shall visit sometime and buy another."

He leaned forward. "It was kind of you to share the bequest with Miss Lovecraft. That was generous and, I think, sensible. After all, she knows the business. Rare and antiquarian books are hardly the sort of thing a tyro can walk into, are they?"

Carter knew Weston was lying; he'd checked the store's ownership soon after the unfolding and knew it had been put into the names of both Lovecraft and himself only a couple of weeks after the execution of the will that gave it to him. It was not possible that Weston had looked up the transfer just after their last meeting. Then again, it was only a small lie. The worst of it was Carter was sure Weston knew full well that Carter would spot it.

"No," he said, "I don't read too much, and I don't know the people she does. It just made sense to share the business."

"Yes." Weston would not stop smiling. It was as if this was the best news the world had ever known. "Very sensible." He suddenly looked at the window. "Doesn't it bother you, the sun coming in like that? You might consider investing in some blinds."

Carter glanced at the window, then at Weston. Weston was looking into the sun and he wasn't even squinting. "Does it bother you?"

Weston's head slowly turned to regard Carter. It looked as organic a movement as a tank's turret coming to bear on its target. "Not at all, Mr. Carter. I am more resilient than I might appear. Very little bothers me." His eyebrows raised as if he'd just remembered a wonderful joke. "To business!" He picked up the same old battered briefcase Carter remembered from

Weston's last visit and took from it a file. Carter had the sense that the file was the only thing in the case.

"A client of the company is in a sticky situation." The phrase displeased him. "A ticklish circumstance. A difficult scenario. He requires help of a certain type that we are not equipped to provide."

"Meaning?"

"Meaning? Ah. Meaning an investigation carried out with the utmost discretion. Your name came immediately to mind."

"Why would that be?"

Weston seemed nonplussed by this.

Carter said, "Why would you think of me? I haven't done work for you in the past. I'm an unknown quantity."

"Well, I *know* you, and my own modest investigation at the time of our first meeting gave every indication that you were an exemplary police officer."

"I'm not a police officer anymore."

"A technicality. I am a good judge of character, Mr. Carter. I won't deny that we may have asked around a little, too, before I came here. You come highly recommended. Mr. Stamford, Miss Van Schloss, Mr. Mendelssohn, all spoke well of you."

Carter regarded Weston with cold eyes. "Can I get you something to drink?"

Weston smiled. "No, thank you."

"You've certainly done your due diligence."

"The firm of Weston Edmunds is well known for it."

"So, okay. What's the job?"

"Of course." Weston started to open the file, but paused before doing so. "I must emphasize that this is a matter of some considerable confidentiality, Mr. Carter. Whether you accept it or not, I must have your assurance that you will not discuss it with anyone else."

"Only with my business partner."

"Miss Lovecraft? She is not a partner in *this* business, surely?"

"She's smart and she knows people." Weston looked at him

blankly. Carter decided this was a point he was going to fight whether it was sensible to or not. "I reserve the right to discuss cases with her. That's part of my working practice."

Weston's eyebrows raised, and his smile returned. "Then by all means, discuss the matter with the estimable Miss Lovecraft, but only on the basis that the information goes no further. You will vouch for her?"

"I will. I do."

"That's fine, then." As Weston returned his attention to the file, his glanced up for a moment at Carter and seemed amused. Carter wondered if Weston had known all along he'd want to bring Lovecraft in on anything Weston might say, and that was what he wanted. Weston took a sheet from the manila folder, glanced at it, and said, "Miskatonic University. Do you have any contacts there?"

Carter made the effort to look thoughtful; internally he was trying to reconcile two sets of memories. Back in the Folded World he'd asked around at Clave College. That no longer existed, nor had it ever existed, but some of the people he'd met who would have gone there had ended up at MU. "A few. Why?"

"Currently there is an experiment in progress in the high energy physics section of the science department. It is an expensive sort of experiment, and it is being carried out as an inter-university project in an effort to spread the cost. A client of my firm is one of the scientists involved. While we were discussing more obviously legal matters, he happened to mention that he is having some misgivings about how the experiment is proceeding. Specifically, he thinks that some of the data may have been manipulated to give a better result than is actually the case."

Carter snorted. "That kind of thing must go on all the time. They must have ways of dealing with it."

Weston nodded. "In the normal run of things, you would no doubt be quite correct, Mr. Carter. But . . . there is a political dimension to all this that makes it a little sensitive to claims of fakery. The other university is the Reichsuniversität, Berlin."

Carter barely had to examine his new memories to know that the Reichsuniversität was Hitler's very own pet project in the years following the end of the Second World War in 1941. It was an internationally renowned place of learning, and the beating heart of German claims to leading the field in arts and, particularly, sciences. It was Caltech, Cambridge, and MIT all rolled up into a single center of excellence.

"And the cheating with the figures . . ."

"A German physicist. It is all very unfortunate. My client would like his suspicions confirmed before acting further. There is a time factor involved, Mr. Carter. The intention is that the experiment be restaged on a larger scale and at much greater expense elsewhere if the current round of results continue to be so encouraging. It would be embarrassing to the Miskatonic if those results were shown to be fraudulent only after the money has been spent. As for the impact it would have on future collaboration with the Reich . . ." An inquisitive flex of the brow. "You seem troubled, Mr. Carter."

Carter was troubled by the conjunction of "collaboration" and "Reich," but he doubted that would be explicable to Weston. He was having to unlearn a whole lot of associations and reflexes for things these days. Now, when people wanted a bogeyman to reach for, it was Stalin. The Germans had put out a lot of propaganda about the brutality of Stalin's regime and it had stuck in the global consciousness as a touchstone for inhumanity in the modern world. They had hardly had to exaggerate, after all.

"So why me? If maybe there could be a diplomatic flare-up, why . . ." He leaned back. "Plausible deniability."

"Indeed so. It would never do for an agent of the U.S. government to be found snooping around the project. Also, that would involve actually telling the government, and my client is not ready to take that step just yet."

"Who is your client?"

"That's . . . sensitive information."

"What? It's 'need to know'?"

Weston nodded. "Precisely."

"I need to know."

"I would be the one employing you, not him. I truly doubt you need to or even should know, Mr. Carter. Better you simply go in, without prior preju—"

"No. I'm not going to argue about this. I either talk to your client, find out what he knows and get a better understanding of what's going on in that lab, or I'm not signing up for this."

"I am empowered to offer you twice your usual fee."

"Make it ten times as much—"

For once, Weston seemed surprised. Not angry or shocked, but like a man who's just found the book he was looking for in the wrong place. "I am *not* empowered to offer quite *that* mu—"

"—and I still wouldn't do it. I speak to your client or I don't feel I can take on the case."

"Well." Weston dropped the file back into his briefcase. "I am not at liberty to reveal his identity. All I can do is go to him with your proposal, Mr. Carter." He rose and offered his hand. "I shall be in touch."

Carter shook his hand and saw him to the door. "Don't think I'm being difficult just for the hell of it, Mr. Weston. I just can't do my job properly without doing the groundwork."

"As I said, Mr. Carter, I believe I am a good judge of character. You do not strike me as a man given to frivolous gestures. I shall ask the client. I can do no more."

Carter had closed the door and was halfway to his desk when the brief initial spark of curiosity as to why Weston was even in New York, never mind Red Hook, reignited in his mind. He walked back to the door and opened it out onto the common stairwell all the offices shared.

"Mr. Weston?" He looked over the rail, but the well was empty and silent, with no footfall sounding upon the stairs. "Mr. Weston?" He walked around the stairwell, but could see no sign of his visitor. On an impulse, he went quickly down the two flights of stairs, but didn't pass Weston on the way. It took him longer to make the descent than the time it had taken him to walk out onto the third-story landing, and he had gone down the stairs pretty quickly. He had not heard the buzz the building's front door made when it was released.

Once, not so very long ago, he would have just accepted it as one of those things, an inconsequential mystery whose solution lay in some stupid little detail he wasn't seeing at the moment. Now, he felt differently. Now he had seen things, experienced things that did not fit neatly into that view of the mundanity of all things. Experiences that had started with the involvement of Mr. Henry Weston.

He went back to his office and sat down heavily to think. The sun slanted in, bothering him. Weston was right: he really should get some blinds.

Chapter 4

"The fucking *Necronomicon*. *The fucking Necronomicon*." Emily Lovecraft was not in the mood to be moderate. "Right there." She pointed at the locked safe. "*The FUCKING Necronomicon*. In this store. In that safe." She looked at her fingertips. "I *touched* it."

Carter was leaning on the customer side of the counter and not entirely understanding her concern. He saw her reach for the hand sanitizer bottle that any sane store owner keeps around. "No. No, don't do that. That would be weird."

She glanced at him and reluctantly put the bottle back. "I touched it."

"*The Fucking Necronomicon*. Yeah, I heard. What is that? Some sort of skanky sex manual?"

She blinked at him. "What?" Then she laughed. "Okay. Okay. It's just called the *Necronomicon*. It's . . . fictional. It *was* fictional. Now it's factual. I kind of knew it must be out there since things

34

changed—it or something like it. Just never expected it to be in my place of work. I never expected to touch it." She looked at her fingers again, and Carter caught the longing glance at the sanitizer bottle.

"So what is it? I think I've heard the name." He frowned. "I have. You said it in passing when you first told me about H.P.L. It's a book?"

"It's *the* book. The one that explains everything you might not want to know, but probably need to if you're going to have a chance against the kind of cosmic shit storms the Outer Gods specialize in. Outer gods." She shook her head. "I know it's all true, but part of my brain just wants to say, 'No way. Not happening. Not true. Don't go believing that stuff.'" She looked seriously at Carter. "Did you ever have times, back when the world was folded, when just for a minute or two, you didn't believe in the world around you?"

"Every time I had to talk to my captain."

"Ha ha. I'm serious, Dan. I mean moments when you thought about how complex the world is, and how long history is, and how it had brought you to that exact moment, and how incredibly unlikely it all was that you should be there, right at that moment, doing whatever you were doing. That never happened to you?"

Carter thought of his moments of dislocation, the sense that this was not a false world as Lovecraft was suggesting, but one of many, and the problem was that they were all too real. He shook his head. "Never."

"Wow." Lovecraft was genuinely surprised. "I thought it was a 'human condition' kind of thing. Thought everyone had moments like that."

"Not me. Maybe I lack the imagination." He nodded at the safe. "I have to ask, why do we have a copy in the first place?"

"Yeah. About that. Not sure if this counts as good news or bad news." She reached under the counter and produced a small, black ledger. "This was in there, too." She slid it across to Carter. "At least it ain't bound in human skin. Small blessing."

Carter flicked through it, but it just seemed like a hand-written list of dry book descriptions, dates, and prices. He passed it back, shaking his head. "Your handwriting."

"Thanks for pointing it out. You have any idea how freaky it was to open that thing and find it full of entries the unfolded me made?"

"You *are* the unfolded you."

"Not by choice." She flicked through the pages and stopped on one particular entry, resting a finger on it. "Here. Abd' Al'hazred, author. Translation into English, John Dee. Fragmentary. Royal quarto. Four hundred and eight pages. Date uncertain, but probably late sixteenth century, and almost certainly printed in England." She looked up at Carter and said darkly, "*Illustrated.*"

"Did you look at them?"

She shrugged. "I'm a curious girl. Yeah, I looked. First couple, I thought, *Not so bad*. Next one I looked at it for a full minute, but couldn't figure out exactly what it was supposed to be. Next one, I slammed the book shut, wrapped it up, put it back." She leveled a finger at Carter. "Half an hour later, I realized what the third picture was of. Went to the bathroom, brought up my breakfast."

Carter stared at her. Whatever else she was, Lovecraft was not a delicate blossom. He was suddenly glad he hadn't seen the pictures himself.

Lovecraft turned to regard the safe, tucked in the shadows behind the counter. "Right then, if somebody had pulled up in a truck and walked in here with a propylene torch, offered to weld the safe shut, drive it to a bridge, and drop it in the river, I'd have let them. I'd have thanked them. I'd have paid them to do it." She shook her head and turned back to Carter. "But not now. I've been thinking about it. If we're really going to set things right, we need to know what we're doing. That book's a sanity-eater, but it also might be a how-to guide to getting things folded up again."

"Well, you'd be the one using it. I'm not much of a reader."

"Ignore him, boys and girls," Lovecraft said to the thousands of volumes around them, "he doesn't mean it." Then to Carter, "The full *Necronomicon* is supposed to be in seven volumes and over nine hundred pages altogether. What we've got in the safe over there is either whatever fragments of Dee's translation were recoverable, or maybe just the edited highlights. Either way, this is the light reading version."

"The *Reader's Digest* condensed edition."

Lovecraft laughed, a sound of gratefully released tension. "Yeah. Imagine 'It Pays to Improve Your Word Power' would be full of stuff like 'fhtagn' and 'Y'Golo . . .'" Her smile faded suddenly with her voice. When she spoke again, it was in hushed tones. "Have to be careful even about what we say now. Some things literally must not be named."

"Why?"

She glanced up and off to one side, as if hearing something that he could not. She looked back at him, all traces of humor gone, replaced with great seriousness, and perhaps just a little fear. "Because they might be listening."

Carter tried to raise Lovecraft's mood a little by joking about what else she might have found in the safe, suggesting Captain Kidd's treasure and Capone's hidden millions. The attempt backfired badly when it turned out that, along with the *Necronomicon*, she'd found a copy of something called *Von Unaussprechlichen Kulten* and another book she admitted she'd never heard of before called *Principia Necromantica* that a brief examination revealed to be at least as worrying as its title.

"We've been selling these fucking things," she said, distressed at the culpability and weak morality of her unfolded self. "To collectors! Carter & Lovecraft actually has a rep in the business for being the go-to place for forbidden tomes. How could we? It's like selling assault rifles to kindergartens!"

"Now it is, but maybe . . ." Carter paused. "No. You're right. All the magical shit exists on this side of the Fold. Those books are dangerous."

"I've got a buyer who wants the *Kulten* book. Offered a small fortune for it when I called to tell him we might have a copy. Dumb move, but what was I supposed to say? What am I supposed to say *now*?"

"Say no. There was a mistake, it was a private sale and an intern advertised it without asking. You can't let those things out, Emily. They're not like assault rifles. They are *way* worse. They're more like a biological weapon. They contain thought viruses. You know what they say about stuff falling into the wrong hands. I'm not saying ours are infallible, but we can't just send these things out to people whose sole qualification is that they have some green."

"It was a *lot* of green," said Lovecraft, but didn't argue beyond that.

Carter leaned forward over the counter and nodded at the safe. "So . . ."

Lovecraft regarded him somberly. He half-smiled, decided that wasn't appropriate, sobered again, and looked steadily at the safe on the chance that this might communicate his meaning without him actually having to say anything.

"So?" said Lovecraft. She plainly knew exactly what he was intimating, and had no intention of letting him get away with not saying it.

"So, when are you going to sit down and . . . read those things?"

Lovecraft continued to look steadily at him for several moments longer before saying, "So, when am I going to risk my sanity and life reading those things so that you don't have to?"

"I don't—"

"You don't read much. Yeah, I heard you." She sighed, as much in resignation as exasperation. "I don't know, Dan. They're kind of a big deal. The necromancy book is just going to be gross for the sake of it, and I'd guess it's too specific for us. *Von Un-aussprechlichen Kulten* is supposed to be a trap book anyway, I think. Shit's pretty much bound to happen if you read it. I guess I'll try to focus on the *Necronomicon*. Besides, my German and Latin probably aren't good enough."

"You speak German and Latin?"

"Latin's damn rusty, but yeah. No practice for years. Not that Tudor English is going to be a walk in the park. I think I'm going to have a look around to see if I can find any glossaries for the English of the period. It's Shakespeare's time—pretty much exactly, in fact—so there should be a few. I'll see what I can find before embarking up the river toward that particular 'heart of darkness.'" She drew a deep breath. "Who knew reading could be so hazardous?"

Carter left Lovecraft to run the business while he went upstairs to the small apartment over the store to look after the private investigation end of things. He'd warned her that a potential client was going to turn up soon, Weston having called to say the client had agreed to meet Carter, and to call him when they did so. Then he set up his laptop on the table in the apartment and started clearing a stack of paperwork he'd allowed to build up while acclimatizing himself to the new scheme of things Lovecraft, Harrelson, and he had found themselves thrust into.

He heard the bell chime a few times downstairs as customers came and went, the mutter of conversation, and—his personal favorite—the sound of a sale being rung up. He'd grown used to the ambience of a reasonably successful independent bookstore in action for about an hour when he heard the door at the bottom of the stairs open and Lovecraft call up. She did not seem pleased.

"Mr. Carter!" She said his name like a disapproving teacher. "There's a *Nazi* to see you!"

Carter made his way downstairs quickly, finding Lovecraft

standing by the lower door with her arms crossed and wearing a judgmental expression. She nodded into the middle of the store at the counter. Standing there was a man of around forty years, lean, sandy-brown thinning hair, wearing a dark wool suit and a horrified expression.

"Emily . . ." Carter muttered warningly.

"What?" She walked with him to the newcomer. "Look. Swastika lapel pin. What's a girl to think?"

"Please," said the newcomer, his German accent evident, "don't use that word."

"Which word?" said Emily, looking forward to using it again, and repeatedly.

"The 'N' word."

Lovecraft froze for a long second, her eyebrows up, her lips slightly agape. She looked at Carter, not quite able to process what she had just heard.

Carter said quickly before she would recover her equilibrium, "I'll take Mr. . . . ?"

"Lukas," supplied the man. "Torsten Lukas."

". . . Mr. Lukas upstairs where we can discuss business. I'll . . . ah. Thank you."

He led Lukas to the stairs, although he was pretty sure he heard Lovecraft mutter, "Make yourself at home. I'll make you a nice cup of Buchenwald, you Nazi fuck" in his wake.

Upstairs, Carter bid Lukas sit and offered to make coffee, which Lukas accepted. As he busied himself in the kitchen area of the open plan apartment, Lukas said, "Who is that black downstairs?"

"That's my business partner, Mr. Lukas. I'm sorry if Miss Lovecraft was less than respectful, but she has her reasons. Please don't respond in kind, or I won't be able to work for you."

Lukas looked confused as he accepted the coffee. "What did I say?"

Carter sat down and wondered how to explain, or even if

he should bother. The Unfolded World really could be a pain in the ass. He decided that talking a Nazi (the guy really did have a party pin on his lapel) out of reflexive racism in one sitting was not something that was going to happen. Instead, he said, "I gotta admit, Mr. Lukas, I'm surprised to see you. I got the idea I'd be dealing with a member of the American side of the project."

"Mr. Weston said that?"

"No, but he didn't mention you'd be a German, plus he told me the trouble was from one of the Germans, so I drew what seemed like the natural conclusion. Okay, that was wrong, but you can see why I thought what I did. How do you know Mr. Weston?"

"Weston Edmunds handles our patents in the U.S. I was discussing one such with them when I mentioned some possible . . . troubles with the project at the Miskatonic."

"And Weston himself took an interest?"

Lukas nodded. "That surprised me. He is the owner, yes?"

"Yeah. He's kind of eccentric, though. So, you have doubts somebody on your team is playing straight with the results? Why don't you take it up with them? Or, I don't know, do you have some sort of governing body?"

"This would be considered a security matter. It's Gestapo business."

Carter laughed. "I can see why you don't want to get them involved." Lukas didn't even smile. If anything, Carter's amusement made him uncomfortable. Carter stopped laughing. "Oh. I see."

Lukas shrugged slightly. "I *am* Gestapo."

Carter felt how Lovecraft had looked a few minutes earlier. "I don't understand, Mr. Lukas. If you're Gestapo, why do you need me?"

"Because . . ." For somebody in one of history's most feared secret police forces, Lukas didn't seem very self-assured. "I'm a scientist. My Gestapo rank is more of a . . . detached role."

"What does that mean?"

"I am not a field agent exactly. More akin to an intelligence gatherer."

A *snitch*, thought Carter, but he kept that intelligence to himself.

"You've reported your concerns?"

Lukas looked more uncomfortable. "In a manner of speaking. I have written in my reports that the results the detector has been giving have been far, far better than we might have expected."

"That sounds more like an endorsement."

"I begin to fear that is how my reports have been interpreted. The desk I report to is a policeman, not a scientist. I do not think he understands my concern."

Carter tried his coffee. "Explain this to me from the ground up, Mr. Lukas. What exactly are you working on?"

Lukas seemed surprised by the question for a moment. He tilted his head to the side, and Carter felt sure he was going to say it was irrelevant and none of his business. Instead, he looked at the tabletop in silence for a moment, opened his mouth, hesitated, and finally said in a quiet voice, "Mr. Carter, we intend to steal power from God."

Inevitably, images of Indiana Jones appeared in Carter's mind, although in this world he was disappointed but unsurprised to discover that Jones mainly went up against the Japanese, except for *Indiana Jones and the Last Crusade*, in which rabid Bolsheviks hunted the Holy Grail in an attempt to resurrect Stalin.

"That doesn't sound like the kind of thing that will turn out well," said Carter, thinking of Ronald Lacey's face melting. Lukas smiled hesitantly, and Carter suddenly knew he was in for a lecture.

"Have you heard of 'zero point energy,' Mr. Carter?" Without waiting for an answer, he continued, "Allow me to explain. Classical physics predicts a state of no energy at absolute zero, which is to say, zero degrees Kelvin, or minus 273.15 degrees Celsius. Indeed, the very definition of absolute zero is this predicted temperature. But, it doesn't actually work. Real matter doesn't behave like an ideal gas. Even at zero, there is still entropy and enthalpy, because there is still energy there, even though there theoretically shouldn't be. The famous example is helium. At absolute zero, everything should be a solid, yet helium is still a liquid. Something must be moving those atoms around. *This* is 'zero point energy.'"

He took a draft of his coffee, but Carter didn't take the opportunity to jump into the conversation; sometimes it's just better to let a man run.

"For many years, it has been a dream to use this energy, this literally free energy, but there have been difficulties. Taking the idea seriously has been a major problem in itself, Mr. Carter. As you might imagine, to many physicists the whole thing smacks of a perpetual motion engine. Getting this project off the ground took a lot of work. German academia wasn't prepared to look kindly upon it, but luckily Miskatonic University has a reputation for taking chances and carrying out research in new, sometimes problematical fields. With a cooperative program like this, we were able to move ahead.

"A very necessary part of research like this is obviously being able to detect the tiny amounts of energy we hoped to liberate, and that was part of the Reichsuniversität's responsibilities, to build such a detector." Here he paused, and his expression, which had been full of enthusiasm for his subject up to this point, grew thoughtful and troubled.

"It wasn't built in Berlin. The first time any of the team saw it was when it was unpacked in Arkham. We *think* it was built at a reputable instrumentation manufacturer in Bavaria—that is what the plate with the serial number upon it says, anyway—but the way it just turned up with an operator was . . . troubling."

"This is the operator you're suspicious of?"

"Yes. Perhaps I'm wrong to be, but suddenly the government—"

"Ours or yours?"

"Ours. The Reich—the Ministry for Science, Education, and Public Instruction, to be exact—provided the funds for the detector and . . ." He trailed off, took a moment to organize his thoughts, and said, "Lurline Giehl. A spotless *curriculum vitae*. We were glad to have her, at first. That was before she proved so jealous of the machine."

"Jealous? How d'you mean?"

"She won't let anyone else near it. If one is blessed, she will permit his readings to be verified, but she does all the calibration herself."

"Let's go back a little. What exactly is the detector detecting?"

Lukas looked surprised. "Energy, of course. Our experimental rig is a variation on the Casimir experiment. Without going into technicalities, there is a pair of conducting plates in vacuum very, very closely mounted to one another, but with the tiniest gap between them. Classically, there should be no field, but there is one."

"This . . . zero point energy?"

"Exactly. Our experiment is to not just detect the field, but to draw upon it. The yield is tiny, but that's unimportant."

"You're just demonstrating a principle, right? If you can get a little out of this, then scaling up is an engineering problem, not a theoretical one?"

Lukas nodded, clearly pleased at not having to spell everything out. Then his expression darkened once more. "There is a political element to all this. My government seems very, very keen that we should succeed. I am concerned that Giehl might be producing numbers to match her own ambitions. It will prove very embarrassing if she is exposed as a fraud. It will taint the whole team and field of inquiry, and damage prospects of future cooperation between our countries."

Carter was having misgivings; this was all beginning to sound pretty career threatening to anyone involved, including himself if he took the case. "I'm not clear on what you expect me to do, Mr. Lukas. It's a closed site and whatever evidence there is is going to be on that detector. Which I know nothing about. What *do* you expect me to do?"

"I have the machine's schematics. There's nothing wrong with those. If that's how it's built, then it's giving accurate results. What I need is to see inside the detector. If you can get me pictures of the circuit boards, good high-resolution pictures showing the components, then I can check it against the schematics. If there are any discrepancies, then I have something to take to the project leader."

"It's still a closed site. If you're expecting me to rappel in through a skylight during the night, Mr. Lukas, you've come to the wrong place. I'm an investigator, not James Bond."

Lukas looked at him blankly. Carter belatedly summoned from his new memory the knowledge that the James Bond novels never became a big deal in the Unfolded World. Something else to dislike about it. "What I mean is, I'm not going to break the law to get these pictures. I'm sorry, Mr. Lukas, but I don't think I can help you."

Lukas sighed, disappointed but not surprised. "I told Mr. Weston I doubted you would be able to. What I've told you, you understand that it is in complete confidence?"

"Absolutely, sir. Client confidentiality comes as standard, even if I don't actually end up taking you on as a client."

Carter walked him to the door, mainly as a courtesy but also to shield him from the Medusan gaze of Emily Lovecraft, which was currently frosty enough to be close to absolute zero itself. As Lukas stepped out onto the sidewalk, Carter asked, "One thing. Something about the science. You say this energy is always there, even when there shouldn't be any. Where does it come from?"

The corner of Lukas's mouth turned down. "We are talking of the quantum world, where things are very different, Mr. Carter. There are theories, of course, but to speak frankly, we do not really know. All we *do* know is that the energy is there, and that it comes from somewhere else. Goodbye, Mr. Carter."

Chapter 5

HELIUM ICE

Dave Koznick had the cushiest job in Arkham. Not the best paid—far from it—but definitely cushy. He was the security officer for a building full of things too big and too boring for anyone to steal. This was the good life. All he had to do was wander around once every ninety minutes during the night shift (his contract said hourly, but the route didn't include any checkpoints to monitor him, so fuck that), make sure the big, boring stuff was still where it was supposed to be (most of it was bolted down, which made it suddenly vanishing even less likely), and make a note that it was exactly where it was last time, being careful to lie about his patrol times, and completely fabricate one for every three he had actually done. This complete fabrication consisted of an incorrect time and some ditto marks in the Comment column—"Nothing unusual." It was the best job he had ever had, and it was improving him as an individual, too, giving him time to do an online course in website design. He worked shifts with a couple of other stiffs like himself, but the ten-to-six was far and away his favorite. Nobody to hassle you, nobody to ask dumb-ass questions, nobody to bother you while you're wrestling with HTML.

He checked his watch. One o'clock and time for his third patrol. He was doubly glad he wasn't on days that week; the previous week he'd had the two-to-ten, and a lot of the brainiacs hung around past normal office hours. He got on okay with the home team, but the Krauts bothered him. With all the stuff about how efficient they were, he had got the idea—weird and unsubstantiated though it was—that they knew he skimmed on his night patrols and were judging him for it. They watched him a lot, and—his second paranoid theory—he wondered if they thought he was an OSS plant. Either way, he felt like an intruder when all he was there to do was to look after their stupid, heavy, boring shit. He was also kind of glad they didn't know his surname. His family had never really cared about their roots, so he didn't have an ax to grind about the Germans dissolving Poland as a state and scattering its citizens. That was history, and wartime. Thing was, if the Kraut scientists found out his name, they might *think* he did, and he'd lose this easy and very fulfilling job.

The route was always the same, although he liked to randomly decide whether he was going to go around it clockwise or counterclockwise on the flip of a coin at the beginning. He left the reception cubby that doubled as the security station in the hall and looked through the glass frontage of the building out onto the Miskatonic campus. He saw a couple of students walk by, heading away from the math building, talking intensely about something, bless their nerdy little hearts. He smiled as he dug into his pocket, found a quarter, and flipped it. Heads, he'd turn left and go around his usual route counterclockwise, tails and he'd go clockwise.

As the coin dropped, its path seemed to kink in the air as if caught in a breeze, and it fell past his waiting hand. It landed on its edge and rolled a couple of yards before coming to a rest, still on its edge.

"Well, lookit," he said to himself, looking at the coin. He considered taking a picture on his phone, but decided not to. If he'd filmed it happening, fair enough, but any fool can balance a coin on its edge and claim that was how it landed. Oh, well. Looked like he wouldn't have a reason to make a YouTube channel this week, either. Still, it had made his choice for him, covering the beginning of the counterclockwise path. Good enough. He picked up the coin and started walking.

The building had four stories, if you included the basement offices, which—as he had to patrol them—he did. The clockwise patrol went up to the top of the building first, then spiraled and zigzagged its way down to the basement before coming back up one flight of stairs and a well-deserved coffee. He preferred that way—it got the climb out of the way early on and after that it was mainly a descent. Going the counterclockwise route meant going to the basement, then a series of small slogs upward, and then the deferred gratification of coming all the way down in one go. He liked that part, but the fragmented ascent irritated him for its incoherence.

These were the concerns of a solitary security guard looking after a building full of shit too big and boring to steal.

So then, the basement. He didn't envy the guys who had to work down in the basement. It was laid out with the work area around the edges so they could glory in the few rays of sun that came through the long, narrow windows running along the upper walls, the center of the floor being taken up with window-less storage rooms, toilets, and a kitchen area. It was mainly about as open a plan as it could be, given it was holding up the rest of the building including all the big, boring, heavy shit in the upper stories, but there were still some rooms down there—a meeting room and three offices. The Krauts had grabbed two of the offices, he knew, because he'd heard some of the homegrown nerds bitching about it. They didn't mind the main guy from the

German university having an office, but there was another dude the Americans called "the political officer" behind his back who'd got the other. Koznick was pretty sure they were exaggerating for gossip; the guy seemed like he'd have to fill out forms in triplicate before even thinking about saying "boo" to a goose. Really, if he *was* Gestapo, then it was a much less scary organization than he'd been led to believe.

The offices were shut and locked, and he only had keys to the meeting room and the American project leader's. That was cool; he wasn't going to go into them, anyway. He just stopped by the door and shone his flashlight through the glass panels. Yep, no desperate thieves making off with a box of paper clips to be seen. Cool.

The Germans usually pulled down the blinds on their doors when they left them, although one wasn't consistent about that—the one they called the political officer, so that was another strike against him being Gestapo, Koznick figured. What kind of secret policeman would be sloppy about security, huh? That's right—none of them. He flashed his light inside to see if any juicy secrets of the Reich had been left out where he could read them from the window, but there was nothing. The guy might have been laid back about the blind precisely because he was so careful about clearing his desk before leaving. Koznick mentally erased the mark against him being an agent. He nodded respectfully; a clever move, Herr Gestapo. You play a deep game.

The meeting room earned only a brief glance. As usual, it looked like the garbage monster had shat on the table, but the one time the cleaners had gone in there to tidy the mess, they'd been screamed at like they'd entered a holy place. Okay, brainiacs. Just wait until the mice move in.

He shone his flashlight on the whiteboard in there and saw it covered in equations and weird squiggles, freehand graphs, and a cool one with a sort of descending spiral like a tornado that he kind of liked. He had no idea what it was—there was a mass of

numbers and Greek letters next to it that meant squat to him—
but it looked good, unlike the graph next to it, which was just a
pile of lines this way and that making an ugly mess. He clicked
off his flashlight, did a circuit to check the windows were secure,
and moved on.

He skipped the first floor, as he'd give it a quick once-over
when he returned to the security station. Besides, he spent most
of his time there and was sick of the sight of it.

The second and third stories were where all the science
happened. He didn't know what kind of science, exactly, apart
from physics, because it was a physics building. It was something
they weren't supposed to talk about, either, and he knew that
because he was supposed to report any open files, loose papers,
or unsecured computers. Plus, there was the guy who might or
might not be the mildest Gestapo agent in history. So, secret
physics.

Koznick had zero interest in physics. He'd patrolled the chem-
ical engineering building before being assigned to this one, and
that was way cooler. That place had big distillation columns that
made weird plumbing noises at night, and he had kind of liked
that once he got used to it. In contrast, the physics building had
fuck all. The second story was largely floor space for a two-story-
high volume big enough to hold the big, heavy, boring shit that
no one in their right mind would want to steal. It was bland and
didn't interest him at all. A big cylinder over here. Some kind of
pump, he guessed, over there. Lots of instruments. When he first
got the job and was told he would be covering the science buildings, the first image that had jumped into his mind was a
Frankenstein-type lab with fuming bottles and stuff bubbling.
Maybe something with sparks coming off it. The reality was
that modern science didn't live up to that, and he resented it
maybe a little for that unwitting betrayal.

The one good thing about the big rig the physicists were playing with was that at least it didn't take too long to walk around,
and the floor above wasn't much more than a ring of offices with

a walkway overlooking the floor below, the rig standing proud almost to the glass roof. Like the basement, there were low-power emergency lights burning 24/7, but they didn't do much except lead to the fire exits. If he'd been a stickler for the hourly tour he was supposed to do, he might have switched on the room lights when he entered. Those did too much to advertise when he actually made his rounds, though, so he patrolled in the murky green illumination of the emergency lights and used his flashlight sparingly. It slowed him down a little, as visibility wasn't great, and he had to walk around every desk to make sure that the sheet of paper left on a desk was just a lunch order and not something classified. In fairness, they'd been pretty good about putting away sensitive material at the end of the day, and he hadn't had to report anyone yet. This he was fine with. They were all working stiffs in their own way, after all.

Now up the last flights of stairs to the topmost level. Nothing much to do there—just some more lab space, a couple of offices, and the server room, which was another one he didn't have a key for, just a list of things he should do in a series of possible events, like fire, power cut, and so on. It mainly consisted of calling people who could come out and do some informed panicking, he guessed. Just so long as he got to pass on responsibility as soon as the shit got within a mile of the fan, he was good.

He paused on the stairs. Why was it taking him so long to get to the third floor? Hadn't he already gone past the landing? He looked back; nope, there was the door from the second floor. He must just have got distracted and not noticed where he was up to. So, up to the landing . . .

There was a piece of paper in the corner, a dropped receipt.

He remembered that, remembered thinking the cleaners were goofing off if they'd missed that. He must have noticed it on his last patrol, and yet the memory of seeing it was so fresh, as if only seconds old. He grunted, impatient with himself. *Just check the floor, go back to your damn desk, and keep on reading about web sockets.*

He opened the door and entered the third floor. He usually liked it up there, but the glitched memory was making him angry. He didn't understand the glitch, and he didn't know why it would make him angry, and that made him angrier still.

Koznick walked to the handrail of the walkway around the open area and leaned on it, breathing deeply while he regained his composure. Below him was the main laboratory floor, before him was the upper part of the test rig, and above him . . .

It can sometimes be a mistake to look up when in a high place, but Koznick was used to the building, used to the glass roof, used to looking up and seeing the moon, or ragged clouds, raindrops smashing against the glass or even snow collecting on it. He wasn't used to seeing the stars. Even the dim green glow of the emergency lights on the lab level and around him was enough to give the roof a mass of ghostly reflections of the building's interior bright enough to hide the stars. Even if they hadn't, while Arkham's light pollution wasn't as bad as some cities, it was still enough to bleach the sky and obscure all but the brightest points of light.

That was what he was used to seeing when he looked up but, this time, he saw them. He truly saw them. The glass of the roof may as well not have been there. All Arkham's streetlights may as well have been turned off. Earth's atmosphere might as well have been gone, such was the stark, penetrating, unadulterated, unmediated light of the stars upon him. The light-years that separated him from them may as well have been inches. There was no sense of him seeing the stars as they appeared three, seventy, six hundred, ten thousand years ago; he knew—somehow, he *knew*—that this was how they appeared that very instant, against a sky so black it hurt to look upon it. The darkness crushed him, and the light speared him like needles of frozen helium.

He couldn't bear to look at it, so he looked down and saw the laboratory floor a story below. It wasn't a long drop, and he'd never felt vertigo looking into it before, yet now it was its very lack of distance and scale that horrified him.

It all looked so fake, like a set for a low-budget sixties science fiction movie. The computers, the instrumentation, even the mass of the test rig felt no more real than plywood and aluminum foil props. It seemed fake, pathetic, and small. So small. Unimportant. Barely worth the effort of looking at it. And around him, an inconsequential city raised in a laughable country on a mote of a planet by a joke of a species.

Koznick's legs gave out. He fell to his knees, and then onto his back, and so he could not help himself, but could only stare up at the hungry stars as they fed upon him.

Carter was at his desk the next day at around noon when he received the call. It had not been a good morning; it was a dreary day in New York, and Red Hook, not the most charming corner of the city at the best of times, looked surly after half an hour of heavy rain. That had passed, but the sun was sullen and barely visible behind the banks of cloud that mired the city in a dismal place.

The gloom extended to his casebook, as he liked to call it on the off-chance that somebody might mistake him for Sherlock Holmes. He'd been promised . . . well, not *exactly* promised a retainer to be on call by the hotel where he had so brilliantly solved *The Adventure of the Purloined Bedlinen*, but now the manager had told him that the chain had some deal with a major security company and weren't interested in freelancers. Given that the possibility of a retainer was what had tipped him into taking the job in the first place, Carter was not pleased. If he picked up the casebook and gave it a good shake, nothing remotely like a steady cash flow poured out of it.

Given the silence of his phone, and the dearth of anything useful in his e-mails, he was concentrating on putting together ideas for a cheap media blitz. Looking at his budget, he figured he might just be able to stretch to stapling flyers on poles. If it wasn't for the steady income that Lovecraft's running of the shop brought in, he would barely be getting by at all, he realized, and he didn't like that feeling. He needed work, and he needed it urgently. He glared at the desk phone, willing it to ring, but it ignored him, like usual. Carter returned his attention to the free poster design software he'd found online. He couldn't remember if it was a good idea or a bad one to use lots of different typefaces. Good, surely? It must be. People like variation.

New York was saved from a horror of six fonts by Carter's cell phone ringing.

"Mr. Carter? This is Torsten Lukas. We spoke the other day, if you recall?"

"I do, Mr. Lukas. How can I help you today?"

"You turned down the commission I offered you on the grounds that you would need access to the site, and there was no way to do that discreetly, yes?"

It wasn't the only reason, but it was the main one. "Yes."

"A situation has developed here. A post for a security guard has opened."

A rent-a-cop? Carter didn't like the idea of that at all. "Sir, I'm sure you can find—"

"I brought it to the attention of Weston Edmunds, who apparently have some influence at the university. The job is yours for the taking."

Carter was just wondering how to say "No" with sufficient diplomacy given how much trouble had already been made over this when Lukas added, "Obviously the university will just think that you're an ex-cop who needs the work, and will pay you for the role. This will be in addition to the fee I shall be paying you."

A rapid monetary calculation rattled through Carter's mind, adding the security guard fee to his own—no, wait, *double* his own—and then his share of the receipts from the bookstore. He suddenly felt pretty well off. Or, at least he would be, providing he accepted the job. He weighed the fact that he'd be taking a Nazi's money along with the faint sense that something was a

little hinky about the job, and then set that against the emaciated state of his casebook. It was not a complex equation, and
the result did not surprise him.

"Okay, Mr. Lukas, you have yourself a detective. I'll send you
a contract and we can get started."

"Bring the contract along tomorrow, Mr. Carter, and I'll sign
it then when I'm unobserved."

"At the university?"

"At the university. It will be your first day on the job."

Chapter 6

Lovecraft was not sympathetic. It was way, way too funny to be in any way diluted by sympathy. When Carter had arrived at the bookstore wearing a sky-blue shirt with navy-blue pocket covers, a belt bearing a flashlight, a stun gun, and a holster for a Walther PPQ M2 in .40 caliber, her delight had been uncontained. The pistol itself was sitting in a weapons safe at the security building at Miskatonic University.

"They gave me a German pistol," he complained. "Why couldn't they buy American?"

Lovecraft really didn't care about that. "Put on the hat! Put on the hat!"

Carter looked sourly at the peaked cap with a Miskatonic security logo on the front of the hat band. "I'm not putting this thing on."

"Aww, come on, Dan. You'll have to wear it on duty. Might as well get used to it."

He looked stonily at her. "Right. Fine. Don't laugh."

She adopted a very sober face that didn't fool either of them for a moment.

"Fine." Carter put on the cap.

Lovecraft's composure disintegrated immediately. She whooped loudly at him from a range of less than a yard, making him flinch. "Strip-o-gram! Strip-o-gram!" She opened the till and pulled out a ten-dollar bill. "Make momma happy and I'll tuck this in your thong." She leaned expectantly on the counter, her grin broad, the bill dangling between two fingers. Carter glared at her and went to remove the offending cap. Lovecraft whooped again. "Take it *all* off, baby!"

"Are you finished?"

"Sure." Still smiling, she replaced the bill and closed the till drawer. "Like it would be worth ten bucks to see *your* action. I don't think so."

"Don't push me, Lovecraft." Carter dropped his hat on the counter. "I'm carrying a stun gun. You really don't want to provoke me."

"So you're undercover? Or are things just tough in Gumshoeville?"

"Both. Not enough people walking through the door looking for dirt on their significant others. Still, been a long time since I was last undercover."

"Weird kind of undercover where you're pretending to be a security guy."

"I'm not pretending. They're paying me to do that work, so I'll do it. It's just, I might be doing a couple of other things while I'm there that they're not paying me for. Somebody else is."

Lovecraft's smile faded to nothing. "The Nazi the other day."

"His name is Lukas. I've been asking around about the 'Nazi' thing. It really is considered impolite to use it these days." He didn't like the look evolving on Lovecraft's face and added, a little weakly, "Go figure."

"*The 'N' word?* Really? He stood right there and . . . holy shit. What did he call me when you two went upstairs?"

Carter was reasonably confident that telling her would be a mistake, so he said, "We talked business. It doesn't all have to be about you, you know."

"What do we call the Nazi fucks if we can't call them Nazis? I need to differentiate my common, workaday fucks from the Nazi ones. How?"

"They prefer to be called 'the NSDAP,' or 'the Nationals,' or just 'the Party,' if it makes sense in context."

"Do they?"

"They do."

"You looked that stuff up."

"I did."

She considered the options. "The NSDAP, huh?"

"Yeah. It means something in German."

She picked up his cap, put it on, gave herself an impromptu toothbrush moustache with her left index and middle fingers against her upper lip, and threw a Nazi salute with her right. "Nationalsozialistische Deutsche Arbeiterpartei," she said in guttural little barks. Her attitude softened as she took the cap off and dropped it back on the counter. "Out of all the things that are fucked up in this world, the last one I was expecting was Nazis marching around as a superpower. I'd kind of managed to brace myself for all sorts of supernatural shit, but this . . . *this* I was not ready for."

Carter went to the door, put up the *Back Soon* sign, and pulled the blind. "We have to talk about what we're going to try and do."

"About? About all this?" Lovecraft spread her hands to encompass the Unfolded World in all its profound disorder. "What can we do?"

"Whatever Randolph and H.P.L. did. The Fold isn't destroyed. It's still there. Somewhere. We *can* reverse it."

"How? Waite's Bill has gone. Your cop friend—"

"I have *lots* of cop friends . . ."

"Harrelson says the spit's gone. According to city records, it was deliberately dug out to make a marina in the late forties. Then the owners—the . . . Waites, I'm talking about here . . ." She hesitated as she said the name, a sudden vision of what the Waites truly were flickering across her mind's eye before she could shoo the image away to somewhere in her memory where it would do less harm. ". . . changed their minds. Sure they did. They knew we might fix their shit and they took away a piece of the coastline to stop it happening. Every day, Dan, every day I half-expect somebody to walk through that door and kill me."

Carter nodded at the counter. "You've got the Mossberg."

"Whoever they send will laugh at a Mossberg. *Whatever* they send. I keep going through what I can remember of H.P.L.'s stories in my mind, just thinking about what might come after us. If they want us dead, we're dead. Fuck, we're *worse* than dead."

Carter shrugged. "Well, they obviously don't want us dead or we would be by now."

Lovecraft sighed, unsmiling. "Mr. Sunshine."

"I have an optimistic disposition."

"Let's be real about this. They haven't come after us because we are beneath their notice. Like, bacterial level to them. Don't be going making us out to be occult-sassin', eldritch-slingin' bad-asses who they're afraid of, 'cos we ain't and they ain't. We're alive because those fuckers forgot about us. I thought I could live with that. Arkham's prettier than Providence ever was. Wiser. More character. I like this town way more."

Carter wasn't sure what to say. He'd taken it for granted that Lovecraft would want the Folded World back, just like him. When she put it that way, though, maybe she had a point. So this world had a background hum of weirdness emanating from the deepest recesses of space. He'd been born under the threat of mutually assured nuclear destruction, had lived in a world of religious terrorism, antibiotic failure, and anthropogenic climate change. What was a bunch of Elder Gods and Old Ones on top of that? If they wanted to bring an apocalypse upon humanity, they could just take a ticket and wait.

"But"—Lovecraft angled her head and looked Carter in the eye; he saw her old fire rekindling there—"I am *not* putting up with fucking Nazis. White supremacist jerk-offs are a big enough pain in the ass without them forming friendly societies to cheerlead for the real and actual motherfucking Third Reich." She shook her head adamantly. "No. Not happening. I could not physically care less about Cthulhu and all that shit as long as they keep leaving us alone. But Nazis? I can't be cool with that, Dan. I can't be going, 'Oh, Arkham in the springtime. So nice, I don't mind the planet's sticky with all this *Mein Kampf* bullshit.' I *do* mind. I want to refold the world. I want to crush those fuckers like ants in origami."

Carter nodded. "Nice image."

"Yeah. I should send it to *Reader's Digest*." She leaned on the counter and looked seriously at Carter. "One thing I'm wondering is, can we do the Fold *just so* and come out the other side still with Arkham? I mean, Arkham instead of getting Providence back?" She shrugged. "I really love this place."

Campus security at Miskatonic had some interesting foibles. The senior officer was dubbed "the Sergeant," while his subordinates were all "constables." There was nothing contractually that said anything like that, but it was tradition and Arkham loved its traditions, the more "olde worlde," the better. Under the circumstances, Carter was relieved he just had to contend with a peaked cap and not a Keystone Kops–style helmet.

Constable Carter arrived at the security building—a grandiose sort of name for a small one-story structure by the main road entering the campus—in plenty of time to start the six-to-two morning shift. Sergeant Graves was just finishing up signing off some expense claims when he entered.

"Good morning, Constable," he said. Graves had seemed okay on their first meeting when Carter had gone through the formality of an interview for a job they both knew was already his. A big man carrying some weight he didn't seem in much of a hurry to lose, Graves was marking time before retirement. Carter had made a guess from his accent that Graves was maybe ex–Detroit PD, but—beyond confirming he was a former cop like all of campus security—hadn't asked right then.

"Good morning, Sergeant. Thought I'd come in a little early and learn the small stuff."

"That's good." Graves put away the papers and smiled at Carter, and Carter realized with a small shock that Graves actually liked him. He had somehow got it into his head that there would be some fencing since he was the new guy. "Sign in here, then come through and I'll issue you your weapon."

Carter signed the entry log, then went behind the counter area into the back room were the gun safe was. It used a key and code combination, and Graves waved Carter to the safe to open it himself. He'd be expected to put the gun back himself at the end of his shift, so it made sense to make sure he knew how to open the thing. Once he had done so, he stepped aside while Graves removed a Walther from the interior, checked its serial against the weapon log, gave it a quick field strip and reassembly on the desk while talking Carter through it, and formally handed it over to Carter. He signed it off as issued, and then passed the log to Carter to sign it as accepted.

"In the future, you only need to sign it in and out of the safe," said Graves, loading a clip with hollow points and handing it to Carter.

"What are these things like? I don't have any range time with a Walther."

"They're nice. Reliable and really flows well when you aim, if you get me. Say what you like about the Germans, they make good firearms. You should get some shooting in with one, though. What are you used to?"

"A Glock."

"Ah, you'll have no problems. They handle pretty much the same. Must admit, I prefer the Walther, though. More natural in the hand."

Carter slammed the magazine home, chambered a round, checked the weapon was safe, and holstered it. "Just the one clip?"

"University policy. To be frank, I've been here eight years and rarely even had to draw. Had to fire a warning shot once a while back when some idiot came on campus with an assault rifle. Otherwise"—he reached down and tapped the stun gun and pepper spray on his belt—"these are your weapons of choice. Remember: shooting students is bad for the university's reputation. The regents frown upon it."

"I'll bear that in mind. I hate to upset regents."

Graves smiled again. "That's the attitude. Okay. All easy stuff. Hourly patrols, but try and be unobtrusive when people are actually in and working outside normal hours. Keep it to public areas, the foyer and a circuit of the outside in that case. From nine to eighteen hundred, somebody has to be at the security station, so that's you from nine to two. Keep your rest breaks as short as you can, because somebody will always bitch if there isn't a uniform at the station every goddamn second." He took a breath. "Anything else you need to know?"

The guard just coming off the ten-to-six shift was called Ward, and he looked very glad to see Carter. "Man, I am bushed. Cannot wait to get home."

"I'm Dan Carter, the new guy." They shook hands. "Rough night?"

"My circadian rhythms are all screwed. Be easier tomorrow when I'm back on the six-to-two."

"My shift?" This was news to Carter. Maybe he should have asked the sergeant more questions.

"My shift. I was just doing this while they got a new hand. Moving forward a shift isn't too bad, but going back one? Whoa, mama. Painful."

"Was the previous guy fired or something? Didn't they have a chance to get a new hire before he left?"

Ward looked at him like a man wondering how to couch bad news diplomatically, and then deciding, *Ah, fuck it.* "Dude, your predecessor went crazy. I found him curled up in a ball at the beginning of my shift two days ago." Again he momentarily considered diplomacy and, again, decided not to bother. "He'd pissed himself, wasn't making sense. I thought maybe he was high or something. Tried to rouse him a little bit, pull himself together, right? Didn't want him to get reported or nothing. Dave was a stand-up guy. Nice guy. So, no trouble. I try, he starts screaming. I mean fit-to-spit-up-a-lung screaming. I saw guys shot and burnt on the job—you're ex-NYPD, Sarge said. That right?—and they didn't scream anything like that." He signed out as he spoke. "Anyway, that was Dave done and gone." He pointed. "The john's over there. Otherwise you're pretty much on your ass at the station from nine till two, so you should get some walking in now while you still can. You'll miss it later. Have fun."

He paused at the door on the way out. "Hope I didn't freak you out about Dave. It's not like the lab's haunted or anything. Take care and don't shoot the geeks."

"Yeah, Sarge told me about that."

"Rules to live by. See you, Dan."

And Carter was alone in the building. Just him and the lingering ghost of sudden insanity. This, he concluded, was probably not the smoothest induction into a job imaginable.

What he did like was the general attitude that they were all grown-up enough to just get on with the job without handholding. That was excellent. What was also nearly excellent was, here he was, all alone in the building where he was supposed to be, with a good hour or so before even the early birds might be expected to show up. It was all excellent, but for the minor details that he wasn't inclined to take the pictures of the detector's internal components without first having a contract in place, and secondly, he had no earthly idea what the detector looked like.

Before even settling in at the security station, he went up to the second story and wandered the laboratory floor to familiarize himself with where he would be carrying out a tiny bit of petty larceny, providing the client came through. The contract he had printed off for Lukas's signature was not quite standard as far as emoluments and expenses went; with some chivying from Lovecraft at his shoulder acting as the anti–Jiminy Cricket, he had upped his usual fee a little before doubling it in line with Weston's promised payday. "Stickin' it to the *Übermensch*," she had called it.

Carter had not been convinced. "I'm not sure overcharging one Gestapo stooge is going to bring down the Third Reich."

Lovecraft remained optimistic. "Death by a thousand cuts."

In any event, he wasn't going to do any industrial espionage for Lukas until he had his name on a contract.

The equipment in the laboratory was precisely as baffling as he had expected. He walked around it for a few minutes, looking up into the open atrium formed by the partial third floor and glass roof. The space was dominated by a tall cylinder perhaps a couple of yards in diameter, skinned in gleaming sectioned steel panels and stretching up close to the glass. Assorted pipes and important-looking boxes were attached to the exterior, and Carter gained the impression that it was a pressure vessel of some kind, probably—based on what he had been told by Lukas—one intended to withstand an internal total vacuum. Lukas had said that the measurements were conducted between two plates an almost unimaginably small distance apart. As a result, Carter had expected the test rig to be no more than bench-sized; the great thirty-foot-high cylinder was therefore unexpected. He wondered if it was from a different project and just too expensive to remove for the period that the American-German team would be working in the building, but a glance around didn't indicate anything else that looked like it might be able to generate and maintain as near a perfect vacuum as human science could manage. He looked up at the cylinder again; perhaps somebody was overcompensating for something.

At five past seven, the first of the scientists arrived. Carter was relieved it was Lukas, who eyed him with some surprise as he approached the reception counter.

"Good morning, Mr. Carter. I was not expecting to see you quite so early."

"I work quickly." He produced an envelope containing two copies of the revised standard contract. "But until you sign that, I'm not working for you. I'm on shift until two. Read it and—"

But Lukas had already taken out the contracts and signed both without reading them. He slid them over to Carter. "Now you sign and we have a deal." Carter took the pen and, hesitating for longer than Lukas had despite knowing exactly what was in the contracts, he signed both, passing one back to Lukas.

"There. Now we're all legal. Now show me the thing I'm supposed to be getting pictures of."

Lukas led the way back up the stairs onto the lab floor. "That." He pointed at a bland unit about four feet high by four wide and two deep painted in gray-blue paint. It bore a flat-screen monitor on its top surface, and an odd keyboard sat by it, half the size of a standard one, the keys labeled with a mixture of numbers, Latin and Greek alphabetical characters, and some faintly mathematical squiggles. He frowned and looked at Lukas, who shook his head. "It baffles me, too," he admitted.

At the back of the unit were power and data leads, as well as connections to the screen and keyboard. There was also a lock. "Only Giehl has the key. It is ludicrous."

Carter quickly audited his lock-picking skills and found them rusty. "I didn't think the machine would actually be locked."

Lukas looked at him blankly then, understanding, shook his head. "No, the lock is not for the cover. It is for the operation of the detector. No one else can use it. I do not think the Americans . . . our American colleagues have noticed Giehl unlocks it in the morning and locks it again when work is done for the day yet. I hope they do not; it would be embarrassing."

Carter was beginning to understand Lukas's concerns about the numbers the detector was producing; it seems a bizarre level of security for something that was just a fancy ammeter. Farther down the back of the machine, he saw the access cover. "I'll bring in a power drill. Should make pretty short . . . Ah, shit." He straightened. "Nonstandard heads." He checked his watch. "You ever try to get into this thing by yourself?"

"I am rarely alone, and the boards will have to be removed for photographing. It is not something that can be done quickly."

Carter could see that; his original estimation of ten or twenty minutes to get the pictures was now heading upward toward an hour. He took out his phone and took some quick pictures of the unusual screws. He straightened, looked around, and spotted a poster stuck to a supporting column bearing the image of a red stop sign Photoshopped to read *If this sign looks blue, slow down.* He went to it and misappropriated some of the generous quantity of Fun-Tak used to put it up before returning to the detector and wedging the lump into the screw head. It came away again bearing a reasonable impression of the shape of the screwdriver head to deal with it. He placed it by a ruler he found on a desk and took a couple more pictures.

"That will have to do. We can't expect to have the place to ourselves much longer." As he squashed the putty into a ball and put it back under the poster, he said, "I'll see about getting a tool to undo those screws, although I won't have a chance to do that until tomorrow at the earliest. Seems I'm back here this evening for the ten-to-six shift as well."

Chapter 7

NECRONOMICON

Lovecraft liked her sleep. She liked to stop looking at any illuminated screens after 9:00 p.m. Who needed them, after all, when you had books? She liked to be in bed sooner rather than later, and she liked to do so in the company of a good book or, occasionally, an entertainingly bad one. Sometimes work precluded this; she would break her screens rule to check her e-mails perhaps once an hour and once immediately before putting the lights out, but she would only open them if their subject lines piqued her interest. She liked to sleep deeply until the alarm rang at seven in the morning. She didn't mind dreaming, even if some of the dreams had been disordered and even harrowing immediately prior and subsequent to the world's unfolding. Yet these dreams had been half-remembered and faded quickly.

The one she experienced that morning was unusual in that it was as vivid as reality. She dreamt that she was no longer in her

apartment, but in her bookstore. This was not unusual in itself—she spent much of her waking life there and it would be extraordinary if that experience did not impinge upon the workings of her sleeping mind. That she dreamt that she was in the bookstore wearing the baggy T-shirt and comfortable pajama shorts she preferred to sleep in was unusual, however. Even in the dream she knew this was odd. Why was she wearing them there? Had she walked the streets dressed like that? She didn't remember doing that. Had she sleepwalked? On an impulse, she checked the soles of her feet, but they were clean. Okay, she hadn't walked. Maybe she'd gone to sleep in the apartment over the store and forgotten about it. She never had before, but it was more reasonable than unheralded somnambulism, so she accepted it with the easy assent of dream logic.

She wasn't just there to stand around, though. There was something that she was pretty sure she should be doing. She looked around and caught sight of herself in the glass of the Edwardian bookcase mounted on the wall behind the counter in which were kept some nice old volumes, too valuable to go out on the shelves yet not valuable enough to go in the safe. Her reflection had bed head, which even within the dream struck her as a very thorough detail for her unconscious mind to include.

There she wavered on the edge of a lucid dream, aware she was dreaming, yet too caught up in the milieu to impose her own will upon it.

She blinked. She was supposed to be doing something. Something important. She realized she was holding a key in her hand and remembered. Oh, yeah. Of course.

She bent before the safe and unlocked it in actions so reflexive they felt as natural as breathing. She had one of the storage boxes out and on the counter before she knew what she was doing. It was only when she went to open it that she began to wonder why she was doing it at all. Her hands wavered over the lid and she began to form an intimation that all really was not well.

"I should wake up now," she said aloud. "There's going to be tentacles and shit if I open that box. I've seen this movie before."

Her hands continued to waver. She told her arms to relax, to fall by her sides, but they would not. Unbidden, her traitorous fingers took hold of the edge of the hinged lid.

"It's *really* important," she said, but she wasn't sure if they were her words.

She opened the box.

There were no tentacles, which was good. Instead, the box contained what it was supposed to contain, and that was bad. The volume of collated fragments of Dee's translation of the *Necronomicon* lay before her. She stared at it, and suffered an ugly sense that it was staring back.

She had been through the records to find where the books in the safe had originally come from. She was not surprised— indeed, she was relieved—that the unfolded her had not bought them. They had been her uncle's purchases, and he had never tried to sell them himself. She knew why; these were for reference, not profit. Besides, as she had said to Carter herself, she'd as soon sell these as she would anthrax bombs to a teenager. God only knew what they might inspire if let loose in the world. Better they stay here, contained and impotent in the safe.

The *Necronomicon* wasn't in the safe, though. It was lying there being indefinably malign, and she hated the sight of even its closed cover. Suddenly she realized why the unfolded her had decided to sell *Von Unaussprechlichen Kulten*. She didn't believe in what these books contained. They were just a valuable curio like an early edition of the *Malleus Maleficarum*. The *Necronomicon* hadn't been sold not because it was an apocalypse in handy take-home form, but because she had never found the right buyer.

The folded version of her knew better, though. Maybe being so close to the Perceptual Twist, or Fold, or whatever the fuck it was when it did its thing had put the folded her and Carter and even Harrelson in control over their unfolded variants. She didn't know. Maybe the answer was in the black book before her, but she was damned if she was going to open it and find out. She had a concrete sense that she would be damned just by opening it right then.

Lovecraft noticed her right hand was on the edge of the cover. Her eyes widened.

"No! No no no no no no! Don't do that!"

Her hand might as well have flipped her the bird. Instead, it flipped the book open.

Carter's guess as to how much time he and Lukas had for his *in situ* briefing was about right. He was barely back at the reception desk when the scientists began to arrive. Most ignored him as they came through in dribs and drabs. Some flashed IDs at him, while others just made a point of having them clipped to their shirts or dangling from lanyards. This saved him the hassle of demanding to see IDs just to show enthusiasm, as there was nothing in his list of standing orders to cover it beyond "Ensuring only authorized persons are on site at all times." If he hadn't been aware of the political dimensions of the project up to now, the dithering nervousness of the security protocols would have made him wonder. They bore an air of "This is a scientific institute, but I suppose we should make an effort." The result wasn't the tightest site imaginable, but intruders would still be spotted fairly quickly. It was astonishingly fortuitous he was being paid to be there.

The serendipity of his predecessor's sudden breakdown was becoming more suspicious by the second, the more he saw of the project's functioning. Any other way in here would have had him pegged as an intruder in five minutes flat. Instead, he was invisible under a peaked cap that he wore with perfect legality. He did not have to pretend to be a security guard; he *was* a security guard, and he would be earning his paycheck and fulfilling his contract, except for the minor detail of covertly opening and examining a piece of equipment that might as well be filled with pixie dust and tumbleweed for all he understood of its working. He was pretty sure that, at least, fell above his pay grade.

It was easy to tell the German contingent from the Americans, although not quite as easy as Lovecraft had implied. It was true that the Germans were homogeneous in their whiteness, unlike the Americans, who almost reached parity between Caucasians and Asians with a handful of African Americans in the mix. The Germans, on the other hand, were doing much better with regard to sex, with a fifty/fifty split between male and female. Nor, Carter observed, were the women in subordinate roles; he watched as a covey of six German physicists entered the building, five trying to convince the woman at the center of the swarm of some eldritch point of abstruse physics in terms made further obscure to him by their being couched in rapid German. She listened with an expression of distant interest until abruptly stopping in the middle of the foyer, turning to her chief interrogator, and briefly replying in a couple of sentences—both of which were, however, heavily laden with syllables. The other physicist asked her a new question, although it was clear from his face that he'd just had the carpet pulled from beneath his feet and was just realizing it. The woman smiled at him, shook her head, and said something short and, it seemed, devastating to his argument. The other scientists betrayed a mixture of enlightenment at her answer and amusement at their colleague's discomfort as his carefully constructed theory augured into a field in Ohio with no survivors, to judge from his face.

As she led the party to the fire doors leading into the stairwell, she glanced at the reception desk and saw Carter watching them. A small frown crossed her brow, but then she looked away and she and her group were gone. Slightly discomfited by the meeting of eyes himself, Carter sat down and tried to reconcile his knowledge that every one of that group was a paid-up member of the Nazi Party, and that he had found the woman attractive. He decided instantly and reflexively that he would not mention this observation to Lovecraft at any point, for fear of subsequently dying a slow death by scorn and derision.

Carter arrived back at the bookstore at half past two and was surprised to find it closed. Letting himself in, he almost fell over Lovecraft who had stationed herself close by the door on a stool.

"What the hell?" he demanded, startlement making him loud. "What are you doing, Emily?"

She gave him a look he had seen before, and that never boded well; she was afraid, and angry about it. His surprise changed to concern. "What's wrong? Has something happened?"

She was silent for a moment, looking for the words. Then she said simply, "It's started again."

"It" was a wide and generic term that had arisen unconsciously in their conversation before and after the unfolding of the world. "It" meant a variety of things, but all of them could be brought under the umbrella of "weird shit."

They had been given a hiatus from the more hard-boiled end of "it" until now, their lives being filled for weeks and months with the encroaching and constant background radiation of "it" that living in the Unfolded World gave them. Every day brought a deluge of "it," and the best strategy was just to let "it" slide by. Nobody in the Unfolded World said, "Lock and load," for example, because the phrase was supposed to be "Load and lock," but John Wayne fucked the line up in *Sands of Iwo Jima* and it had become part of the vocabulary of the Folded World.

Here, however, the Duke never got a chance to transpose the words, because the movie was never made, because the battle for Iwo Jima had never taken place, because the USA never entered the Second World War, because the Germans talked the Japanese out of Pearl Harbor and redirected their attention to mainland Asia, and the Japanese listened because "the fucking Germans fucking vaporized fucking Moscow" (this being Lovecraft's exact phrase to Carter on discovering the schism), and if the Japanese hadn't had a proverb about respecting the wishes of a country that can vaporize cities before Moscow sucked on twenty kilotons of atomic airburst, they sure did afterward.

"It" also covered the misty details of a world that was not simply a historical counterfactual brought into actual, vibrant existence, but something that was skewed from what Carter and Lovecraft had known in many small ways. The most obvious was that Arkham and its near neighbors existed at all, but there were a vast multitude of other things that plainly predated the folding of the world in the 1920s. Things like whispers of lost cities, and peculiar episodes in the lives of the great, the good, and the not so good.

And then there were the unusual books.

Lovecraft was pointing at a book lying open on the counter beside an open storage box.

"*That*," she said, and she didn't use anything like the tone she often adopted when talking about books, "*that* was not on the counter last night."

Carter tried to remember whether it had been there when he went to work that morning, but he had been in a hurry and had barely glanced around the store before leaving and locking up. The book looked familiar.

"Isn't that the . . . uh, *Necro* . . . What was it called? *Necronom*—"

"Yeah. That's exactly what it is. I dreamt I took it out of the safe last night. I dreamt I opened it when I really, really didn't want to."

Carter nodded at the book open on the counter. "Just like that?"

"I opened the book, took it out of the box. I couldn't help

myself. Then I woke up all sweaty and shit." She realized how that sounded. "Sweaty. Just sweaty."

Carter began to walk toward the counter.

"What are you doing?" said Lovecraft.

"Seeing where you opened it. It might be important."

"It *might* be dangerous."

"It's just a book." He allowed a slight dismissive tone into his voice and regretted it immediately.

Lovecraft grabbed his arm, pulled him around, and glared in his face almost nose to nose. "It is not *just a book*. There is nothing *just a book* about that thing. It's a metaphysical virus. It's a mind killer. It's the fucking apocalypse with page numbers. It is *not*"—she placed the flat of her palm against Carter's chest and pushed him hard enough to make him step back—"light reading."

"It still might be important. You're right; it's happening again." Lovecraft frowned again, but this time with curiosity, and Carter quickly added, "This job I'm doing. It's beginning to feel a lot like somebody is pulling strings. If Henry Weston offering it to me in the first place wasn't enough, it turns out that the only reason I'm able to do it at all is because the guy before me had some sort of breakdown."

"The previous security guard?"

"The night after I turned the job down precisely because I couldn't get in there unseen. Now I can."

"You think that Nazi—?"

Carter shook his head. "Just because the man's got Party membership, it only makes him a Nazi by name. I don't think he's a bad guy."

"A nice Nazi."

"Yeah, a nice Nazi. Look, Emily, this is this world, not ours. You're going to have to get past the whole Nazis being elemental-evil thing."

She looked at him as if he were simpleminded. "Nuh-uh. We know. We *know* what they would have done in a New York second if things had just been a little different."

"But . . . they didn't do them. They nuked Stalin instead and became heroes of the Western world. They gave back almost everything they'd conquered in Europe. In this world, the Swastika is a symbol for . . . I don't know. Civilization."

"Fuck that." Lovecraft said it sullenly and Carter knew then that she would never change her mind. If he was honest with himself, he wasn't sure he could, either. He was trying to be pragmatic about their situation, but he just succeeded in making himself feel like a hypocrite.

Lovecraft went to the counter, opened a drawer, and took out a pair of white cotton gloves and a slip of brownish, unbleached paper. She put the slip into the *Necronomicon* as a bookmark while making every effort not to look at what was on the page, then closed it, using one of the gloves as a buffer between her skin and the cover. Still using the gloves without bothering to put them on, like somebody using cloths to protect herself while handling a piece of hot metal, she picked it up, put it back in its box and shut it with a distinct sigh of relief.

She looked over the box at Carter. "Speaking of just what a solid the Nazis did for the heartlands of capitalism, doesn't that whole thing bother you?"

"So the Germans developed the atom bomb before we did. Nobody's ever called them scientifically backward. What are you saying?"

"Historically . . . in our history . . . they didn't get within spitting distance of a workable bomb. A lot of the best guys for the job were Jewish, and they'd run off. A lot of them ended up on the Manhattan Project. So, they didn't have all the best minds they could have, plus they didn't have easy access to uranium, plus pretty early on the British working with the Norwegian resistance blew the Germans' only supply of heavy water to shit. Even if that last thing didn't happen here, the other two are still plenty problematical. Yet somehow they got a nuke that worked to specification the very first time."

"They didn't test?"

"I've been reading up on that. The official line is a smaller version that was detonated in a mine someplace in Austria. It worked perfectly, so they upscaled and sneakily got it into Soviet airspace, right over Red Square. Blew up a bunch of their guys, including their senior ambassador to the Kremlin, but, y'know, acceptable losses and shit." She put the storage box back in the safe, locked it away, and came back to lean on the counter. "Some really interesting conspiracy chat about all that. Seems that Moscow is a ghost city to this day. When the Reich rolled into Russia and conquered as much of it as they could eat, they walled off Moscow because of 'contamination.' The wall's still up. Nobody's allowed inside. Now, if it's a relatively low-powered atom bomb compared to what came later, why is there still contamination? That didn't happen with Hiroshima and Nagasaki in the Folded World. Uranium ain't like plutonium; contamination goes pretty quickly 'cos the half-life is that much shorter. So, tell me, what's going on inside that wall?"

"That's rhetorical, right?"

"No, Dan. I thought you could ask your nice Nazi. Yeah, it's rhetorical." She sat on the stool behind the counter and propped her chin up with her hands. "You think you're being manipulated?"

"Again." He gestured at the safe. "Maybe both of us."

"For what reason?"

"How would I know? I thought H.P.L.'s weird gods' schemes were beyond the understanding of mere humans."

"Maybe on a grand scale, but we're only seeing what's going on close to the metal. Down here with the bugs and the germs, we can see aims maybe, even if we don't see the big picture." She seemed distant for a moment, remembering something that was not pleasant to recall. "Charity Waite . . ."

The name hung in the air like a draft of nerve gas. Carter unconsciously stepped back.

Happy not to have to say the name again, Lovecraft continued, "*She* said something the last time I saw her. When she went.

When she left. She said, 'We have common interest with so many.' She said everything that happened with Colt wasn't to do with her, at least not to start with. There are factions, Dan. Now they've got their sandbox back, fuck only knows what games they're playing in it."

Chapter 8

THE HAUNTED PALACE OF SCIENCE

Carter made his apologies, but he really needed to get some sleep if he was going to be in any kind of shape to take on another eight-hour shift starting at ten that evening.

"Can you do me a favor?" He fished out his phone. "I'm sending you some pictures I took today of some weird screws and an impression I made of the kind of head a screwdriver would need to have to remove them. Could you find a supplier, please?"

Lovecraft was just finishing making a notice that read, *Closed for inventory. Please knock for attention.* She went to put it on the door and pulled the blinds.

"Right. So if your exciting adventure in scientific espionage goes to shit and I get cops in here, or—better yet—the Feds, they can find that I helped you from my search history. Sound plan, Dan."

"Don't worry. They'll be too busy laughing at your tentacle *hentai* porn to find it."

He'd said it as a joke, but he saw her eyes slightly widen.

"Oh, my God. Emily . . ." He couldn't help laughing.

"Once," she said, mortified. "*Once*. Just out of interest. And that was in the Folded World, anyway."

"Yeah. You'd never have a sly look at squid porn in any other version of the universe, right?"

She thought about that and her face fell. "Shit."

"If you find anywhere that sells a screwdriver that fits those heads, order one with express delivery, okay? I'll pay you back." He went to go up to the apartment.

"Yeah, yeah," he heard her mutter behind him. "Can't talk now. Searching my browser history." As the door closed behind him, he heard her whistle low and mutter to herself, "Why, you *dirty* girl."

The test chamber was in the process of being worked toward the most perfect vacuum attainable to terrestrial science. This was substantially more perfect than such poor vacuums as, say, outer space, around which peripatetic atoms and micrograins of complex matter might be found floating around, making the spaces between the stars grubby, and unsuitable for serious science.

While the chamber once again reached such a state, there was little to do in the lab except check and recheck figures, run the sensors through software tests, catch up on general paperwork, and—for everyone else—goof off in scientifically stringent ways. The American and the German teams were polite enough to each other, but they spent little time fraternizing. Part of this was the language barrier—not all the Germans spoke good conversational English, and just about none of the Americans spoke German—and partly the slightly disquieting sense the Americans had that the project was a done deal and they, the Americans, were only being permitted involvement to provide a patina of international collaboration. Results so far had been so good, without false starts or ambiguities, that although no one said as much there was a feeling of stage management, as if they were spear carriers in a play whose script they were not permitted to see.

It didn't make for a good working atmosphere, which wasn't helped by the visits every American scientist had received at home from FBI agents telling them not to become too familiar with their counterparts as it was a working certainty that one or more of them were Abwehr agents. The German intelligence service—just as with most other intelligence services—was not above setting honey traps to ensnare the unwary. Thanks to the FBI intervention, the American contingent was now all too aware, and treated their counterparts as if they were potentially radioactive.

Only those that needed to be near the chamber during pumping out were. The vacuum was maintained as much as possible, but the limits of engineering meant it had to be scoured for rogue molecules now and then, and the pumps that held the chamber in its near-pristine state were not quiet. The dull thudding of the early evacuation was long past, but the rapid beats of the finer-grade pump was too close to that of a penetrating headache to be tolerated by most for long.

Dr. Lukas was checking the almost-but-not-quite implausibly good figures for the last run when he felt a presence by his shoulder. He looked up.

"Still going though those, Torsten?" asked the woman standing over him.

Lukas fought down the urge to behave like a guilty schoolboy and hide what he was doing. Instead, he said, "Just being diligent, Lurline."

"You're an example to us all." Her tone was lightly mocking. He was used to that.

"Is there anything I can help you with?"

"No, no. Just killing time until we're ready for the sixth series. If the second half of the program returns results as convincing as the first, I think we may be well on our way to Nobel Prizes, don't you?"

Lukas couldn't make himself get excited about such a prospect. A small nagging voice told him the experiment would be discredited well before then. "Perhaps. We need to do much more than we're doing here to create convincing results."

"Of course." She perched on the side of the desk. "But we are doing good science here. Soon we shall be ready to use a larger apparatus. Perhaps even draw a useful amount of energy."

"That is presuming much."

She stood up, and laughed once. "I am an incurable optimist, and optimism is how things get done." She looked up at the rig for several seconds before adding, "There's a new man on security."

The change of direction caught Lukas by surprise, and he found himself saying, "Is there? I can't say I'd noticed."

"Hmmmm." She looked off in the general direction of the security desk, as if she could see the new man there. "You don't think he's a plant, do you?"

Lukas wheeled his chair back to look at her over his glasses. "A *what*?"

"You know," she continued, entirely unabashed by his tone. "An agent."

"A spy?" He kept his tone neutral. "For who? Another university, here to steal our results?"

She snorted. "No, for the American government. OSS or FBI or something like that. You know they don't trust us. They're sure we're all Abwehr or Gestapo." She smiled, looked off once again at the chamber, and added as an afterthought, "Instead of just *some*."

Lovecraft had gone by the time Carter came down to go to work. There was a note on the counter saying, "No joy finding your weird screwdriver. This is what you get for ordering hardware through a bookstore, idiot. Will try again tomorrow. Enjoy patrolling the Haunted Palace of SCIENCE. E xo"

He smiled and pocketed the note. Then he'd decided it might take some explaining if he dropped it in the lab so he balled it up and dropped it in the trash instead.

He arrived at the Miskatonic campus with ten minutes to spare and entered the building at five to ten. The cleaning crew were just putting away their gear as he entered and was hailed by Pete Jenner, the guard who'd relieved him what seemed like only a few minutes before.

"Wow, *déjà vu*," said Jenner, signing himself out, and—Carter noticed—marking the time as ten on the nose. "Wouldn't surprise me if you're actually a different guy than I saw earlier, and they're replacing us all with clones. I'd believe anything in this place."

"Nah," said Carter, signing himself in and sticking to the fiction it was a few minutes later than it actually was when he entered the time. "That's policy over at Genetics. Here, they're pulling in multiple copies of me from different dimensions, but only paying us once." That was almost the truth, when he came to think about it.

"Wouldn't surprise me." Jenner pulled a coat over his jacket and tossed his cap into a plastic carrier bag. "Regents of this place are fuckin' chiselers."

Carter was looking at the duty log. Jenner had reported leaving the desk between normal patrol times, and it wasn't marked as a bio break, "bio" being the notation the guards used to indicate going to the restroom. "What was this?"

Jenner looked at the notation Carter had his finger rested upon and shook his head, dismissive and perhaps a little embarrassed. "Something or nothing. Thought I heard somebody in the lab, so I went to check it out. Wandered around for ten minutes, but there wasn't even a mouse." He grinned. "Mice are smarter than to hang around scientists, am I right?" He picked up his bag. "Just asking for trouble. Anything else?"

"No, I'm good. Take care, Pete. Sleep well."

"Thanks, man." Jenner hesitated by the door. "You should have a drink with me and Kev Ward and the Sarge sometime when we can get some schmuck to fill in for a shift."

Carter nodded. "Sounds good." And it did.

Jenner waved, closed the door, made sure the lock had engaged, and walked out into the night.

Carter was finally alone. Nothing would have pleased him more than to give it a couple of hours, then—when he was supposed to be touring the facility—take the back off the detector and take the pictures Lukas was so desperate for. But, he'd tried to order a screwdriver from a bookstore and look how that had turned out. Idiot. He smiled, and settled down to read a book he'd brought with him from the store.

He'd noticed he was reading a lot more since he'd ended up as joint owner of a bookstore. He had always been an occasional but steady reader before—maybe four or five or six books a year, which made him a dangerous intellectual if you listened to some of his old NYPD buddies—but now he didn't like watching TV so much. Part of that was the news was full of people he'd either never heard of or whose roles in the Folded World had been different. It was strange being in a world where JFK had died of undiagnosed prostate cancer in 1978; maybe Lee Harvey Oswald really *had* been a Soviet assassin the whole time. It was strange that no one had ever taken a shot at John Lennon and he was still around, but that Ringo Starr died in a car crash in 1983. It was strange that the Nazis were regarded as worthy and respected rivals to the U.S., and not stinking turds of evil.

The British still loathed them. They'd been stripped of an empire in a humiliation that made the Versailles Treaty look like kid-gloves handling. They'd been marginalized, and left with a huge war debt that took generations to pay back. When the American media mentioned them at all, it was either pityingly or patronizingly, often both. The British were like savages living in the ruins of Atlantis. The French had barely done any better, but they had fallen to the Third Reich during the war, and the Germans had been magnanimous in victory. The British had held out, right up until the moment the future dawned in a brilliant mushroom cloud over Moscow.

Carter could sympathize with them. The U.S.'s "business as usual" attitude when the rest of the world had fallen in the toilet depressed him, but there it was, and here he was, and he would just have to get used to the idea.

The other reason he hated watching TV was that it was terrible. He'd left a world in which TV was in a new golden age, and arrived in one that was artistically mired in what would have been the late seventies or early eighties to him. It was beautifully shot most of the time, but it was a long way short of challenging. Every new cop series was about a mismatched pair, one wacky, one straitlaced. Every new sci-fi series seemed to involve a cyborg protagonist.

He'd watched an episode from a top-rated spy series a few nights previously. There was a biological weapon placed in a crowded public place by a "Neo-Communist" group that couldn't be evacuated because "it would cause panic." The hero, who had no skill shortages in any area, managed to defuse it with one second on the clock. There was some "America! Fuck, yeah!" air-punching, the episode's romantic interest implied that, yeah, she'd be very happy to blow the hero after or maybe during the credits, and then the show's theme played with enough screaming guitar power chords to light New York for a week. It was shit, and it was at the top of the ratings.

Existential reasons aside, Carter wanted to refold the world just so he could bear to watch TV again.

The book Carter had brought with him was *From Berlin with Love*, one of a series of books by Ian Fleming that were never very popular outside the U.K.—the copy he was reading was an import—and that fizzled out after maybe six titles. From what he had read so far, it seemed pretty close to the movie he could still remember if he focused, except obviously the

Russians had been replaced by Germans, and SMERSH by the Abwehr.

He patrolled as he was supposed to, although he varied the exact time by about ten minutes before or after the hour. After all, an intruder might depend on evading him by hiding on the hour. A little variation might make all the difference. He did his eleven o'clock patrol at 10:51, his midnight patrol at 12:03. He'd just finished a chapter at 12:59, though, so he decided to tour then and there, at one o' clock.

On an impulse, he decided to reverse the direction of his previous two patrols, just to bring at least one unusual factor to it to catch out the unwary, hypothetical intruder. He'd start in the basement offices and work his way up.

He descended the steps and walked through the open area, it looking very much as it had last he saw it less than an hour before. His impulse was to sink into routine and just wander around, shining his flashlight into any dark corners along the way and simply fulfilling his own idea of diligence. Yet, the impulse foundered as he entered the level. Perhaps it was simply that he wasn't used to seeing it first on a patrol, but somehow, the place seemed out of kilter.

It was a sensation that he would have been unable to describe if asked, yet that was all too familiar to him, a curious, quivering, inherently unwilling disbelief that he felt as much in his gut as in his mind. He hadn't felt anything like it since the last time he had been on Waite's Bill, as he and Lovecraft had run from the unfolding of the world and all the realities adjacent. He hadn't missed it in the slightest. Yet here it was again, and there was no reason for it. He'd been through the offices several times already, twice already that evening, and not felt a thing except boredom. Yet now those self-same offices were redolent with a foreboding usually reserved for the abandoned mansion on the edge of town, or the stark Carpathian castle set upon a mountain slope. He saw a gel wrist support before a keyboard and it reeked of a dreadful alien quality, as if it were only a copy of the real thing. The whole room felt like a copy, a set of a real office. No, not even that; its artificiality was deeper still. It was like looking at a photograph of a not-quite-convincing office set, as if the set dressers had never seen one and were working from a brief written description.

Carter was aware he was sweating. The sensation always, *always* boded ill. Any second now, weird shit would happen, or somebody would try to kill him, or somebody would try to kill him in a weird way, but something would happen. He moved so his back was to a wall, rested his hand on the butt of his pistol, and waited, mind and gut quivering, as the world rotated off its axis and slid ugly feelings through the room.

Presently, it stopped, which was the most threatening thing it could possibly have done. It left Carter backed into a corner, pale and sweaty, standing in a gunslinger's crouch, all ready to draw, but no one to plug, goldarnit. He felt stupid, and hoped he wasn't on camera. As he straightened up, a man who wasn't there developed into existence by the stairwell, and walked out.

"Oh for fuck's sake," said Carter, and went after the ghost.

He hadn't hallucinated it, he felt reasonably sure. Then again, the essence of a good hallucination is that you buy into it. Making a mental note to check the security camera footage later, he climbed the steps to the first story and found himself alone. The door through to the steps leading up to the next floor wasn't moving, but he felt it was, or at least should be. It had swung open a moment before, though he had not seen it, and swung shut, though he had not seen that either, and now it was still just slightly in motion, although it did not move at all. Without hesitation he followed the nonexistent man. It did not feel absurd to Carter; it would have been more so not to pursue.

Up the stairs and onto the first laboratory level. There was the vacuum chamber—"God's dildo," he'd heard one of the American team members call it—and the detector, the sight of which he was already coming to hate. And there was the figure. It walked casually, unconcerned that it was being observed or even that it did not truly exist. It wandered here and there, and it seemed to Carter that there was something familiar about the way it walked. Not a distinctive gait so much as the degree of relaxation and purpose to the steps, the posture of the blurred man, an ink drawing on the fabric of reality that had been smudged into near incoherence.

It occurred to Carter at about this point that he had pursued the specter for all the wrong reasons. Because he was angry with himself for standing there with his hand on his gun like Billy the Asshole. Because he had been unnerved by the experience of fugue that had descended upon him. Because he was nursing outrage that the Powers had decided to piss around with him again. These had occupied his mind when he made the decision to chase the figure when, really, running the other way may well have been a profitable option.

Now here he was, with a blurred man wandering around the project's scientific gear like an unenthusiastic visitor to a museum of arable farming, and he had not the first idea what to do, or whether he should be frightened or angry. He settled on nonjudgmental ambivalence—a suitable mode for the venue—and followed the figure around.

As ghosts went, it did not seem very interested in making its haunt entertaining. It—no, *he*, Carter became convinced from the build and movement—gave every impression of being very at home in the laboratory, and with no great desire to detail the events of his grisly death or to provide cryptic clues to his murderer's identity. As ghosts went, it seemed as bored with haunting as Carter was with patrolling.

The thought stayed with him as he followed the entity up the stairs to the topmost level of the building. It hesitated on the top landing, seeming to notice something in the corner, but Carter could see nothing there. Losing interest in the unseen object, the ghost went through the doors onto the third story, pushing open a door that wasn't there and leaving the one that was entirely motionless. Carter followed, less dismissive about interacting with matter.

He found the ghost standing on the balcony overlooking the laboratory floor, looking up at the glass panels of the roof. Behind Carter, the door thudded heavily shut. For the first time, the ghost seemed to notice that it wasn't alone. It looked at the door and then—as if seeing Carter for the first time—it looked him in the face.

Carter's stomach and heart and mind all lurched, and none of it was through fear. That would come later. The sensation of nothing being right, of things being out of joint, was with him again, but this time the feeling was in itself wrong. It wasn't quite what he had experienced before, and the difference speared him and opened like a steel blossom in his chest.

The lines of the ghost grew more discrete and defined with every second. He could see eyes there now, a nose, a mouth. Yet with every iota of definition it gained, he felt that he was being robbed of one. He was losing the ability to feel like a human, to feel human, to feel anything but himself as an expression of vectors and energies in space. He reached for his gun, an action born of instinct and soul-souring panic rather than any hope it might do any good. He wasn't just dying; he was being unwritten, reduced to factors on existence's flyleaf before inevitably being forgotten. He wasn't just dying; he was being unlived. The ghost was sapping him away, and it didn't even care. It was wearing his uniform, drawing his gun. It aimed right at his chest where silver-toothed nothingness was eating his soul, and the ghost demanded, "Who the fuck are you?"

Chapter 9

THE NECESSARY TOOL

But it didn't demand it in his voice, or from his mouth, or from his face. It was solid now, in the form of a Miskatonic University guard. Carter couldn't find anything to say, or any way of saying it even if he had. He himself was the ghost now, wet ink smeared under the thumb of an uncaring god with no name a sane man would ever want to utter. He was drawn thinner than thought across an expanse that separated worlds, and—when he could stand it no longer—he hoped for some shade of oblivion.

He came around forty minutes later, alone on the top-level balcony with his leg folded under him and asleep. He limped downstairs, riven with pins and needles, falsified his "Patrol completed at" time, logged a bathroom break, went into a cubicle, and threw up.

* * *

The rest of the shift was uneventful. Carter didn't even feel wary as he went out on the subsequent patrols; there was a muting in his sensibilities, and he didn't much care if it was because the phenomenon he had endured had packed up its wagon for the night or whether whatever sensitivity he possessed to such things had been beaten into quiescence by the violence of the vision. He completed his work robotically, and tried not to think about anything much. He did reengage his mind, however, long enough to find the closed-circuit file for the camera in question, copy it to a thumb drive, and then replace it with an earlier example. There wasn't a great deal to see; he was spared both the sight of the ghost and the potential embarrassment of watching himself mime existential terror in response to a manifestation invisible to the camera. Instead, the video showed some sort of interference, but nothing he was familiar with. It wasn't snow or lines, and he didn't care to watch it for too long in case it resolved into a scene of a Japanese woman crawling out of a well.

It was while he was pulling up the earlier files with matching time stamps that he noticed something odd. The system automatically date-stamped the files, which was a security oversight of which he took full advantage, simply using the deleted file's name to overwrite its replacement. There was the small matter of the file's creation metadata, but—by the simple expedient of unplugging the router and then manually setting the time to what he needed before creating the fake—he was able to fool the system and made himself feel like some sort of hacker to boot.

He wasn't so busy congratulating himself that he didn't notice a file in the same time slot from a previous week showing a red exclamation mark, though. He tried to run it out of little more than curiosity, but the player glitched and put up a message saying the file was "damaged."

In the fraction of a second the file ran before failing, the corrupted image looked very similar to the one from his one o'clock patrol that night. He copied it onto the thumb drive, too.

When he was relieved at six o'clock, his relief asked if anything had happened during his shift. Carter said, "No."

When Carter got back to the bookstore, he knew he wouldn't be able to sleep for a while. Instead, he lay on the bed in his underwear—the unlovely and unloved security uniform draped over a chair back—and looked at the ceiling until he heard Lovecraft unlock the front door and come in. He dressed in his own clothes and went down to see her.

He found her with her head under the counter, sorting out her stationery. "Hi," she said without looking up. "How was work?"

Carter considered. "It was okay, I guess. I saw a ghost, was nearly erased from reality, and threw up afterward. Same old, same old."

"Yeah, well"—Lovecraft finally got the office supplies organized to her satisfaction and straightened up—"that's blue collar jobs for you." She looked at him properly for the first time that morning, and his expression made her brow lower. "You're not shitting me, are you? You saw a ghost?"

"The Haunted Palace of Science turns out to be haunted, maybe. Or I'm crazy, maybe."

Lovecraft waved a finger at him. "No. No, no, no. We are not at home to Mr. Self-Doubt. We start doing that, and we unravel. You saw a ghost? Then, unless it turns out to be Old Man Jenkins the Janitor in a rubber mask, you saw a ghost."

Carter nodded. "Thanks. I did need that."

A knock at the door distracted them. "Hold that thought," said Lovecraft, and went to answer it. Presently she returned with several packages. "Say what you like about the Unfolded World, but couriers turn up damn early. I like that." She put them on the counter and went back behind it to begin sorting through them. "Tell me about your ghost."

She worked as he told her, but he was never in any doubt she was giving him the bulk of her attention. She asked about his routine, what he remembered about the briefly seen true face of the phantom, and about how he'd doctored the video files.

"You were expecting to see yourself?"

Carter nodded. "It was like I wasn't there after a while. Like it started off as a copy of me, but I ended up as a copy of it. Does that make sense?"

She looked at him long enough to turn down her mouth and shake her head at him. She returned to the packages. "Nope. You're the delicate and sensitive ex-homicide cop. I'm the two-fisted thug of a bookseller. I don't feel nuthin'." She laughed under her breath and Carter smiled, too. "Seriously, you're the descendant of Randolph Carter. I'm just the descendant of the schmuck who wrote about it. I can't imagine how it feels when the weird hits. Kind of envious. Kind of relieved." She tore open the end of a short package fashioned from packing tube. "And what do we have here?" She pulled out the contents, unwrapped a cocoon of green bubble wrap, and produced a very sharp-looking screwdriver. "Excalibur, my liege."

"Thanks."

Carter reached for it, but Lovecraft held it away from him. "This thing cost me twenty-five bucks, including the overnight. No money, no . . . man, this thing looks even weirder in the flesh than it did on the website."

"Where did you find it?"

"Importer. This is a genuine piece of Reich technology. Ahh . . ." She dropped it on the counter. As it rolled to a halt, Carter saw a symbol embossed into a pommel-like stud behind the grip.

"You made me handle a swastika, Dan."

"Come on, Emily. How was I supposed to know that was there?" He reached for the screwdriver, but she picked it up first.

"Then again, you made a swastika get handled by me." She adopted a bad German accent in a high piping voice, dancing the screwdriver in her hand like a puppet. *"Ach nein! Eine schwarze Frau!"*

Carter held out his hand. "Please can I have the screwdriver?"

Holding the screwdriver by the blade, she rested the handle on her shoulder and held out her other hand. "Sure, but it'll cost you twenty-five wholesome American dollars, you dirty collaborator."

Across the street from Carter & Lovecraft Books was a coffee shop. It had been there for several years, certainly long enough to remember when the bookstore was called Hill's Books. Under that name, however, the bookstore predated the coffee shop, and so they had settled into an easy symbiosis of things to read while drinking coffee, or something to drink while reading.

The name of the coffee shop was Poppy's. There had been an actual Poppy some time before, but she had died, and the new owners were not egotistical enough to change the name of the beloved venue simply because it had changed hands, nor so cruel as to obliterate the name of the shop's equally beloved former owner, nor so stupid as to antagonize regulars by doing so. The spirit of Poppy lived on in the place in a far more benevolent mode than the haunting Carter had endured the night before.

The coffee shop was moderately to very busy throughout the day, certainly when Miskatonic U was in session, but the waitress still managed to maintain a good grasp of who was in and where they were. Currently on the edge of her radar was the birdlike man at the two-seater table in the window. He was on his fourth cup of tea now, and he drank them like an automaton, looking out of the window roughly in the direction of the bookstore across the street the whole while. He was polite but unengaging when she brought fresh cups over, and declined any food to go with the drink.

Abruptly, he pushed away the half-finished cup in front of him, gathered up the battered leather satchel by his chair, tossed a bill onto the table, and left without a backward glance. The waitress was at his table in a moment, fearful that he'd bilked her, but to her grateful astonishment the bill bore Grant's face, not Washington's. She looked out of the window and watched the man cross the street and go into the bookstore.

It was probably a coincidence that the man pushed away his teacup at the exact moment that Dan Carter lapsed from light sleep into deep sleep in the apartment over the store. Exhaustion from the double shift and his experience during the second had finally overwhelmed him and he was now dead to the world. Certainly, the tinkling of the bell over the store's door would not wake him, nor would any conversation, even if it were to become heated.

Emily Lovecraft looked up as the bell sounded and the man came in. She took his measure quickly: a nice suit, unfashionable, but comfortable; a hat, not such a rarity in the Unfolded World; a battered old-school leather satchel; a gentle, aesthetic face; a mild and faintly benevolent expression. She had him tagged as a Miskatonic U professor before he'd even taken one step inside the store. He was clearly not there for browsing, either, as he made straight for her.

She closed the book she'd been reading, put it aside, and said, "Good afternoon. How can we help you today?"

"Good afternoon." He paused, smiling, and looked off to one side as if a thought had occurred to him. "That's an interesting thought, isn't it? How can you help me today? That implies that you have helped me on previous days in different ways, or that you anticipate helping me in the future."

A professor of semantics, Lovecraft decided.

"Well, return trade is always vital for any business," she said.

"I suppose it is. I would like to return. I like books." He looked around. "And you have several."

"We do." The man amused Lovecraft, and—now that he was close enough for her to see the cut and material of his suit—she also recognized him as probably well off. She liked both of these factors. He could amuse her while buying large quantities of stock. She hoped that he was one of the old breed of dilettante intellectuals who bought books by the yard to give his library gravitas. She'd read about rich Victorian guys doing that. How cool would that be?

Then he ruined it all by placing both hands flat on the counter, looking her in the eye, smiling pleasantly, and saying, "I understand you have a copy of the *Necronomicon*."

Lovecraft's smile wavered. "The *Necronomicon?*" She hoped it wasn't too obvious that she was playing for time, although she knew she couldn't have been more blatantly short of raising a hand and asking him to wait a minute while she thought of a workable evasion.

"Well, yes." The man seemed mildly surprised. "Fragments of the Dee edition. Surely I haven't come to the wrong store?" He looked off to one side as if thinking, then back at her. "No. This is definitely the right place. Of that, I am sure."

"It's a very rare book, sir," she said, belatedly adding, "I believe. I think the university might have one in their restricted collection."

"They do," said the man conversationally, as if they were discussing the weather. "An original, one of only eight, to my knowledge, but it's in medieval Arabic, and I'm a little rusty. They also have the Olaus Wormius Latin translation, but he could be such a prig somet—"

"Eight?" interrupted Lovecraft. She had researched the *Necronomicon* when she found she held a copy, and that did not jibe with her findings. "Five, you mean? Miskatonic, Buenos Aires, Harvard, the British Library, and the one that used to be in the Bibliothèque nationale de France, but ended up in the Reich-Bibliothek in Berlin."

"Oh, yes," said the man. "Five. My mistake." His smile stayed at its initial intensity throughout the exchange, as if this was the factory setting for his face.

also recognized him as probably well off. She liked both of these factors. He could amuse her while buying large quantities of stock. She hoped that he was one of the old breed of dilettante intellectuals who bought books by the yard to give his library gravitas. She'd read about rich Victorian guys doing that. How cool would that be?

Then he ruined it all by placing both hands flat on the counter, looking her in the eye, smiling pleasantly, and saying, "I understand you have a copy of the *Necronomicon*."

Lovecraft's smile wavered. "The *Necronomicon*?" She hoped it wasn't too obvious that she was playing for time, although she knew she couldn't have been more blatantly short of raising a hand and asking him to wait a minute while she thought of a workable evasion.

"Well, yes." The man seemed mildly surprised. "Fragments of the Dee edition. Surely I haven't come to the wrong store?" He looked off to one side as if thinking, then back at her. "No. This is definitely the right place. Of that, I am sure."

"It's a very rare book, sir," she said, belatedly adding, "I believe. I think the university might have one in their restricted collection."

"They do," said the man conversationally, as if they were discussing the weather. "An original, one of only eight, to my knowledge, but it's in medieval Arabic, and I'm a little rusty. They also have the Olaus Wormius Latin translation, but he could be such a prig somet—"

"Eight?" interrupted Lovecraft. She had researched the *Necronomicon* when she found she held a copy, and that did not jibe with her findings. "Five, you mean? Miskatonic, Buenos Aires, Harvard, the British Library, and the one that used to be in the Bibliothèque nationale de France, but ended up in the Reich-Bibliothek in Berlin."

"Oh, yes," said the man. "Five. My mistake." His smile stayed at its initial intensity throughout the exchange, as if this was the factory setting for his face.

a bill onto the table, and left without a backward glance. The waitress was at his table in a moment, fearful that he'd bilked her, but to her grateful astonishment the bill bore Grant's face, not Washington's. She looked out of the window and watched the man cross the street and go into the bookstore.

It was probably a coincidence that the man pushed away his teacup at the exact moment that Dan Carter lapsed from light sleep into deep sleep in the apartment over the store. Exhaustion from the double shift and his experience during the second had finally overwhelmed him and he was now dead to the world. Certainly, the tinkling of the bell over the store's door would not wake him, nor would any conversation, even if it were to become heated.

Emily Lovecraft looked up as the bell sounded and the man came in. She took his measure quickly: a nice suit, unfashionable, but comfortable; a hat, not such a rarity in the Unfolded World; a battered old-school leather satchel; a gentle, aesthetic face; a mild and faintly benevolent expression. She had him tagged as a Miskatonic U professor before he'd even taken one step inside the store. He was clearly not there for browsing, either, as he made straight for her.

She closed the book she'd been reading, put it aside, and said, "Good afternoon. How can we help you today?"

"Good afternoon." He paused, smiling, and looked off to one side as if a thought had occurred to him. "That's an interesting thought, isn't it? How can you help me today? That implies that you have helped me on previous days in different ways, or that you anticipate helping me in the future."

A professor of semantics, Lovecraft decided.

"Well, return trade is always vital for any business," she said.

"I suppose it is. I would like to return. I like books." He looked around. "And you have several."

"We do." The man amused Lovecraft, and—now that he was close enough for her to see the cut and material of his suit—she

It only struck her later that the man's claim that there were eight copies of the original *Necronomicon* in existence might have been neither an honest mistake nor a ruse to catch her out.

Having blown any chance of carrying on the pretense of ignorance about the *Necronomicon*, Lovecraft tried a new tack.

"The Dee edition is one of the rarest subsequent editions, though. Maybe even rarer than originals."

"Oh, yes. It is rarer. Undoubtedly so."

"Well, it's hardly likely to turn up in a small bookstore in Pro—in Arkham, then." The near slip bothered her. She thought she'd gotten the whole "it's not Providence anymore" thing down pat. Why was the little man putting her off balance so much? She had her twelve-gauge pal under the counter if things got unfriendly in a gross material way, but things looked like they were going off in their own direction and it wasn't one where the Mossberg might be useful.

"I would agree with you, but for the fact I was told you have a copy." He smiled pleasantly at her, unwaveringly at her, as if he'd just inquired about buying *The Little Book of Calm*.

Lovecraft raised her eyebrows. "Told?"

"Yes." The smile seemed permanently stitched onto his face. "By Alfred Hill."

In the pause that followed, Lovecraft realized that she had stepped back from the counter. "That's my uncle."

"Hmmm." It was unclear if the man was indicating that he knew that, or merely that he was showing polite interest.

"He's dead."

The man's smile finally toned down to an expression of curious interest. She might have just said her uncle was a Jesuit missionary. "Dead? Oh, I'm sorry to hear that. Might I ask when, if it's not too upsetting a subject?"

"He's been missing for over seven years. He was legally declared dead a few months ago." She stepped back up to the counter. "When exactly did he speak to you?"

"Oh, a while back. It might have been seven years, I suppose.

Tempus . . ." He seemed to relish the word for a moment, then abruptly added, ". . . *fugit.*"

"You put off coming here for seven years?" If Lovecraft made any effort to keep the disbelief from her voice, it was a weak one.

The smile returned. "I have been busy."

Lovecraft had had enough of Mr. Nice Suit and his shit. "I'm sorry, but if we ever had a copy, my uncle must have sold it between him telling you about it and . . ." She hesitated.

"His disappearance," supplied the man. "Yes, I suppose he must. Such a shame, but I should have struck while the iron was hot. Such a shame. I'm sorry to have wasted your time, Miss Lovecraft."

Lovecraft wasn't about to let him suddenly name-dropping her add to the low-level freak-out she was already experiencing. If he'd known her uncle, then presumably Alfred would have mentioned the Lovecraft connection, and from that and the new name of the store it wasn't an amazing deduction to arrive at her name. "That's okay. Kind of wish we did still have it. I'd like to see a copy myself." She had no idea why she felt the need to embellish the lie like that, and as soon as she said it, she realized it was true. She really did want to look at the book again. Properly this time. After all, it was only a book. She wasn't some delicate violet from an H.P.L. story whose mind would crack like an eggshell after reading a line. She realized she had become distracted and covered by saying, "Out of curiosity, why did you want a copy, sir? It's not exactly light reading."

The man shrugged. He was still smiling, as if he were pleased even at not getting the book he wanted. "A gift for a colleague."

Lovecraft raised an eyebrow. "That's a hell of a gift."

The smile, if anything, deepened. "She's a hell of a colleague. Good day, Miss Lovecraft." He headed for the door.

Lovecraft called after him, "Should I take your contact details, sir? In case we get another copy, or hear of anyone who has?"

Tempus . . ." He seemed to relish the word for a moment, then abruptly added, ". . . *fugit*."

"You put off coming here for seven years?" If Lovecraft made any effort to keep the disbelief from her voice, it was a weak one.

The smile returned. "I have been busy."

Lovecraft had had enough of Mr. Nice Suit and his shit. "I'm sorry, but if we ever had a copy, my uncle must have sold it between him telling you about it and . . ." She hesitated.

"His disappearance," supplied the man. "Yes, I suppose he must. Such a shame, but I should have struck while the iron was hot. Such a shame. I'm sorry to have wasted your time, Miss Lovecraft."

Lovecraft wasn't about to let him suddenly name-dropping her add to the low-level freak-out she was already experiencing. If he'd known her uncle, then presumably Alfred would have mentioned the Lovecraft connection, and from that and the new name of the store it wasn't an amazing deduction to arrive at her name. "That's okay. Kind of wish we did still have it. I'd like to see a copy myself." She had no idea why she felt the need to embellish the lie like that, and as soon as she said it, she realized it was true. She really did want to look at the book again. Properly this time. After all, it was only a book. She wasn't some delicate violet from an H.P.L. story whose mind would crack like an eggshell after reading a line. She realized she had become distracted and covered by saying, "Out of curiosity, why did you want a copy, sir? It's not exactly light reading."

The man shrugged. He was still smiling, as if he were pleased even at not getting the book he wanted. "A gift for a colleague."

Lovecraft raised an eyebrow. "That's a hell of a gift."

The smile, if anything, deepened. "She's a hell of a colleague. Good day, Miss Lovecraft." He headed for the door.

Lovecraft called after him, "Should I take your contact details, sir? In case we get another copy, or hear of anyone who has?"

It only struck her later that the man's claim that there were eight copies of the original *Necronomicon* in existence might have been neither an honest mistake nor a ruse to catch her out.

Having blown any chance of carrying on the pretense of ignorance about the *Necronomicon*, Lovecraft tried a new tack.

"The Dee edition is one of the rarest subsequent editions, though. Maybe even rarer than originals."

"Oh, yes. It is rarer. Undoubtedly so."

"Well, it's hardly likely to turn up in a small bookstore in Pro—in Arkham, then." The near slip bothered her. She thought she'd gotten the whole "it's not Providence anymore" thing down pat. Why was the little man putting her off balance so much? She had her twelve-gauge pal under the counter if things got unfriendly in a gross material way, but things looked like they were going off in their own direction and it wasn't one where the Mossberg might be useful.

"I would agree with you, but for the fact I was told you have a copy." He smiled pleasantly at her, unwaveringly at her, as if he'd just inquired about buying *The Little Book of Calm*.

Lovecraft raised her eyebrows. "Told?"

"Yes." The smile seemed permanently stitched onto his face. "By Alfred Hill."

In the pause that followed, Lovecraft realized that she had stepped back from the counter. "That's my uncle."

"Hmmm." It was unclear if the man was indicating that he knew that, or merely that he was showing polite interest.

"He's dead."

The man's smile finally toned down to an expression of curious interest. She might have just said her uncle was a Jesuit missionary. "Dead? Oh, I'm sorry to hear that. Might I ask when, if it's not too upsetting a subject?"

"He's been missing for over seven years. He was legally declared dead a few months ago." She stepped back up to the counter. "When exactly did he speak to you?"

"Oh, a while back. It might have been seven years, I suppose.

"No." The man paused at the open door. "That won't be necessary. I'm sure the book is in the best place for it already." He left before she could point out that his reason didn't seem to have much to do with his decision.

Chapter 10

INSIDE THE MACHINE

Carter was distracted after he slept, focused on that evening's planned petty larceny and something that he found difficult to separate from corporate espionage in his mind. He was certainly too distracted to notice Lovecraft's slightly edgy demeanor and her limited, unsuccessful attempts to drag their brief conversation around to the freaky guy who had spoken to her uncle seven years before and knew all about the copy of the *Necronomicon* lying in the safe. So Carter left the store preoccupied, and carrying a messenger bag that contained a book, a sandwich, a Nazi screwdriver, a small camera that took good high-resolution pictures, and a mountable LED light. He said, "catch you later" at Lovecraft over his shoulder, and didn't see her unhappy expression or hear her say "Yeah" in a "For fuck's sake, will you please get your head out of your ass and ask me what's wrong" voice.

After he'd gone, she sighed and sat heavily on the stool behind the counter. She swore at herself inwardly for not just saying what was on her mind, but she did it unenthusiastically. She knew full well she'd been reluctant to bring the subject up because it seemed a little thin when she tried to find words to express how the strange little conversation had gone. *Yeah, so this guy came into the bookstore, and . . . he wanted to buy a book!* She could see Carter's expression in her mind's eye; the brow was down and the eyes were pretty quizzical. He'd come out with *And?* And she would just have a lot of nothing to explain how she felt. *He said he knew my uncle Alfred? He knew how many copies of* Kitab al-Azif *are in existence! But he got it wrong! In a way I found kind of threatening for reasons I can't say!*

She could see that expression on Carter's face all too well.

And?

Lovecraft turned on the stool to look at the safe. She looked at it for a long time.

Carter started his shift very aware of how much of a fraud he was. He felt like an actor in an extemporized scene at a theater school. When he said, "Good evening, Sergeant," to Graves, the older man flicked his eyes up at him from his computer for a moment too long, as if he felt something was off. But then he just nodded.

"Settling in, Constable?"

"I think so." He looked at the lights in the security station, considering, and added, "There's not a whole lot to this gig, really, is there?"

Graves smiled as he returned his attention to the computer. "Nope. We're just warm bodies providing a presence. Sorry you took the job?"

Carter shook his head. "I need the money." It was true, but it still felt like a line coming out of his mouth. "See you around, Sarge." And he left the security building to head for the high-energy physics building to commit what he was pretty sure was probably some sort of crime.

The toughest part was carrying on as normal for the first part of his shift. He'd decided to do the job on the two o'clock patrol, because that was the deadest time of the night in his experience. Three was good, too, though. Maybe he should put it off until three. Maybe four. Carter knew he was procrastinating, but he liked the feeling of putting off the inevitable. It was a degree of control over his destiny that he treasured and that control felt rare these days. He carried out the initial patrol and the three following pretty much on the hour, and not exactly on the hour because that was his choice and within his control. Then it got to two in the morning, and he knew he didn't have to do it right then if he didn't want to. So, nursing theories about the illusion of self-determination, he went off to do it anyway.

He'd neutered the screwdriver's vicious point by finding a cork in the apartment kitchen over the bookstore and pushing it over the tip. Now he could carry the thing in his jacket without it working through the cloth and shivving him in the spleen, which was a bonus. The money for the job was good, but not that good. He transferred the camera and the LED light from the messenger bag to his pockets, took a deep breath, and set off on his normal patrol route.

The patrol quickly took on the same air of theater of his earlier conversation with Graves. Here he was, pretending to be a security guard by going through the basement offices, flashing a torch around. Here he was, working his way up the building. Here he was, walking onto the lab floor as if everything was entirely normal.

This performance was unnecessary. He had been blipping the lab's security camera off and on intermittently all evening by just pulling its USB plug gently from the feed socket in the cabinet in the security station, then plugging it in and out a couple of times. It wasn't exactly a USB, he noticed, but close enough. In the Unfolded World it was called an SDS, which meant something in German, because—of course—the standard protocol had originated in the Reich. The logo was different, too: a spiral where the line turned at a right angle to the circular path and finished in a simple arrowhead, making the thing look like a fancy question mark. All evening, he had created the illusion of a sketchy feed and, five minutes before 2:00 a.m., he had finally pulled the plug and left it out. He'd stood by the cabinet for a moment, hoping he hadn't fucked up, and while he did, he found himself looking at the logo and deciding he didn't like it. He'd never been very attached to the USB logo, either, but there was something kind of pagan about the SDS spiral, like it had been copied from a cave painting or a carved stone at a Paleolithic site or something. He'd let go of the feed cable as if he'd found himself absentmindedly holding a snake, and closed the cabinet door.

Now here he was unobserved, yet he still couldn't help but go through the motions of being a disinterested security guy. Yep, looks secure in here. Heh, cleaner missed that wastepaper basket. Gee, look at all that science shit on the whiteboard. These eggheads, huh?

He strolled around the laboratory, fighting the urge to put his thumbs in his belt and walk like a deputy in a program-filling thirties western. He had every right to be there. Nothing was wrong. Nothing was unusual. It was part of his usual routine to take a knee by the detector, produce a screwdriver from his jacket, pull a cork off its head, and use it to start extracting screws from a maintenance cover on the machine's casing. Nothing to see here. Just as well the camera isn't working right now. Be a waste of memory to record something this mundane.

He worked carefully. A scratch on the anodized metal surface would be obvious to anyone taking a second to look, and the dumb-ass screwdriver was just aching to scratch something if he didn't keep it under close control. So he worked steadily, and used his off hand to keep the screwdriver's barrel in place. The screws moved easily—the depth of the head gave perfect purchase and the handle provided plenty of mechanical advantage. The plate was irregular in shape, and every corner had a screw, five altogether. Carter dropped them into a plastic bottle cap he'd brought along to hold them.

He considered just loosening one of the lower screws so it would hold the cover while he slid it out of the way, but it turned out there was a recessed lip around the opening that took the screws, and he worried that the cover might scratch the detector casing, so he removed all five before gently easing off the cover.

He couldn't see much inside the detector even as low as he was and had to go on hands and knees to look inside. There was a little light in there—a dull green glow from an LED somewhere—that he guessed was to show the unit was on standby or it had a backup battery for its firmware or something. It didn't matter. It wasn't enough to see anything except the outlines of the circuit boards, what might be the power unit, something else that might also be the power unit, and a braid of cables running up the machine's rear wall.

Carter fumbled in his pocket and found the miniature LED work light. The base had a simple clamp, but its flat side was a magnet and this he attached to the detector casing by the opening. He angled the head to face through the gap and toggled the light on.

By the harsh white light of the ring of LEDs in the gadget's head, he could see the circuit boards in strong detail, the cables, the fan mountings. The second dark shape he had guessed might be a power transformer was exactly that. The first shape he'd thought might be, however, he could now see was actually maybe three kilos of quarrying explosives attached to a trigger mounted on one of the boards.

"Ah," said Carter. "Ah, shit."

He sat back on his haunches and looked at the bomb. Maybe he should be running, he thought, but surprise and a sense of dislocation prevented his fight or flight reflex from doing anything but putting him on his haunches with a thoughtful expression.

He'd seen bombs before, back when he was a cop. Never an armed one in the flesh, thank fuck, but plenty of pictures and neutralized devices and dummies brought in by the bomb squad so the beat cops and detectives knew what not to give a kick to. This one didn't look very sophisticated at all. He guessed it was wired to the power bus so it would detonate when the detector was turned on. It looked too simple to have a backup timer or any antitamper measures. Of course, maybe he wasn't seeing the whole thing, and maybe he was presuming a lot based on very limited experience.

He weighed his options. He could try to defuse it, and possibly get blown to shit. He could just put the cover back, pretend he hadn't seen it, and let one or more of the scientists get blown to shit instead. He could call his client, spend the next twenty minutes listening to what a panicking German scientist sounds like, and finally arrive at the same conclusion he would have reached by himself, but with less time to do it. He could report it, and then have to explain why he had been poking around inside somebody else's very delicate scientific apparatus at two in the morning. He could call in a bomb alert and let the professionals deal with it. He'd have to wipe everything down, but that wasn't such a big deal. Yep, that was the plan. Get some cleaning product from the janitor's closet to dissolve grease, wet a tissue with it, wipe down anything around there he might have left fingerprints or DNA on. Wake up Lovecraft, put up with two minutes of being fluently sworn at, ask her to go out, find a phone booth nowhere near her apartment, and call it in while trying to sound like a terrorist with a pathological hatred of high-energy physics. Or Nazis. Yeah, a pathological hatred for Nazis sounded more likely.

It probably wasn't the best plan, but it was the best one he could come up with at short notice. Sizing it up, he thought it stood a pretty good chance of success.

"Don't move," said somebody from behind him, and the plan's chances nose-dived pretty badly.

The voice was female and accented in German, so Carter didn't have to perform much of a deductive leap to say, "Dr. Giehl?"

"What are you doing with that machine?"

"That's a little complicated," he said. He wasn't sure if he should raise his hands or not. "Are you pointing a gun at me?"

"Yes," she said, and the lack of hesitation made him believe it. "Why have you opened the detector?"

"Like I said"—he raised his arms slowly as he spoke—"that's complicated. Not really sure where to start with that." He looked at the screws in the plastic lid, the screwdriver on the floor, thought of the camera in his pocket, and then he said. "Have you heard of the CIA, Doctor?"

She didn't reply immediately, and that was fine because there was no CIA here, only the OSS, which in this world liked its name and never changed.

"Say that again."

"CIA. Central Intelligence Agency."

"Never heard of it. That's who you're with?"

"It's a suboffice within the OSS. They deal with peripheral threats and practice deniability. I'm not 'with' them because nobody is, apart from some higher-ups and office staff, I guess." Carter marveled at the high-quality, smooth-as-chocolate-mousse bullshit that was flowing out of his mouth. "I'm a detached agent, like all the agency's field agents. I get hired for a job, and if it goes to hell it doesn't matter, because I can't prove I was ever hired by them."

No reply. On the plus side, he hadn't been shot yet, so that was good.

"'Peripheral threats.' What does that mean?"

It was a good question. The phrase had felt good when he had said it, and he knew vaguely what he was getting at when he had, so he trusted his subconscious to pull the rabbit out of the hat and let himself go to the Zen of bullshit.

"Partially defined threats compiled from disparate sources, ma'am. Nothing solid enough for a main intelligence or security agency to act upon, but worrying enough to spend a few bucks checking out." He shrugged. Slowly. "I don't cost much, really."

He half-believed it himself. He deserved a round of applause for all this.

"What sort of threat?"

Holy crap, thought Carter. *She's buying it. Thank you, lying Baby Jesus.*

"Not sure. Domestic, I think. I was just told to look out for anything weird."

"Weird."

"Out of the ordinary. Y'know?"

"And what is so 'weird' about that piece of apparatus?"

"This thing? Nothing. But . . . Ma'am, may I move a little? I just want to show you this." He didn't wait for a reply, but slowly reached for the screwdriver before holding it up between his forefinger and thumb. "I found this on the floor."

"A screwdriver? So what?"

"It's German, ma'am. A specialized tool. I don't think you can even buy these things in the U.S." Before she could come up with any more arguments, he said, "If you're asking me why finding it lying around when this place is usually pristine made me suspicious, I got to say again, I'm paid to be suspicious. So, I thought, what might it be used for? This machine is the only one that needs a tool like this to get into." This was true. He'd examined the other machines previously. Even the German ones used standard screw heads. "I looked inside." He cautiously looked over his shoulder, making sure his hands were held up. "Ma'am, there are six sticks of explosive in here. If you'd turned this thing on in the morning, there wouldn't have been enough left of you to identify from dental records." This wasn't true—teeth were amazingly resilient and often made it through explosions—but it sounded good.

The doctor hadn't been blowing smoke about being armed. She had some nasty little pistol in her hand that looked like the kind of thing Walther might make. She looked down at him over the sights, her shock evident.

"There's a bomb?"

"Yes, ma'am."

"How do I know you didn't put it there?"

That was a good question, and it took him a moment to think of an answer. "Try and think back. When you came in here and saw me, did I look like somebody who'd just planted a bomb, or just found one?"

She pointed the gun at him for several more seconds, then lowered it. "*Scheiße*. A bomb. *Scheiße*." She lowered but did not put away the pistol, and Carter saw he had been right about it. It was a Walther PK380, and being shot by it would have been no fun at all. "Show me."

He scooted back a little and pointed into the open side of the detector. As she approached, she pointed at the base of the wall. "Sit there with your hands behind your head, fingers interlaced. If you make any sort of move I don't like, I will shoot you."

She hadn't tried to take his gun, but if he went for it while sitting, it would be difficult to draw and certainly give her plenty of time to raise her own weapon and empty the Walther into him. Carter did as he was told. "Yes, ma'am."

She crouched by the detector and looked inside. She looked more exasperated than shocked now. She said something harsh in German that sounded like she was spitting nails. She glanced over at Carter. "What were you intending to do?"

He was relieved to realize that cover story and truth were now in alignment. "I was going to close it up again and call in a bomb warning. Let the bomb squad deal with it."

"Anonymously?"

"Well, yeah. Gets complicated if I call it in as myself. The whole deniability thing is going to bite me in the ass, isn't it? I can't really tell the cops why I was looking inside the machine because no one is going to corroborate it. I get thrown under the bus, and it's game over for me. That's not a good plan for me. Do it anonymously, and I get to stay out of it."

Giehl thought it over for a moment. "No."

"No?"

"You're not going to call it in at all, anonymously or other-wise."

"Ma'am? The bomb?" He nodded at the detector, as if there might be another bomb they were talking about.

"We'll defuse it."

Carter slowly unlatticed his fingers and looked at her as if she'd just suggested they forget the bomb and tango. "We'll *what?* Wait. *We'll?* Lady, I have no idea how to defuse a bomb." It wasn't entirely true. He did have a small idea how to, but he was pretty keen not to apply that idea in case it got him vaporized.

"You don't have to. I know what I'm doing. The device is very simple." She put the gun away and Carter saw she had a holster mounted on the back of her belt, hidden beneath the long jacket she wore over jeans.

"Have you got a conceal-carry license for that?" The States were much softer with concealed firearm laws here than on the other side of the Fold, but Carter knew they didn't extend to for-eign visitors.

"No," she said as she reached into the machine. She shot him a sideways glance. "Are you going to report me?"

"Just keep your mind on what you're doing."

"I always do." He could see from her expression and the ten-sion in her forearm that she was applying pressure to something. Then her arm moved suddenly as whatever the something was came free. She didn't hesitate, but extracted the device, now de-tached from its mounting, and tossed it onto the floor by her with a weighty clatter.

"Holy shit," said Carter.

"It can't explode. It has no power source. Also"—she held up a brass-colored cylinder about the dimensions of a pen—"I pulled the detonator."

Carter was sitting with his hands by his side now that the threat of death by pistol-toting physicist seemed to have passed. "Where exactly is your doctorate from, Doc?"

She didn't trouble to look at him as she sat on the floor and picked up the device, treating it with about as much respect as a TV dinner. "I think I must have got it from the same place you got your guard qualifications." She examined the trigger. "Crude, but practical. It would have taken the capacitor about ten or fifteen seconds to charge, then it would have fired the detonator. Any idiot could have built this." She looked at him. "Carter, isn't it?"

Carter wasn't sure he was so happy about "Any idiot" and his name being so close together in the doctor's speech, but he let it go. "Yeah. Look, I got to ask, what was so bad about my plan that you decided it was better to arm wrestle an IED than call it in to people who have the equipment and training?"

"IED?"

Oh, right, Carter reminded himself. IEDs weren't called that now. They were just booby traps or improvised bombs or whatever. "Improvised explosive device."

"That's what they call them in the CAI?"

"CIA, and yeah. You haven't answered my question."

She got to her feet. "Because your bomb squad would have decided the safest thing to do would be a controlled explosion, and they would be right, too. They would destroy a unique device in the name of safety, and put this project back months while a replacement was built and calibrated. I was not prepared to let that happen."

"Okay, so your gadget's safe." She flinched slightly at the description, which Carter enjoyed more than he should. "Can I call the cops now?"

Chapter II

MASTERS OF DESTINY

Harrelson was not enjoying his morning. Arkham had the same crimes as everywhere else, but Miskatonic University loomed far greater in the life of the city than any of the seats of higher education of Providence, now lost in the mists of probability, and somehow the tone of crime seemed colored by the presence of MU. He had two homicides on his desk: a student who'd been found in the river having suffered an antemortem blow to the head, and a teaching assistant who'd been shot in a parking lot. If what Lovecraft had told him about the U was true, then it was like a weirdness magnet anyhow, but it just seemed to attract trouble. The kid in the river could still be an accident. The parking lot shooting might just be a snafu mugging. But . . .

But he'd gone through old case files soon after the unfolding, trying to get a feeling for a town that wasn't his anymore, and what he'd found had freaked him out a little. Miskatonic U wasn't just a weirdness magnet—it was a death trap. Students and faculty dropped like flies out of any sort of sensible proportion with a similarly sized institution anywhere else. Yet it was very Ivy League and had more endowed chairs than any other institution. The supersmart and the superrich came to Miskatonic University, and a statistically weird number of them would never leave. Yet still more came, and the cases of their predecessors ended up closed real quick. The boy in the river? On balance, Harrelson thought he was looking at an accident there, but he still wanted to ask around a little to make sure, pull some CCTV and so on, see if anything shook out to change his mind. In Providence, he'd have been given the slack to do that. Here, his captain had started out by calling it an accident before they knew anything at all, and now every time past Harrelson's desk, it was, "Have you finished your report on that tragic accident yet?" Harrelson almost felt like keeping the case open just to piss off the captain, but he knew he wouldn't. Miskatonic U's gravity was crushing, and those who tried to resist it ended up places they didn't want to be.

Like Innsmouth. Being assigned there was like a Fed being reassigned to Alaska. He'd heard scuttlebutt about how cops, some of them good cops, had been sent to Innsmouth PD because they couldn't or wouldn't toe the line in Arkham. It wasn't the shittiest burg in the Unfolded—that was Dunwich—but it was the shittiest one with a police department. Most bailed for new pastures at the first opportunity. The ones who didn't ended up worn down and washed out. Having seen the place, he wasn't surprised. He'd also seen people on the street who looked familiar somehow. It had taken him a couple of days to figure out that he hadn't seen them, he'd seen people who had the same kind of look. The Waites, back in the folded. Innsmouth had way, way too many people who had that weird Waites look about them—the men too stupid and the women way too smart and all of them with those eyes that just looked a little too big. Harrelson had drunk a half bottle of Jack that evening before he told himself that wasn't the way he wanted to go.

So, he had two murders on his desk that were going to snap shut like mousetraps any second now whether they were resolved properly or not, and a guy from the DAPFG telling him German cops were great and there was a natural friendship between the countries. DAPFG stood for some nightmare in German— Deutsch-Amerikanische Polizei Freundschaft Gesellschaft, he thought the guy said, although he wasn't clear on that and thought he'd maybe remembered one "*schaft*" too many.

"Harrelson's a good Teutonic name," the guy said, a detective from vice. "You'd fit right in."

"I might," admitted Harrelson, "if it was the Scottish-American Friendly Club. The name's Scottish."

The man laughed. "Whatever. Look, there are exchange trips, hands across the ocean, it's a good thing to belong to."

"I'll pass," said Harrelson. He was trying to will the vice cop to fuck off, but it didn't seem to be working. "Sauerkraut gives me the shits."

"Yeah, me, too," he said with enough sincere sympathy that Harrelson now felt he knew more about the man's medical history than he had ever or would ever want to know. "But beer, man! The beer! C'mon, give the club a try."

"If it'll get you to leave me alone so I can get on with my caseload, okay."

"Cool!" The vice cop pulled a glossy printed circular from his inside pocket. Harrelson saw it wasn't the only one in there. He gave it to Harrelson and went, finally, with a cheery nod, which made Harrelson wonder if vice was such a bad gig in this city. No vice cop should be *that* happy. He returned the nod and smile a little tightly, and dropped the circular unread in a desk drawer as soon as the cop turned his back.

His cell rang.

Lovecraft was unsympathetic. "Let me get this straight: you're really working for the Gestapo, but now you have to pretend to be working for the CIA so you can work alongside the Abwehr?

Is that *right?*" She snorted. "Jesus fucking Christ, Dan, how'd you manage that?"

"Just lucky, I guess." He didn't want to get into this right now, but he just couldn't help but say, "And the man's a Gestapo stooge, not actually one of your leather overcoat guys, and I only *think* the woman last night is maybe Abwehr."

Lovecraft sighed. Her momentary anger had been the product of surprise more than anything else. "She's the one you're supposed to be watching? Well, I guess you can watch her from close up, now she thinks you're some sort of fellow traveler."

Carter narrowed his eyes at her. "What was I supposed to do? And, come on, 'fellow traveler'? That's not cool."

"I didn't say you were, just that she thinks you are, kinda. Oh, look. I've hurt your delicate feelings. It must be tough being a white, blue-eyed, blond guy in a world where the Nazis are a big thing."

"Not that you're bitter."

"Not that I'm . . ." She stopped and the half smile left her lips. "I can't even joke about this anymore. I can't carry on being a good soldier if we ain't going to fight some fucker to make things right." She nodded at the safe. "Some guy came in yesterday asking after the *Necronomicon*. Said my uncle Alfred had clued him into it before he went missing, like, seven years ago."

Carter wanted to eat some eggs and sink into a deep sleep all afternoon, but he forced himself to focus on what Lovecraft was saying. "And?"

"And"—she made a short pantomime of vague hopelessness—"I told him he was mistaken and we didn't have it."

"I thought you wanted to get rid of it?"

"I do. I did. I just ain't so sure anymore. If we are ever going to stand any kind of chance of putting a crease back in the universe, we are going to need to know a shit ton more about how these things work than we do now."

Carter glanced at the old black safe, lurking in the shadows behind the counter. "You said those books are dangerous."

Is that right?" She snorted. "Jesus fucking Christ, Dan, how'd you manage that?"

"Just lucky, I guess." He didn't want to get into this right now, but he just couldn't help but say, "And the man's a Gestapo stooge, not actually one of your leather overcoat guys, and I only *think* the woman last night is maybe Abwehr."

Lovecraft sighed. Her momentary anger had been the product of surprise more than anything else. "She's the one you're supposed to be watching? Well, I guess you can watch her from close up, now she thinks you're some sort of fellow traveler."

Carter narrowed his eyes at her. "What was I supposed to do? And, come on, 'fellow traveler'? That's not cool."

"I didn't say you were, just that she thinks you are, kinda. Oh, look. I've hurt your delicate feelings. It must be tough being a white, blue-eyed, blond guy in a world where the Nazis are a big thing."

"Not that you're bitter."

"Not that I'm . . ." She stopped and the half smile left her lips. "I can't even joke about this anymore. I can't carry on being a good soldier if we ain't going to fight some fucker to make things right." She nodded at the safe. "Some guy came in yesterday asking after the *Necronomicon*. Said my uncle Alfred had clued him into it before he went missing, like, seven years ago."

Carter wanted to eat some eggs and sink into a deep sleep all afternoon, but he forced himself to focus on what Lovecraft was saying. "And?"

"And"—she made a short pantomime of vague hopelessness— "I told him he was mistaken and we didn't have it."

"I thought you wanted to get rid of it?"

"I do. I did. I just ain't so sure anymore. If we are ever going to stand any kind of chance of putting a crease back in the universe, we are going to need to know a shit ton more about how these things work than we do now."

Carter glanced at the old black safe, lurking in the shadows behind the counter. "You said those books are dangerous."

So, he had two murders on his desk that were going to snap shut like mousetraps any second now whether they were resolved properly or not, and a guy from the DAPFG telling him German cops were great and there was a natural friendship between the countries. DAPFG stood for some nightmare in German— Deutsch-Amerikanische Polizei Freundschaft Gesellschaft, he thought the guy said, although he wasn't clear on that and thought he'd maybe remembered one "*schaft*" too many.

"Harrelson's a good Teutonic name," the guy said, a detective from vice. "You'd fit right in."

"I might," admitted Harrelson, "if it was the Scottish-American Friendly Club. The name's Scottish."

The man laughed. "Whatever. Look, there are exchange trips, hands across the ocean, it's a good thing to belong to."

"I'll pass," said Harrelson. He was trying to will the vice cop to fuck off, but it didn't seem to be working. "Sauerkraut gives me the shits."

"Yeah, me, too," he said with enough sincere sympathy that Harrelson now felt he knew more about the man's medical history than he had ever or would ever want to know. "But beer, man! The beer! C'mon, give the club a try."

"If it'll get you to leave me alone so I can get on with my caseload, okay."

"Cool!" The vice cop pulled a glossy printed circular from his inside pocket. Harrelson saw it wasn't the only one in there. He gave it to Harrelson and went, finally, with a cheery nod, which made Harrelson wonder if vice was such a bad gig in this city. No vice cop should be *that* happy. He returned the nod and smile a little tightly, and dropped the circular unread in a desk drawer as soon as the cop turned his back.

His cell rang.

Lovecraft was unsympathetic. "Let me get this straight: you're really working for the Gestapo, but now you have to pretend to be working for the CIA so you can work alongside the Abwehr?

"They are. Freak-your-eyeballs-out-of-your-skull dangerous. Accidentally-summon-things-it's-suicidal-to-even-name-never-mind-meet dangerous. Get-yourself-way-worse-than-killed dangerous. But, I don't see we got a choice, Dan. We either roll over, accept all this, and pretend we're cool with a world where Hitler died peacefully in bed surrounded by his loving relatives, or we take some risks to make sure he eats his gun in a bunker like he's supposed to."

"That means bringing back the Holocaust. The Cold War."

"The Nazis offed way more than six million during this world's version of Barbarossa. As far as anyone knows, they're still exterminating in the East. Not much news comes out of what's left of Russia. No matter what we do, a lot of people die. But there's a difference. In the Folded, it's all down to us. Here, we're puppets, or pawns, or cattle for gods who only get worshipped out of fear. If humanity is going to hell, I'd prefer it if it was all our own fault."

"Masters of our own destiny."

"Yeah. Even if it's shit."

Chapter 12

THE WEED OF CRIME . . .

"The morning I've had," said Harrelson after the waitress left. He picked up the black coffee and stared into it, seeking answers to the problems of his life. It offered none, so he drank a mouthful of it instead. He looked at Carter. "Hot," he said.

Carter sat opposite him in the booth. Under his coat, Harrelson could see a rent-a-cop uniform, one he recognized as Miskatonic U security because he spent way too much time walking the campus there, dealing with this death or that. Harrelson decided not to ask; MU was enough of a pain in the ass for him without asking for another helping.

"I got a kind of a problem," said Carter. He looked uncomfortable as he said it, and it struck Harrelson that he'd never seen Carter look uncomfortable before, not even the time they were dealing with the problem of Waite's Bill in the least legal way possible.

Chapter 12

THE WEED OF CRIME . . .

"The morning I've had," said Harrelson after the waitress left. He picked up the black coffee and stared into it, seeking answers to the problems of his life. It offered none, so he drank a mouthful of it instead. He looked at Carter. "Hot," he said.

Carter sat opposite him in the booth. Under his coat, Harrelson could see a rent-a-cop uniform, one he recognized as Miskatonic U security because he spent way too much time walking the campus there, dealing with this death or that. Harrelson decided not to ask; MU was enough of a pain in the ass for him without asking for another helping.

"I got a kind of a problem," said Carter. He looked uncomfortable as he said it, and it struck Harrelson that he'd never seen Carter look uncomfortable before, not even the time they were dealing with the problem of Waite's Bill in the least legal way possible.

"They are. Freak-your-eyeballs-out-of-your-skull dangerous. Accidentally-summon-things-it's-suicidal-to-even-name-never-mind-meet dangerous. Get-yourself-way-worse-than-killed dangerous. But, I don't see we got a choice, Dan. We either roll over, accept all this, and pretend we're cool with a world where Hitler died peacefully in bed surrounded by his loving relatives, or we take some risks to make sure he eats his gun in a bunker like he's supposed to."

"That means bringing back the Holocaust. The Cold War."

"The Nazis offed way more than six million during this world's version of Barbarossa. As far as anyone knows, they're still exterminating in the East. Not much news comes out of what's left of Russia. No matter what we do, a lot of people die. But there's a difference. In the Folded, it's all down to us. Here, we're puppets, or pawns, or cattle for gods who only get worshipped out of fear. If humanity is going to hell, I'd prefer it if it was all our own fault."

"Masters of our own destiny."

"Yeah. Even if it's shit."

He didn't want to ask, but he guessed he should. "What kind of a problem?" Carter looked even more uncomfortable, then nodded at something under the table against the wall. Harrelson frowned, looked, and discovered a plastic bag. He picked it up and looked inside. He continued to look for several seconds, his expression unchanging. Then he put the bag down again and looked at Carter.

"You're cooler about this than I was expecting," said Carter.

"Nah," said Harrelson, "I'm in shock. Probably going to freak out in a minute. Let me get there." He took another mouthful from his coffee, swallowed it while looking thoughtfully at Carter, then said, "What the fuck are you on? A diner? You bring a . . . *this* into a diner?"

"It's deactivated and I've got—" Carter lowered his voice. "I've got the detonator in my pocket." He nodded at the tabletop to indicate the bag packed with explosives beneath it. "It's safe. It's commercial dynamite. I checked it—it's stable. Quarrying stuff. I think they use it as an ANFO initiator."

Harrelson looked at him as if he'd started speaking in tongues. "You think they use it as . . . Man, I turned off after *dynamite*. Where did you get it?"

Carter hesitated. "I'll tell you, but I don't want you making this official. There's no case here."

It's a bomb, Harrelson mouthed at him, disbelief on his face.

"It would . . ." Carter leaned forward. "Look, you want the State Department to get involved? This has to do with the Germans."

"The *Germans* did this?"

"No, the Germans were supposed to be the targets. High-energy-physics joint project team at the university. That was inside a machine the Germans use."

Harrelson's morning was not improving. "Always the fucking U," he muttered under his breath. He looked at Carter, plainly not wanting to hear how this particular hairball had happened. "Okay. Tell me how this particular hairball happened."

Carter told him all the main points, just skipping the stuff about the ghost, because Harrelson really wouldn't have responded well to that kind of shit. He did, however, tell him about Dr. Giehl, her unexpected appearance in the wee small hours, and the fact that she was carrying.

"That don't seem very normal to me," said Harrelson.

"She said she couldn't sleep and wanted some results she'd left there. She's got an apartment in a block the university owns about half a mile away."

"She went armed?"

Carter adopted a mild German accent. " 'Your country has a crime problem,' " he quoted. "She says she was carrying for personal protection."

"You believe her?"

"Kind of, but it's not the only reason. She just came over as way too at home with a weapon. She had no problems pointing it at me, or . . . She said something that bothered me. She told me to get down and put my hands behind my head—"

"Kinky."

"She also told me to interlace my fingers. Now maybe she just picked that up from a book or movie or something, but the way she said it, it came really easily to her."

"You think she's some sort of cop?"

"I think she's some kind of agent. My dude's Gestapo, so she ain't that, or at least they didn't tell him about her. Thing is, Gestapo is a security outfit. I think she might be Abwehr."

Carter wasn't aware of putting any emphasis on one word more than another, but Harrelson seemed to pick up on something anyway.

"She *might* be? Abwehr's like OSS, right? Intelligence? If she ain't with *them*, who else is there?"

Carter shook his head. "Fuck if I know. I could have understood another Gestapo stooge, but she is way too at home with a weapon for that. Abwehr might want to turn some of our scientists, I guess, but . . ." He rattled the back of his fingernails against the side of his coffee cup while he thought. "She's a scientist first. If they had some big scheme, they'd plant an agent as an assistant or some kind of hanger-on, somebody who has time. She spends all hers worrying over that machine like a mother hen."

"Maybe you're reading too much into how she handles a gun. Maybe she belonged to her college's practical shooting team or something, I dunno. She reads a lot of procedurals. It could be anything." Harrelson checked his watch. "I gotta go soon. What do you want me to do with the . . . bag?"

Carter picked it up and put it on the bench by him. "Nothing. I'll take care of it."

"You really do want this on the down low, don't you?"

"I wish it had never happened. I wish I'd just got the damn pictures and some joker hadn't put a bundle of dynamite right where I needed to be."

"Yeah. The perp. I was wondering when we were going to get to them. Thoughts?"

"Really amateur hour. The trigger's primitive and had no backup or antitamper on it. I think it stretched whoever built it. Probably never handled explosives before."

"Does dynamite have like, I dunno, serial numbers on it?"

"This stuff didn't, I looked. Still worth checking for reported thefts, though." He looked hopefully at Harrelson who rolled his eyes. "Anyway. I don't know why the explosive was planted or who by, but it doesn't look like it's 'Spy vs. Spy,' which is kind of a relief. I'll keep my eyes open. Maybe they'll make another attempt."

"If they do, and you miss it, and people die, it's on your head, Dan. I think you're crazy not to report it."

"I can't do that. I'm already wading in Shit Creek. Reporting it would drown me."

"Okay, your funeral. We never had this conversation and as far as I'm concerned you got an oven-ready chicken in that bag there." Harrelson started to leave, hesitated as he thought about what he'd just said, and pointed at Carter. "Do *not* put it in the oven."

Carter smiled wanly. Tiredness and hunger were catching up with him. "Thanks for the advice, Detective."

The man in the hat and coat returned to Poppy's coffee shop, again ordered a tea, and sat by the window. He entered exactly ten minutes before Carter & Lovecraft Books was due to close, although the waitress didn't notice this or even care very much, intent as she was on earning another large tip. He had turned up at this time the day before, after all, and done just that.

The hour arrived, and he watched the sign in the bookstore's door flip over to read *Closed*. Presently Emily Lovecraft came out with a hook on a pole to push up the canopy over the storefront and then pull down the shutter over the window. She locked it, and went back inside. The man sipped his tea, and continued his surveillance. Soon, the door opened again, and Lovecraft exited wearing her street jacket, a tasseled shoulder bag across her chest and, the man was particularly interested to note, a large artist's portfolio in her hand. She paused as she was about to close the door to glance at the portfolio, and the man could see her frown. She seemed on the cusp of going back inside, but instead seemed to steel herself, drew the door closed, and locked it. Holding the portfolio a little away from her side as if carrying a case containing a venomous reptile, she walked down the sidewalk and out of view.

The man pushed his cup away and rose, pulling on his coat and picking up his hat. The waitress was at his side in a second. "Was everything good for you, sir?" she said. The teacup was barely touched, and she feared a negative.

"Callooh," he said. "Callay."

"I'm sorry?"

The man smiled. "A little project of mine seems to be coming along very well. A frabjous day indeed. For you." He passed her a fifty-dollar bill without fanfare or pause for thanks and walked toward the door, the smile stamped upon his face as if it were a permanent fixture.

The man turned in the opposite direction from where Lovecraft had gone, and kept his head tilted slightly so his face would be hidden should anyone happen to look out of the apartment window over the bookstore.

A little way along the block was an alley, and the man took it sharply, as if eager to be out of sight of the store. Immediately after turning the corner, the tilt of his head righted itself, and he walked along, his smile as placid and radiant as when he had spoken to the waitress.

The blow was meant to put him off balance, but he was heavier than he looked and what was intended as a hard push to the back of the head turned into a punch of sorts. The man staggered all the same, his hat falling off onto the oil-streaked asphalt. He was silent, but threw his hands up to cover his head.

There is little point in exploring the life of the man's attacker, Billy Hoskin, in much detail. He had a reasonably paid job in a body shop, but he also had a charge sheet dating back to juvie, and an impulse control problem when he saw expensively dressed men reeking of money entering dark alleys.

Hoskin thought the sight of the man clutching his head was both funny and aggravating, since he hadn't hit him that hard. He moved in close and started going through the guy's pockets, hunting for his wallet. "Just give me the money and we're done here, fucker."

The man said nothing, which wasn't unusual in Hoskin's experience, but he wasn't making any sound at all, which was. He wasn't breathing hard, or whimpering, or sobbing or making little incoherent noises under his breath or any noises that Hoskin had heard these people make when you got a little physical with them. He stood, half-crouched, half-bent over, clutching the back of his head, and something in the pose irritated Hoskin. He hadn't been hit that hard, so what the fuck was his malfunction?

It occurred to him maybe the guy had already had a head injury and the blow had reopened it.

"You'll be fine. Money, and then I'm gone. Come on."

The man's pockets were remarkably empty. No forgotten receipts, tissues, there hardly seemed to be any lint. Finally, just as he was becoming desperate, Hoskin found the man's wallet in an inside pocket of his jacket. He grabbed it, relieved he could finally get out of there. In fact, the relief was so great it surprised him, as if he'd dodged a bullet, as if he were escaping from real danger.

His hand was barely out of the man's jacket, the calfskin wallet firmly gripped, when the man's hand snapped down from his head to grab Hoskin's wrist. "No," said the man firmly. "You may take the money, but you may take nothing else."

Hoskin tried to pull his hand away, but the guy was strong. Hoskin pulled hard and it was like his wrist was held in a clamp. The man didn't even move an inch. How could a little guy like that weigh so much?

The man reached up and pulled the wallet easily from Hoskin's trapped hand; he couldn't have stopped him if he'd wanted to, not now he seemed to be losing feeling in it. He released Hoskin as if dropping a dead rat, and then ignored him as he drew a wad of maybe twenty fifty-dollar bills out. The man held the money out to Hoskin. "There. That's what you wanted. Take it and leave."

It took a minute to get through to Hoskin that he had completely lost control of the situation. It kind of made him angry, but the wad of green just floating there made it hard to get too mad. He snatched the money and glowered at the man. "What's your business anyway, man? Who the fuck do you think you are?"

The man didn't say anything. He didn't move. It was suddenly like talking to a waxwork. There was something else wrong. Now that the man was no longer holding his head, a flap of something, hairy on the underside, was hanging from it, lankly bobbing off to the left side. Hoskin started to laugh; the guy was wearing a hairpiece and Hoskin had dislodged it when he shoved the guy. That was why he was being so weird. Nothing like injured vanity to upset people in strange ways.

Then he saw it wasn't a hairpiece at all. It was skin, but it wasn't, and the skull exposed beneath it was not a skull. Hoskin looked and then he made the mistake of seeing, and wheels spun inside his mind as gears of logic and simple causality disengaged. He couldn't be seeing what he was seeing but he was seeing it so he could not be seeing it and the gears ran rapidly and with no letup or control, spitting out sparks that were Hoskin's sanity being ground away.

He screamed, once, a high-pitched scream he was hardly aware he was making, and ran from the alleyway. The man, animated once more, lifted the strip and tamped it more or less back into place. Out in the street, the man was screaming and people were stopping. It was all a great nuisance to the man. He put away his wallet and walked rapidly the other way.

Harrelson was on the knotty last paragraph of his report, the last thing standing between him and going home, when the nutcase was dragged in. The guy was pretty big, a raging mess of a red face, dirty-blond hair, and a lot of shouting. It took three uniforms to keep him in check, with two more hovering about. One had his hand on the butt of his gun, which irked Harrelson, but not enough to get up from his cozy warm desk and venture out toward the tank. He returned his attention to his report and had got most of the way through typing "unconfirmed" when the guy screamed a bunch of stuff, the only word of which that made it to Harrelson's ear ungarbled was "monster." He looked up again. Now the lunatic was saying somebody wasn't human.

People got dragged in all the time ranting about orbital mind-control lasers, and how the Bilderberg Group was hiding in the attic, and stuff that was almost boringly similar to paranoid rants on the other side of the Fold. Harrelson had been hoping for a better class of conspiracy theory in a world where there really was some dark shit going down, but he'd been disappointed in this. Carter had told him to keep his ears open for anything that was a little different as an SOP for the Unfolded, but so far nothing had given him much pause. This, though . . . not many of the nut jobs actually mentioned monsters. V had never been a thing here, so the folded weirdos' obsession with reptile people infiltrating society was never a thing either. That was one of the cool things about the Unfolded: no lizard people bullshit.

Well against his better judgment, Harrelson typed the last few letters of "unconfirmed," got to his feet, and went over to where the nut job was screaming about monsters.

"You called for psych yet?" he asked one of the officers.

"Yeah, but they can't be here for an hour." The cop was maybe thirty, but clearly never going to rise to any higher rank. He looked pleadingly at Harrelson. "What do we do with this freak?"

Harrelson looked at the square, flushed face of the screamer and turned down his mouth. "I know this guy. Hey, Billy! Billy! Focus, man, and stop screaming! You're upsetting people."

The man looked vaguely at him, not really seeing him, but at least he stopped screaming. "Put him in the interview room. If you put him in the tank, he'll set off every idiot in there. I'll sit with him until the doc turns up."

The uniforms were grateful, but wouldn't say it, nor did he expect them to. They took Billy Hoskin into the interview room, made sure his restraints were in place, and left Harrelson with him. Harrelson sat down and regarded Hoskin with disdain mixed with curiosity. Yeah, he vaguely knew Hoskin: bad Irish kid from a bad Irish family, ended up working a chop shop, broadened his skill set into stealing the cars in the first place, then carjacking because he wasn't the most patient guy. Last he'd heard, Billy was out on parole, but nobody was expecting that to last long.

"Hey, Billy."

Hoskin's eyes held a vacancy within and behind them. Harrelson tried again.

"I'd get you a coffee, but I ain't spooning it into your mouth, so I guess you'll have to do without." Still no response. "Not that you look like somebody who needs caffeine right now. You using, Billy?" It seemed out of character from what Harrelson could recall, but people change. "Have you taken anything?"

Hoskin looked slowly around the room. There was a weary depression in his face, as if he were on the edge of tears. Harrelson decided to stop fucking about and just ask.

"So, Billy, what's this monster you're all upset about, huh?"

He knew it was a risk. Maybe Hoskin would clam up, or maybe he would freak out and they'd have to Tase him or something. But just maybe he might actually say something useful, and do it before the psych arrived.

Hoskin's gaze settled upon him and Harrelson saw he was looking at the top of his head.

"What is it? I got something in my hair?" He reached up and touched it, but found nothing. He realized the interview room's one-way mirror was behind him and looked over his shoulder. "You think somebody's watching? Believe me, Billy, you ain't that newsworthy."

When he turned back, he realized it really was his hair that Hoskin was finding so fascinating. "Okay, can you stop staring at my hair, please? Maybe I should use some conditioner, I know, but who's got time?"

"His hair wasn't hair."

Harrelson leaned forward. "Who's this we're talking about? The monster guy?"

Hoskin's gaze slid down until it was looking Harrelson in the eye. The expression of hopeless dread started to return. Harrelson had never been in an interview quite like this one before, but he knew how to read a suspect well enough.

"Hold it right there, Billy. If you think I'm some kind of monster, too, ask yourself a few questions first. One, if I was in cahoots with your monster man, why would I be bothering to ask *you* any questions when *they* could just tell me what I wanted to know? Two, if I'm in on the big monster conspiracy, why didn't I just uncuff you and shoot you first thing? I coulda claimed I thought you'd calmed down and stupidly showed a little compassion in letting your hands go. Then—gasp—you attacked me. Bang. You see what I mean?"

Hoskin was silent for several seconds and Harrelson thought he was probably just going to curl up mentally and that would be that. But then Hoskin leaned forward and said in a harsh whisper, "It looked like a man. Fruits."

Harrelson blinked. "Fruit? What, the guy propositioned you? I dunno what you mean."

"Fruits," said Hoskin again in the same whisper, then slowly started to tell Harrelson things, some of which were relevant, and some of which were true. By the time the psych arrived, Harrelson was happy to leave the room.

He sought out one of the officers who'd brought Hoskin in. "Yo, Torres. A word." He took the uniform to one side. "The doc's in with Billy Hoskin now, but I gotta tell you, I know Billy a little, and he ain't never seemed to have enough of a mind to lose, if you see what I mean. What went down?"

The policewoman shrugged. "I wasn't the first on the scene, Detective. Got there and found Basker, Hunt, and Albers trying to get him out of traffic. First we thought he was on meth, but then Hunt says he knows him and he's no tweaker. Hoskin kept talking about a man with a full empty head and some stuff about fruit. Some kind of breakdown, maybe? Oh, one weird thing. He had a wad of bills in his hand, nineteen hundred dollars in fifties. They all looked brand new, but they were nonsequential. Numbers not even close to each other. That's weird, isn't it?"

Harrelson nodded. "Yeah, that's weird."

Torres nodded back. "Yeah, it's weird. Captain's saying they might be counterfeit, that we should pass the buck to the Treasury and let them deal with Hoskin."

Harrelson grimaced. "For fuck's sake, Hoskin can't even spell 'counterfeit.' Had to get the money from someplace though, so . . ." He thought for a moment. "Where'd this piece of street theater happen?"

"Havilland, right outside the sporting goods, outdoor gear place. You know the one? Carson's?"

"Just down from the antique bookstore on the corner," said Harrelson, the sense of a lot of shit flying toward a really big fan growing in him. "Yeah, I know the one."

Chapter 13

PROPERTY RETURNED

Torsten Lukas made a small jump of surprise when he realized there was a car following him as he walked the sidewalk. The atmosphere at the laboratory the previous day had been strange, and he had found himself becoming unaccountably anxious.

He was momentarily relieved, then angered to see it was being driven by Dan Carter. He looked quickly around, then bent to the lowering driver's window as Carter pulled up alongside him.

"What are you doing? We can't be seen together! If Giehl sees—"

Carter glowered back. "We work together, Doctor. Remember? I'm just giving you a friendly lift. Get in." The tone in which he said "friendly" was not even close to friendly and Lukas walked around to the passenger door with misgivings.

Once he was inside and before he'd had a chance to fasten his seat belt, Carter was already out in traffic. "Two nights ago, I broke into that"—he swallowed the desire to add "fucking"—"detector at two in the morning."

Torsten's antipathy evaporated. "You did it, Mr. Carter?" He looked around for a manila envelope stuffed with incriminating pictures. Unfortunately, it didn't exist. "You took pictures of the boards?"

"No, I didn't." Lukas started to say something, but Carter talked over him. "Two reasons, both doozies." Lukas frowned at the unfamiliar term, but Carter wasn't in the mood to explain it. "Reason one. Your pal Dr. Giehl just happened to turn up a few minutes after the detector was opened. I had to bullshit her a little bit." Lukas was frowning again, and this time Carter did explain. "I lied to her. She thinks I'm a U.S. agent for a suboffice within the OSS made up of deniable assets. Long story short, she thinks I'm OSS, okay?"

"She went into the laboratory? At 2:00 a.m.?"

"Yeah."

"That's . . . Did she say why?"

"Some stuff about having left some work there that she needed. That was bullshit, too. I don't know how, but she knew I'd opened the case. Which kind of leads me to the second reason why I didn't get any pictures when I opened the detector." He paused long enough for Lukas to glance inquiringly at him. "There was a bomb inside it."

He returned Lukas's glance at that moment, and saw something he'd been kind of hoping not to see. Utter confusion. Either Lukas was a brilliant actor, or he truly knew nothing about it.

"A bomb? A bomb like—"

"In like *boom*. Yeah. Nothing to do with you?"

"No!"

Carter was glad he'd caught Lukas's expression when he thought he wasn't observed, because the denial was the kind of bluster both the innocent and the guilty roll out.

"Well, I'm pretty sure Giehl didn't put it there, although she was pretty handy at defusing it. I'm also pretty sure she's Abwehr."

Lukas was quiet for a moment, trying to take it all in. "Abwehr," he said finally. He followed it with a few heartfelt words of muttered German. "Those stupid bastards. We're just tripping over one another. You're sure?"

"Well, she didn't have a spy badge or a decoder ring or anything like that, but I'm making a guess. She's had field training from somewhere." He didn't need to add that this was unlike Lukas, who'd been let loose by the Gestapo after a cup of coffee and a pep talk. His abrupt look away showed he was already thinking that himself.

"You're sure *she* didn't plant the bomb?" said Lukas. "To protect that damned machine?"

"It wasn't an antitamper device, Doctor. It was wired to the power unit. It was meant to kill Dr. Giehl. Maybe even all of you; it was a good-sized bundle of dynamite. With all the shrapnel from the detector's case, anyone in the lab would've been lucky to get out alive."

Lukas shook his head. "This doesn't make sense. I didn't do it, you didn't do it, she didn't do it. So who did? Who would want to close the project down that much?"

Carter had no idea. "Scientists don't try to blow up rival scientists, do they?"

Lukas shook his head. "No. Scientists carry out their assassinations in scientific journals. The worst thing you can do to a scientist is destroy his credibility. Blowing him up is . . . inelegant. And dynamite, you say? Using commercial explosives would just be unprofessional. Anyone with laboratory training, and access, and any sense at all would make their own explosives. Why risk discovery by getting them from elsewhere? I will say it again, Mr. Carter. This does not make sense."

Harrelson felt like a turd in a ballroom. The reception foyer was gleaming with polished marble and art deco glass and steel, and there he was, waiting on a chair that was better than him and knew it. He had a feeling the woman at the front desk with whom he'd spoken took home a bigger paycheck than him, too. Occasionally she would glance over at him and smile, but it was the kind of smile reserved for waifs and strays. Harrelson had rarely felt more out of place, sitting there in his cheap suit with a plastic store bag on his lap.

It was a relief when he was finally told he could go up and was directed to an elevator. The relief evaporated when he discovered it contained an elderly man in a bellboy uniform who operated the controls.

"Uh, top floor, please," said Harrelson, suddenly realizing how much he liked pressing elevator buttons.

"Top *office* floor, sir," said the man with a genial cackle of laughter underpinning his words. Harrelson feared the guy might give him candy and tell him about the old days. "The shaft doesn't go all the way to the top of the building, you see."

"Oh?" Harrelson watched the floor indicator progress too slowly for his liking.

"No, sir. The top floor is a penthouse suite. The elevator doesn't go there for *security* reasons."

The emphasis on "security" was as if Harrelson might think of several others and the elevator guy just wanted to nip those kinds of silly ideas right in the bud. Harrelson realized he was supposed to say something.

"Penthouse, huh? The boss's?"

"Indeed so, and his father's before him, and his father's before him. A true family company. So rare these days."

The elevator finally arrived and Harrelson had to fight not to say, "So long, Pops," as he exited, making do with "Thanks." A young man was waiting for him and took him through the busy office down a long corridor to a dark wooden door set in a dark wooden frame. The whole place felt like some sort of throwback, as if the nineteen twenties had got its hands on computers and assimilated them somehow.

The corridor opened out into a small desk area before the doors, and at it sat a middle-aged woman with a view clean down the corridor. She had the air of a guardian rather than a personal assistant, but she accepted the nod the man with Harrelson gave when they were still thirty feet away, spoke briefly and quietly on the intercom, then rose to be at the door by the time Harrelson arrived. She swung the door open and ushered him through. "Ten minutes, Detective," she said in a low voice as he went by, and he realized she was the woman he'd spoken to when he'd called ahead. She'd been very specific about how long her busy employer could spare.

The inner office felt like even more of a throwback than what he'd already seen. Paneled walls, a large desk that couldn't be less than a century old, and—tellingly—no computer on it, just a big old-fashioned blotter, a neat stack of papers off to one side, and an inkstand that looked as old as the desk. Standing beside the desk, as if posing for a picture, was its owner. The man smiled and held out his hand.

"Detective Harrelson. A pleasure to meet you."

Harrelson approached, aware of the door clicking shut behind him, and shook the man's hand. It was a firm handshake. Almost too firm, like shaking the hand of a waxwork.

"Mutual, Mr. Weston," said Harrelson.

Henry Weston ushered Harrelson into the chair before the desk, and started to walk back around to his own. "I would offer you a drink, Detective, but as you can see, I'm presently very busy indeed." Harrelson looked at the neat stack of papers set out on the desk like a museum exhibit, and didn't trust himself to reply.

Weston suddenly stopped. "No, I shan't sit there. It will look like some sort of job interview, won't it, with this great piece of wood in the way?" Then, to Harrelson's distinct and ineffable horror, Weston perched on the corner of the desk like a school counselor. He guessed that he managed to keep that sensation off his face, because Weston smiled as happily as if he'd just conquered Everest.

"Now, Detective," he said, smiling sweetly down from on high, "how can I help you? Your telephone call was vague."

Harrelson wondered how he knew that. It was true—he had deliberately steered around his reason for coming by talking about ongoing police investigations and Weston maybe being able to help out in some kind of peripheral way. Had his assistant reported it to him like that, or had she recorded the call? Had Weston listened in on the call? Maybe he had; the request for an interview had been okayed there and then. That hadn't bothered him too much at the time, but now, having seen what kind of operation Weston Edmunds was, it nagged at him. As if having the richest man he'd ever met sitting on the edge of a desk an arm's length away, grinning at him, wasn't awkward enough.

"I was wondering if you could look at something for me, sir." Harrelson opened the plastic bag and took out its contents. He held it up for Weston to see. "Do you recognize this hat?"

If he was expecting Weston to act suspiciously or evasively, he was disappointed. In fact, Weston did the thing that was at the bottom of his list of expectations. "Why, yes!" He took the hat from Harrelson without asking, and examined it with obvious delight. "Wherever did you find it?"

"It was recovered from a crime scene, sir." That was only true if you really stretched the definition of "crime," but Harrelson didn't mind that. "I was wondering if you might have any idea how it got there."

Anyone else might have been put on their guard by a line like that, but Weston continued to toy with the hat, a slightly whimsical smile on his face as he looked inside the crown as if expecting to find Narnia in there. "Not much of a crime if you're returning this to me, Detective. And *that*"—he nodded at the plastic shopping bag—"doesn't look like an evidence bag to me." He turned the smile upon Harrelson. "I *am* a lawyer, you know."

Harrelson knew better than to argue the point. "Yeah, but we still have to collate evidence before it gets kicked over to the Feds."

He was almost surprised when his words had the first palpable effect he'd yet seen with Weston. The smile dialed down a little on the attorney's face, maybe by 10 percent, and he canted his head around to look at his visitor. "The Feds?" The term should have sounded comical coming from a man like Weston, but it did not.

"Yeah, the Treasury might be getting involved. We collared a guy who'd mugged somebody and got a wad of interesting money off him."

"Not forged." The way Weston said it, Harrelson couldn't make out if it was a question or a statement.

"I can't comment on that, sir, but something fishy's going on. We'll be glad to hand it off to the Treasury, to be honest. We're busy enough. But, we have to put together a full file before their agents turn up. So"—he pointed at the hat—"your hat was found near to where this mugging took place. It's an expensive piece of head wear, sir, made to measure. I went to the makers, and they gave me your name."

"Did they?" Another 10 percent flickered out.

"They did after I showed them the warrant, Mr. Weston." This was a lie; he'd given them some soft bullshit about returning the hat to its rightful owner. He'd wandered in, told them he happened to be in the neighborhood, and he just wanted to give the thing back as it was obviously an expensive chapeau. If they hadn't, he'd have chased a warrant, although he had doubts he'd have gotten it. "After all, there's potential currency crime here. It's serious stuff."

He looked at Weston and found it strange that the man had so little body language. Apart from that smile, which seemed attached to a rheostat, he gave nothing away. Harrelson decided he would just have to gauge when to throw the man a rope by gut feeling, and his gut said the moment was now. "I was wondering if maybe you saw something."

That's right, bub. I'm not after you. Cheer up and let your mouth run off.

Weston didn't react for almost two seconds, then the smile recovered 10 percent of its luminescence. "I don't see how, Detective. The hat wasn't taken from me. I simply forgot I had taken it out with me and left it in a coffee shop. Cappella, two blocks from here." He pointed eastward and slightly downward. Harrelson wondered how accurately he was pointing at the coffee shop, invisible from the desk. "It must be three days ago now."

"You weren't mugged?"

"I think I would have remembered that, and reported it."

"This joker got nineteen hundred bucks from somewhere, and it wasn't through hard work, sir."

"Have you tried asking him where he got it from?"

Harrelson decided not to tell Weston that Billy Hoskin wasn't being very coherent at the moment, raving about monsters, men with empty heads, and a weird obsession with fruit. "The suspect is being uncooperative."

"Ah, the criminal mind. Its first instinct is to deny everything. Perhaps when he passes through this state of denial and understands his situation properly, he will be more forthcoming."

Harrelson knew a brick wall when he saw one. He rose from his chair. "Maybe so. Sorry to have wasted your time, Mr. Weston."

Weston slipped easily from the edge of the desk back to his feet. "Oh, not at all. It has been an interesting moment in an otherwise humdrum day. And I got my hat back." He looked pensively at it. "Do you want it back for evidence?"

After he had found it in the alley Hoskin had been seen running from, the hat had made the trip back to the precinct in an evidence bag, where a friendly CSU had used tape to lift hairs and potential DNA evidence from inside the crown. There was no case, exactly, and Harrelson had decided to run fast and loose with things after he'd realized how close the incident had occurred to the Carter & Lovecraft bookstore. His captain would've laughed in his face if he'd tried to explain, so he didn't try. This would all have to be his hobby for the time being. So, he'd transferred the hat from the evidence bag to a plastic shopping bag in the hope of not spooking Weston, and here he was.

"No, sir. Looks like it has nothing to do with the mugging."

After Harrelson had gone, Weston looked at the hat in silence for a long moment. In a sudden movement he brought it to his face and slowly inhaled the lower inside edge of the crown, where the hat met scalp. There were enough molecules to detect, but he only needed a few. There was something he identified as a hydrophilic molecule, already bonded to atmospheric water, and there was a stray molecule of ethylene oxide which, among other uses, was a denaturant used to scour materials of stray DNA contamination during manufacture. Putting the two together suggested the sort of tape used for lifting forensic evidence. Weston walked to the hat stand by the door and placed the hat carefully upon a hook. Already, he was thinking far, far ahead.

Chapter 14

LOST COUNTRIES

The good news as far as Carter was concerned was that Lukas wanted to know what was going on more than ever and was prepared to pay a bonus on top of his usual retainer to keep Carter on the job. The bad news was exactly the same. He was of two minds whether he wanted to walk away or not. Defusing bombs and playing Piggy-in-the-Middle between arms of Nazi intelligence and security seemed like a potentially dangerous place to be. Weighing against that was the money, his curiosity, and the growing conviction that the weirdness about the case that didn't involve bundles of dynamite instead somehow involved the Fold. He hadn't forgotten the ghost he'd seen—he'd have given good money to be able to—and he wanted to, *needed* to know what significance it had, if any. He had seen it, it had seen him, it had challenged him. Carter couldn't ever remember a campfire ghost story finishing with the teller—flashlight under chin—saying, "And the ghost said, 'Who the fuck are you?'"

There was also the question of the phantom bomber. It would have been peachy keen just to hand that over to the police, but that avenue now had a large, Abwehr-issued *Verboten* sign across it, so he would just have to hope whoever was behind it didn't have any more sticks of explosive in reserve. Whoever they were, despite Giehl's derisive comments about the device's lack of sophistication, she'd avoided mentioning that they'd still managed to circumvent the alarm she'd put on the detector, an alarm that Carter had triggered without even noticing it was there. So, somebody who wasn't a complete idiot.

Carter had made an arrangement to arrive at work half an hour before he was due to take the night shift. Dr. Giehl wanted to compare notes with her American counterpart now that they'd had a chance to consider the events of the night before. He hoped to Christ she hadn't had a chance or the volition to get in touch with her handlers and ask them about the CIA, because if she had then things could get real shitty real quick.

He was supposed to meet her in the parking lot by the building's service door, and he approached it with reasonable apprehension, half-expecting Giehl or some Nazi stooge in a slouchy hat and overcoat to step out of the shadows and shoot him with a suppressed Luger. If it came to that, he'd rather it was Giehl: being murdered by a pretty attractive doctor with a sexy European accent was marginally better than being murdered by some square-headed thug from central casting.

The reality turned out to be better than being shot by anyone at all, but still not as interesting as he'd expected: Dr. Giehl was not there. Carter checked his watch and found he was right on time. He'd got it into his mind that being both German and a physicist would make Giehl pathologically punctual. It looked like he was wrong. Maybe she'd just got buttonholed at the last minute and was—

There was a muffled shot from inside the high-energy physics lab and a male cry.

Not being an idiot, Carter reached for his radio before even thinking about drawing his gun. "Sergeant? This is Carter. I'm outside the high-energy building, and I'm pretty sure I just heard a shot fired in there."

There was a moment's silence, then the return channel opened. "Carter? What are you doing there? You're . . . Wait a minute, did you say there's shooting?"

"I think so. I heard a shot, or something like one, then a man shouted and—"

Another shot, and a high scream. It was impossible to tell if it was a man or a woman, but it was the sound of somebody in terror and maybe in pain.

"Did you hear that? I got to get in there, Sarge. Call APD, and tell them there's trouble here. Tell them no sirens."

The sergeant started to say something, but Carter was already moving toward the front entrance, his issue Walther PPQ M2 nine mil in hand. He would have preferred to go in through the service entrance, but it doubled as a fire exit and could only be opened from the inside by overriding the door alarm and pushing on the panic bar. So, he'd have to go in the front way, and just hope it wasn't covered.

The building's foyer was empty, including the security station. Carter vaulted the desk and landed inside the cubicle. A quick glance around showed no sign of Jenner, the guard he was supposed to be relieving, either dead or alive. He checked the monitors, but every camera in the place seemed to be down. A cursory examination down the back of the unit showed why: every feed cable had been pulled. He could see it would be easy to get working again, but time consuming, and time was probably short.

He left the cubicle—by the door this time—and stopped by the stairwell leading down into the basement offices. It seemed quiet down there, which was not unusual at that time of the evening. If anyone was still hanging around, they would most likely be on the laboratory floor.

Aware he was heading into trouble, a feeling he never enjoyed and that he would never get used to no matter how many times he took up the opportunities to walk into it that his life offered, he quickly and quietly climbed the steps to the second story. The sarge had been right: the Walther did sit in his hand much like a Glock. He was grateful for that small familiarity. It was not a moment for discords in his experience to distract him from what might happen.

He considered going up to the floor above, where he could look down from the mezzanine onto the laboratory and get some idea what was going on. But, two shots had already been fired. He needed to . . .

He reached the top of the first flight of stairs and found himself looking at a large pool of blood, leaking out from under the right-hand side of the double doors that led into the laboratory. It was a lot of blood, dark and venous, a creeping shape that shone sharply beneath the strip lighting. Carter couldn't see how anyone could lose that much and, at best, not be in shock. He stepped over it to the left and braced himself below the window set in the door on that side.

He could hear voices: one—male—raised and angry, and others answering him. He listened intently to try and make out what was being said, but whoever was doing the shouting wasn't clear, a product both of being nearly incoherent with rage and— Carter hoped—having his back to the door. Carter made out "destroyed," "murdered," and a lot of repetition on "fucking." Okay, that was likely the shooter. As for whatever was being said back, that was said in low, calm tones, trying to talk the shooter down. More than one voice, there. They didn't seem to be making much headway, though. Carter noticed that none of the voices had German accents.

Carter raised his head far enough to look through the very

corner of the glass. The eastern side of the lab seemed to be empty of people. He would have to move farther into view himself if he was going to check out the entire area. Hoping he wasn't about to collect a bullet in the head, he shifted slowly to the right.

He needn't have worried. At least, not about that. The man with a drawn gun had his back to the door and was shouting at a small cluster of terrified scientists. Fronting the group was Ian Malcolm, the head of the American side of the team. Carter realized there were three German physicists, and they were all cowering at the back. Then he saw, no, they were being shielded by the Americans.

Jenner was the man with the gun. Malcolm was telling him to be cool, but Jenner was a long way from being cool. He was walking in short, angry bursts of activity, here and back, here and back, his attention wandering off the group, then back a second later, running his free hand over his scalp as if trying to wipe away his anxiety and anger, and—oh, fuck—was he angry. His finger was also on the trigger, which worried Carter a lot. The Walthers didn't have a safety catch, instead settling for two internal drop safeties and a firing pin block. In short, they were designed not to go off if knocked or dropped, which was all cool, but the trigger *was* the safety. All Jenner had to do was twitch his finger and somebody else might get shot, and seeing how twitchy he was right then, that was a likely scenario.

Carter didn't have much choice. Jenner had obviously already done one stupid thing and was working himself up to doing another. Carter couldn't do much from the other side of a door. He could probably shoot Jenner through the window, but he didn't want to. Ideally, he didn't want to shoot the man at all, but that meant talking him down since Malcolm wasn't making much headway, and that meant entering. With plenty of misgivings, he tapped on the door, and waved at Jenner when he swung around to see who was slowly opening the door.

"Hi, man," he said, slow and calm, while trying to remember whatever he had ever known about crisis negotiation. He'd been taught a five-step system, but all he could recall was that first came active listening, then empathy, then rapport, then some other stuff he'd have to wing through. Ultimately, he wanted the gun off Jenner and no more shots fired. All he had to do was to remain cool.

He glanced down and to his right as he stepped into the lab. Lukas was on the floor, the blood pool emanating from his body. He looked very, very dead. "Well, fuck," said Carter, forgetting to be cool. He looked over at Jenner. "Hey, Pete. What's up?"

Jenner's nerve slipped still further. "Carter? What are you doing here? You shouldn't be here yet!"

"Yeah, well, I wasn't doing anything else, so I figured, heck, might as well go to work a little early." He nodded sideways at the body. "Man, did you shoot Doc Lukas? Why'd you do that?"

Jenner didn't look like he was going to talk for a moment. There was an expression of barely controlled horror running around just under his skin and it might burst out any second now. Whatever else Jenner was experiencing, he had not gone robotic as was often the case with spree shooters, turning off any and all empathy so they could carry on with being assholes without any remaining splinters of humanity getting in the way.

Carter pulled up his training. Active listening. Okay. "Talk to me, Pete. I'm listening."

"My name," said Jenner, slowly, clearly, stepping back so everyone in the room was in his field of vision, "isn't Jenner."

Carter had a sense of foreboding that all the five-step plans in the world weren't going to bring this to a conclusion with no further bloodshed.

"They did it to him, they did." Jenner gestured violently at the cluster of scientists, causing some to flinch, some to shy away. "The fucking Germans did it to him."

"They killed Lukas?"

"No!" Jenner changed from uncertain to furious in a second. Carter wished he could remember more from his crisis management training. He seemed to be fucking up. "Dave! They fucked with his head somehow!"

"Dave?"

"Koznick," said Dr. Malcolm. "The guard who suffered a breakdown."

"No!" Jenner pointed the gun squarely at Malcolm's head. "Not a fucking breakdown!" Malcolm slowly raised his hands to shoulder height in a sign of submission and surrender. "Those fucking Krauts *did* something to him!"

"Hey, Pete, just take a minute," said Carter, trying to bring Jenner's attention back to him. "I need to understand what you're saying. Dave Koznick had something done to him? Something that made him have a nervous breakdown? How?"

"I don't know!" Jenner couldn't stop shouting, which Carter reckoned his crisis management trainer would have described as "counterindicative to a preferred solution." "I don't fucking know how they did it, but they did it somehow!"

"Okay. Just . . . okay. So, they did this . . . why?"

Jenner looked at him like he was an idiot. "Koznick!" He saw no comprehension in Carter's eyes. "He was Polish! And those motherfuckers"—the gun swept off Malcolm and at the Germans huddled behind the Americans—"they wiped out Poland! Genocidal fuckers! That's what they do! That's what they do! Millions dead, and nobody gave a fuck. They're just tidying up now! Every Pole in the phone book, might as well be a fucking death list!"

Realization finally came to Carter. "Pete, so if your name's not really Jenner . . ."

"Janowski. My parents changed it to fit in better. That's what they said. They also said a Polish name is like having a target painted on your back with some people. I told Dave, told him he should change it, but he just laughed . . . just laughed and said the war was a long time ago. He didn't care. He didn't care what those motherfucking animals did to Poland."

Carter couldn't take his eyes off Jenner's—Janowski's—gun. What was it? Less than a six-pound trigger pull? Less than half an inch of travel to fire, tenth of an inch reset before the trigger could be squeezed again? Barely a twitch of the finger to let off two rounds. Assuming two rounds fired, then he still had thirteen to go. Three surviving Germans, and four Americans to go through to reach them.

"But they cared. Hunting us down. *Him.*" Janowski jerked his head toward Lukas's corpse. "He was fucking *Gestapo!*" He spat the word out, but it was a word made for spitting.

The revelation created a murmur among the Americans. "Gestapo?" said Malcolm. "Are you sure?"

"I heard them arguing about it! Her! Her!" He jabbed the gun at Dr. Giehl. "I heard her call him Gestapo!"

"No." Giehl's voice was clear. "You misunderstood. I said he was behaving like Gestapo."

"No! My German's fine! You can't tell me I didn't understand that! I heard you! I fucking heard you! I—"

Carter shot him. In the moment when Janowski's gun was raised to bear over the heads of the scientists as he raged, Carter took his chance and fired. His gun hand had been by his side, so there was no chance of aiming properly, just a snapshot gauged for the right bicep in the hope of disarming him. Maybe it was a bad shot, maybe it was years of training to go for the center of the body, but the bullet hit Janowski in the armpit. He made a shocked sort of whinny and clenched his arms against his body, the gun pointing down. Carter tackled him and took him down, disarming him immediately.

"Oh, fuck," muttered Janowski. "Fuck. Dude, you shot me."

"Call an ambulance!" Carter barked at the scientists. Malcolm was already heading for a landline handset, cell phones being discouraged around the sensitive gear.

"Where'd I get hit?" Janowski's face was gray. "Hurts like a bitch. My whole side. Ribs?"

"Armpit. I was going for your arm, Pete."

"Armpit, huh? Shit. Guess I'm fucked then. All kinds of arteries and shit in there, ain't there? Yeah."

There was a lot of blood. Carter was aware of it soaking into his pant legs as he knelt by Janowski. "Keep your arm down tight against your side. No, wait. Just a minute." He took out a pocket pack of tissues and stripped the wrapper off. He lifted Janowski's arm to find the wound. Blood pulsed rapidly from his armpit, obscuring the hole on the shirt cloth, but Carter found it, pushed the wad of tissues on top of it, then pulled Janowski's arm back down. "Now, hold your arm down. Keep the pressure on it." Carter pushed Janowski's upper arm against his body. His hands were covered in blood. "Medics are on the way. You just have to hang on for a while."

"Nah." Janowski spoke as if Carter were suggesting they go see a movie. "Nah, they'll just get me in the hospital. Fuck. Look after my cat, okay? He's called Misky. He's . . . Jesus, this hurts." His eyes were looking around at the ceiling. They settled on the glass of the atrium roof. "I can see the stars."

Carter glanced up, but the glass just looked like a dark square to him, the glare of the laboratory lights making it impossible to see more.

Janowski was still talking. "They'll just get me in the hospital. They'll get all of us. One way or another, the fucking Nazis will kill everyone. Including themselves . . . including themselves." He looked Carter in the eye. "They will get all of us."

The police arrived to find Constable Carter of Miskatonic Security administering CPR to Constable Jenner, while the sergeant of the guard stood uselessly by with a defibrillator pack in his hand. There was no fibrillating pulse to shock back into beating steadily, however. By the time the paramedics arrived Carter had been talked into giving up, and there was no hurry at all.

Chapter 15

2D, 3D, 4D, nD

It was the beginning of a very long night for all of them. The detectives arrived, and Carter was relieved to see Harrelson leading the investigation. Harrelson seemed less happy to see him. He drew Carter to one side to take a statement, and they communicated in terse little sentences when nobody was nearby to overhear.

Harrelson's first informal statement when they had found a quiet corner was, "The fuck, Carter? Bombs and now this? What the fuck is going on here?"

"I'll explain what I know, but not now. We got to make this look on the up and up. I'm going to tell you exactly what happened, but I'm going to leave out a pile of shit you already know—"

"And wish I didn't."

"But that can't go into your report. Also"—Carter looked

around cautiously—"this place isn't going to be taped off-limits, is it? No police guard overnight?"

Harrelson looked at him suspiciously. "Why?"

"'Cause I have to put that bomb back."

Harrelson snorted. "The fuck you say?"

"I'm not going to rig it to blow. I'll leave a wire loose or something. The thing is, your guys are going to search Jenner's place and chances are they'll find bomb-making gear, but no bomb. They're also going to find the tricksy screwdriver you need to open the German instrument cases and put two and two together. Best solution would be to smuggle the bomb to his place before your people arrive, but that's not going to happen. Just no time. So, I put the bomb back. They find it; loose end tied up."

"Yeah? And what if the bomb squad decides to just blow it up instead of trying to defuse it? What are your Nazi pals going to say about that?"

"I had precisely one Nazi client, he wasn't my *pal* by any stretch, and the poor fucker is dead anyway, so Christ only knows how I'm going to get paid now."

Harrelson winced. "Cold."

"The point is, all this Spy vs. Spy bullshit turned out to be just that. It was down to one guy who got a weird idea in his head and people got hurt. Does it have to be any more complicated than that?"

"You tell me, Carter. Tell me the story. I'm supposed to be taking a statement here."

Carter did so, being absolutely honest in as many details as he could, although that resolution suffered a bad start when he had to lie about why he'd arrived at work early. After that, however, he was able to stick rigidly to the truth, at least about the events of that evening.

Harrelson stopped at a couple of points, signaling it was off the record by clicking the point of his pen in. "This guy Koznick, what do you know about him?"

Carter knew next to nothing, only that it had been Koznick's resignation on health grounds that had opened a job for Carter to take. Harrelson nodded, clicked the pen point out again. "Seems kind of a coincidence, though, wouldn't you say? You should check him out in a few days, after the heat from tonight's had a chance to die down a little. Find out if that sick leave story's true or if he was pushed, y'know?"

"Why should I care? Client's dead. I'm out and clear."

Harrelson gave a short, derisive bark of a laugh. "Yeah, you wish, like it's your choice." He tilted his head and gave Carter an appraising look. "Let me just run something by you, and then you can tell me again how easy it's going to be to walk away from this cluster fuck." He squared to Carter as if they were about to start a staring contest. "Does the name Henry Weston mean anything to you?"

Carter's face told him everything he needed to know. Again the short derisive laugh. "Yeah," said Harrelson, "you *wish* you were out and clear."

The sun was long up by the time he got back to the bookstore. He had a change of clothing in his locker, which was lucky, as CSU wanted the ones he was standing up in. That was fine by him; he'd almost got used to the smell of blood, but when the fresh air mixed with it, it was as if his nose had become resensitized, and reminded him that there was nothing to love about that scent.

He'd had to hand in his weapon, but as it wasn't really his, this he was also cool with. He wasn't worried about any legal comeback on the shooting. It had been a "good shoot," fired to prevent a likely further homicide or multiple homicides by a man who had already killed once that night. Carter had taken the shot in front of, and to protect, four American citizens of impeccable character and three Germans who were probably okay, too. None of the witnesses had anything to say about Carter that wasn't flattering. How he'd tried to talk Jenner/Janowski down, how he'd avoided violence as long as he could even at risk to his

own life, had only fired when it looked likely Jenner/Janowski was about to shoot somebody else, and how he'd shown control in firing only once, putting the gunman down with a single bullet.

This last point bothered Carter. He'd always been trained to fire twice in a situation like that. He said he had no idea why he'd only fired once. That was a lie; he guessed it was because he liked Pete Jenner, and had no desire to reset the trigger of his own Walther a tenth of an inch, then put a second round in the guy.

He was surprised to find the store locked up, and the note he'd left Lovecraft about a display case she wanted for some of the store's more expensive (but not the most expensive) books was still lying in the middle of the counter where he'd left it. Maybe she was sick. He checked his phone, but there were no messages, or any from her on the landline's answering machine. It wasn't like her, but at the same time he was so tired it was hard to care. Tired and sick at heart; he'd killed once during his police career and—although he'd weathered it better than some— it still gnawed at his conscience sometimes. That was for somebody he only knew by rep, all bad. Pete Jenner was somebody he knew, had chatted with, joked with. Even as his head was hitting the pillow, Carter knew he was going to need some closure on this. He'd look into Koznick's breakdown and find out the truth of it, a favor to a dead man.

She'd started with drawing curves and arcs on paper, using her old high school compass and a French curve, both of which were stored in a "drawer of things that might one day be useful." It was nice to see the line, graphite gray on white, and what it meant became a little more solid in her mind. But it wasn't enough. It wasn't nearly enough. Emily Lovecraft went back to her "drawer of things that might one day be useful" to look for more art supplies.

She'd found string and thumbtacks. This was more like it. It was a large ball of white string she'd bought for something—a parcel, maybe? she couldn't remember—and only used a few inches. There looked to be a lot left. Good. She'd be needing it.

She reconstructed the curve she'd drawn by stretching string between floor, walls, and ceiling (she'd considered using the space under the table, but there were no walls there, and not enough room). Each length formed a tangent and, as the lines proliferated, the curve emerged from their intersections. Unlike the curve on the paper, however, this one warped in the third dimension. It still wasn't perfect, but it was getting there.

She'd started with a large tub of thumbtacks, but they gave out before the ball of string, and she went out to the store to buy more. It was only then that she realized it was just past dawn. She had been working on it for the better part of twelve hours. Part of her said she should rest and, anyway, wasn't this all getting a little psychotic? The rest of her said, no. It was the most glorious thing in the world. For the first time in her life, she truly felt as if she was communicating with something greater than herself, seeing a truth that was larger than any truth she had ever known or even imagined could be. She had always liked to think she was a spiritual creature at heart, but she was beginning to see how infantile a belief that was. She was seeing things now as if she'd been blind her whole life and the book had finally given her the gift of 20/20 vision. Well, not quite. There were still aspects that were occluded, but if she worked toward them, she was sure she'd be able to see clearly. It amused her that "occluded" and "occult" had such similar meanings and yet the Latin roots from which they were derived were subtly different. The former was from *occludere*, meaning to shut off, and the latter from the frequentative of *occlure*, to conceal. She'd checked in the dictionary, just to be sure.

She looked a little too bright-eyed and intense to the man at the counter of the twenty-four-hour convenience store when she dumped six boxes of thumbtacks and four balls of colored string and three of white—the store's entire stock of these items—in front of him along with a pack of energy bars and a six-pack of caffeine drinks. He decided she was probably wired on some-thing, and just wanted her to get out of the store quickly. Then again, it was Arkham, and Arkham had a reputation for eccen-tricity among its citizens.

"It's for an art project," she said, unsure why she was lying, or even if it was entirely a lie. She scratched her head fiercely as she said it.

"I didn't ask," said the man, pushing her change across the counter to her.

"That's bad customer relations," she told him as she walked for the door. "Really bad. You should take, like, a polite inter-est. I won't be coming here again."

Four hours later she was back again to buy more energy bars and caffeine drinks, and to ask if they'd restocked thumbtacks and string yet.

Carter had been told not to report to duty until the police inves-tigation was settled, but he was assured he would be maintained on payroll until that time. It took him a moment to realize they were giving him a paid holiday, at which point he gracefully ac-cepted. Even if he resigned the minute they asked him back to work, he'd have made up the money Lukas owed him. Merce-nary, he knew, but he had bills to pay. In any case, he thought maybe if he could work up the ladder a little or took limited shifts, the job might provide a bulwark against insolvency while he tried to get more PI work.

He'd been asked to come to the precinct to go through his statement once again—Harrelson would be doing that and had assured him that it really was just routine—but that wasn't until the late afternoon. He'd woken at a little after 1:00 p.m., and dis-covered that the store still wasn't open, nor were there any mes-sages from Lovecraft. He showered, dressed, and went out.

He had never visited Lovecraft's apartment in the Folded World, but in the Unfolded about the only positive was she'd found herself living in a small house, a cottage to all intents.

Here, she'd shown him around shortly afterward, but the change was still taking up most of their attentions, and little about the visit had stuck in his mind. He hadn't been around since.

It looked quiet enough when he arrived. It was the kind of "olde worlde" place that typified Arkham, and appeared on every postcard ever sold in the city. Gambrel roof with gable end carvings, finials, and a wrought iron cresting, with a useful attic bearing its own large and ornamented dormer at the front. It was a fine little house, and more than once while in a positive mood Lovecraft had said that, if and when they refolded the world, they must find a way to bring the place through with them. In fact, they could bring the whole of Arkham through with her blessing; she much preferred it to Providence.

The curtains, Carter noticed, were still drawn. Given what a habitual early riser Lovecraft was, that worried him. Maybe she was ill. Maybe she'd had an accident. He pushed the doorbell and heard the sonorous clang of the sixties-style tubular bells arrangement she'd pointed out to him. Apparently it had come with the house, and she found it too incredibly kitschy to take out. Besides, she liked the low mellow tones it produced, "like an old Avon ad." Now he could hear those tones reverberate around the house for long seconds until they slowly died. There was no reply.

He stepped back in time to see the bedroom curtain on the second floor twitch. He walked straight back to the door and pounded on it. He'd hardly started when the door swung open, and there was Lovecraft. She looked a little disheveled, but she seemed very happy about something. She grabbed his wrist and pulled him inside.

"Dan! I was about to call you! You have to see this!" She scurried up the stairs so quickly she dropped a hand to a riser to prevent herself from stumbling.

Carter watched her go with incredulity. "Aren't those the clothes you were wearing yesterday?" But she'd already gone.

He followed her up to the rear room that she used as a study.

On his previous visit, it had been set up with a desk with a PC, a large table against one wall, and bookshelf units. Now he passed stacks of books left out on the upper hallway and, on entering the room, found all the bookshelves empty and pushed up against one another in front of the window.

How she had reorganized the room was not the center of his attention, however. Running across the center of the room like a web built by a giant and deranged spider was a mesh of strings, mostly white but with some colored threads running through it, centering in a spindle of reds, blues, and greens running slant-wise from ceiling to floor.

Lovecraft looked at him as if seeking approval. "You see it? You can see it, right?" Her eyes were bright. Carter saw discarded caffeine drink cans lying on the floor and thought of how up-tight she got about any litter in the store. "You can see it?"

Yes, he could see it. Lovecraft had built a three-dimensional model of the Fold.

Chapter 16

. . . BEARS BITTER FRUIT

Lovecraft kept saying, "No."

She said it to whatever Carter said, and what Carter was saying was things like, "You need to step away from this and rest," "We should go downstairs," "I think you've had enough caffeine for today. And tomorrow. Jesus, Emily, how much of that robot piss did you drink?"

When he finally got her sitting at the kitchen table, he gave her a glass of milk, sat down opposite her, and said, "What the living fuck were you thinking?"

She smiled at the gratuitous swearing, which he found heartening. "We have to start fighting back, Dan. We're the only ones who know what happened, so we're the only ones who can put things back the way they were. To do that, we've got to take chances. We've got to *arm* ourselves."

As she said "arm" she leaned forward and glared at him.

Carter thought long about what to say next. He settled on, "Maybe there's some other way—"

"Guns? You think we can defeat the Old Ones with firepower? Heh." She leaned back again. "Nope. The only tiny bit of this playing field that is even close to level is the Fold and what goes with it. We have to figure out how it works, and lever it back on those sons of bitches before they realize we're still a threat, if they ever thought that, which maybe they didn't."

"You want to mess with this stuff after what it did to William Colt?"

She half-laughed again at the mention of their erstwhile nemesis, now spread thinner than thought in the dank corners between dimensions. "Him? C'mon, Dan, he was an asshole from the moment he was born. The Fold didn't do that to him, it just gave him an outlet to grandstand his assholery from. H.P.L. and Randolph handled it and didn't go crazy." She thought about it. "Actually, it's a hard call with H.P.L. That whole 'fear of the other' thing did kind of eat him up."

Carter pushed the milk glass to her and looked significantly at her until she picked it up and drank from it, all the while making "Fuck you, you ain't my mother" eyes at him over the glass's upper rim.

As she drank he said, "How did you even manage to reconstruct that thing? We don't have the cube here."

She put the glass down. She had a white moustache of milk on her upper lip. She really wasn't herself, Carter realized. She closed her eyes as if to brace herself to say something unpleasant and shocking, and then said precisely that. "The *Necronomicon*. I read the *Necronomicon*." She shrugged. "Well, some of it, anyways. There's a lot of stuff in there. Language is kind of Shakespearian vocabulary-wise, but not in iambic pentameters, thank fuck."

Carter didn't trust himself to reply for a moment. When he did, he only said, "Emily."

"I know. I know. I've been the one talking about it like it's a sanity sink, and full of things-man-was-not-meant-to-know, but I thought, hell, I'm not a man, so what the fuck." She looked up at him. "Have I got a milk moustache?"

Carter nodded. She wiped it off with the back of her hand. "Let me show you something." She picked up a memo pad and pen from the counter, and started to draw. First she drew an odd humpbacked curved line. "Recognize this?" Carter shook his head. "You wouldn't, because it's this"—she sketched in a few lines over one another that suggested a skein of wool, twisted— "from the side." She looked him in the eye. "A Nobel Prize can only be given to a team of three at most, and never posthumously. That's why you've never heard of Rosalind Franklin."

The change of tack caught Carter off guard. "Who?"

"Watson and Crick, the DNA guys on both sides of the Fold. They won the Nobel Prize back in 1962. Third name on the ticket was a guy called Wilkins, a crystallographer. But, they'd never have managed to work out the structure of DNA without Franklin. She was brilliant, and had pretty much worked out DNA's structure by photographing X-ray scatter. Don't ask me how. That stuff's kind of like magic itself. Cancer took her in '58, though. So, no embarrassing woman to make things complicated for the boys by pointing out they took her work without permission."

"Okay," said Carter. "And this is relevant, because . . ."

"Structure. She looked at a zillion points of data, and Rosalind Franklin said, 'Well, lookit, a double helix.'" Lovecraft shook her head. "She was English. She probably wouldn't have said 'lookit.' But William Colt looked at the Silver Key and he said, 'Twist,' and it wasn't, and now he's dead, and we're fucked, and it's all because he didn't have a sense of perspective. That guy Suydam had a better idea."

"Suydam was a child killer."

"Doesn't mean he was stupid. He let himself get killed. That shows how smart he was. I think he saw right at the end what he was really dealing with and that he didn't dare make anything of it for fear of letting . . ." Her vocabulary let her down, or maybe

she didn't want to name names. Whatever the case, she contented herself by just rolling her eyes upward and wriggling her fingers at the ceiling, ". . . who knows what back into the world. He saw we were all living in a puppet theater. This"—she gestured around and then slapped both hands on the table—"is the reality. Well, I preferred the puppet theater."

"Only half of what you're saying makes sense."

"That'll be because you're only understanding half of it. The *Necronomicon* is a gold mine. Nasty, dirty gold that corrupts. So, not so different from *gold* gold. I know it's dangerous, Dan. Believe me, I wouldn't have cracked it open if I thought we had a choice. I've got two anchors to keep me sane. First is a Carter and a Lovecraft have already done this shit once before and pulled off the trick. Second is I don't want power, I just want things back the way they were, back to the good old days when we didn't have to be polite to Nazis. We pull it off, that copy of Dee's translation can go into a dark corner and stay there for all eternity as far as I'm concerned."

"You wouldn't destroy it?"

She looked at him as if he'd just suggested she take up practical coprophagy. "No. The sanctity of books *always* takes precedence over existential threats to reality. Jesus, what kind of philistine are you?"

Carter, whose priorities were different, skipped answering. Instead he pointed at the ceiling to indicate Lovecraft's newest art project, and not any alien entities that might overhear. "That thing you made, you found instruction for it in your reading?"

"Of course not. It's the *Necronomicon*, not a hobby crafts book. I just . . . look, it's easier just to show you the book."

"No." Carter said it firmly. "No. I am not looking in that book."

Lovecraft looked at him oddly. "Anxious much?"

"Yeah. I'm anxious to stay sane. One of us has to."

She scoffed at him. "It's not that bad."

"Slippery slopes never look that bad, or else they'd be cliffs."

"That's deep."

"Thanks."

She crossed her arms on the tabletop and rested her chin on the uppermost. "Okay, if you won't look, I'll try to explain. There's a lot between the lines—that's the quick way to describe it. Not subtext, though. Not the way we usually mean subtext, anyway. I'd put money on most people reading the *Necronomicon* and coming away afterward no wiser, no more or less sane, no different than they were before. It's a weird book. Anecdotal, and metaphorical, and kind of a bestiary in places, and it's all mixed up. A real mess. Old man Alhazred, the guy who wrote the original, was nicknamed The Mad Arab. Not by other Arabs—that would have been weird—but even they thought he was mad. The original edition, the *Al-Azif,* doesn't do a thing to change anyone's opinion of Alhazred. Thing about occultists is that they don't write a thing that isn't obscure. I bet they write shopping lists as acrostics. They're paranoid about their discoveries being stolen, or falling into the wrong hands, or whatever. Doesn't matter whether they're writing truth, near truth, or utter bullshit, they hide stuff. Sometimes it's in cipher, sometimes it's by using coded language. The *Necronomicon* reads like a lot of random garbage from the mouth of a medieval lunatic, unless you happen to know or at least have a good idea of the truth behind it. Then it decodes, right there in your head. Like decompressing a file. It's the damnedest thing. That's what a proper, honest to god"—she corrected herself—"*gods* revelation feels like. I was reading some stuff about birthlines which seemed totally irrelevant to anything and then suddenly the image of the Fold jumped into my head, *Boom!* sharp as the day we saw it in the flesh. Before it was just a lot of light floating there, but now I understood it. Early days, but I think I understand it better than Colt ever did already."

Carter felt uncomfortable hearing it. The knowledge William Colt had possessed had proved dangerous for everyone including, ultimately, Colt. "Are you telling me you can pull the sort of shit he did?"

She grinned. "Nope. Wrong side of the Fold for that, and if I *was* on the right side, I wouldn't do it, because that's a good way to end up back on this side. And this sucks, apart from this house. I really like this house."

All the cops looked the same to Billy Hoskin. Now that he'd had a chance to calm down a little and what he'd seen in the alley off Havilland was becoming distant to him because his mind knew better than to dwell on it, he'd realized that he was in a police station and cops kept talking to him. They mostly wanted to know where he'd got the money and who he'd got it from, but his mind didn't want him thinking about these events for its own good, so the memories were vague and frustrating to the cops and, to a lesser extent, himself. He kind of wanted to remember, and he really kind of didn't. It made his mind itch.

They kept saying, "Well, it's a federal case now," and "Wait til the Feds get here, then you'll wish you'd talked to us," but he didn't really understand why the Feds would take an interest and how they could be worse than the police. He knew he wasn't the smartest guy around, but he was smart enough, and he should have been able to understand it. It didn't help that his mind kept itching.

They were keeping him at the precinct until something happened. He'd been charged with some kind of currency felony, and was just waiting until the mythical Feds arrived to make something of it. He'd lawyered up straight away, because that's what smart people do, but the lawyer had just looked at the indictment and seemed out of his depth. His plan was, "Let the Feds talk to you. They'll find there's no case and walk away. Then the police will have to let you go." That was easy enough for him to say, but Hoskin had never been in trouble like this before, so he didn't have much choice but to do what the lawyer said. He sat in his cell under the ancient police station, and waited for the Feds to arrive.

Two cops arrived before them. They walked in off the street and made straight for the cells as if they were very familiar with the place, but they were strangers there. They wore their caps the whole time and, later, when the surveillance recordings were examined, no one recognized them. The shadows under the brims of their caps were very deep, very dark, and their faces were obscured.

Those that saw them didn't notice the shadows. They didn't notice anything at all. They had things on their minds, or something distracted them as the cops went by, or they simply decided to close their eyes for a few seconds. Just to rest them, you understand. There was nothing suspicious about the cops. They belonged. They just felt like they belonged, and noticing them would be like noticing a particular light fixture, or a scuff on the floor, or a scratch on the wall. They belonged. They were of and with the building. Why would anyone notice them?

They walked in a steady, unhurried walk, but nothing slowed them. You might call it inexorable. When they arrived at the elevator, the elevator was waiting for them. Later, when they left, it was waiting then, too.

Hoskin looked up from where he lay on his cell bunk as the door swung open. It took him by surprise; the viewing slot was invariably opened before the door to make sure he was on the far side of the cell and not ready to jump anyone. But this time he hadn't even heard the door unlock. A cop stepped into the cell and stood over him. With the light above him, the shadow his cap cast made his face invisible. Hoskin just had a vague impression of eyes.

"You're being transferred," said the cop.

"What?" Hoskin sat up. "Where to?"

"You're being transferred."

"Does my lawyer know about this? I want to speak to him."

"You're being transferred."

Every time the phrase was repeated, the tone and intonation was identical. By the second repetition, Hoskin thought it sounded like a recording.

"I ain't going anywhere until I talk to my lawyer. You don't just get to move me around without anyone knowing where I am."

The other cop stepped forward. "The charges have been dropped," she said. "You're free to go."

"You're being let loose," said the first cop.

Hoskin looked from one to another. The guy sounded like a heavy from a fifties gangster movie. The woman sounded husky, with a Midwest accent. Both of their faces were in shadow, but that didn't matter because they were letting him go. There were no charges to answer.

"So what was that about me being transferred?" he asked.

The cops said nothing, but stepped out into the hallway and waited.

Hoskin had based an entire career on never looking a gift horse in the mouth, even if it turned out that his definition of "gift" was pretty much synonymous with "belonging to somebody else." The cops said he could go, so he was all set to go. He walked out of his cell.

Fourteen minutes later, the duty sergeant found the cell empty, and the alarm was raised. It didn't take long to find Hoskin. Even as cops were running around the police station to find the missing man, a patrol who'd been called out to an incident at the Chapman Park projects found him.

The responding officers made their way to the top of a four-story block and into the roof space. Most all buildings, new and old, in Arkham had tiled roofs by local ordinance, and this was no exception. The officers found a hole smashed through, shattered tiles scattered near and far. In the middle of the debris lay Billy Hoskin, staring up at the starry night sky. He seemed to have fallen a long way, although where from was a difficult question. Whether the fall would have killed him was moot;

being frozen solid had ended his life long before he ever hit the ground. How this had all happened within the eight minutes between the moment he walked off the surveillance recordings and the moment he hit the rooftop was the sort of question for which Arkham PD had no answers at all.

Carter was a hero. This came as a surprise for him when he was asked back to Miskatonic University. He had been told to go directly to the high-energy physics building to meet the sarge, and on walking in, he found a bunch of scientists applauding him. Dr. Malcolm of the U.S. contingent walked straight up to him and shook his hand. "I have never been happier to have somebody turn up early for a shift," he said, smiling and shaking Carter's hand with both of his.

The shock of seeing two people shot to death in front of them was clearly still with them, and Carter noted that many of the scientists there were not ones who'd been at the incident, while half of those who had were absent. Dr. Giehl read out an official communique from the Reich's science minister commending Carter's actions and character, which Carter made a mental note never to tell Lovecraft about as she would surely mock him for the rest of his life.

Some halfway decent wine, apparently direct from the German consulate, appeared, and people took it as an opportunity to blow off some steam. That the focus seemed to slide off Carter pretty quickly after the speeches was both a relief to him and also made him wonder what else was going on that was absorbing all the scientists so much.

He found out when Giehl took him to one side. "Lukas's death is doubly painful, Mr. Carter. The very next morning we received confirmation that the project has achieved its aims, and is going to the next stage." She glanced over to the knots of scientists, and Carter could see that they were talking shop with more enthusiasm than he'd seen so far. "He would have been so happy. We're scaling up. Making the first moves toward seeing if zero point energy can deliver power on a practical level. We could be on the verge of freeing ourselves from all other forms of energy forever. A whole new world." She looked down into her wineglass. "Poor Torsten."

Carter did not trust himself to offer his views on waking up one morning to a whole new world. Instead he said, "When you say scaling up, you mean how much bigger than that thing?" Carter nodded at the column of the ZPE device. "Will you have enough room here?"

She laughed at such naïveté. "It is vastly larger than this. No, it will be built elsewhere. We shall be leaving Arkham. The construction will not take very long. Most of the component parts have already been built by my country in response to how encouraging the results were here right from the beginning."

"You'll be setting up in Germany? Are the American scientists still involved?"

"Oh, yes. You need have no fear of your country suddenly being cut out of the project, Mr. Carter. For one thing, the new test rig will *not* be built in Germany. The measures we used to cut out extraneous interference here will not scale up economically, so we must build the rig a long way from civilization." She looked seriously at him. "We considered New Jersey."

Carter couldn't keep a flicker of a smile from the corner of his mouth. "Why, Doctor, I do believe you just made a joke."

"No need to call attention to it. It will pass. No, the project is moving to one of the farthest islands in the Aleutian chain. There is a former military base there, part of the early-warning radar network from the days of the Cold War. There is a concrete dome there that is in very good condition and will house the new ZPE device easily. We're all going." She looked at him seriously. "I would like you to go, too."

Carter blinked. "Me?" was all he could manage.

"Certainly. We will need a head of security. What happened

the other night showed you take your responsibilities seriously. Also, surely your Uncle Sam would like some official presence on site?"

Carter belatedly remembered he was supposed to be a secret agent. "I'm barely on payroll," he said, looking for an out. "Moonlighting as a campus constable at Miskatonic U is one thing, but—"

Dr. Giehl said a number that stopped him in his tracks. "That is per week," she clarified. "In dollars. Berlin thinks you would be an asset to the project. Yes," she said, noting his raised eyebrows, "I've already discussed it with my superiors. We know all about you, Mr. Carter."

Carter was confident that, no, they didn't. He changed the subject. "The Aleutians really are at the back of beyond. I'm not sure there are any animals bigger than seabirds on them. Why do you need security?"

"Jenner isn't the only person out there who hates us. There are whole countries who would happily steal the research. Being in 'the back of beyond' makes us as vulnerable as it does secure. If anything happens, we'd be a long way from help."

"If I do accept, you said I'd be the 'head' of security. How many others would I have? I mean, I'd have to sleep sometime."

"We have the budget for one more, but they'd have to be good at other things, too. Administrative skills would be useful. We generate a lot of information, and we have to keep two governments happy with reports. Do you know anyone?"

Carter was thinking of Harrelson. The detective had been talking about taking some leave. "How long will this take?"

"The equipment will be there when we arrive. A week to set up, a fortnight to test and calibrate. A month of actual experimentation. Perhaps eight weeks altogether. We should have some solid results at the end of that time."

Carter considered. Harrelson would need to negotiate a sabbatical with his captain to get that kind of leave. He also won-

dered where she'd picked up such an English word as *fortnight.*
"I'll have to think about it."

"Well, don't think too long." She went back toward the other
scientists. "This facility is being dismantled. We leave in ten
days."

Chapter 17

THE CASTLE ON THE HILL

"Me?" Lovecraft echoed Carter's astonishment. "I can't! What about the bookstore?"

"It's just for two months. We don't get much walk-in traffic, anyway, and the place has Internet so—"

"Which is where?"

"The Aleutians."

"The Aleutians?" She leaned back from the table and Carter knew he was about to get hosed down with industrial-strength scorn. "The *Aleutians*? The fucking Aleutians? Have you looked at a map? Do you know where they are sending you?"

"Of course I know where they're sending me. It's in the North Pacific."

"No! It's on the *edge* of the Pacific! Right on the other side of those islands is the Bering Sea. It is cold, miserable, and remote, Dan. And, as I don't think UPS does regular pickups from there, it's a shit kind of place to run a mail company from. 'The Internet,' he says, for fuck's sake."

"Find somebody to run the place, then. You were saying your friend was between jobs."

Lovecraft paused, unwillingly considering the suggestion. "Petra's got sense and, Jesus knows, she could use a paycheck. Why me, though? You must have some ex-cop friends somewhere who'd be happy to go to a cold, wet rock at the edge of creation if the money's so good."

They were at Lovecraft's house once more, drinking tea in the kitchen. She had been doing half days at the store, mainly to clear mail orders, but wanted to carry on working on the model of the Fold. That she was controlled enough to be able to walk away from it for hours at a time was a relief and a consolation to Carter. She wasn't about to go full-on Cthulhoid cultist on him if his brief readings of H. P. Lovecraft's works were to be believed. He wouldn't get another chance to read them unless they managed to refold the world, though; on this side, H.P.L. was only famous for a series of pulp high-fantasy stories. Lovecraft had shown him an entertainment news story that a big budget film was in development based on his character Randu the Swordmaster. "I don't get a penny," she'd ruefully admitted. "The old bastard's copyrights lapsed years ago."

On this side of the Fold, the only people who'd heard of the Cthulhu mythos other than Carter, Lovecraft, and Harrelson were dangerous people, and—Lovecraft hinted—some of them weren't people at all.

"I asked Harrelson if he could take some time off, but he just laughed at me. The APD is buzzing right now and he's leading on a bad case."

Lovecraft was interested despite herself. "What kind of bad case?"

"You know that story about somebody hiding in the wheel well of an airliner and falling through a roof in the projects?" She nodded; everyone had heard that story. "Yeah, well, half of it's bullshit. What really happened is a guy was taken illegally from holding at the main precinct house in Easttown, then frozen to death, *then* shot into a roof in Chapman, and whoever did it did it all in less than ten minutes. Christ only knows how. Harrelson was talking about hunting down any 'renaissance faire' nuts who might have a siege catapult and access to liquid nitrogen. I'm not sure he was joking."

Lovecraft ruminated for a long second. "Ever read any Algernon Blackwood?"

"Should I have?"

"Yep. I was going through a collection of his stories a week ago. One was missing. Probably his most famous. So I looked it up and it doesn't exist here. It's called 'The Wendigo.' Just . . ." She wafted a hand with frustration, took up the empty cups, and carried them to the sink. "I can't recall it well enough. Something about frozen bodies falling from the sky. Something like that. I wish I'd read it more recently. But the idea of the Wendigo being a conceptual monster and part of the mythos has been around a good while. And the story doesn't exist here—that's significant. It must be. For one thing, it predates the original Fold, which probably happened somewhere around 1927. Of course, time is kind of a flexible concept to some of the things we're now sharing a universe with. The Fold covered up a lot of old shit and just left echoes." She put the cups back on their hooks and turned to Carter. "Why the Aleutians?"

"Doc Giehl told me it was to get away from interference. I guess she was talking about radio and TV waves. Cell phones, that kind of thing."

"Plenty of deep mines here and in the Reich. Wouldn't those do the job just as well?"

Carter shrugged. "I think there's an economic factor. Attu had an old military base. It's perfect for the experiment. Just means they don't have to build any facilities, I guess."

"Attu. Rings a bell. Something to do with World War Two, but we never got to go to war here, so whatever it was didn't happen anymore. Must have been a battle with the Japanese, I guess. That sounds right." She went out of the kitchen for a minute and returned with an atlas. She opened it on the table and flicked through to a world map. "Attu. Wow. You can barely see it at this scale. The army put a base there?"

"Air Force, I think. It was an early warning station. There's a concrete dome the scientists have set their hearts on as a laboratory, and a bunch of blockhouses. It'll be home away from home."

Lovecraft grimaced as she looked at a larger-scale map of the islands, although they were still tiny even at 1:6,000,000. It was a grimace of self-disgust, as she was starting to like the idea. "I don't guess many people can say they've been to the Aleutians," she murmured, half to herself. Then, louder, "Admin, you say?"

"And you'll need to carry a gun. Open carry in a hip holster."

"Heh. I'll feel like a sheriff."

"A deputy. You'll answer to me. I answer to Dr. Malcolm, who's the project manager. I'll ask them to supply you with a shotgun, too. I know you love your shotguns."

"I do love my shotguns. Get me a semiauto like my Mossberg. Better yet, get me a 930 with a folding stock so I don't have to learn anything new. Tactical sight, too." She thought about what else could go on her rider, but remembered something more pressing. "Money. What's the money like?"

He told her. She whistled. "Sounds like business is good in the lawman industry these days. Do I get a badge?"

In the state of Westphalia, Germany, a few kilometers southwest of Paderborn, lies the town of Wewelsburg. It is, to some significant people, the center of the world because of the castle that stands over it.

Weweslburg Castle was built on the site of several predecessors and, indeed, built from their bones, the stone of earlier iterations being pressed into service to raise the curious, triangular structure. It had originally been built as a residence for the Prince-Bishops of Paderborn at the beginning of the seventeenth century. Thereafter, the castle had a checkered history, changing hands by deed and act, in peace and in war. It was abandoned for some years, fire hollowed out one of the towers, and it was left to decay and crumble for decades. In the early twentieth century, however, it was rebuilt with the intention of it becoming a cultural center for the historical area, containing a museum, youth hostel, and banquet hall.

In 1933, however, Heinrich Himmler toured the castle and took a fancy to it. When his plans to take over Schwalenberg Castle, some forty-eight kilometers away as the eagle flies, for a center for the SS fell through, he immediately turned his attention to Wewelsburg as an excellent second choice. Overcoming resistance from the district authority, Himmler was able to negotiate a hundred-year lease for the castle for a nominal rent.

Initial plans for the castle to be a school teaching a broad spectrum of ideologically sound subjects for fresh, young SS recruits quickly became derailed by Himmler's personal obsession with the occult.

Such is the history of the Weweslburg in both the Folded and Unfolded Worlds. The primary difference is that these hopeless desires for powers beyond those of conventional thought and science in the history of the Folded World were weak echoes of the far more successful research in the Unfolded. In the Folded World, Hitler was largely unimpressed by Himmler's forays into the supernatural. In the Unfolded World, he had cause to be more accepting.

The triangular form of the castle had been extended twice: once immediately after the abrupt end of the world war that never was in 1941 when the village church was demolished on Himmler's orders, and again in 1984. The building style had been maintained throughout, and only the age of the materials was an outside indication of how the building had evolved. Even then, it took a close inspection to tell where the 1941 stonework began, and it would surely be as difficult to tell the eighties extension was new in a few decades.

As a general principle, the closer to the northern tower one came, the greater the security. This had been Himmler's scheme for a "Black Camelot," a searing focus point of all that the Nazis in general and the SS in particular stood for. Thousands of slave laborers had died in the reconstructions, and a well of darkness filled with their unwilling sacrifices. In the northern crypt, rites had been performed, and associations formed of a sort that could only be sanctified far away from the sight of those who were too weak-willed to understand that the path to power is neither pretty nor painless. One of the great advantages of the annexation of so great a portion of the former Soviet Union was that most of the pain could now be so easily outsourced. The people of the town below the castle had long since learned not to question the arrival of large trucks that rode low on their suspension, and through whose thick walls it was still just possible to make out shouts and thuds as of fists against steel, yet rode high and silent when they left.

Director Mühlan's office was in the north tower, a broad, arcing room that gave an excellent view out over the town and onward toward Paderborn. It had been fitted out to the specifications of Heinrich Himmler, its first occupant in 1946, and Mühlan felt the presence of his illustrious forbear every time he entered the room and sat at the very same desk. Himmler would not have recognized the computer that occupied the space once occupied by a blotter, but he would have appreciated the level of security it bore. He was, after all, the *de facto* ruler of the Third Reich, even if General Warner Richter, the current Führer, was under the impression that it was he. Then again, Richter was no fool; he understood that running the Reich and guiding it toward its destiny were two very different things. So he fussed over finances and kept the rest of the world sweet or intimidated as they deserved, while Mühlan took care of the greater truths. Richter made sure that the Ahnenerbe got whatever it asked for, and—if he ever knew about the trucks that came from the east to Wewelsburg heavy and left light—he had gone to pains to forget about them.

Across from Mühlan's desk was that of his secretary, Irmgard. He admired rather than liked her, but the depth of that admiration was great. Plain and oddly sexless, her whole life had been dedicated to the Party, from the Hitlerjugend as a child, to induction into the SS as soon as she was able. Her loyalty and ideological purity were unimpeachable in every respect. She knew full well what occurred in the crypt of the northern tower and it did not lessen her enthusiasm in the slightest. If anything, she had become more steadfast. She had researched the history of the Ahnenerbe in detail, and Mühlan suspected she knew more about it than him by this point.

She looked across at him. "Herr Director, there is a Triole request incoming from Arkham. Do you wish to receive it?"

"Of course." Triole was a simple yet pleasingly sound concept in secure Internet communications. The program ran three popular commercial chat clients, encoding and splitting the message at one end to be pieced back together and deciphered at the receiving end in real time. Between the cipher, the fragmentation, and the security protocols of the clients themselves, the Gestapo has pronounced it breakable only with extreme difficulty, not least because the system randomly selected which of several clients to use every time.

A flash appeared on his screen telling him about the request, which he immediately accepted. A chat box appeared, an ugly, functional interface with current security and protocol data streaming off on one side. The coders who had developed Triole had gone to some pains to avoid the program looking in any way cute.

"Stage 2 Seidr confirmed. Hosts in full agreement. Security head confirmed, subject 434. Subordinate request problematical."

Mühlan allowed himself a frown. All the project site needed was some goon who could hold a gun as a subordinate to subject 434, Daniel Carter. He waited a moment for clarification, but none

was forthcoming. His patience exhausting itself quickly, he typed, "Explain."

The answer came back. "Female," he read. "Black."

It was hard not to laugh. He permitted himself a quiet snort of amusement that made Irmgard glance at him. "Understood," he typed. "Remain watchful. Anything else to report?"

"Not at this time. Message ends."

The ugly little interface told him that the connection had been terminated. He closed the program, thought for a moment, then rose to look out of the window. "I sometimes wonder if our Dr. Giehl is really cut out to be an agent," he said.

Irmgard had a security rating equivalent to most high-ranking officers; she knew probably more than was safe for her, but that is the very definition of a secretary, after all. She knew full well who Giehl was, having handled any amount of documents pertaining to the Abwehr's woman on the spot.

Irmgard said nothing, for it was not her role to ask for secrets, merely to process and keep them. Mühlan sometimes wished she'd show a little more curiosity if and when he wanted to talk, such as now. "She's worrying over the ethnicity of one of the Americans, as if it matters."

He looked out over the town, over the land, over the world. An attempt had been made to change the world, but it had failed. So the sensitives told him. An attempt to snuff out the Third Reich by preventing Unternehmen Sonnenuntergang from ever happening. They said in that awful world of shadows, the Third Reich fell yet the Soviet Union survived for decades afterward. That the power that would secure the Reich was taken from them before they even had it in their hands. That the beloved first Führer died in ignominy and was labeled a monster by the Jewish Bolsheviks. They could not be sure how the attempt had been made, or why it might have failed, but the scientists were confident it could be prevented from ever happening again. Yes, the world would be changing again soon enough, but in a way conceived and executed by the Reich.

Everyone at the so-called ZPE site in the Aleutians would, in all likelihood, die as it happened, but that was a small price to pay, and would come with the bonus that he would never again have to contend with any of Lurline Giehl's ridiculous taste for melodrama.

Chapter 18

THE JOURNEY WEST

Even Carter, the more enthusiastic out of he and Lovecraft when it came to the Aleutian posting, balked when he realized just how long it was going to take to reach the distant island of Attu. The flight to Anchorage would take twelve hours in itself, and there were almost another two and a half thousand miles to go after that. Attu was an unpopulated island, now receiving its first substantial number of visitors in years as the technicians and the first wave of scientists arrived to start setting up the ZPE rig. It may have been blessed with regular flights when the USAF operated there, but now it would take an ungodly number of little hops to reach Adak Island, a little over halfway along the chain as it heads westward. From there they were to rendezvous with some of the other support personnel and then, to Lovecraft's profound horror, go the last four hundred and some miles by ship.

"A little cruise," Carter described it, unwisely.

They were talking over coffee at the bookstore. Lovecraft almost snorted hers out of her nose. "Cruises are on cruise liners. This is on, what? A fishing boat? An icebreaker? An *iceberg*? What?"

"A research vessel. I forget what it's called, but it'll take about a day and a half to get there. It's carrying supplies for the site, too. We're the designated adults who'll be keeping an eye on them."

"In case of Somali pirates? Polar bears in fast attack boats?"

"Maybe. This isn't our world anymore. Maybe we'll be attacked by a giant squid or something and have to fight it off."

"Don't even," said Lovecraft, so Carter shut up about giant creatures with tentacles trying to kill them.

"At least we'll be armed. The weapons will be waiting for us at Adak, too."

Lovecraft laughed and shook her head in self-deprecation. "I'm just acting up, Dan. It's all an adventure." She looked at him and the smile slipped when she saw his distant expression. "Unless there's something you're not telling me?"

"I don't know if it's significant. It might be a coincidence. Hell of a coincidence if it is."

"Go on." She said it reluctantly.

He reminded her of the man who'd vanished from police custody only to reappear almost immediately as a frozen corpse plunging through a rooftop several blocks away. "Before he died, Harrelson took an unofficial interest. The guy was in custody in the first place because he'd been found standing in the street shouting wildly about a man with an empty head and some stuff about fruit. He had almost two thousand in fifty-dollar bills on him. Harrelson goes to have a look around, finds a hat down an alleyway right by where this all happened. Traces the owner. Henry Weston."

Lovecraft frowned. "I know that name."

"You should. He's the lawyer who handled your uncle's estate back in the Folded. Turned up out of the blue to tell me this place was mine."

"Okay. So? Coincidence."

"He's also the guy who put me in touch with Lukas."

"Still a coincidence."

"Harrelson beards Weston in his offices, puts a little pressure on him to find out how his hat ended up where it did. Weston bullshits him. Doesn't even try very hard, but there's nothing to say definitively that he's lying. Only thing that can put him at the scene is if the man with the unexplained money can ID him. Within twelve hours, he's dead and frozen."

"I don't see—"

"Let me finish. Where this all happened"—Carter pointed down the street outside the store—"thirty yards away, if that."

Lovecraft grew quiet.

"So I did a little footwork myself. Talked to Jen over at Poppy's."

"Poppy's?" Her eyes flicked to look through the storefront window toward the coffee shop across the street.

"The day the guy went crazy in the street, just before then by a few minutes, she remembers a customer. She can't remember much about him, just how he behaved."

"Jen? But she remembers everything."

"Not this time. He bought tea. Second time in two days. Barely touched it, then suddenly left. Both times he paid with a fifty buck bill and told her to keep the change. Harrelson told me the dead crazy man was pulled in holding nineteen hundred dollars he couldn't account for. You see?"

Lovecraft did. "The one in Poppy's started with two grand. Dead guy got it how? Mugged him?"

"Worst decision of his life if he did. The only description Jen could give me of the tea drinker is he wore an expensive but not flashy suit, nice overcoat, and hat."

The description suddenly clicked in both their minds. They looked at one another. "Oh, shit." They said it so nearly together as to make no difference.

"He was in here," said Lovecraft and reflexively looked at the safe.

"The man in the Clave College parking lot," said Carter, then quickly added, "He was *what?*"

"He knew about the *Necronomicon*. Shit. Shit, shit, shit. We've been had right from the start." She looked at Carter with frightened eyes, and he couldn't blame her. "What do we do? I mean, if this whole pleasure trip to the ass end of creation comes from him . . ."

Carter thought for a moment, or at least tried to think. The ramifications of this were sending shock waves through his mind and trying to think of a coherent plan was like trying to build a champagne fountain during an earthquake. "If we're right, then if Weston wanted us dead, we'd be stone dead by now. Harrelson may be in danger, especially if he tries to rattle Weston's cage again. We got to warn him to back off. In the meantime . . ." He tried to focus away from the stupid idea that had come into his head. It wouldn't let him. "In the meantime, I have to go and talk to my lawyer."

Lovecraft was not very happy about the idea of Carter seeing Weston again. Her happiness did not multiply when he suggested that she accompany him.

"And what if we're right, and he's in with the opposition?"

"I'm not sure if he's with us, but I'm pretty sure he's not against us."

"And you're basing this on what? Male intuition?"

"On the fact that we're still breathing."

He'd called Weston's office, but they had told him he was at the courthouse, arguing a complex tort case on behalf of a major client. Later they called back to say he would be happy to speak with Mr. Carter if Mr. Carter could make his way to the courthouse, and not be insulted if the interview was necessarily brief. Mr. Carter had said that was fine, and there they were, waiting for Weston to show up.

The courthouse was an impressive stack of marble and granite; Arkham had long taken its law seriously. They waited in the corridor between the counsel offices and courtroom number two.

"What are you going to say to him?" said Lovecraft.

Carter pursed his lips; he had next to no idea. "Ask him if he's an agent of extraterrestrial forces from beyond the fifth dimension, I guess."

Lovecraft's expression indicated this wasn't the time for levity. Then her brow tightened as she looked past him up the corridor. Carter turned, and then rose to his feet as Henry Weston made his way toward them, his old leather briefcase in his hand. He seemed delighted to see them.

"Miss Lovecraft! Mr. Carter! Well, this is nice. Would you mind if we walk as we talk? I'm in court in a very few minutes."

"You don't seem very surprised to see me here," said Lovecraft, preempting Carter winding up to pitch his own question.

"Should I be? You've begun studying the book, no doubt? Splendid! Its reputation is deserved to a degree, but exaggerated. Your ancestor tended toward hyperbole, I'm afraid. Still, you seem a very grounded young lady. I'm sure you'll be fine. I wouldn't have suggested you look at it otherwise."

"You didn't suggest it at all."

"I'm sure I must have. You're reading it, after all, aren't you?"

Carter cut in. "You've been manipulating us from the beginning."

Weston pursed his lips "Now *that* is certainly an exaggeration. I simply led you to information pertinent to you. After that, it was all your own doing. And, may I say, you've done splendidly. The business with the Waites and that awful fool

Colt, sterling work. Sterling!" He was smiling like a favorite uncle applauding enthusiastically from the auditorium during a school play.

"We don't want your thanks."

"Ah. You feel ill done to." His expression shifted toward contrition. "If it's any consolation, if you hadn't become involved, the Fold would have been destroyed. All those potentialities on the other side lost forever. This"—he gestured around him—"would have become all that has been and all that may ever be, at least within the next few millennia." He glanced at Carter and an impish smile appeared. "You're going to ask me why I just didn't do it myself, aren't you?"

Carter was, but didn't admit it.

"Well, two broad reasons, which merge into one. Deniability, and personal weakness. I had few allies, so an aspect of avowed disinterestedness was my best armor. The Waites' . . . sponsor, I suppose you might call her, would never have tolerated interference from me. From you two, however, she assumed it was the usual bumbling."

"Meaning what?" said Lovecraft sharply.

"To err is human, Miss Lovecraft. Ah, we're here. I'm afraid I must leave you. I understand you're both undertaking a long journey?"

"How did you know that?" asked Carter, though he would have been more surprised if Weston hadn't.

"Enjoy yourselves while you may. It will be something of a busman's holiday, I fear."

"And if we don't go?" said Lovecraft. "We can still back out."

Weston regarded her sadly. "Well, then it has all been for nothing." A bailiff held the door open and he entered the court, leaving Carter and Lovecraft behind.

"Son of a bitch," said Lovecraft under her breath, the sound of somebody just realizing that they've been outmaneuvered.

"So we're still going, right?" said Carter.

Lovecraft merely sighed, and that was answer enough.

* * *

Lovecraft's friend Petra agreed to look after the bookstore for a couple of months and did so with pleasure; Lovecraft had been right that she needed a job. She also saw them off from Ulysses Airport for the long flight to Alaska, consistently referring to Carter as "your friend Dan" with a significant look. Lovecraft was relieved when the flight was finally called.

Carter for his part was more distracted by the aircraft out on the tarmac. "Look at that," he said, pointing out of the lounge window. Lovecraft followed his finger.

"What am I looking at? Just a bunch of . . . Wait, is that a Pan American plane?"

"It is. It is." Carter was grinning like a kid. "Pan American didn't go down the shitter here."

"Hey." She slapped him gently in the ribs. "We're still changing things back if we can." She turned to see Petra grinning at her. She scowled.

Carter wasn't paying attention to the pointed conversation in mime going on behind him. The view outside still had his full attention. "Yeah, yeah," he agreed, "but . . ." He looked out at the white-and-blue airliner again. "Wow."

Their flight took them to Chicago, and then on to Anchorage. From there they spent time between connections at progressively smaller airports, until they became little more than airfields, and finally, thirty hours after they had left Arkham, they landed at Adak, the last island in the Aleutians to have a permanent human population. Earlier Lovecraft might have been unhappy about the last leg being by sea instead of flying, but now they were both glad of a chance to walk on land for a few hours and to freshen up before joining their ride, the RV *Frederick Cook*.

Naturally, the settlement on Adak Island was called Adak, not least because it was unlikely there would ever be a second settlement there in the imaginable future. It was on the site of a former army and navy base, and felt vaguely Icelandic in that it shared Reykjavik's taste in colored roofing—in Adak's case, red, blue, brown, and white. It did help make the place look happier than a settlement on a bleak island few had ever heard of might be expected to look. The entire enduring population of Adak was less than 350, and they worked mainly in fishing and services. The airport was far larger and more sophisticated than they'd been anticipating, and Lovecraft went off to ask about it. She came back angry.

"It's a good airport because it's ex-military. Did you know they have a direct service from Anchorage? We could have got here in half the time and done it in comfort in a 737."

"You'd have missed the boat," said the technician who was loading their bags into a pickup. "It's got its own schedule, and the 737s only fly twice a week." He grinned. "We got here a few days ago, so we came in one of them. You're right. Way more comfortable than island hopping in those crop dusters." Lovecraft's mood was not improved by this intelligence.

Carter didn't much care about how they'd got there; he felt like a hobo. Thirty hours' beard growth for a man who was almost obsessively clean shaven was not something to be enjoyed and he could barely tolerate it. He disappeared into the restroom with his shaving kit the first chance he got, and emerged a quarter of an hour later with his hair washed and wet, his chin bare of bristles.

"You sure you were never in the military?" asked Lovecraft. "Or do you just like feeling a blade against your skin?"

The wet hair was a mistake, though. The islands were still a good way south of the Arctic and the temperatures were usually bearable, but it was the fall and the air was barely above freezing. Carter found his cabin aboard the ship, and stayed there until they were ready to depart. The ship was awaiting a full research team from the University of Washington and, rather than lie idle, had accepted the commission to carry part of the Arkham ZPE team and most of its supplies out to Attu, returning to Adak in time for its assigned mission. As a result, the ship carried only its crew and a handful of Arkham personnel. This suited them just fine; no having to share cabins.

Carter and Lovecraft had shared all their flights with Drs. Ian Malcolm and Jessica Lo, the senior Americans on the team. At the ship, they met up with Jerry Rendall, a postgraduate researcher, and, from the German contingent, Drs. Hans Weber and Lurline Giehl, both of whom had arrived earlier aboard one of the coveted 737 flights. Even with the four technicians, they were still spoiled for choice from the twelve double-occupancy staterooms assigned to research crew.

Carter was grateful that he didn't have to be polite to a roomie. He had hardly managed more than a few minutes' sleep at a time during the last two days, and he was expecting to sleep for most of the journey to Attu. The sea was calm, but the ship's medic handed out sea sickness meds to all the new passengers just to be on the safe side, warning them that they could cause sleepiness. To Carter, this was a feature, not a bug.

Somehow he managed to stay on his feet for the departure, waving at the few who came to see them off. As soon as the ship was a quarter of a mile out from the dock, however, he made his excuses and went down to his cabin.

Carter swallowed the meds with a gulp of water and clambered naked into the lower bunk; climbing into the top one looked too much like work. For a few minutes he lay awake, worrying more that perhaps he was too exhausted to sleep easily than any concerns about where the RV *Frederick Cook* was taking him or the "busman's holiday" that Weston had mentioned awaited them.

Then either the meds kicked in, or the exhaustion finally consumed him, or both, because he fell quickly into a deep sleep.

Deep, but not dreamless.

Chapter 19

BURNING BLOOD, BURNING BONES

Carter missed the days when he dreamt and it was about not knowing where to go on the first day of school, or of his long-dead dog Sharky, or his car running out of gas and having to walk such a long way to a gas station that somewhere along the way he forgot what he was doing and had ice cream instead. Then the Suydam case had gone south and, after that, his dreams became a minefield.

Yeah, sometimes they were still harmless enough. Most of the time, in fact. But there was always the nagging little fear that tonight, a dream was going to turn out to be *different*, to have significance, to drill through layers of reality that were impervious during the waking hours and bring something to him that he really didn't want to see.

Lovecraft had warned him this would happen far more often

now that the world was unfolded, and that such dreams were important and that he should note them down whenever he had them. "How will I know a normal dream from one of these 'important' dreams?" he'd asked. She'd shrugged. He bought a notebook and tried to write out as many dreams as he could remember immediately after waking.

So far, he hadn't had many, and the ones he was pretty sure meant something were really difficult to understand. He'd been expecting something Freudian like in *Spellbound*, all vistas designed by Salvador Dali and willful symbolism, but it wasn't like that, if his experiences during the Colt affair were anything to judge by. These dreams felt brutally real and showed things in far too much truth to be easily taken in. Lovecraft told him he was a dreamer from a line of dreamers and that he'd be able to handle whatever was thrown at him, but it didn't feel that way sometimes, not all the times when he'd awoken in a pool of sweat from having seen something his memory censored.

He was kind of glad about that, although he would never have told Lovecraft as much. She was envious of his ability to "dream" and for it to mean more than the random babblings of most people's unconscious minds. She was adamant that it was a gift, and he didn't want to disappoint her by failing to use it when it might be their ticket to setting things right. Still, sometimes when he awoke with just the last vaporous memories of what he'd experienced beyond the wall of sleep, he very deliberately didn't note down what he remembered in the hope that his mind would obliterate the memory all the sooner.

On these occasions, however, he was in something like normal REM sleep. As he lay sprawled across the bunk aboard the *Frederick Cook*, he was bone tired and drugged. He sank through the stages of sleep quickly, enduring some momentary anxiety dreams about missing plane connections, and down, down into deep sleep, much too deep for dreams and nightmares to exist.

Not conventional dreams, at any rate.

* * *

Carter wasn't sure where he was, but was pretty sure he wasn't meant to be there. It was a round stone room with twelve columns around it, and he was confident that he'd never been there before, nor even seen it in pictures. The day was fading outside the tall windows set into thick walls, but he could feel that this was a place that never slept. He had a sense of conversations being held just out of sight, and of footfalls on stone floors.

The thought of the hard floor beneath his feet made him look down and he saw there an intricate design worked into the stone, a complex symmetrical shape consisting of an outer circle and a much smaller one set concentrically within it, and twelve lines emanating out from the center, each performing a sharp right and then left turn before finally reaching the outer circle. The kinked arms made it look like some sort of superswastika, and no sooner had the thought occurred to him than one of the several doors that led into the room opened.

Two men entered, chatting in German. One was in a suit, the other in a military uniform. Carter had no idea what rank he was, but he seemed pretty senior. He wasn't so badly informed about the Third Reich, however, that the fact that the uniform was black and bore a double-lightning-flash insignia on the right-hand side of the jacket collar didn't tell him he was looking at an SS officer. The uniform's design wasn't exactly like the wartime ones he'd seen in a hundred movies and TV series—the modern Third Reich had lost its obsession with jodhpurs, for one thing—but it was still clearly a descendant of Hitler's personal paramilitary army.

Carter couldn't understand a word they said, yet he still had a sense of what they were talking about. They walked over by one of the tall windows set into alcoves between each pair of columns on—he guessed by the angle of the sun—the northern side of the room, and there, by the fading light, the man in the suit showed the uniformed officer something on a clipboard. The officer nodded, checked his watch, and Carter understood him to say something of how he couldn't believe they were still having to do this shit after all these years. His plainclothes colleague said something reassuring. "Not long now." Something like that.

They moved on to exit by a different doorway, unlocking the door to do so, and Carter felt he should follow them, so he did, out onto a spiral staircase that looked like the sort of thing Errol Flynn would've enjoyed fighting Basil Rathbone on. The door locked itself behind the men as they closed it.

They went down the stairs and Carter felt like a ghost as he followed them unseen. The staircase seemed to descend forever, yet they arrived at the end of it too soon for his liking, and then they were in a chamber that was mostly subterranean, judging from how small and high the windows in the wall were. In the center of the round crypt—Carter wasn't sure if that was the right name for it, but it seemed fitting—was a shallow recessed stone-sided pit in the center of which burned a flame. It was clearly fed by gas, and he wondered if it was an eternal flame of some kind and if maybe this was some sort of war memorial.

Looking up at the walls made him doubt it. There was a swastika there, but it was part of a larger, complex design on a wall hanging. The upper part was an oval with a sword running vertically down it, the blade caught in a loop of something that might also be meant to be a blade, Carter wasn't sure. The oval had what he guessed were runes running around it, but whatever they meant was beyond the sympathetic translation the dream lent to speech. Beneath this design was a smaller one of a swastika held within a square diamond with tails running off the lowest point. Written on the square in the same kind of chicken-scratch script as the runes he could read "Volk" and "Sippe." He knew "Volk" meant people, as in "Volkswagen," but "Sippe" meant nothing to him.

Electric lights were mounted around the wall, each over a rounded stone bench, presumably meant to seat one, and on each lay a folded black cloth. Carter counted twelve of them, and twelve wall hangings, one above each bench. Carter spotted one more swastika, although it had curved outer arms and was the backdrop to a weird-looking *T* shape that looked like a stylized moustache on a stick, although he doubted that was the intention. The whole thing was surrounded by a wreath picked out in golden thread, and he had little doubt that the thread was real gold. Every one of the hangings looked handmade to very high standards, hand-stitched with gold and silver on luxuriant fields of dense velvet, even if what was on them just seemed like an endless stream of Nordic bullshit.

The door opened. Two more men and a woman, all dressed as if they were highly placed executives—perhaps they were— entered. Then came another SS officer, followed immediately by a couple of soldiers pulling the sort of large trolley Carter had seen in warehouses.

The trolley was stacked with bodies, two deep. Carter counted eight, both sexes, and all of them white. The two soldiers lifted the bodies from the trolley like sacks and hefted them over to lie by the pit of the flame. As they were laid down, one of the plainclothes men went around, placing a finger to the throat of each in turn, and Carter realized they were unconscious, not dead. The man stopped by one body and checked for a pulse for longer than the others, then with obvious irritation summoned the soldiers to remove it. That one was dead. They carried the corpse out, and Carter knew they would return with a live replacement.

Carter did not want to be there anymore. He did not want to see what was going to happen. But struggle as he might, he could not walk out and, even though he knew he was sleeping, he could not force himself to awaken. He could only stand and watch, an unwilling witness.

Things started to happen quickly. The soldiers left and returned with five more unconscious people. Carter could see they bore Slavic features, and he remembered what Lovecraft had said about how the West had never really cared about what the Nazis did in the former Soviet Union, how one holocaust had been exchanged for another, more politically acceptable one. All of them showed signs of a hard life, but—while thin—were not emaciated. Nor were their clothes the uniforms of a prison or a concentration camp; they were work clothes, aged and patched. These were people who had been snatched from their everyday lives of working the occupied lands of Greater Germania in the East, growing wheat that they saw precious little of once it was harvested.

Each was dumped around the edge of the central pit on the raised bench-like lip that surrounded most of it but for a break at one point that seemed to be there to provide access to the flame. As Carter watched the twelve unconscious people being crammed almost shoulder to shoulder, hoisted to lie over the bench like bags of potatoes, he saw the room had filled with more people. The two soldiers, sweating from their exertions, pulled the empty trolley from the room and closed the doors behind them. They looked to Carter to be relieved to be leaving.

Now there were twenty-four people other than him in the room, twelve unconscious, and twelve conscious. Twenty-five if he counted himself, but he didn't feel as if he were really there, or only as an observer at some *avant-garde* dramatic performance in the round. None of them looked familiar to him. He had half-expected Führer Richter to be there, but no. Some political observers said he was just a figurehead. Perhaps they were right.

There was that odd dreamlike sense of time not running quite as it should. He looked at a wall hanging for a moment that featured a black tree picked out upon a silver circle, but as he watched it, he started to doubt it was a tree and, just perhaps, was the image moving slightly? Did the branches move, not as branches on a tree might in a high wind, but as the tentacles of a sea anemone, swaying blindly in a slow tide?

Then he looked away and saw that the black cloth squares on the benches were not cushions, but were black robes. All those present—he now counted five women, two in SS uniform, and seven men, four in uniform—were drawing the robes over their work clothes and uniforms. They seemed bored by this, even faintly derisive of the dark pomp and hidden ceremony of it. They slid the robes over themselves, some more elegantly than others. Most of the military officers removed their gun belts and Sam Brownes.

Carter distantly remembered reading somewhere that SS during the war carried a dagger, but he was surprised to see these officers carried one at their belts and another, longer knife in a long sheathe running across their chests along the Sam Browne's chest strap. Every one of the officers drew the knife and put it to one side before removing the Sam Browne, and every one of the others in civilian dress had a similar knife waiting wrapped in black paper on top of their robes. Carter was standing close enough to see one of the temporarily unattended knives in detail and was surprised to see the weapon looked antique. The blade was maybe ten inches long and the steel—if it was steel— was pitted. It wasn't a dagger, either, but only sharpened along one edge. The tip was pointed enough to allow it to be used as a stabbing weapon, but that seemed almost an afterthought. It made Carter think of a huge blade for an outsized cutthroat razor more than anything else. The handle did nothing to diminish this illusion, being of aged ivory. Something was carved into the handle, but when he tried to read it, it was as if the light made the lettering squirm and change beneath his gaze.

Then the woman to which it was assigned finished pulling the robe over her head and fixing her hair after its passage, and took the knife. She held the black paper in her off hand and drew the blade down it to test it. It was terrifyingly sharp, shearing through the sheet as easily as if it had been cutting water. The paper did not bend or curl under pressure at all, because no pressure was required. The woman's face did not show pleasure at how sharp the blade had proved or any form of satisfaction, but only impatience. She turned toward the center of the room, and Carter saw all the twelve were ready.

The officer Carter had first seen in the room upstairs stepped forward. He started saying something, and whatever it was, it wasn't German. It wasn't anything Carter had ever heard before. His voice rose, and the words became clearer and more distinct and less bearable with every syllable.

Carter didn't need to guess what was going to happen, he hadn't seen any number of shitty films with sacrificial scenes in them to not know where this was going, yet at the same time, it felt off, as if the cultists (robes, daggers, and weird rites in a secret location said "cult" to Carter) hadn't bothered reading the script properly. The guy doing the chanting was doing it alone, and he did it with all the passion of somebody reading from a dictionary. Carter realized the man was bored and, looking around the circle, most of them shared that boredom. This was something they had done before, many times, and grown inured to. It was necessary, but dull. They were going to take twelve lives and they regarded it like taking out the garbage or filling out their tax returns. Carter had seen some evil in his life, but he'd never seen it looking anywhere near this banal. He wanted to wake up before the inevitable happened. He needed to wake up.

He could not. He did not.

The senior officer stopped his chant abruptly. There was a change in the room. Carter couldn't seem to feel much in the dream, but he felt cold now, an aching distant cold as if he wasn't just losing heat to his immediate surroundings, but to somewhere else a long, long way away. It seemed the circle of twelve felt it as well. They looked at one another a little warily, but they were not worried. Not really.

One of the unconscious people—a Russian? Ukrainian? Pole? none of those places really existed anymore—groaned like they were sick and stirred where they lay by the flame. The woman standing behind them tutted, said something, *Hurry up*. The leader stepped forward and lifted the head of the man lying before him by the hair. The man's hair was thin, and the officer's grip slipped, leaving him with a hank of hairs torn out by the roots. The man's head thudded painfully against the flame's stone surround, but he did not stir from his sleep. The dull thud of the head against stone was loud in the room, and a couple of those present snorted with amusement. The senior officer glared at the unconscious man as if it were his fault. He lifted the man's head again, this time by cupping his chin in the palm of his hand, and when the throat was exposed he quickly slashed it with his knife, clean across from jugular to carotid, parting the cartilage of the throat as he went.

Carter cried out then, but nobody heard.

The blood flowed quickly and, *Jesus Christ*, thought Carter, there was a lot of it. It poured into the gutter around the flame, gushed into it, but it did not simply pool there.

The blood caught fire. Carter had seen a lot of blood in his life and he was pretty familiar with its properties, but he had never once considered it flammable. Yet there it was, burning in strange wide flames, like liquor on crêpes suzette. Carter belatedly realized that, whatever was feeding that "eternal flame," it sure as fuck wasn't a butane cylinder out back. The flames leapt high, and they burned in colors that hurt Carter's mind, and those of the other watchers too, judging from the way they turned their heads and half-closed their eyes. The flame eagerly devoured the flood, the sibilant roar of the flames almost hiding the sound of the man dying, his last breaths hissing and wheezing out of the open trachea. As the blood slowed, the officer picked up the man by his feet and shoved him into the flame headfirst. He burned quickly, like a cordwood bundle soaked in gasoline, and his bones burned fastest of all. Inside a minute, there was nothing but some spiral ashes dancing in the air.

To the frustration of the woman whose assigned sacrifice was coming round, the victims were murdered in strict counterclockwise order. Some handled themselves more efficiently than others; one of the men had trouble maneuvering his victim into the fire and had to have help from a neighbor to his embarrassment and a subdued chorus of sighs. Not one of them showed the most momentary sign that they felt compromised, barbaric, or monstrous. They had become accustomed to the unspeakable, and atrocity was humdrum.

Eventually the stumbling process of murder was enacted eleven times in ways that ranged from the workaday to the sort of humiliation you usually only see when somebody screws up a PowerPoint presentation for senior management. At the last of the twelve stations, the woman who was assigned to it was all but stamping her foot with impatience when her turn to kill finally came. It arrived a little late. The twelfth victim was almost conscious and was stumbling to her feet.

The robed woman wasn't in the mood for shit from some blue collar who didn't know her place. She swung the long, ugly knife in her hand from a chef's blade-up grip to a knife fighter's blade down, stepped up to the confused Russian—at least the few words she said sounded Russian to Carter (*What happened?*)—and swung the knife into her right breast. The woman screamed, the pain punching through whatever was left of the veterinarian level of tranquilizer she'd endured, and stepped back. The edge of the raised bench-like circle around the flame caught her in the back of the leg, and she almost fell, but recovered herself in time. She staggered, trying to catch her balance, almost falling sideways but grabbing at the edge of the break in the circle to recover her balance.

The senior officer muttered something that felt in Carter's mind like *For fuck's sake*, the twelfth cultist blushed angrily, and in anger more than guile, she punched the Russian woman. The Russian gave ground once more but this time, there was no bench to stop her.

Only the flame.

She stepped into it and . . . nothing happened. The strangely colored fire lapped around her legs as high as the knees and did not burn or hurt her. She stood there confused, the flames circling her shins like an affectionate cat. Then a dribble of blood ran from between her fingers where she had her hand over the wound in her breast, and, as it entered the flames, it burned like gasoline. The fire climbed the falling trail of droplets faster than they could fall and, in a moment, had reached the wound.

The Germans, no, the Nazis, no—Carter realized with a squirming shock that it was truly possible to be more evil than Nazis—the cultists in their secret little murder room stepped back as the unnatural fire wormed its way between the woman's . . . the screaming woman's fingers, and in a second, it was inside her. It was something new to the jaded circle. There were gasps, cries, and at least one laugh.

The Russian woman's blood burned brightly in her veins and arteries and, when it reached them, her bones burned more brightly still. Yet, for all the fury of her immolation, it took her a long time to die, and Carter was forced to watch every second. Nor was he alone as an unseen observer; something stood by his side, watched the final sacrifice, and was satisfied by it for reasons Carter could not and dared not guess at. It was as aware of him as he was aware of it. He did not look upon it because he feared above all things he might see. It did not look upon him because he was not worth the trouble.

The Russian woman's screams were like the roar of a furnace, but presently died away as she was consumed and shrank away to nothing in the contaminating fire.

When she was all gone, one of the cultists said something that the dream told him meant *We should do them all that way next time*, and there was more laughter.

Once more, said the leader. *Then Case Seidr will finally make this unnecessary.*

The presence by Carter left, and he found the iron grip of *being* that had held him there fade away, and he tumbled from the scene like a man half-waking.

Chapter 20

THE DARK ISLANDS

The dream became less real and therefore more bearable. Carter felt able to relax and rest in the warm nonexistence of sleep, which he was vaguely aware was the point of sleep after all, and not an excuse for his strange and unwanted talent to drag him off unbidden into cisterns of European depravity, which even unconscious he found irritatingly classier than American depravity.

He enjoyed the small pleasures of oblivion for some time, and his mind tumbled down avenues without letup or focus. His breathing steadied, he stopped sweating, his heart beat slowly and steadily. He was aware of little in that deep well.

Scent came to him first. A human smell of skin, close and intimate, and he fell to wondering how long it was since he'd slept with a woman, and it seemed like a very long time, back, back, back long before the world was unfolded and since then he'd been too focused on fixing the universe as he understood it and maybe hadn't spent enough time meeting new people, which, in the abyssal, velvet well of deep sleep, now seemed like a good and worthwhile thing to do, and he was sorry he hadn't seen that before.

Even before the world unfolded, it had been some months since he'd been in any sort of relationship, since before the Suydam case. There'd been what he'd hoped might turn into something with Gina who was a PAA at the precinct but that ended up as only a one-night stand because she hadn't mentioned she was changing jobs and would be working at an NGO in Baltimore, and—Carter remembered as he tumbled down the rabbit hole of fractured and unreliable associations—was definitely a shame as the one night in question had been a good one, and he had made a point of not drinking too much beforehand, even though he was nervous and worried he was going to fuck things up, but that had turned out to be a good call and he thought then, knowing he was asleep tried to remember for when he wasn't because it was a good thought, that maybe she wasn't at an NGO in Baltimore in the Unfolded World and maybe they could meet up again and just maybe fuck again because it had been very good and . . .

Smooth soft skin. Dear fucking god but he loved skin against skin, the scent and the touch, and he suddenly realized he was having an erotic dream and that he was too asleep to wake from it even though he knew it was an erotic dream and that was just excellent, yes. He just wished he knew who his unconscious mind was fixating on.

Was it Emily Lovecraft? The idea settled upon him like a warm hug and he was happy to be in its embrace. It grew hotter and tighter around him, and when a voice whispered a question, he said, "Yes."

Lovecraft had been pretty pleased with herself that she'd managed to get some sleep during the fragmented journey to Adak, especially as it had given her the opportunity to mock Carter, who had barely managed a minute. Yep, calling him a zombie and him being so tired all he could do was accidentally play along with the joke by going "Murrrr . . ." out of exhaustion had been pretty sweet. She was pretty confident he'd passed out as soon as he was in his bunk, though. She, on the other hand, had brushed her teeth, sighed, and got dressed again, because no way was she going to be able to sleep.

She felt tired, yes, but nowhere near enough to get her anywhere near sleep, so she decided she would go for a walk around the deck, tire herself out that way, and maybe the sea air would work its magic and make her drowsy. She could but hope. Shrugging on her jacket, she went up the short corridor running by the staterooms assigned to researchers on the port side—Carter's was on the starboard, she knew—went up the stairs at the fore end—the ladder, as the crewman who'd directed her to her room had called it—and so up onto the deck.

It was cold, but not bitterly so. The Aleutians weren't really that far north for all her making out they were essentially Arctic when Carter first told her where the ZPE team was bound. In fact, she'd seen later when she'd opened the atlas and looked, they were more or less on the same latitudes as, say, Belgium. The big difference was that they didn't have the Gulf Stream to keep them warm. Even now beneath an almost clear sky, a low sea fog hung across the waters where the Pacific met the Bering.

She was leaning on the rail when one of the crew came by. He greeted her and they stood in silence as the RV *Frederick Cook* made its way westward through the silent waters. Lovecraft nodded at a shape looming up from the sea no more than a mile to the north. "Where's that?"

"Amchitka," he said. "We're going the scenic route, or you'd never have seen it."

"Scenic route?"

"Sailing south of the islands. Forecast is for strong northerlies and if we're going to get blown off course, better that it takes us away from them. The shallows around them are dense with rocks. Add a couple of hours to the trip, but better safe than sorry, eh?"

"No argument from me." She nodded at the island. "No lights. I guess no one lives there?"

The crewman half-laughed. "Not if they have any sense. The government used it for underground atomic tests in the sixties and seventies. It's not supposed to be radioactive, but who'd want to live there to find out? Kind of a shame, though. Two good-sized airstrips on it, but the place has been abandoned for more than twenty years now. Only usable in an emergency, otherwise it's off-limits. This is as close as we're allowed to go. It is a shame. It would have made a good island-hop between Adak and Attu for helicopters maybe, if there was a fuel dump there."

Lovecraft was looking at the island. "They let off nukes there?" The knowledge made the dark mass of bleak stone seem haunted.

The crewman nodded at the sky. "You're privileged to see the stars here. The skies aren't clear here often. Not often at all." He bid her a good night, and continued toward the bow.

Lovecraft looked at the stars. She couldn't remember ever seeing so many. So far from the light pollution of any city, they only had to contend with the ship's own lights, and they were nowhere near powerful enough to make the sky glow and obliterate the smaller stars.

And there were so many of them. Lovecraft had never lived outside a town, had rarely traveled outside built-up areas during the night, and she realized now how much she had been missing. She could see the phantasmal glow of the Milky Way, and the knowledge that she was looking toward the core of her own galaxy, that the glow was made up of uncountable millions of stars great and small, young and dying, made her feel tiny. Tiny, but not insignificant, because to her mind significance was a very human value in itself, and as a human, she carried at least a few grains of it. In fact—and she smiled as she thought it—she had been directly involved with an event of cosmic significance. Maybe more than a few grains, then, even if few people knew it.

Then she remembered that one of those few people was Henry Weston, and her smile faded quickly. She looked up at the stars, but perhaps a few of them looked down upon her, and minds of unimaginable sophistication and impenetrable processes played games with her and her "significance" for goals beyond the comprehension of any human.

The night sky lost its charm for her then, and she didn't feel so very privileged to see it. As the menacing bulk of Amchitka Island, force-fed nukes and left to cool, diminished in the ship's wake, she went below.

She'd come up the port ladder, but now the starboard was closer and she did not desire to be under the leering stars a second longer than necessary. She'd have to walk back to the bulkhead to get on to the connecting corridor, which would add a minute to her journey, but that was still preferable. As she reached the bottom of the ladder where the corridor turned before the starboard hallway of staterooms and was just turning the corner, however, she saw a door open somewhere toward the end. She truly didn't want to run into anyone who might get between her and her bunk by hassling her with friendly conversation when she just wasn't in the mood. She stepped around the corner of a small open cubby that held a fire extinguisher and a few cleaning supplies. If whoever it was happened to see her, she'd say she'd thrown up in her cabin and was just looking for something to tidy up.

She needn't have worried. The person in the corridor walked straight past and through the bulkhead door, opening and sealing it behind them as the crew had instructed them to do during the night watches. Lovecraft watched them go through narrowed eyes. It was the scientist who she'd been introduced to at Adak, Dr. Lurline Giehl, to whom Lovecraft's internal annotation system had added the labels "Abwehr," "Nazi," and "bitch." She had not liked Giehl at all on first meeting, yet had glued a fake smile on and stayed civil so far. But now Giehl had a light sweat on her, obvious under the lights, and a suspicion was forming in Lovecraft's mind.

She entered the corridor and walked quietly down to the door she'd seen the doctor exit. As with all the newly assigned staterooms, it had the temporary occupant's name in a card holder on its laminate surface.

"*Daniel Carter*," she murmured under her breath. "You slut."

Carter felt the best he had in months the next morning. He felt alive in a way that had evaded him for a long time now, and real in a way he hadn't felt once since the world had unfolded. Now, he felt a part of the world instead of just an observer. He still intended to change it back at the very first opportunity, but the new reality did not grate on him so much. He could hardly account for it after what he had seen in his dreaming vision. He should have been soul-sickened by what he had witnessed, but instead he was purely angry at those Nazi fucks and their carny occultism. The anger lent him a spark, and the spark gave him purpose.

He was ravenous at breakfast. His bunk had smelled of sex in the morning, although he didn't seem to have made a mess of the sheets, which was a relief. He'd had a cold, invigorating shower before running it hot for a few seconds. He had read a James Bond book years ago—he wasn't sure which one—and Bond did something like that in the morning to wake himself up. It certainly seemed to work. He went into the mess feeling like a lean, mean, fucking-up-the-plans-of-Weird-Gods-and-Nazis machine, got himself a plate of bacon and eggs and a big mug of black joe, and sat down opposite Lovecraft with a broad smile and a heartfelt, "Good morning!"

Lovecraft looked up from fitfully stirring her oatmeal around as if he'd just invited her to join the Arkham branch of the KKK.

She held the look for a moment, and then returned her attention to her bowl.

Some of Carter's pep deserted him. "You okay? How'd you sleep last night?"

"I slept just dandy," she said, stabbing the oatmeal with her spoon. She looked at him from beneath a lowering brow. "How about you? Disturbed night?"

He shook his head. "No. I went out like a light. Between the lack of sleep and the motion-sickness meds, I was dead to the world. Glad of it, too. I really needed some rest and last night was just what the doctor ordered. Feel great this morning."

He noticed she was looking at him oddly, as if he'd just said something contentious. Then he remembered the "dream" and his own expression clouded. Bizarrely, Lovecraft's changed to show some satisfaction. Carter wondered what the hell was going on inside her head. It was like they were having a conversation from two different scripts.

"Yeah," he said, deciding to plow on regardless, "I had a dream." She looked blankly at him so he clarified with, "A Randolph Carter kind of dream."

She frowned, her own script apparently still getting in the way. "A dream? A 'dream' dream? What time was this?"

Carter had taken the opportunity to start on his breakfast, and Lovecraft had to wait until he'd chewed and swallowed for an answer, having to make do with his expression of frustrated consternation while his mouth was full. He took a gulp of coffee to clear his mouth, and said, "How would I know? I was asleep all night. I told you. I only woke up half an hour ago."

"How can you remember a dream if you don't wake up during it?"

"That's how normal dreams work. These are different. I remember them like I lived them." He thought back to sometime in the early hours, and a different dream, which he also remembered albeit in a fragmentary kind of way. Yes, he must have awoken for that to have stuck. He had a blurred memory of turning over and being half-awake to do it.

He glanced around; the mess was still almost empty, and the only other people in were a couple of techs in the far corner who were bemoaning that Attu's supply of booze would be tightly controlled and they'd be spending most of the next couple of months boringly sober unless they got a still working. Satisfied that the mechanics of distilling and the avoidance of going blind were the techs' main focus for the moment, he leaned closer and told her quickly the main points of what he'd seen.

When he finished, he added, "It was nothing like in the movies. It was just a job for them. They were bored for most of it."

Lovecraft had finished her oatmeal while she listened and was now eating an apple. "Still kind of vaudeville though, ain't it? You're sure this was the real deal?"

He looked at her soberly. "They were real people, Emily. I saw twelve people murdered. It was for real. I don't know where it happened. I don't know anyone's names. But it was as real as we're sitting here."

Lovecraft thought for a moment. "We need to get every detail down while it's fresh in your mind. You tell it to me, every single damn thing you can remember, I'll keep pushing with questions, and you write it down. No, better idea—I'll type it. You type like you got bottles on your fingers."

"I made some notes in my dream journal." That a hard-nosed man like Carter kept something as New Age as a dream journal no longer amused either of them—not given the nature of some of his dreams. "We'll do this in my stateroom."

"Yeah," said Lovecraft, "let's check out your bachelor pad," and she was on her feet and making to leave before it struck him that it was an odd thing to say.

Chapter 21

THE DOME

Carter hadn't left the stateroom's porthole open when he'd gone out earlier, an oversight he regretted when he returned with Love-craft close on his heels. He muttered something about the air being close and made his way straight to the porthole to unlock and open it.

Lovecraft closed the door behind her, leaned by the frame, and inhaled through her nose. "Gee, Dan," she said with heavy irony, "kind of funky in here, ain't it? Smells like a bordello." She enjoyed herself far too much, enunciating every syllable of the word.

The screw mechanism that held the rectangular porthole shut wouldn't come undone easily, and Carter fought the locking nut with growing irritation that was undeniably tinged with embar-rassment. "Yeah. It's kind of close in here. Didn't realize."

"You had a lady friend in here? Show her your etchings or something?"

"I was asleep all night. I must've sweated when I had that dream." The damn nut would not move. "Just let me get this thing loose."

"Sweat." Another melodramatic inhalation as if testing a wine's bouquet. "Yeah, I get the sweat. But, what *is* that underneath it? Smells . . . *sexy*."

He turned to find her looking at him with arms crossed and an unfriendly smile on her face.

"Okay. Fine, I had another dream. More conventional dream. Do I have to spell this out?" The bolt finally moved, and he quickly disengaged the lock and swung the porthole inward. The air that flowed in its wake was breathtakingly cold, but it was also odorless.

"A sexy-times dream? You still get those? Wow. And there I was, thinking you had help."

Carter's patience, already shortened by humiliation and the recalcitrant screw lock, was wearing very thin. "What's this about, Emily? You've been weird all morning."

Lovecraft's smile faded, and she thought for a long moment before speaking. "What you do in your spare time is your business, but not when it's got an impact on why we're here, and sure as fuck not when you are literally sleeping with the enemy."

Carter frowned. "When I'm 'literally'? I literally have no idea what you're talking about."

"Give it up, man. You can come up with all the cutesy stories about you having an adolescent wet dream you like—"

"*Cutesy?*"

"—fact remains, you fucked a Nazi, and I am having a hard time being cool about that."

Carter was stunned. He looked blankly at her and said, "What?"

"Lucille Gayle, or whatever her name is."

"Lurline Giehl . . ."

"I saw her come out of here in the small wee hours all aglow and looking damn pleased with herself."

Carter's jaw had dropped with surprise. "What? Doc Giehl? In here? Are you sure?"

"Sure as I'm sure I'm in your sexy den now." She looked at Carter's face. "Holy shit. This is actually news to you, isn't it?"

Carter didn't trust himself to say anything, but just stood there staring at her like an idiot.

"How did you miss being jumped by the sexy Nazi, Dan?" The smile that had been forming faded suddenly. "Fuck. That's rape, ain't it?"

"I . . . don't know. I guess? It's . . . You're sure it was her? In here?"

"Yes. Totally, on both scores. You don't remember any of this?"

Carter shook his head, feeling more stupid than he had for a long time. "I thought it was a dream. But I don't remember seeing her. I can't have opened my eyes."

"You have to be kidding me. She's going to be pissed if she finds out you didn't even know it was her. I mean, who the hell did you think you were fucking in your dream?"

Carter had a vague memory of who that had been, and couldn't look Lovecraft in the face. Her eyes widened. "Oh, that's beautiful. That's just fucking beautiful."

"I'm not responsible for what happens in my dreams. For Christ's sakes, Emily."

"Don't you dare say I should take it as a compliment."

Carter, who'd been considering exactly that, said, "Of course not." He sat down heavily on his bunk, looked at the bunched up and fragrant bedding, and got up again to sit at the corner desk. "Why'd she do it?"

Lovecraft shrugged, bored with innuendo. "Who knows? You're not bad looking, and you've got that blond, blue-eyed, thug look all the Nazi chicks dig. Also, you saved her life. Maybe she just snuck in here to 'thank' you and thought you weren't as asleep as you were. I don't know. It's your body. You're the only one who can decide how upset you wanna be about it."

"I don't remember. It was a nice dream. I don't know what I should think of it now." He shook his head. "I can't get upset about it right now. Still too surprised. Maybe later. I don't think I will. Unless she's given me an STD. That will piss me off."

"Yeah. That Hitler herpes is the worst." She took a chair by the door. "Look, Dan. I'm sorry about what I said earlier, being a bitch about it. I didn't know that . . . *you* didn't know. Whatever you want to do about this, I'll back you up, even if it's nothing. Gotta say, though, I'm hoping it's something. If you want to throw her over the side, I'll tell people a giant squid got her."

Carter couldn't help but give a half laugh. "You're a pal, Ms. Lovecraft."

"Happy to be so, Mr. Carter."

They sailed into sight of Attu Island shortly after dawn on the second day. Carter made a point of locking his door that night after a day where it had proved almost surprisingly easy to dodge contact with everyone but the ship's crew. Instead he accepted an invitation to Lovecraft's stateroom where she waited with a pot of coffee, their assigned weapons still in their packing, and cleaning kits.

"Face it, tiger," she said as she held a lint-free cloth below her eyes like a veil, "this is hotter than bumping it with Doc Giehl."

Now it was impossible to avoid anyone, however. Just about everyone was in the bow to watch their destination heave into view, and perhaps they all felt just how isolated they were for the first time. The strong northerly winds had finally arrived, and the RV *Frederick Cook* was lashed by spray as she altered course to take her into a cove protected by a high ridge running along an isthmus onto a peninsula.

Dr. Malcolm made a very short speech about how what they were going to do there might change the world, but the wind stole half his words, and the bitter sea spray robbed his audience of their enthusiasm, so they were all glad to get back under cover. Up on the bridge, the helmsman was working hard on keeping the ship in a narrow deep-water channel edged with rocks, the navigational buoys that had once floated there largely torn away and lost in winter storms, and never replaced. Nobody thought it wise to break his concentration, so they went below and finished packing belongings and gear to get ready to disembark.

Attu Island didn't look even as inviting as its slightly radioactive cousin to the east in the early light. The arctic winds had brought clouds with them, and the ship's crew, who'd seen enough of the local weather's eccentricities to last a lifetime, said the inmates of the scientific establishment would be unlikely to see another star—including the sun—for days or weeks. They might not see another clear sky for the remainder of their stay, in fact. This prediction of a persistent literal gloom cast a metaphorical one upon many of those preparing to leave the vessel, but not Lovecraft. She looked at the low cloud and thought that what the eye don't see, the heart don't grieve over, or quail at. No, she'd be just fine without stars for the time being, thank you.

The docking facilities at the island had left something to be desired. Formerly, there had been two wooden piers out into the cove, but after the early-warning station was abandoned, the harsh conditions had destroyed them slowly yet surely. Now just enough of them survived to be navigational hazards. The crew who'd arrived first on the island and who would be traveling back on the *Frederick Cook* had helpfully rowed out to put red flags on the pilings farthest from the weathered concrete dockside. As an alternative way to dock, they'd emplaced cleats so the ship would have something to tie off to, even though it meant a tricky approach. The helmsman took his time and no risks, however, and a quarter of an hour later, they were casting ropes down to the building contractors who'd been making the place livable.

Visible from the landing were the prefabricated buildings that had been set up in the shadow of a large ridge to the west, the bright blues, whites, and yellows of the plastic outer walls showing absurdly against the dour darkness of the rock, and the unhealthy scraps of green grass and scrub that were all that could grow in that wind-blasted place. The buildings looked like toys left by giants on a day trip. About a hundred meters away lay the blockhouses they'd been told about, but they looked uninhabitable even at a glance, and presumably a closer survey had proved just that.

Lovecraft reached the three waiting cars that were to ferry their gear, flatbed Kübelwagen transports donated by the Reich. She looked over toward the temporary settlement.

"So where's this dome where the experiment's taking place?" she asked the contractor who was helping her load her bags.

He grinned and pointed up the ridge. "Up there, on Mount Terrible."

She looked at the dark massif disbelievingly. "You're shitting me? Who calls a mountain 'Mount Terrible'?"

He laughed. "Somebody who's had to climb it. Don't worry, ma'am, the military built a road up to it. It's safe to walk, but a 'wagen will have you up there in twenty minutes. Great view when the weather's clear, but, yeah, there's not many blue skies around here."

The prefab units sprawled across what had once been an aircraft staging area for the military base. The runway was still there, and in good enough condition for light planes to operate from it, but no plans for an aircraft to be stationed there had been made. With no aircraft and no boat, the scientific expedition would be trapped on the island in an emergency until they could be evacuated, but no emergency so catastrophic that immediate evacuation was necessary had been envisaged. Only two cases potentially filled that ticket—a volcanic eruption or an outbreak of food poisoning—but seismic surveys indicated the former was currently very unlikely and, if that changed, there would be warning, while in the latter case a regime of the encampment never all eating from a single round of cookery at the same time plus scrupulous supply and medical checks made it unlikely.

The contractor who'd told Lovecraft about Mount Terrible further compounded her growing love for the place by telling her the entire island chain was volcanic. "Sure. The whole ridge is where two plates have smashed into one another. Just over there"—he pointed southeastward into the gloomy horizon—"is Agattu. Had earth tremors from there not so long ago. But don't worry. There haven't been eruptions for years." He shrugged. "Well, apart from the one on Atka. That keeps blowing its top, true." He thought for a moment. "And there's that big dormant one on Umnak. But those are all well to the east. Really not much activity around here." He looked like he'd said his piece, but then he remembered something. "Apart from Mount Kiska on Kiska Island, of course. You'd have passed that on the way. That's a huge volcano, but it's dormant. Don't worry. No volcanoes on Attu." And with these comforting words, he left her to settle into her room.

She sat on her bunk for some minutes, trying to remember why this had all seemed like such an exciting idea in Arkham.

The first days went very quickly. The building contractors left aboard the RV *Frederick Cook* on the same afternoon that the remaining scientists and their two-person "security detail" were dropped off. Carter felt like a complete fraud as he discovered there was actually a security station included among the prefabricated buildings; it seemed he wasn't alone in feeling like a third wheel, as a very professionally painted sign reading *Sheriff's Office* appeared hot glued to the door during the night. Pranks aside, he was relieved that the supplies of alcohol on the island were very limited. Two months of people sitting around with, as it turned out, very-limited-bandwidth Internet was bound to lead to tensions. The Internet connection was supplied by satellite link. It was ruinously expensive to maintain so its use was strictly rationed. Indeed, satellites were their only link with the outside world at all. Nobody had ever bothered to lay telephone cable to the end of a chain of islands even most Americans didn't know about, and it was so remote that conventional radio communications were problematical. The base contained a long-range HF set that could bounce signals off the ionosphere, but this was regarded as a last resort, the satellite Internet link being more convenient and often more reliable.

As soon as they found out about the Internet rationing, both Carter and Lovecraft booked their bandwidth for the next couple of weeks. Carter was expecting news from Harrelson, and Lovecraft wanted to be sure Petra hadn't burned the bookstore down.

"I thought you said she was reliable?" said Carter.

"She is. I'm allowed to worry about my baby."

"*Our* baby," Carter reminded her just as a technician was going by, earning them both an odd look.

It would have been nice to sit on the veranda outside the "sheriff's office" in a rocking chair with a shotgun across the lap, chewing tobacco and tipping their hats to the good citizens of Attu Station, but their office didn't have a veranda, they didn't have any rocking chairs or chewing tobacco, and the weather had turned, by popular agreement, "fucking freezing." The good citizens of Attu Station stumbled around anonymously in huge parkas, buffeted by unfriendly winds and swirls of snow brought down from the North Pole. Unsurprisingly, leaving the buildings for anything short of real necessities became rare.

One such necessity, indeed the whole point of their presence, was to set up the experiment. Carter and Lovecraft went up to the experimental site on the second day, both because it was important they be familiar with all the station's areas and also purely out of curiosity.

The drive the contractor had promised them would take twenty minutes took twice that time, largely because snow was beginning to collect on the freezing rock and nobody relished the thought of an uncontrolled skid on a steep mountainside. The road itself, thankfully, was well engineered, wide and even with a mild inside camber to drain it of rain, and plenty of boulders along the outside edge to act as improvised barriers. There were still plenty of large gaps between them, though, with anything from a 45-degree escarpment to a vertiginous drop of fifty or sixty feet onto rocks. None of it looked very survivable, so the driver, a technician called Bowles, took his time and whistled tunelessly under his breath the whole journey up to calm his nerves.

Attu currently held a grand total of five motor vehicles, all of them Kübelwagens with the project logo painted on the sides. Dr. Malcolm had told Carter in an unguarded moment that the Reich had supplied the first logo. It had looked like the results of Wagner, Nietzsche, and Speer spending an afternoon playing with Photoshop after eating too much sugar. The American scientific community had seen the oddly familiar lightning bolts raining down across the Earth, quietly said "Nope," and offered up something way more anodyne but less contentious. This had been accepted with diplomatic speed by the Germans, and so that particular barrier was hurdled.

Trying to make conversation, Lovecraft said, "This is going to be a slow climb when the snow arrives."

Bowles paused in his whistling to grunt with dour amusement. "It'll take two or three times as long. Don't know why they couldn't have waited until spring to do this project. It's not like the mountain's going to go away or anything. Got some solutions back at base I'll break out when the snow comes—and it *will* come—but this is a bad time of year to be out here." As he spoke, they turned the last corner of the road, and arrived at their destination.

Bowles parked alongside a pair of the Kübelwagens outside an impressive concrete dome, some 150 feet in diameter, at the mountain's peak. By it was an open area, concreted flat, with short lengths of steel girder thrusting up to the uneven end where it looked like they'd been severed with cutting gear. Bowles saw Carter looking at these and said, "That's where the radar was, back when this place was operational. The dome's where the operators worked. A hundred and fifty-five feet wide, that mother. Bigger'n the Pantheon in Rome."

They made their way to the entrance on the dome's southern side. On the western side was a new building, which they guessed contained the generators to supply the large amounts of power the experiment might require. The northern side of the dome partially merged with a rocky spire, perhaps all that was left of the mountain's original peak before the engineers finished blasting it flat.

The entrance was accessed by a short stoop of steps descending ten feet into the rock. "It's underground?" asked Lovecraft.

"No," replied Bowles, undogging the door's heavy locking mechanism, "just kind of inset. Not really sure why they bothered with a dome since they went to all the trouble to dig down like this, but that was all sixty-some years ago. Nobody left to ask. Maybe the dome was the only prefabricated structure available or something. Here we are." He swung the door open and waved them through. "Guys, welcome to ZPE Central."

Lovecraft, who had never seen the facility at Miskatonic U and who had been hoping for crackling Jacob's ladders and massive bayonet switches like a Universal Studios Frankenstein set, was slightly underwhelmed that it looked like somebody had set up a sales office in a nuclear bunker, the base of an evil villain who was going to achieve global domination by cold-calling the world into submission. Yes, there was some sort of huge cylinder gizmo in the very center of the chamber that stretched almost all the way to the dome's apex ninety feet above them. "This place was just for radar operators?" she asked Bowles. "But it's *huge*."

He frowned. "Yeah. Does look overengineered, doesn't it?" He shrugged off his parka and hung it on an array of hooks driven into the concrete by the door. "Amazing heat insulation, though. Once the contractors get the place up to a shirtsleeves temperature, we only have to warm the air up that comes through the ventilators to keep it that way. The dome itself barely bleeds any heat at all."

Lovecraft turned to hang up her parka and found Carter looking around the chamber as if he'd just been tricked into an ambush. She took his arm and led him to the hooks. "You're gawping, Sheriff. What's wrong?"

He didn't reply immediately, instead looking around the dome's lower edge. "Those . . . what do you call them? The supports . . . stanchions? Buttresses."

"Uh-huh? What about them?"

"There are twelve."

Lovecraft understood him at once. "It's a very popular number. You should look at a clock face sometime."

"I know. I just . . ." He gazed around the dome, the air of a trapped man not diminishing at all. "Just, the coincidence of it. Round chamber. Walls curving into the ceiling. Twelve supports. Freaks me out a little."

"Yeah, I can see that, but you really need to suck it up before anyone else sees it. You got a pistol at your hip and people don't need to see the armed guy have an episode, you understand me?"

Carter felt the weight of the Colt .45 on his belt. Ironically it was the very model he had been thinking about getting, but now that he had been issued one, he'd gone completely off the idea. It really was too much gun for his usual work, was bulky, and he was glad he was permitted to open carry here at the back of beyond, because it was too big a lump of firepower to conceal easily. He found himself missing his Walther from MU, and feeling like a traitor for doing so.

"Yeah," he said, "I understand you." He took his time shucking his parka so he could get over himself a little. It was just a coincidence. Domed rooms weren't uncommon, and if you're going to build a circular room, why wouldn't you use twelve supports? It was just a coincidence that he'd recently seen a dozen people die in a . . .

He took a breath. *It was just a coincidence*, he told himself, and left it there.

He glanced at Lovecraft settling her own gun at her hip, and felt a small pang. Lovecraft, in contrast to a monstrous Colt .45 ACP, had been issued a British pistol, a Webley PD-12, which Carter was sure didn't exist in the Folded World. It was a snug little .38 WS automatic that held twelve rounds in the box and was well regarded in the reviews he'd looked up. He'd called it "nice" several times while examining it, and he'd been reluctant to return it to Lovecraft, although he'd hidden that from her. He couldn't help thinking that he'd made a mistake asking for the Colt and had definitely made a mistake about being dismissive of Lovecraft's vague request for "something that will put people down if need be without making a song and dance about it. Oh, yeah, and a motherfucker of a semiauto twelve-gauge, please."

With all the technology manned by earnest scientists arrayed around the massive central cylinder, it made Lovecraft think of any number of low-budget sci-fi films and TV reruns from the seventies. "Needs more flashing lights that don't do much," she murmured to Carter. "Isn't real science without flashing lights."

In fact it looked very familiar to Carter, all very similar to the equipment he'd grown used to at the lab in Arkham, right down to Dr. Giehl's energy detector doohickey. It was exactly the same unit from Miskatonic University. After the Jenner incident, the bomb had been smuggled back into it and Giehl removed all traces of the tinker-detecting setup that had detected Carter's tinkering but—critically—not Jenner's. The unit had sat there with a bundle of dynamite in it for several days until it was due to be packaged up ready for the Aleutians journey, and then Giehl had spirited it away using her Abwehr connections, Carter guessed. Presumably New York and Washington were stiff with Abwehr stooges, so it wasn't such a big deal for one to go up to Arkham long enough for a few sticks of dynamite to be surreptitiously handed over and subsequently dumped in the river or something.

Carter didn't much care about the logistics of how the Reich disposed of the bomb nearly as much as he was bothered that APD never bothered checking inside the detector despite all the clues that there was a) a bomb and b) that it was inside a German-manufactured piece of equipment. On the one hand, it was a relief; on the other, it pissed him off that they couldn't seem to add two and two.

That was all in the past, though. Now he and Lovecraft were in a concrete dome in a place that most people couldn't find on a map with a dozen tries, overseeing an experiment that promised to change the world for the better forever, yet had shadows of high weirdness falling across it. He had no idea who Weston was working for, but he doubted you'd find them in the phone book.

Chapter 22

A VIEW FROM MOUNT TERRIBLE

"Ah, good morning, Sheriff! Deputy!" Dr. Malcolm enjoyed the whole Wild West vibe far too much. He could only have been happier if the dome had been fitted with bat-wing doors. The physicist's whole demeanor had changed from Arkham. There he had been a sensible, thoughtful man of science. Here, he was a frontiersman, metaphorically and very nearly literally. Apparently he was known for walking up the mountain before starting work rather than traveling by car, simply because it made him feel more . . . nobody was sure what. "Manly" had been suggested, but that wasn't right. It seemed to be more something about rediscovering himself in nature, now that they were surrounded by the stuff and their work was scraping away layers of the natural world as it had been hitherto understood to expose something vibrant, primal, and exciting beneath. Malcolm had also been seen wearing a checked lumberjack shirt, and none of his colleagues were entirely sure how to process this new datum.

Certainly the site having a couple of de facto law officers—even if most of their time was spent helping out with the maintenance with the technicians in Carter's case and running administrative matters in Lovecraft's—seemed to make Malcolm's day every time he saw them.

"Hello, Doctor." Carter liked the man, even if he was personally expecting the Wild West shtick to grow thin much sooner than later. It seemed unkind not to let the man have his fun, though.

Malcolm proceeded to show them around the facility. The ZPE wasn't online as yet, but the components and the test gear were undergoing individual tests before everything was connected and, so far, it was all going exactly to schedule. As long as nothing failed at this stage, they would be starting two weeks of calibrations on the following Monday, and then it would be a solid four or five weeks of experimentation. The hope was that they would be detecting definite traces of zero point energy on the first day, and the rest of the time would be spent confirming those initial results and then proceeding through a thoroughly planned program of experiments intended to boost the energies released.

"Realistically, if we finish the program and we're producing as much power as a double-A cell out of thin air, that's a shattering advance. But . . . but I have hopes this thing"—he gestured at the central column—"will actually be putting out as much as a small portable generator. Say, two or three kilowatts. If it turns out to be that easy, the world changes tomorrow. The old saw about nuclear energy and then fusion energy, 'power too cheap to meter,' might finally come true, just from a very different area of physics." He turned to them, and there was a true, selfless joy there. "There are very few times you can say, that *anyone* can say, 'What we are doing here will change the world for the better.' I feel so lucky, so *blessed* that this might be one such time."

"Well, let's hope so, Doctor," said Carter, and smiled, and felt like horseshit for doing so. But what was he supposed to say? "Well, the truth is we're all just pawns in a cosmic chess match and we don't actually know the rules or even what 'winning' looks like, but it's probably going to look a lot like losing from our perspective, because all chess matches look like massacres when you're a pawn. And your project is either a fraud or the worst thing that will ever happen to the human race, unless it's the best, which is also a possibility. In the meantime, Go, Science! Yay."

"Well, let's hope so, Doctor," just seemed a lot briefer and kinder to Carter.

Malcolm showed them around the dome's main room and the couple of small rooms off it—a room containing electrical gear and capacitors, a common room, and a restroom that could best be described as "functional." Then he showed them around the main floor in more detail, but Carter was losing interest.

This was all new to Lovecraft, but he'd seen this all before at Miskatonic U, albeit on a smaller scale. His attention wandered, and then he realized it had wandered onto Dr. Giehl, who was sitting cross-legged on the floor while she sorted out a bunch of cables that had just been thrown into a box instead of being properly coiled and tied off in Arkham. She looked up and caught him looking at her. A small smile appeared at the corner of her mouth, and she returned to her chore. Some conspiratorial tic in the expression solidified what he had already strongly suspected, that Giehl was under the impression that he'd been fully conscious during their encounter in his stateroom. While it did his ego good to think he was a satisfactory lover while on autopilot, it meant there was going to be a very difficult conversation between them at some point, and Carter knew it would be wiser for it to be sooner rather than later. So, feeling paradoxically more fearful than when he'd confronted Jenner at gunpoint, he went over to Dr. Giehl.

"How's it going, Doctor?" he asked. It sounded lame, and he

suddenly felt like a fourteen-year-old again, asking out Sally Pine. That had been an unmitigated disaster, and he could feel another about to break.

"Sheriff Carter," said Giehl, smiling as she untangled a trio of leads, "how kind of you to mosey over and ask."

He sighed. "Did everybody hatch this cowboy theme while I was looking the other way?"

"Welcome to Attu," she said, still without shifting her attention from the cables, "population twenty-four. The biggest, wildiest, westiest town in the U.S. Yes, Dan. There were a couple of bottles of schnapps, a boring voyage, and we may have got a little drunk and silly. You didn't know about it because"—she glanced up at him then, and there was steel beneath the smile—"you were avoiding me."

"Yeah." He crouched by her and lowered his voice. "Yeah, I was. About that . . ."

"You were virtually asleep and probably drugged with motion sickness medication. Yes, I worked that out a little too late to do anything about it. I thought you were taking 'strong and silent' too seriously."

Carter raised an eyebrow. The last thing he'd been expecting was that she already knew. "I'm sorry," he said awkwardly.

"No. I should apologize. You said yes—more than once, in fact—and I thought we were mutually engaged in"—she half-smiled and perhaps blushed a little—"the activities. So I tiptoed back to my cabin and thought it wise to avoid you for a little while. I needn't have troubled myself, as you had the same idea." She returned her attention to the cables. "I have no idea how much you remember but, for whatever it is worth, I enjoyed myself. Even after I realized you were in some sort of dream state. Sneaking back, it all felt very transgressive."

"Oh." Carter was wondering whether to feel complimented or insulted. "So, you and I?"

"We're both professionals, Sheriff Dan. If you are content to let things lie, then so am I. We shall, of course, continue to work together as we have done to date. And no"—she dropped a coiled cable back into the box and started on some more of the tangled mess—"it won't be happening again, no matter what your level of consciousness. We shall put it down to a moment of weakness on my part."

"Okay." Carter was now fairly sure he was being insulted, or at least his masculinity was, yet he didn't think this was the time and the place to make an argument about it. When he thought about it more later, he doubted there was ever any suitable time or venue for arguments like that. "Well, if you need anything, Dr. Giehl, you know where to find me."

She said nothing, but he noted the half smile still at the corner of her mouth and realized that he had no idea what it meant. As he straightened up, he saw Dr. Malcolm was still deep in his spiel, but Lovecraft was only half paying attention. She couldn't have heard a word of their conversation, but she still gave a small shake of her head, one corner of her mouth lifted in an expression of thoughtfulness, but her eyebrows down, overall giving an aspect of disappointed opprobrium. Carter had the feeling he had succeeded in disappointing two women in different ways in the space of a minute. This was a record.

To Lovecraft's disbelief and Bowles's respectful surprise, Carter said he'd walk back down the mountain rather than be driven down. He waved goodbye to them as they drove away to descend the counterclockwise road that wound around most of the mountain's upper quarter before turning to zigzags that descended into the glaciated valley below. The snow had stopped for the time being, and the cold wind had diminished to a breeze, but the weather report indicated both would be back within a few hours. Bowles's last words to Carter had been not to dawdle; there were still four hours of day left, but he would have the better part of ten miles to cover in that time. No matter how tempting it looked to save himself time by climbing down between meanders on the mountainside road, he should stick to the road, and that if he wasn't back by nightfall, Bowles would come look-ing for him. He also ducked back into the dome to warn them that there was a pedestrian on the mountain road and to drive even more carefully than usual. All the precautions irritated Car-ter, who'd just wanted a quiet walk to himself and not this big production of safety theater, but he had to admit it was neces-sary. When he was finally by himself, it was a relief.

Mount Terrible wouldn't have offered much of a challenge to a competent mountaineer from most aspects, but that wasn't to say it would be a pushover. The ridges concealed sudden steep inclines and more than enough cliffs to punish the unwary and overconfident. Carter wondered if he was in the latter category as he started walking along the access road. The snow had stopped before very much of it had had a chance to stick or drift, but even that short fall had been enough to make the path treach-erous. When Bowles had driven away, Carter wasn't even sure if he'd taken it out of bottom gear. It had certainly taken a while to disappear from view around the first bend.

Carter paused there for a minute, taking out the binoculars he'd found among his equipment in the security station and look-ing down toward the temporary settlement below and to the west. He could see the project's other two Kübelwagens parked by the garage unit, and figures walking by. Beyond the living quarters lay the rocky coast and the cold sea, and beyond that—a *long* way beyond that—lay Alaska, and then Canada, and finally home.

Carter had traveled less than he would have liked in his life, but when he'd been abroad there had always been the sense of it being a temporary state of affairs, and that an invisible bungee cord would presently twang him back to his home. That sense deserted him now. He felt adrift, cut loose. There was no impe-tus to go anywhere except as necessity dictated. Yes, he wanted to keep on walking to the station, but mainly because it was warm and there was food there, not because it was in any sense "home" to him. Nowhere was "home" now. He wondered if Lovecraft and Harrelson felt that way, too.

He put away the binoculars and continued his descent. At the end of the near revolution of the peak, he found himself at the top of the meanders the U.S. CoE had cut into the mountainside decades before and looked down. It looked a long way. Near the bottom, he could see the Kübelwagen cautiously negotiate the last hairpin and then drive out into the valley before turning west. He was relieved Bowles and Lovecraft had made the descent without problems, less so that he wasn't with them. It looked a long way to walk, even if it was all downhill. He felt like an idiot for not bringing his walkie-talkie, but he hadn't planned to be by himself like this. At least people knew where he was, and he had no intention whatsoever of leaving the road.

He took a couple of steps, and paused again. He'd happened to look to the southwest where the sea glittered darkly in Temnac Bay and, just for a moment, he thought he saw something out there. He took out his binoculars again and scanned the surface. There was nothing. Carter lowered the binoculars and looked with his naked eyes upon the bay, frowning. The sky was overcast, so at least there were no strong reflections from the waves to trouble him, but the cloud layer was thin and the water seemed to glow in the dull light. Perhaps his eyes had deceived him, and he'd only thought he saw something large and dark out where the bay opened into the cold Pacific. He knew whaling used to be an industry in the Aleutians; had he seen a whale? It wasn't impossible, but something told him he was wrong.

Something flickered in his mind, and he knew it had been no whale. He hated the fugues that settled upon him now and then, and he especially didn't want one now, out on a bare mountainside with snow threatening. A sense of a double-exposed world cluttered his vision, yellow and black. The road he was on ceased to exist, though he could feel the smooth camber beneath his feet. Out at sea, there was nothing but the dark waves. He'd been mistaken. He hadn't seen anything. But there was movement. Without meaning to, he raised the binoculars to his eyes and it was as if they were a kaleidoscope, the world shattered into shards and prisms. There was nothing out there, just jagged lines and blurred tangents. He willed himself to lower the binoculars before the lines cut into his brain and left him with, at best, a migraine, or at worst, a seizure. Just before he did so, he saw the beach of black volcanic sand close by where the Temnac River ran into the bay, and he saw a dark figure rise from the water there and shamble clumsily across the thin strand to be lost in the contours of the land.

Carter lowered the binoculars with a jerk and muttered, "Fuck!" under his breath in a mixture of anger and, he realized a moment later, fear. The fear made him angrier still. He clenched his eyes and forced the Fold to leave him alone for just one fucking second while he tried to ensure his grip upon the here and now. He opened his eyes, and now there was only a gloomy vista across a gloomy bay. There was nothing on the sea and nothing on the beach. He braced himself, and raised his binoculars once more. There was nothing on the beach. He breathed easier; of course, there had never been anything on the beach. The Fold had been fucking with him, maybe seeing something that might have happened in the Unfolded if . . .

He'd snorted with contempt when he'd first found the binoculars in his office and discovered they had a zoom function. A martinet to functionality, he preferred single magnification binoculars for their consistency, sharpness, and collimation accuracy. Now, however, he blessed whoever had decided a pair of zoom binoculars was what the sheriff of Attu Station really needed. He went to one of the roadside boulders, braced himself against it to cut down vibration, and looked again, cranking the zoom function to its full fifty-times magnification.

There was nobody on the beach he could see, but there were tracks. Strange, wide tracks. Something walking on two huge, probably webbed feet had been there.

Carter thought of the Waite man who he'd spoken to a couple of times back in Providence when it had still existed, the man who wanted to swim. The first time, he *had* been a man, if a borderline case. The second time, no, not anymore. He had changed into something else, something aquatic or at least amphibious. Something with huge, webbed feet.

Carter put away the binoculars, checked his pistol, and set off down the mountain as quickly as he dared. He and Lovecraft had talked about this. They knew beyond reasonable doubt that weird shit was incoming. They'd both been sure it wouldn't happen this quickly though. It would wait for the experiment to go online, obviously. After all, what was the point of all this if not to get the experiment online? It looked like they had been terribly, perhaps fatally wrong; the weird shit had preempted them.

Chapter 23

DARK WATERS

Lovecraft's reaction when he finally reached the encampment and told her the happy news was predictable. "You are shitting me," she said, but from her expression it was clear that she thought anything but.

He'd found her gratifyingly quickly after reaching the prefabs; walking straight into the security office, breathing hard from the "forced march" pace he'd maintained from the mountain, sweating inside his parka, he discovered her with her feet up on his desk, reading a Fortean magazine she'd picked up back in Arkham explaining that—these days—such magazines counted as current events. She'd drawn a breath to make some ironic remark as he burst in, taken one look at his face, and instead said, "What happened?"

After he'd told her what he'd observed out in the bay, he said, "I know what I saw. It was as big as a man and it walked on its hind legs like a man. It wasn't a seal. I'm pretty sure it was one of those fish/frog bastards like the Waite men turned into."

"Deep Ones," said Lovecraft. "H.P.L. called them Deep Ones."

"That is a shit name."

"Pithier than 'fish/frog bastards.'" She glanced down to her pistol in its holster. "If I remember properly, they don't die easy, either." She looked back at Carter. "What's the plan?"

"We have to get back out right now, out to the bay and see if we can find it. Find it and kill it."

"Slow down there, Sheriff. It's dark and all we got is flashlights. Those fuckers can probably see in the dark if they can see underwater, and we'll be giving them all the advantages of seeing us before we see them. *If* they let us see them at all."

"But the tracks will be gone by then."

"Tracks are already gone. High tide was about twenty minutes ago." She saw Carter's expression. "Oh, yeah. I am the queen of the telling detail. Just struck me like the kind of thing a girl should know on a small island. We'll save our trip to the beach for the morning, tell folks we're off to scout out the island and maybe do a little target shooting. We'll take one of the Kraut jeeps."

Still slightly stung that he'd been caught out by Lovecraft's knowledge of the tides, Carter said, "Kraut? Not very politically correct."

She raised her eyebrows. "Given what I get called out on the street these days, fuck political correctness. Anyhow, these Germans . . . these *Nazis* call us shit all the time. I heard it on the ship, I hear it here. I think they think that 'cause I'm black, knowing two languages is beyond me. Well, newsflash, assholes. Back in the Folded, I did a lot of trade with Germany, I got pretty good conversational German going." She got up and went to the coffeepot. "And that's another reason we've got to get back to the Folded World; I *like* the Germans, and they deserve better than these Nazi fucks and their joke one-party democracy where there's always a top asshole who was best at playing the *Füh-rerprinzip* game."

She paused, thinking. "That's weird in itself, don't you think? Hitler always talked about a thousand-year Reich, but he never really left a framework for how power was supposed to be inherited. It just happens." She held up the magazine. "Theory in here that he never really died. He'd be 120, 130 years old by now, but they use weird science to keep him alive and he's calling the shots from a freezer up in the Adlerhorst. That's also weird; on both sides of the Fold, the Nazis have got this rep for using weird science." She nodded in the general direction of the dome. "Like they're doing up there."

The site was already running up quite a junk heap after even a few days, all of which was corraled for being taken off the island when they left. Lovecraft helped herself to a few institutional-size coffee and food cans, explaining to the galley chef (nobody was quite sure why the kitchen ended up being called the galley, but it did) that "Sheriff Dan's goin' to larn me how to use mah shootin' iron proper." The chef said she should have fun, but to bring back the cans when they were done; one of the project's briefs was to keep the island clean of as much trash as they could.

Nobody seemed to think it so extraordinary that Carter and Lovecraft should take time out to plink at cans, but then several of the project's senior members owed their lives to Carter staying cool under pressure and taking the shot only when he had to, not a second later, and making it count.

"You realize we're going to have to find somewhere to massacre some cans now, don't you?" said Lovecraft as they drove away from the settlement in one of the Kübelwagens. "We can't go back with virgin cans after telling them that story."

"I could just tell them you're that bad a shot."

"I could just shoot you and tell them it was an accident."

Bowles had told them that the vehicles had excellent off-road characteristics, and they shouldn't have any problems driving out to the bay. The first part of the route was easy anyway, simply following the road to Mount Terrible along the Ukudikak River. Attu was too small for any rivers to get much above ten or twenty feet wide and, on the rocky terrain, they flowed shallow. That was just as well, as the Kübelwagen would have to ford the Ukudikak and the smaller Namada Creek a little farther to the west before they reached Temnac Bay.

Carter was driving, both because he was the only one of them with off-road experience and because Lovecraft had a license but had driven only rarely in the previous couple of years. She also didn't enjoy driving much, regarding it as a chore, and was content to let Carter take the wheel. As a bonus, riding shotgun (literally, her Mossberg twelve-gauge lying alongside her) allowed her the luxury of looking around the terrain as they traveled, and this she definitely did enjoy.

"I'm glad I came," she said as they drove in the shadow of Mount Terrible. "The ship and those little planes, and all this. I've never done anything like this before."

"We don't know what we might find in the bay. You might change your mind real suddenly."

She snorted dismissively. "If we don't seek the weird shit out, the weird shit does it to us. It's why we're on Attu in the first place. We're never going to get to sit any of this out, you know? Not until either we flip the world somehow, or the weird shit kills us."

He glanced across at her. "That's fatalistic for you, Emily."

"Nah." She was looking up the slope of the mountain. The dome was invisible from that angle, but the access road was obvious as it switchbacked its way up toward the peak. "Realistic. It's cool. The existential dread doesn't bother me like it used to. We're lucky; humans are so stupid we even get used to cosmic horror given half a chance."

"You think that's true? H.P.L.'s stories were full of people going crazy, weren't they?"

"It's still happening. There was the guy near the store Harrelson was talking about."

"Yeah, and I've been asking around about the guy whose job I got at the U. He had a 'breakdown.'"

"Sure he did."

"I've asked Harrelson to pull his background security check and e-mail it to me here. Anyway, the insanity that seems to be part of all this, it's like a sickness. Like something you can catch. You think in reality we're resistant because we're too dumb to take it all in?"

"Maybe. Maybe not. I think maybe we are, specifically us, because we're wrapped up so close to all this that the supernatural scary shit is no more likely to drive us insane than any other scary shit. We both saw the Fold. We saw other stuff, too, and I don't feel any crazier."

"The insane never know they're insane."

"Yeah, but we're not in soft rooms being told we're wrong about reality. We're still rational, logical human beings and we're still buying into the consensus of reality . . . apart from the stuff about godlike aliens controlling the world from behind the scenes, which I admit would get us thrown through the nut hatch if we went public with it. But three of us having exactly the same delusion—"

"Four, if you count Weston."

Lovecraft fell silent. A minute or so later, she said, "Yeah, about Weston. Just who the fuck is he?" Carter didn't reply and, when she looked at him, she saw his lips were drawn tight, as if considering an unpalatable possibility. "Yeah," she said. "That's what I think, too."

The Kübelwagen crossed the Ukudikak easily. It looked like the military had deliberately created a fording point just off where the road turned up toward Mount Terrible, and it was still in good condition. Certainly the Kübelwagen's high clearance made easy work of the short, rugged span of rocks. Navigation subsequently became more complicated. Carter was using GPS to guide him to the eastern end of the bay. First it led them across a rugged table of exposed rock, crossed here and there with small gullies formed by erosion, many of them deep enough to tear off the car's wheels if they drove into one too quickly. They could be negotiated if taken at an angle, and driven through slowly, but it was a painstaking business, and there were many of them. Then, when they finally arrived at the southwest side of the stone plain, they found there was a steep slope that ended in a cliff where the Namada Creek had eaten away the volcanic rock.

Carter swore. Lovecraft said, "You *did* plan this all out on a map before we left, didn't you?"

"No. It's only a few miles and we have a car. What do we need a map for?"

"Dan, don't take this the wrong way, but you can be a real jackass sometimes. You ain't in Red Hook now." She pulled a map from her jacket and unfolded it. "Give me our coordinates from the GPS, would you? I figure we're about *there*"—she tapped the map—"but we'd better be sure before we start moving again."

"Look, we just drive south until we find a slope and can get to the beach."

"Or we find it finishes with another cliff. Coastlines do that kind of shit. Just give me the goddamn coordinates, would you?"

They were very nearly where Lovecraft had reckoned their position. She traced farther south until the land gave way in a steep slope.

"The car could handle that," said Carter, aware that whatever small reputation he might have as an outdoorsman was already in the process of burning to ashes.

"Yeah, it probably could, but we'd end up on this dinky little beach that's separated from where we want to go by this outcrop here. Last time I checked, this is a Kübelwagen, not a Schwimmwagen, so that's not an option."

"A what?"

"Amphibious version of what we're in. Kind of wish we did have one. That would be awesome. We could go fishing. With guns."

Carter rested his hands on the steering wheel and stared at her. "How do you *know* this stuff?"

She didn't look up from the map. "I read. Reading's good. Now, looky here—we head northeast, cross that stream we went over before, north over this one, then back west. That slope looks steep, but it's not as bad as the one you were talking about to the south, so we should be okay. If not, we'll find a way around, or maybe we'll just have to get out and walk the last little way. If we're good on the slope, you drive down the creek—I mean actually in it if it's as shallow as the last one—and that brings us out there, at the east end of the beach." She looked out of the windshield and pointed at the dark strand some half a mile away. "About there. Okay?" There was no reply, and she looked over at him. "Okay?"

Carter was staring out into the gloomy waters of the bay. "I've been so focused on the Deep Thing I saw on the beach, I'd almost forgotten about what made me use the binoculars in the first place. There was something in the bay. Something big. I only saw it for a second, out of the corner of my eye almost, but I did see it. I thought it might be a whale, but then I saw, on the beach . . ." He turned to her, suddenly animated. "How deep's the water out there? Is it on the map?"

"All the Aleutians are along a humongous volcanic ridge. They're the tops of submarine mountains poking out of the surface. I'd guess the water gets real deep real quick as you go away from shore. Yeah, look." She pointed at the map. "This ain't a nautical chart, but it does have a few soundings around the island. There's one about there"—she looked out at the sea, and pointed to an area at the mouth of the bay not far from where Carter thought he'd seen something—"that says forty. That's fathoms, so that's . . . six feet to a fathom . . . holy shit, that's 240 feet deep! You could hide fucking Godzilla in that bay, never mind a whale." Carter looked at her stonily, and she smiled, a little embarrassed. "Yeah, okay. My bad. Forget I just suggested that a giant primeval monster would be able to hide out there. It was a whale, okay? It was a whale."

Carter started the engine and turned the car to head northeast. "Something else to hate about the Unfolded," said Lovecraft. "No Godzilla movies. And it's Deep *Ones*, not *Things*. Although I've got to admit, your version doesn't sound any lamer than H.P.L.'s."

Chapter 24

BLACK SAND

The route was frustratingly roundabout, almost three miles to arrive at a point less than half a mile from where they'd started, and it was difficult terrain that meant low speeds and a lot of wariness. More than once Lovecraft was obliged to get out and guide the Kübelwagen across gullies and past potholes. The car was a feisty machine and good on the terrain, but it would only take one mistake to end up stranded if they asked it to perform the impossible. At least the return trip would be easier; most of their troubles had been caused by going so deeply onto the stone table due to Carter's overreliance on the GPS in the first place. Going back, they would skirt it and be back onto the road that much quicker.

They drew up at the end of the creek where its bed opened into the beach, and climbed out to survey the bleak strip of black sand beside a black sea, beneath a sky that was growing darker as more clouds moved in. North-northwest, the top of Mount Terrible was already lost in wreaths of stratus. Lovecraft watched the weather close in with a sense of foreboding.

Carter, meanwhile, was looking the other way, at the sea. "What times does the tide come in?"

"Hmmm?" Lovecraft turned and looked out at the Pacific, wallowing slowly with an air of oily, indifferent menace. "About three hours. Look at where the grass starts, though. We're above the high tide mark. The car's fine as long as it stays here." She nodded at the waves, barely bothering to break on the beach, viscous and loathsome. "First time in my life I've looked at the Pacific with my own two eyes, and just look at the thing. Why couldn't they have decided Hawaii was the perfect place for their damn experiment? Dan, why we're here . . . you don't think the explanation about radio interference and all that is just bullshit, do you?"

"What, like there's something important about this particular place?" He shook his head. "I don't think so."

Lovecraft took a long breath and blew it out. "I just keep thinking maybe this is another Waite's Bill, except without the dumb guys and the creepy women. Well, Doc Giehl's kind of creepy, and God knows, you're pretty dumb, but you know what I mean."

Carter couldn't get angry with the mild chiding in her tone. "I do, but I don't see it. This place would have to have history, wouldn't it? Waite's Bill had stories going way back. Stuff happened there. What happened here? There was an early-warning station and now there isn't. End of story."

Lovecraft leaned into the car and took out her shotgun and a shoulder bag containing spare ammunition and some survival supplies. She slung it over her shoulder crosswise right shoulder to left hip, and then the shotgun the other way.

"*That*," she said, tapping him gently in the chest with one finger, "is what we call white privilege."

"Ah, c'mon . . ."

"Seriously, Dan. The Aleut lived here for centuries. Maybe millennia. You saying they don't count?"

"Emily, come on now. Don't put words in my mouth. We know next to nothing about what the Aleut did here. They didn't leave a written record."

"Exactly the point I'm making. Maybe they had their own creepy-ass version of the Waites here, but they died out, or swam out to sea one day and never came back." She looked to the north; the clouds were thickening. The weather report had said the snow wouldn't arrive until that evening, but she was beginning to think that was optimistic. She turned her attention back to Carter. "Unless they did. Maybe that's what you saw from the mountainside."

She started walking along the beach. Carter watched her go for a second, then dogtrotted to catch up with her.

There were still drifts of snow from the brief fall of the previous day. Given how cold it was, barely above freezing, it seemed unlikely to thaw before the new fall came. White streaks lay across the dark stone, and the straggly, unhealthy heath grass lay buried in places, a few stalks sticking up through the crust here and there. Under the attenuated light, the snow didn't look crystalline at all, but more as if it had grown there, a dull, fungal growth sprouting fitfully across a landscape that felt lunar in its forbidding aspect. Lovecraft muttered something along the same lines, and it struck Carter as a poor sort of omen that they were both thinking of fungi and corruption, of the feeble touch of life on that barren island, and of the alien fruiting bodies that might make better use of it.

A vague memory, something Harrelson had said, slid into Carter's mind, but before he could grasp it, Lovecraft said, "What's the plan if we run into a Deep One? Try to talk to it? Shoot it? Run away? Just give up and go insane? I know old man Howard P. would approve of that last one, but I'm open to suggestions."

The thought slipped away, leaving the smart sting of something precious or at least interesting lost, leaving only the memory that it was precious or interesting. "I don't know. Talk to it first, I guess. The one I saw on Waite's Bill didn't mind chatting. First sign of trouble, shoot it."

"Yeah, that's what I figured. Pretty much describes my social life." Even as she was joking, Carter saw her hand drift down to touch the ATI Scorpion grip on her Mossberg as it hung by her side on a long strap. She'd asked for a 930, as it was a model she was used to, but, when she opened the box, she found somebody had decided a 500 ATI tactical was a better choice. She'd bitched about it some at first, but she got over it quickly and now actually kind of liked the badassery of the pistol grip and of the three shell holders mounted down the left side. Unlike the 930, the 500 was a pump action, but once she got into the habit of a good, positive racking action before firing, she was cool with that.

Not that she'd had a chance to fire it yet. "This thing had better handle like a 930 if I have to put out some lead. Should've got some of the cans and tried it out by the mountain before we got here."

"Coulda, shoulda, woulda," said Carter reflexively, and instantly regretted it. He deserved the sour look Lovecraft gave him. "Sorry. This whole day just keeps going wrong in little ways. I don't feel confident about this field trip at all."

"Chances are we won't find anything anyway. You could hide a small army around here with all these little creek beds and gullies and runnels and shit. You'd have to be up in a helicopter or something to see them. One fish guy out here? If he wants to hide, we won't find him."

Carter ground his jaw, but more from the knowledge that she was probably right than the negativity.

That was when they saw the tracks.

The tracks started not far from the eastern edge of the Temnac River where it opened into the bay. They wandered onto the side for a few yards, then backtracked to the river once more. It was noticeable that they reentered the water slightly upstream from where they had originally exited, the line of footprints turning by 45 degrees to the north. The implication seemed to be that whatever had made the huge, finned footprints had returned to the river, nine or ten yards wide there but barely knee-deep at most, specifically to avoid making any more tracks, and was heading inland.

Lovecraft took out her phone, currently useless for communication, and snapped a picture of the tracks with its camera. "These tracks are *huge*," she said in a near whisper. "How big are these things?"

"The one I saw at Waite's Bill towered over me," said Carter. He unconsciously reached for his gun and tested how well it sat in its holster, loosening it for a quick draw. Lovecraft noticed the action and looked apprehensively out to sea and up the river. "It said its size depended on how much it ate. There must be good feeding around here. Seals, I guess."

"I read a little about this place before we came out. Seals, sea otters, and all kinds of birds. Seems it's a badge of honor for birdwatchers if they come all the way out here."

"Birds." Carter looked at her. "I haven't seen any birds here at all. Have you?"

She started to say, sure, of course there are birds, but she hesitated, thinking back over the few days they had been there since their arrival. "Yeah, there . . . No, that was on Adak." She looked at Carter, her eyes widening. "Shit. How can there be no birds out here?"

Carter said nothing, but the glance he gave to the tracks was eloquent enough. There was a strange tone in the air, like a moment in the dying of a note from a tuning fork, but held indefinitely. It was below the threshold of mundane perception, but Lovecraft could feel something that paced slowly through them like a ghost wind. She saw Carter look to Mount Terrible, now hidden by low, lambent clouds from a hundred feet up its sides.

The weird shit index had climbed too high around here, and the birds had moved away for the time being. Maybe the west end of the island was full of them, or maybe they'd flown away to another island altogether. Wherever they'd gone, they weren't here. Something had spooked them and, being wiser animals than humans, they'd left.

Two humans who were beginning to question the wisdom of coming there checked their weapons and started to head up river.

The river was a fractious thing, and clearly changed its course across the hard land frequently. They found signs within the first hundred yards of their advance that the river had slid its bed this way and that in the not-too-distant past, and even went by where a full meander had been cut off by the river finding a quicker route between the bends. If the Temnac had been much of a river, the isolated meander would have been an oxbow lake, but as it was it looked more like an oxbow ditch.

The landscape felt primeval and half-formed, massive outcrops and boulders littering the rugged, glacial terrain all around them. They both felt they were in a losing proposition, yet neither wanted to be the first to say it. The landscape could hide a dozen Deep Ones riding mammoths within a mile and they wouldn't see them until they turned a corner or crested a rise, by which point they'd be pretty much on top of one another and things would probably escalate quickly.

"What choke has that thing got?" said Carter in a low voice, indicating Lovecraft's shotgun with a nod. It was in her hands now, and she carried it ready to shoulder at any moment.

"Bare cylinder. Didn't think we were coming out here to shoot game, so I figured if I had to shoot, it would be pretty close up." She looked down at the weapon. "Should I rack a shell in? My instructor would be pissed at me walking with a chambered shell, but I'm feeling a little anxious at the moment."

Carter patted his Colt .45 in its holster. "You and me. I got one in the spout myself. Be my guest."

Lovecraft hesitated, the wish to rack the gun properly battling with her desire to be as quiet as possible. Finally she girded herself and pumped the action in two sharp, positive actions, as per doctrine. The racking sound seemed to echo around the landscape, silent but for the low groaning heaves of the lazy sea behind them.

"Well," she murmured, barely loud enough for Carter to hear, "*that* was loud." They moved on.

Another couple of hundred yards on, they encountered another of the pissant oxbows, but this time the island of land cut off by the old meander on one side and the new course on the other was higher than head height and whatever lay on the far side was hidden from them.

Carter paused, looking warily up the old course. "What's up?" asked Lovecraft.

"We can't move past this unless we know it's empty. We have to secure our rear."

"We go up there?" She grimaced; by some small miracle she'd managed to keep her boots out of water so far but the small oxbow looked waterlogged, and a small snowdrift had formed at the eastern side. She didn't like the idea of getting her feet soaked in near-freezing water in near-freezing weather.

"No, I go up there. You move ahead to where the two courses join up and wait until I rejoin you."

Her jaw dropped. "Split the party? Are you serious? Fuck, no, man. I've seen this movie and it does *not* end well."

He frowned at her as he drew his pistol. "Come on, Emily. Just do it. It's not like we have a choice. If we go together we can't see this arm, and we could be circled around on. That's more dangerous than us being separated for a few seconds, believe me."

"Jesus. Okay. I'll trust you on this, but if we get ganked by fish guys, I am never forgiving you. Just so you know."

"It'll be fine," said Carter, starting to move into the oxbow. "Chances are there's nothing down here anyway."

She watched him walk for a few yards, and started northward along the extant river herself. "*Nothing down here anyway,*" she muttered scornfully. "Famous last words right there, bro."

It only took her a couple of minutes to reach the point where the new course split from the old, and she waited by the junction. By her reckoning, Carter had about two or three times as much ground to cover, but given how marshy the ground looked down there, he probably couldn't make the same walking speed as her. She thought she might be waiting maybe another three minutes before she saw him. She took a position in the groin where the main flow ran directly south, but a trickle still ran into the meander, and she waited there, hidden beneath the overhanging bank of the little island. Two minutes passed. Three.

Four minutes.

Carter had never struck Lovecraft as the kind of man who played stupid practical jokes. He especially didn't seem the kind dumb enough to take up practical jokes when loaded weapons were in play. She swore under her breath, trying to control a rising anxiety. Maybe he was just having trouble moving through the mulchy ground. Maybe he was stuck up to his shin in mud. Thing was, Attu didn't really have too much soil. Sand? Quicksand? Was that really likely?

Five minutes.

She wanted to call, but if there *was* something just around the corner, calling would just tip it off. She tried not to think what might have already befallen Carter in that scenario. She glanced at the shotgun. Yes, it was a frightening weapon, but her intention had been that, should shit and fan rendezvous during the expedition, Carter would be at her side and keeping him apart from a cloud of lead shot would be pretty easy. If he and a potential target were pretty much in the same place, though, friendly fire—a shitty sort of euphemism for shooting one of your own—was too much of a possibility to be ignored. With great misgivings, because she was a far better shot with a shotgun than a handgun, she double-checked the Mossberg's safety and shoul-

dered it. The Webley felt really small in her hand, but she brought it up in the central axis relock stance Carter had spent a whole five minutes teaching her and, hoping she looked a lot more bad-ass than she felt, she moved into the meander to find Carter.

She'd taken maybe three steps when she heard a splash in the water behind her. The only things that made sound on the island were people and water, and the water burbled in the rivers that were barely more than streams, or boomed and sizzled onto and off the black sand and stones of the beaches. The water only splashed when something fell in it, or stepped in it.

She started to pivot, suddenly very frightened, but she was hit in the back before she'd even got halfway through the turn. It was a hard blow, and something powerful and bulky followed it through, sending her sprawling into the shallow lick of water that fed into the meander. She managed to hang on to the gun somehow, but the weight of the shotgun and her pack bore her down into the water and she had to use her left hand to push her-self up. She managed to get up, staggering forward to get her away from her attacker, but there was water in her eyes and when she wiped it away with the back of her free hand, she saw it was mixed with blood. That would explain the dreadful heaviness and the difficulty focusing: she'd banged her head when she fell. It was strange that she'd deduced that and not felt it, but no, there it was, pain on her forehead, right-hand side. She'd hit her head, and even under the clouds things were far too bright and there was that trouble focusing, and she was being attacked, and she realized she couldn't defend herself properly and she was prob-ably going to die now.

She tried to bring the gun around, but something grabbed her, something with a dark, rubbery skin that was way stronger than her, and suddenly she was on all fours and she didn't have her pistol anymore. She'd been disarmed by a Deep One. She wondered if it would be able to get its dumb-ass toad fingers through the trigger guard and guessed that, with her luck, the answer would be "Yes."

She rolled awkwardly onto her back on the wide bank of the little stream and tried to look at it, but everything was double images and glare, her head was starting to throb, and blood ran into her right eye, making it sting. The Deep One stood over her and she saw it level a weapon, maybe her own although she really couldn't tell, at her. Okay, this wasn't how she'd always envisaged checking out. "Don't shoot!" she shouted at the implacable, inhuman creature, "don't you fucking shoot, you fucking frog-faced freak!"

The monster hesitated. Then it said, "Sir? What's our policy on topping Yanks?"

Chapter 25

THE SECRET INVASION

It was a pretty shitty place for an interrogation. If they'd been taken by the Gestapo, at least there'd be a nice warm cellar to be tortured in. But the men who'd captured Carter and Lovecraft didn't have one handy, so instead they were sitting on a boulder in the lee of the little meander island, disarmed, wrists zip-tied, while their captors made tea. The tea was the sole plus point in this equation.

"You're British?" said Carter wonderingly as a marine corporal tended to the cut on Lovecraft's brow.

The senior officer, a man with a pale complexion and red hair offset by a nose that had been broken somewhere along the line and the shoulders of a rugby player, looked him over appraisingly. "Not sure how much we should tell you. My orders are vague about prisoners."

"Prisoners?" said Lovecraft, and then "Fuck," as her looking up suddenly rewarded her with antiseptic gel in her eye. "What's this 'prisoners' bullshit? You're on U.S. land here. We're U.S. citizens and you sure as fuck ain't. Didn't think we were at war or nothing, so what's going on here?" She allowed the medic to finish his work. "Special relationship, my ass," she muttered.

She was in a foul mood for any number of reasons, but paramount was that she'd mistaken a man in a wet suit for an inhuman monster. It was a reasonable mistake to have made, but between that, and totally failing to defend herself effectively, she was not feeling happy with herself or those that had doused her in the water. "I'm going to die of pneumonia sitting here in wet clothes," she added in an undertone.

"Yes," said the officer. "You being Americans has complicated things."

"It's an American island," said Carter. "Why wouldn't we be Americans?" Then he thought of the concrete dome and realization dawned. "Oh. I see. And if we'd been Germans?"

"That would have been far more clear-cut," said the officer, his meaning very clear to them both. He crouched on the sand spit before Carter and Lovecraft. "How much do you know about your German colleagues?"

Carter looked around at their captors and wondered what was the wise thing to say. There were six there—the officer, the medic, one with some sort of submachine gun who never looked away from them and whose job was pretty obviously to kill them if they tried anything, one at each approach of the meander, and one hidden among the straggling grasses atop the little plateau in the middle. He had a scoped rifle on a bipod, and Carter feared for anyone who came looking for Lovecraft and him. All the men wore wet suits although they had gotten rid of the fins, which lay in a heap nearby.

The enmity between the U.K. and Germany was well known, as was the U.K.'s inability to do anything about it. As a result the Reich treated the U.K. as a joke, and had reasonable grounds to do so. Nobody cared to deal much with them for fear of provoking the Germans. That had been the case in 1941 when the Second World War stopped before it could become truly global, and it was still largely the case today. Isolated and marginalized, the U.K. was a ghost of what it had been in 1939.

In which case, thought Carter, coming all the way out here to mess with the Germans and possibly incurring the wrath of the U.S. in the bargain was a pretty ballsy move. Suicidal even.

He was just beginning to formulate an answer that was cagey without sounding too much like it when Lovecraft said, "One's Abwehr that we know about. Another was Gestapo, but he got shot by a Polish guy in Arkham. He's dead. Both of them, that is. They're both dead now. As for the rest of them, who knows, but I'd guess it's hard getting a gig like that unless you're Party members. So, yeah, Nazis."

She noticed Carter's expression. "What? You think they don't already know all this? What do you think they're doing out here with a sub in the bay? Bird watching?" She looked at the officer. "Disappointing trip if it was."

Carter wasn't about to let her get away with that. "Maybe, but you don't just tell them everything right from the get-go. Jesus, Emily, you must suck at poker."

"Ohhhhh." Lovecraft took this in. "That's what I've been doing wrong. Seriously, though, hey, James Bond, what are you? Royal Navy? Commandos? What?"

The officer looked at her oddly. "You've read Ian Fleming?" He half-laughed. "I didn't think they were available outside Great Britain. Which is your favorite?"

"*From . . .*" She hesitated, clearing away eidetic debris from the Folded World in her mind. "*From Berlin with Love.*"

"That is a good one."

"Kind of wish he'd called it *From Prussia with Love*, though."

"Oh?" The officer seemed sincerely interested. "Why's that, then?"

"It's just . . . I just think it sounds better."

The officer nodded. "You may be right. But, of course, you

run a bookshop, so you may have an insight into which titles work better."

Lovecraft looked at him suspiciously. "How in hell did you . . . ?"

The officer reached over and held up her bag. "Your ID's in here. We've already checked up on both of you. Which makes us wonder"—he straightened and looked down on them—"exactly what a private investigator and a bookseller are doing in a such a godforsaken place as Attu Island?"

"I really doubt you'd believe us if we told you," said Carter.

"I'm very open-minded. Try me."

Briefly, Carter explained how he'd moonlighted as a security guard at Miskatonic University, had ended up defending the scientists against Jenner, and been invited along nominally as security, but more as an honest broker in arguments that would inevitably break out among a small isolated population for a couple of months. "They needed an administrator, so I put Emily's name forward," he concluded, "and that's all there is to it."

There was a short silence during which it was brought home to them just how silent the marines—if they were marines—were. Carter had also noticed the submachine guns they carried had suppressors mounted on their stubby barrels. He guessed they were probably loaded with subsonic rounds, too. They would be able to kill Lovecraft and him very quietly if they so decided, assuming they didn't just use knives.

The officer crossed his arms. "Is it?"

"Is it what?"

"Really all there is to it? How did you know two of the German contingent belong to Reich intelligence and security? You say I won't believe your story, and then trot one out that is entirely reasonable as far as it goes. And then we have what Miss Lovecraft said as she was being disarmed. Ryan?"

"Sir?" The marine standing by with his gun ready responded without taking his eyes off Carter and Lovecraft.

"Remind us what Miss Lovecraft said while you were relieving her of her weapons."

"Yes, sir. She said, *Don't shoot, don't you fucking shoot, you fucking frog-faced freak*, sir."

Everyone was looking at Lovecraft. "I was upset," she said.

"Upset enough to call him a 'fucking frog-faced freak'? I mean, really, look at him. Marine Ryan is a famous ladies' man in the unit, an Adonis in a beret. 'Fucking frog-faced freak' seems a tad unkind, wouldn't you say? Unless"—the officer had been pacing as he spoke; now he stopped and looked at them—"unless you feared being attacked by something that might reasonably be called a 'fucking frog-faced freak.' There's always that possibility, isn't there? So"—he smiled, not unkindly—"why don't you tell me your little story again and, this time, please make it something I'm less likely to believe."

Lovecraft and Carter looked at one another. "You tell him," she said. "I sound like a lunatic to myself whenever I have to talk about this shit out loud."

Carter sighed. So did he, but she'd bailed on the responsibility first, so he guessed he'd have to be the one who sounded insane. "When we came here, to this beach, and came up this riverbed, we weren't looking for anything human."

"Ah," said the officer. "Seals, perhaps?"

"No," said Carter feeling his temper rise. The guy had all the guns; why did he feel the need to bait his captives, too? "Not seals. Not people either. Something else."

"Deep Ones," said Lovecraft quietly, deciding to weigh in after all. "Things that might have been men, but surely ain't now. I felt that neoprene or whatever your suits are made out of and thought it was like frog skin. That's why I freaked out. Sorry, man," she said to Marine Ryan, "I was kind of upset when I called you that. You're very pretty really."

"Thank you, ma'am," said the marine.

Lovecraft looked at Carter. "He called me 'ma'am.'" She grinned.

"So you thought you'd been ambushed by monsters," said the officer. "That's your story."

Carter shrugged.

"Good," said the officer, "now we're getting somewhere. We call them Fomor or sometimes Fomorians, although in the heat of the moment, that usually gets shortened to Foams, or lengthened to 'fucking frog-faced freaks.'"

Carter and Lovecraft looked at him with open astonishment, as if somebody had just told them the content of a secret dream. He smiled benignly. "Now we're past the horseshit stage of our relationship; why don't you tell me everything you know about them and what you're really doing on this island?"

It was a relief to be able to talk to people other than themselves or Harrelson who could listen to tales of outsider dimensions, cosmic horrors, and alternate time lines. Almost too much of a relief—it was hard to hold stuff back. Yet, by mutual unspoken consent, they somehow managed to keep Martin Harrelson out of it (because even alluding to the existence of a friendly cop from the other side of the Fold seemed like snitching) and Henry Weston (because it felt dangerous to do so). Otherwise, pretty much anything was game.

And through it all, the Royal Marine officer listened. He had their hands freed and gave them cups of hot tea. He apologized to Lovecraft that there was little that could be done about her clothes, but they were well chosen with regard to materials, and if she stayed active walking up and down as she talked ("Between here and there, ma'am, and no farther," Marine Ryan had warned her. "I'd hate to have to shoot you."), her body heat and circulation would do a lot to dry them out.

"And then we came out here because of what Dan saw in the bay and on the beach, you jumped us, and now we're all up to date. So"—Lovecraft looked at the marines—"what now?"

"Thank you, Miss Lovecraft, Mr. Carter. You've been very candid."

Carter stood slowly, working out the kinks in his shoulders. "As Emily said, you've got all the guns."

"Is that the only reason you were so forthcoming?"

Carter looked at the officer. The guy looked like he could bull-rush a small elephant, but his questioning had been smart and his eyes were shrewd. "No," admitted Carter. "It was a relief to talk about it. It's crazy, but it's true."

"Alas, it is both. But this Fold of yours, that's new to us. It might explain a lot. The Third Reich fell on the other side? When?"

"1944. U.S. and U.K. and Commonwealth armies in the west, Russians in the east. Russians got to Berlin first. Hitler chose suicide over capture."

"1945 in the war against Japan," added Lovecraft. "We, that is, the U.S., dropped a couple of atom bombs on mainland cities. They sued for peace after that. The German A-bomb project got nowhere near a working bomb. Still can't understand how they managed it on this side with the Operation Sunset bomb over Moscow."

The officer checked his watch. "You should be getting back. If you're missed, it could cause problems we're not ready to cause just yet. We don't want to compromise you."

Carter and Lovecraft glanced at one another. "You're letting us go?" said Carter.

"Of course. We try to avoid killing civilians, especially ones with whom I think we share common cause. What's on the other side of this Fold of yours sounds vastly preferable to what's going on now. I'll leave you with a couple of thoughts. We've had agents in the ruins of Moscow, not long after the detonation. I'd be surprised if your government didn't, too. The only radiation there is from uranium too far below weapon-grade to have been used to make a bomb. The boffins are pretty sure it's from a casing that was around what did the real damage. And this experiment the Reich is so keen on taking place out here rather than any of the isolated spots they have access to in the corpse of the Soviet

Union? If it has anything to do with zero point energy, than I'm a Dutch uncle. Your Gestapo and Abwehr stooges were and are probably the only ones on the team that don't really understand what this is all about. They're good little Party members and do what they're told."

Lovecraft frowned. "What *is* this all really about?"

"Yeah," Carter said, "and why are you talking about the Nazis like they're not behind it?"

The officer shook his head. "To answer your first question, we don't know. We're here to find out. To answer the second, well . . . the NSDAP got into power by behaving like a virus in the Weimar Republic. Now they don't seem to realize they're infected themselves. Ever hear of Thule?"

"No?" said Carter.

"Oh, shit," said Lovecraft.

"Miss Lovecraft evidently has. You can tell Mr. Carter on the trip back." He turned to the corporal who'd tended Lovecraft's cut brow. "Barnaby, give our new friends the spare radio." As the corporal handed over a compact military field radio, he said, "Encoded and secure. Use the channel it's set to. Use the call sign . . ." He considered for a moment, then caught Lovecraft's eye, smiled, and said, "*Fleming.* Do *not* get caught with it. If the Germans find out about you making contact with us, they will kill you. Have no illusions about that."

"Sorry I didn't do a full job on the cut, ma'am," said Barnaby, "but it would have looked odd if you went back with it fully treated. I used some Dermabond from your own field kit, but you should get it seen to properly when you get back."

"That's okay, and thanks." She grinned and looked at Carter. "I think I could get used to being called 'ma'am.'"

Chapter 26

FANCY SHOOTIN'

"It was knowing about James Bond that did it," said Lovecraft as they walked along the beach toward the waiting Kübelwagen. "We bonded right there. Did you see it? 'Hey, I can't kill this awesome American woman because she's read Ian Fleming.' That's what happened. 'Bonded.' Heh."

Carter was resisting the urge to look back. He wasn't worried about being turned into a pillar of salt nearly so much as antagonizing the sniper he suspected was keeping an eye on them. "If you think that's what it takes to talk a special ops team out of killing a potential threat, you just keep thinking that." He looked sideways at her and found she was smiling to herself. "What are you so happy about, anyway? I mean, I'm glad they didn't just shoot us or drown us in the sea to make it look like an accident or anything, but I'm not seeing much else we should be cheering about."

She looked at him as if he were a loved yet slightly slow cousin. "You don't? Dan, we've got a government behind us. Maybe even our own government could be a go-to if what the guy back there was hinting at is true. We're not alone in this shit. I mean to say, apart from the Nazis and the Japanese and some homegrown lunatics, nobody likes the Unfolded as much as the Folded. Maybe we can get help. Hell, maybe we don't have to lift a finger and crack teams of government agents paid for by our tax dollars will swing into action and fix it for us."

Carter did not smile. "If that's true, why hasn't the Fold been fixed before now?"

"Well, maybe they don't know about the Fold yet. Captain Shoulders back there surely didn't."

"Emily, there are a shitload of things he won't have been told because somebody has decided that intel is above his pay grade. When all's said and done, the guy's just a grunt."

"Don't you talk about Captain Shoulders like that. He has a sexy accent, and looks like a younger Daniel Craig, 'cept with red hair."

"What is it with you and James Bond?"

They arrived at the Kübelwagen and climbed in. The engine started from cold the first time. "We'll stop in a mile and shoot up the cans," said Carter as he guided the car up the creek bed. "While we're getting there, tell me about . . . what was it? Tooley?"

"Thule," said Lovecraft, pronouncing it *too-la*. Her good mood, mainly inspired by not being dead when she had thought her luck had run out, entirely evaporated in the space of those two syllables. "The Thule Society. I'm glad I knew something about these guys before things changed, 'cos I tried researching them when things started getting weird with Nazis back in Arkham, and now there's almost nothing. I read about them a couple of years ago in a magazine article, so don't expect any deep knowledge here."

She took a breath. "Okay. The Thule Society. Y'know in the Indiana Jones movies, the Nazis always seem to be hot to trot after anything occult that can be weaponized? Well, part of that's because of the Thule Society. They were there right from the birth of the Nazi Party because they were all about *völkisch*."

Carter was finessing the car around a gulley, but still found time to say, "What's that?"

"There's no exact translation for it in English. It's kind of to do with folklore and folk memory, but also with racial identity. Thule itself is a place the ancient Greeks came up with on a slow Wednesday, a mythical land in the north. The society ran with it and—"

"Aryans. Race theory?"

"You got it. Hitler embraced all that shit, naturally, but he stayed at arm's length from the society's other big obsession: the occult. That wasn't a problem, though, because Himmler couldn't get enough of that Kool-Aid. Now, on our side of the Fold, the nice side without so many tentacles, the Thule Society was cut loose. Hitler wasn't keen on secret societies and freaky occult ones—after all, the shadows are where conspiracies start—so they were all suppressed in the thirties. Same year the Freemasons got closed down, Himmler formed the Ahnenerbe, a new part of the SS that was all about *völkisch* and the occult and those are the assholes Indy keeps running into in the movies back in the Folded.

"Now the thing is, rumors that the Thule continued underground were common in *our* world. Given the materials they have to play with in the Unfolded World, you got to wonder if they're only rumors. Then our friend in the tight rubber suit says 'Thule' and you start to worry. Maybe they did successfully go underground here because the occult shit they knew actually turned out to work." She looked at her shotgun lying beside her. "Man. It's still got a shell in the chamber. Can we start shooting stuff yet?"

Once almost off the small plain of stone, Carter stopped the car. "Here's as good as anywhere. Let's make this quick."

They took the seven empty institutional cans out of the trunk and arranged them in a row running east to west, while they took up firing positions about twenty yards to the north. Both Lovecraft's guns had ended up in the water during her struggle, but she'd forgotten that the estimable Corporal Barnaby had kindly fieldstripped and dried them, so the shotgun's chamber was empty after all.

"So what was he suggesting?" Carter handed Lovecraft earplugs. "That Thule has become like a real-world version of *Spectre*?"

"We keep coming back to James Bond, don't we?" Lovecraft looked up at the dark bulk of Mount Terrible, its peak wreathed in heavy clouds. The snow could not be far away now. "Then again, secret mountaintop bases, sinister societies, spies from different agencies falling over each other." She looked out toward the bay as she put in the earplugs, out into the deep water where they now knew a submarine lurked. "Ian Fleming used to be with naval intelligence. You know that? I guess there are plenty of parallels. Thing is, Goldfinger was never backed up by aliens." She racked her shotgun, addressed a can at the end of the line a little over twenty yards away, and fired. A can spun away from them, its side perforated by the swarm of pellets hitting it squarely. "Yep," she said, smiling a little smugly as she racked in another shell. "Still got it."

She emptied the remaining five shells into five more cans and then stood aside while she reloaded and Carter took a stance. "Over to you, Deadeye."

Carter stepped into a Weaver stance, reconsidered, and moved into an isosceles.

"You shootin' or dancin', Sheriff?" asked Lovecraft.

He ignored her, centered himself, drew, and rapidly fired seven times until the slide locked back. Only one of the cans was still where they'd placed it before Lovecraft had her turn, and he shot that one first with a single round, then acquired, double tapped, and moved on to hit three of the others where they lay farther away and on their sides.

Lovecraft whistled. "Five hits, I make it. First time you used that gun, pardner?" Carter nodded. "Not too shoddy." She slung the shotgun over her shoulder and drew the Webley. "I guess I should try my luck with this thing. Help me out with the legs, would you?"

Her stance wasn't dissimilar to an isosceles and he guided her into it with a few words and a couple of gentle kicks to the sides of her boots until she was standing properly. "That feels okay," she said. "I can live with this." She fussed over her grip for a moment, but didn't ask for advice on that, so Carter didn't offer any. When she was happy, she raised the weapon in a CAR stance, took a second to steady her breathing, then emptied the gun in a series of steady shots, rarely more than a second apart. Not every bullet struck home, but, where she missed, she stayed on target, revised her aim, and tried again until she had scored a hit. When the slide locked back she lowered the weapon and viewed the cans with dissatisfaction.

"Well, that sucked," she said. "And why does this thing only hold eleven rounds?"

"Don't knock yourself," said Carter. "That wasn't bad. None of the cans are at the same range anymore, and that one that took three shots must have been thirty-five yards away. If you have to shoot anyone, they're much bigger targets."

"Yeah, and they'll be running around and probably shooting back. It's all swings and roundabouts in the wonderful world of gun violence." She holstered the pistol, swung up the shotgun, racked in a round, and gave the can that had escaped the Mossberg's attentions a lead pellet shower. "Okay. Let's tidy up and head back. I need to change out of these clothes."

As they approached the settlement, they saw a party of the German scientists leaving the galley, laughing and joking. Carter slowed the Kübelwagen. One of the scientists noticed them and waved, and he smiled wanly, and waved back.

Lovecraft also waved, saying in an undertone, "If they really are Thule, then they believe I'm *untermensch* with every fiber of their tiny, withered hearts. What kind of fucked-up world is this where the nicest guy out of the bunch of them was Gestapo?"

Carter parked by the garage unit and they got their gear together. "You take the radio they gave us, Dan," said Lovecraft. "All that Secret Squirrel 'Roger Roger' bullshit ain't my speed at all. I need a shower. See you in the galley."

Carter shook his head. "I need to swing by the office first. Got some Secret Squirrel 'Roger Roger' bullshit to attend to. Come by after your shower and we'll go in together."

As they parted by the car, the first flakes of snow began to fall.

"Need to know" was eating Lurline Giehl up. More specifically that her handlers didn't think she did need to know. When she had first been attached to the project, her brief had been simple if mystifying. She was to be the guardian and operator of a highly sensitive energy detector for use in the zero point energy project. The detector was quite capable of doing its job perfectly, but its operating firmware held some carefully concealed trapdoors that allowed anyone who knew they were there to subtly influence the readings. Her job had been to cook the results, and make sure the Americans never found out.

Morally, the task had dismayed her; she was a good scientist and to deliberately falsify results was anathema to her. It was explained to her that no permanent damage to the scientific reputations of either the Reich or herself would be incurred, however. It was simply necessary to progress the experiment to the next stage for political reasons. Then the detector's manufacturer would, in a communication of great professional embarrassment, admit that tests on an identical unit to the project's had revealed an insufficiently shielded component that caused the detector to give false positives. ZPE would be revealed as a mirage, and the Reich would offer Miskatonic University some very nice sops as recompense. No shame would be reflected on any of the scientists. It would simply be one of those things.

When the next stage was announced, Giehl had assumed her work would be done and she would be returned to the Fatherland. Yet here she was, carried along with the project like gum on its heel. She had communicated her dismay at this outcome with her contact before leaving Arkham. She had real work back in Berlin that she should be getting on with. The reply had been perfunctory: she would be going where the Reich needed her to be, not where she wanted to be. The Abwehr required an asset on Attu Island, and so she would be going along to act as its eyes and ears.

It irritated her, not least because she was positive that the whole team was rotten with "assets." Lukas had turned out to be Gestapo, and she doubted he was the only one. She had heard mutterings that the Ahnenerbe was somehow associated with real ZPE research back in Westphalia somewhere. The Ahnenerbe connection worried her; they might have started out delving into folklore and alternative sciences, but these days the name seemed to be muttered darkly in the context of some very cutting-edge technologies. She couldn't quite understand how that could be, and what she didn't understand troubled her.

So, here she was, on a remote and unfriendly island for two months, spying on a project that didn't need spying on and expected to send in regular reports that were as brief and unhappy as the "What I did on my holidays" reports she'd had to fabricate after uncomplicated summer vacations in her youth. They knew what she'd been doing. Most of it was a summer camp with the 'Jugend, and what was left was her own time and she didn't enjoy the teacher's demands for it to be pinned to a lined page like a butterfly.

Then, she'd made things up, but she didn't feel she could play games like that with her unseen Abwehr handlers. They had shown an interest in Dan Carter and that was fine, because so had she. That hadn't turned out so well. She was relieved that he had seemed more embarrassed about it than her, as it allowed her to withdraw from the battlefield with some arch dignity in place. Now she just kept an eye on him and the black woman he had seen fit to bring along. They seemed very familiar with one another. More than once Giehl theorized that they were probably intimate, too, although there had been no overt signs of affection greater than friendship between them. There had been a few ribald comments mainly among the Americans when Carter and the black woman had gone off to "practice shooting," but then they had come back with empty brass and cartridges and several shot and bullet-riddled cans. She had seen them herself. The black woman also had a mild head injury and had seemingly fallen in a stream. The innuendo had died down after that. Now a faint sense of disgust that a fine man like Carter might amuse himself by fucking a black had been replaced with a concern that the weapons were not just for show.

This would have to be the meat of her next report with regard to them. Probably nothing the Abwehr didn't already know, but hers was not to reason why. She would simply report what she saw.

She left her room and was walking down the corridor to the galley when she heard the black woman's voice. Giehl paused and looked out of the edge of one of the high windows in the outer wall. There they were, Carter and the black, apparently walking back from their office. Giehl saw the bandage on the black's brow, its whiteness thrown into sharp relief against her skin making it plainly visible even in the dying light, and he saw that their faces were serious. Their voices were muffled, though, and the high windows did not open easily or quietly. She shadowed them with the wall between them as they approached the external door—they were surely going to the galley, too—and stepped into the open door to the currently empty rec room next to it as they entered.

They were wrapping up a conversation that it seemed to

Giehl they didn't wish to hold in public, and she heard just the end of the closing sentence from the black woman. It held a word she did not know, but she memorized it on the chance it held significance. Then they started talking about what they were going to eat and, a moment later, after they shucked the ubiquitous parkas, Giehl lost their voices entirely as they went into the galley.

She counted to ten, and then followed them in.

Chapter 27

COLD BLOOD

Dr. Giehl had booked her Internet usage for the late evening. Attu base didn't stretch to Wi-Fi except for LAN messaging and file access, so everyone had to sit in a small office and use the machine there if they wanted to use the Internet. It had been done that way deliberately as a way of policing usage and, while it made sense, nobody liked it.

As a courtesy, the door was shut while somebody was using it and a door hanger reading *Occupied* was fashioned. This had been altered—probably by the same genius who came up with the *Sheriff's Office* sign—within hours to read *Looking at Porn*.

Before Giehl logged in, she stuck a thumb drive into a SDS port and waited while it scanned the setup for keyboard loggers and other potential security risks. She waited a little anxiously while it completed its scan, checking her watch and

glancing at the door repeatedly. This all felt so ridiculous, yet the sort of ridiculous that it turned out came with a body count. She hadn't liked Lukas much, but when that Polish madman shot him down like a dog, her slightly blasé attitude toward her intelligence work had been shattered. The only one she felt she could even half-trust on the base was Carter, and he was a foreigner. She felt foolish about the whole business aboard the RV *Frederick Cook*. She'd gone to him, full of self-confidence and more schnapps than she was used to, fancying herself as some sort of Mata Hari, and then he'd turned out to be essentially unconscious throughout the whole encounter. She felt sure he'd told the black. They were as thick as thieves, those two. Giehl wasn't sure if they were a couple, exactly. She hoped not. The thought of him lying with an atavism like the Lovecraft woman made her gorge rise.

A pop-up appeared on the screen to tell her the machine was secure. She launched the Triole client. She quickly selected the only address on the program's list and then typed in a request for connection. She wasn't sure exactly what this stage did, but she presumed it would get her from a secretarial desk to the computer screen of somebody who mattered at Abwehr headquarters.

The message "Please wait" appeared on the message screen. Giehl did so, because she had no choice, but the two minutes she had to wait crawled by. Finally a new response appeared. "Go ahead Tamfana."

Giehl had been unfamiliar with the name "Tamfana" when it was assigned to her, and she had looked it up while still in Germany. It transpired that it was a goddess about whom very little was known, which suited her. Indeed, there was the possibility that it was not a goddess at all, but a misunderstanding of a phrase from Tacitus; it might just as easily be a temple or a place. She felt childishly pleased with the code name for a few days, until she fell to wondering how many others had borne it before her, given the predilection of the Reich to recycle Nordic code names as they became free. *What happened to the previous Tamfanas?* she wondered. *Were they even still alive?*

She typed in, "Stage 3 Seidr confirmed. Project proceeding ahead of schedule. Anticipate operational"—she checked her watch and worked out shift patterns—"in 30 hours."

It wasn't much of a report, but she was obliged to make one. She waited. She was just wondering if her connection had failed when a reply appeared.

"Thank you. Report when implementation imminent. Status subjects 434 & 435?"

Giehl blew out an unhappy exhalation. She felt foolish for ever mentioning Lovecraft to her controllers. "Carrying out assigned tasks. Nothing unusual to report." Of course, she was in the dome up to twelve or sixteen hours some days, and now that the weather had closed in, it was useless as a vantage point. Not that being able to see the encampment in the distance was very helpful, even on a clear day. She'd only heard about their shooting expedition after the fact, but had seen the bullet-and-shot-riddled institutional cans in the recyclables containment herself when she was dumping some drinks cans in there.

She racked her memory for something else to report. A small thing leapt to mind, the thing she'd heard Carter mutter to Lovecraft in the galley when they thought they were alone.

"Please advise. Meaning of FOMORIAN."

Over five thousand miles away as measured through the Arctic Circle and across the frozen northern seas, the request appeared on the screen of Director Mühlan in Wewelsburg. If he had been able to see him, Carter would have recognized him as the man in a suit from his dream. He quickly read the line of text, but when his gaze swept across the capitalized word, his eyes widened. "*Verflucht*," he said aloud. His secretary Irmgard looked over in surprise; the director *never* showed anger. "*Verfluchte Scheiße!*"

He started to type furiously in response.

* * *

Dr. Giehl watched in astonishment as the Triole chat box started to fill with new demands for clarification. She answered what she could and promised to try and find out the rest. It had been subjects 434 and 435 who had been talking. No, she hadn't overheard any more. She had only reported it because she didn't know what they meant and wondered if it might be important. After the demands came new directives and orders. One in particular stood out. Giehl muttered *"What?"* with growing horror. They couldn't be serious. She typed back for confirmation.

"Confirmation. Stage 4 Seidr must be attained as soon as possible. American interference must not be tolerated. Speak privately with Dr. Weber. Tell him this exact phrase: 'Case Rosweisse is in effect. Contact immediately.' Obey Dr. Weber in all matters subsequently. Confirm your understanding."

Giehl stared at the screen, unable to bring herself to touch the keyboard. She had long been aware that she was a very small piece in a very large game, but she'd never been given the slightest idea that Weber was Abwehr too. Now to find out he was apparently a senior agent to her . . . her pride was hurt, but she was also afraid. Just what did they mean by "American interference must not be tolerated"? They were on American territory; the Abwehr command could not seriously be intending for them to assault Americans on their own land? That was tantamount to a declaration of war.

A new message appeared. "Confirm your understanding."

With as much reluctance as if she were signing her own death warrant, Dr. Giehl typed, "I understand."

Lovecraft was awoken by her phone buzzing. This didn't happen too often on Attu, and it was the first time it had happened at night. It meant that she'd received a text on the island's intranet, but she knew she wasn't on many people's fast dials. She checked and found, not surprising her in the slightest, it was from Carter.

"Come to the sheriff's office asap. Be QUIET," it said, intriguingly though uninformatively.

That meant going outside. Lovecraft lifted the corner of the blind over her bed and looked out of the window. What she could see in the site's external lights looked very white, and there were flakes streaming across the nimbus around them. The snow had finally arrived and settled in with a vengeance, slowly cocooning the land and the man-made structures upon it. Lovecraft muttered dark imprecations on the head of whoever thought it was okay not to have all the living units joined as she quickly dressed and pulled on her light boots rather than the heavy ones she used if she was going to be out in the cold for more than a few minutes.

Remembering to be quiet, but not enjoying the brief period of pretending to be a bargain-basement ninja that it entailed, she made her way to the office.

There she found the shutter down over the window and reminded herself that she did the same in her room; the last thing she needed was a snowdrift smashing its way through the window, as she'd been told could happen if it fell deeply enough. She knocked gently on the door, it sounding even gentler than intended due to her gloves, and she opened the door a crack, largely out of paranoia. Reassured by the sight of Carter behind the desk—he looked up and gestured her in urgently when he saw her—she entered and stamped snow off her boots.

"Holy Jesus, it is storming out there," she said, pulling her gloves off. "If it keeps up, the units're going to get buried."

Carter ignored the weather report. "Need your eyes on this, Emily. You said you can read German, right?"

"Yeah. Decent conversational, I'd guess you'd call it." She frowned. "So?"

"I need you to look at this." He got up and left the chair out for her. "I've got an English/German dictionary here, if you need help."

Still frowning, she sat and turned her attention to the screen. She seemed to be looking at a transcript in German. "What am I looking at here?"

"I've got a feed to the offsite computer in the comms office. The one we get Internet time on."

"You're kidding me!" She looked up at him. "I didn't have you down as some sort of hacker."

"You're right not to. I'm a PI. Occasionally we buy spy shit. When I heard about the communication setup, I went and talked to a guy I know. He set me up with a hardwired tap. I installed it the first night we were here. All it is is a little gizmo that goes between the monitor plug and socket in the back of the machine. I poked a hole through the wall with a screwdriver, fed the wire through, then closed the hole with sealant. The gap between the units is pretty narrow, so nobody goes down there, and there's a bundle of cables running along it anyway. Now it's all covered in snow, which is good. Other end of the wire comes in here, where I've got an external hard drive set up to take a snapshot of what's on the screen. Nice thing about doing it this way is it's undetectable with malware scanners. They assume somebody is remotely hacking in with root kits or whatever. They don't sniff a physical tap like this." He saw her expression. "No, I haven't been monitoring everyone. Just Lurline Giehl and Hans Weber."

"Wow. This is some heavy-grade intrusion of privacy you've got going on here."

"Yeah, yeah, life's a riot with Spy vs. Spy. Thing is, Giehl uses some kind of chat app that I'm damn sure isn't installed on that machine. She must be running it off a thumb drive. She starts talking to somebody in German. No greetings, no 'Hi, how are you's,' just straight into it. And look what she says."

Lovecraft looked at where Carter was pointing. FOMORIAN. "Well," she said. "Now ain't that a coincidence?"

"Can you translate the rest?"

She glanced up and down the text. "Oh, yeah. This shouldn't

take too long." She pushed the keyboard back and took up a notepad and pen. "Meantime, make yourself useful and get me a coffee."

Nor was she exaggerating. In less than ten minutes she'd sketched out a working translation and showed it to Carter.

"Okay," he said as he read it through for the second time, "so mainly bad news with maybe a little good news."

"Yeah? Maybe it was added in translation, because the only news I saw in that was maybe we should have kept our yaps shut on the corridors even when we thought we were alone. Kind of late for that, but whatever."

"Doc Giehl. Look at what she says. She's all business until they get excited about us saying 'Fomorian.' Then she gets real evasive and tries to talk it down. Her bosses at the Abwehr won't have it, but she tries. The stuff about American interference is what really rattles her. Then there's when her boss tells her to alert Doc Weber. If our information's right, he's probably Thule, but she doesn't know that. She probably thinks he's Abwehr, too, but now she's wondering why she wasn't told that."

"There's such a thing as 'plausible deniability,' Dan. Very popular with the spy crowd, I believe."

"Why have multiple intelligence stooges in a single team? It's bad enough there was a Gestapo simp she didn't know about, now there's somebody attached to the same agency and she wasn't told? Doc Giehl's not an idiot, but they're trying to play her for one. Look at what she says here and here." Carter pointed at lines close to the end of the conversation. "She's backpedaling from her earlier questions. Yes, sir, no, sir, three bags of bullshit, sir." Carter looked at Lovecraft. "She's frightened. I think she's finally caught on that her bosses' loyalties might not be to the Fatherland. Or at least not the same Fatherland."

Lovecraft turned the office chair to face him, and looked up at him with her arms crossed and her expression unimpressed. "Please tell me you're not thinking of trying to recruit Eva Braun to the Scooby Gang."

"We don't have many friends we can rely on out here."

"We got a submarine full of buff guys with sexy accents. We don't need the Ice Queen."

Carter made a backward nod in the direction of Temnac Bay. "They're all the way out there. We could do with friends right here. We can't even depend on the American contingent. By the time we can convince them things aren't how they seem, it could be way too late."

Bowles had been unable to sleep. He was a city boy at heart, and while it had been hard work to adapt to all the changes in environment that the project had imposed upon him since they had left Arkham, he had managed to accept them and get his head down after a hard day's work easily enough. Tonight, however, felt different. It took him a while to realize it was the snow that was doing it, it was the snow that was eating the sound of the sea and making the island as silent as a deep cellar. He tossed and turned, tried reading for a while, and considered quiet masturbation, but the deadness of the night but for the occasional clicks and shudders that ran through the units depressed and distracted him, so instead he decided to go and fix the transfer switch on the reserve generator. There'd been an outage in the late afternoon, and the standby had failed to start automatically. Irritating, but not the end of the world. He'd promised everyone he'd check on the problem in the morning after he fixed whatever the problem with the main generator had been. That turned out to be the first thing he'd checked for—a loose connection on the battery—and once the main was running again, fixing the standby dropped off everyone's radar but his. As he couldn't sleep, maybe an hour fussing with a transfer switch in a cold maintenance shack would make his bed feel more welcoming.

He was just coming to the conclusion that the switch was a piece of shit and they might have to order a new one, or maybe a whole replacement generator if loose switches weren't to be had, when he heard low voices outside the shack.

It never for one moment occurred to Nick Bowles to lay low. Why should he? He was on an isolated island, he knew everyone else there, and everyone knew him. He considered himself a nice guy, and that was not an unreasonable supposition. Most would have agreed. There was nobody on the island who did not at least think Bowles was okay. He did not have a single enemy there.

He opened the shack door and found what looked like the entire German contingent of the project climbing into the four Kübelwagens parked under the covered carport, the fifth being up at the dome. As he watched, three of them moved off in convoy, heading for the mountain road. He checked his watch; 2:00 a.m. local time. They had to be crazy to go up in the dark with visibility down to maybe five yards at most. He ran to the last car, seeing Dr. Weber just loading some gear in the trunk. He couldn't see who was waiting at the wheel, but—as he approached—he caught a glimpse of Dr. Giehl in the backseat. She didn't look happy at all, he thought. She looked almost like somebody who'd just had really bad news. Bowles wondered if something had gone wrong at the dome and the experiment might be a washout. He hoped not. ZPE was going to change the world for the better. How could it do anything else?

Problems up at the dome or not, however, there were protocols in place that had to be observed.

"Doctor!" he called, dogtrotting through the driving snow. "Dr. Weber! Sir!"

The doctor turned to see him. Bowles noticed that the man slouched, sagging at the shoulders, almost as if he was disappointed to see him.

"Nick," said the doctor, "you should get indoors. The weather's getting worse."

Bowles hesitated. He hadn't even known Dr. Weber knew his first name, much less that he was prepared to call him by it. "Look, Doc, I'm sorry to be a pain in the ass, but you can't take the last car. One always has to be at the station in case of emergency."

"There's been an emergency." The doctor said it without conviction, like a man reciting a line from a first read through of a play he didn't want to be in. "We have to get up there as soon as we can."

"I have a paramedic certification—"

"No. Please, no, Nick, it's not that kind of emergency. I do not have time to explain. Please go indoors."

Weber was lying to him, but Bowles couldn't understand why. He had a feeling that whatever was going on was above his pay grade, and that he should hand it off. "Look, I'm going to have to talk to Doc Malcolm about this."

"Dr. Malcolm is up at the dome," said Weber. He seemed tired, almost depressed. "Everything is in order. Go back to bed, Nick. It is a full day tomorrow."

"I can't sign off on this, Doctor, I'm sorry. If Dr. Malcolm's up there, I'll have to talk to Dr. Lo about it."

Weber looked him in the face, then sighed and shook his head. He said something under his breath in German that Bowles was pretty sure was an apology, although he didn't know what for. Weber looked over at the secondary entrance. "Here is the doctor now."

Bowles looked over, but no one was there, least of all Dr. Lo. The door was secure, the station silent. His lips were just starting to form the word, "Where?" when Weber shot him through the back of the head. The snow ate the sound of the pistol as Bowles pitched face-first into the snow.

Weber shook his head. "Why couldn't you just go in when I asked you?" He turned at the sound of one of the Kübelwagen doors opening. Dr. Giehl looked at the corpse with a strange, empty look, the expression of one who is watching an unsought inevitability.

"You cannot leave him there," she said simply.

Weber was standing, looking at the pistol in the palm of his gloved hand. It had forced him across a Rubicon he thought was still a little way away. He took a deep breath and put it back in his parka pocket. "We must catch up with the others," he said with new steel in his voice. He pushed Giehl back into the car and sat alongside her. The fourth Kübelwagen drew out from the parking area and followed the tracks of its predecessors into the white-and-black night.

Chapter 28

RED AND WHITE

They'd concluded there was little else they could do that night and so Lovecraft left the office to go to bed while Carter closed down the computer and put out the lights. He'd hardly begun when Lovecraft came back in, agitated and urgent.

"Nick Bowles! He's dead!"

Carter's first thought was there had been an accident, but Lovecraft closed the door behind her and pointed at the arms locker. "I need the Mossberg."

"What?"

"He was shot. He's out by the motor pool facedown with a hole in the back of his parka hood, getting buried by snow right by the lights. Thought he'd fallen or something, lifted his hood, that's when I saw the hole in his head and then the one in the hood. I thought we were supposed to be the only armed ones on the island?"

"We are." Carter didn't hesitate as he turned to the locker with his keys, opened it, and passed it over to Lovecraft. He looked at the locker's other contents, then pulled out spare magazines for their handguns and a cartridge bandoleer for Lovecraft. She accepted it with evident surprise.

"Oh, God. Really? We going to war or something?"

"I think the war's come to us, Emily."

Lovecraft led him out into the night, the snow coming in harshly angled from the north. Drifts were already becoming deep. Her tracks in the snow, visible in the harsh, oblique lighting of the external lights, were still plain, though; the clear, steady footprints out, and the blurred footprints back, marked by plumes of loose snow thrown by her running feet.

Bowles lay where Lovecraft had found him. Carter didn't spend much time checking the body; Lovecraft had already told him all that was immediate and necessary. Instead, he looked around him. He could see Bowles's footprints, still visible but growing softer by the second. He could see them leave from the maintenance shack toward the motor pool, and its sheltered port. Many people had come from the site's primary and secondary entrances. When he looked closely at the footprints, none of them were toward the doors.

"They've taken all the cars," he said finally, reasonably sure he had worked out the series of events.

"Who have? The Germans or the Brits? This is a Thule thing, right?"

"Yeah. I think Giehl telling her handlers about Fomorians has really poked a hornet's nest."

Lovecraft thought through the ramifications. "So, they figure us for British agents, or American agents working with the British. Nah, must be British agents. U.K. is a pariah state in the Unfolded. OSS wouldn't work with them. If they figure us for, like, MI6, why didn't they come after us?"

Carter had been searching on the ground based on where the tracks stopped. He suddenly knelt and picked something out of the snow—a shell casing. "I think this is pretty much all the evidence we can expect to find here. Help me get Nick into the shack. Take his feet."

It wasn't a task Lovecraft savored, and she was glad Bowles's head lolled back as they carried him so she didn't have to look at his face. As they carried him out of the storm into the shack, the door of which still stood open as Bowles had left it, Carter said, "They're scientists first, evil occultist fuckers second. Whoever shot Nick could just as easily have done it to his face, but it looks like he was suckered into looking away. The shooter didn't *want* to see his face. That doesn't sound like a cold, clinical killer to me. Same goes for us. They didn't want a shooting match, so they just took all the damn cars and left us stranded. I guess they were kind of hoping we wouldn't even notice all this had gone down until morning, by which time I'm guessing it'll be too late."

They laid Bowles down across some pallets and Carter found an opaque blue plastic tarp to put over him.

Lovecraft watched him as she fidgeted with the bandoleer, trying to make it rest more easily across her shoulder. "They've gone up to the dome to do whatever it is they're planning on doing, but what the fuck is that, Dan? The Brits didn't know either."

Carter shrugged. "Weird science, and it must be something major if they're prepared to burn their bridges with the U.S. like this. I'll tell you something—I'm really wondering if the dome ever *was* just an early-warning station. Locations are so important with the occult stuff. Maybe they found something up there and studied it for a while, but they didn't get anywhere, so the DoD or whoever was paying for it pulled its funding. It fell off everyone's radar, so when the Germans said, 'Hey, this place is ideal,' the State Department said, 'Yeah, whatever,' and didn't even tell the DoD because the place had been derestricted years ago."

"We going to stop them, right? We got guns, we're badasses,

we're going to go up there and kick Thule butt. That's the plan, yeah?"

Carter nodded reluctantly. "It's why Weston went to so much trouble to put us out here. It must be. I don't like being his puppet in all this, but I got to admit, I feel motivated to get involved. Maybe now that we know he's a player, next time he'll just ask instead of fucking us around like this."

"'Next time.' Ha. Love your optimism. Okay, first things first. Call the cavalry. The Brits might be able to get up the mountain faster than us, and God knows they're better suited for this kind of bullshit. Then . . . I guess we start walking . . ."

As she spoke, her voice slowed. She was looking at the crate that had been covered with the blue sheet Carter had used as a makeshift shroud. "Son of a bitch. Remember when Nick was talking about 'solutions' to the snow for getting up and down the mountain? I figured he just meant chains or spikes or something. This is a Ski-Doo."

Carter fetched a pry bar and lifted the lid. Inside was a ski-mobile in packing material, fresh from the factory. It was also in pieces. "Nick was the mechanic, Emily. I'm pretty handy with engines, but I can't put this thing together quickly."

She looked at him as if he were an idiot. "Duh," she said, tapping his forehead. "We've got a camp full of scientists and engineers here. At least one of them is going to be able to get it up and running pretty quickly. You go and call Captain Shoulders. I'm going to kick some doors and do some recruiting."

The arrival of all the Reich scientists at the dome was a huge surprise to the night shift as they worked on finalizing the installation of the experiment's systems, even to the German scientists who were on the shift.

Dr. Malcolm looked in astonishment as the inner door opened and a gaggle of eight scientists led by Dr. Weber entered, shaking snow from their parkas.

"Hans?" said Malcolm. It was four in the morning. He and

the three with him were there because they wanted to be. They called themselves the "night shift," but there was actually no real shift system in place; they just wanted the project to be under way as soon as possible and were prepared to work long hours to do so. After all, it wasn't as if there was much else to do on Attu. They had gotten used to working through the nights and the one thing every such night had in common was that nothing unexpected happened. Usually they would drive back down about now and sleep for seven hours, but the snow had made that unsafe, so they planned to work a little longer, and then nap on the cots set up in the dome's rear, before driving back down when the sun came up. This had been the only break in their routine for the last six days, and now here were a bunch of men and women stamping the snow off their boots, and wearing expressions that ranged from determined to ashamed.

"Hans? What's going on here?"

"I'm sorry, Ian," said Dr. Weber, stepping forward. "There has been a change of plans. Would you, Hamer, and Cortez please leave? I am sorry, but you may not take a vehicle. You will have to walk back to the camp."

"What?" Malcolm could not find anything more intelligent to say for a moment. As he was trying to think of something, the one German member of the night shift walked by him to join her compatriots. "Gabi? What the hell is going on here?"

Weber spoke again. "I am truly sorry, Peter, but I must insist you leave immediately."

"Walk down the mountain? It's a blizzard out there!"

"No. It is snowing quite heavily, but I would not call it a blizzard at this stage. It may worsen, however, so you should go now before it does."

"I'm not going anywhere without an explanation! What's gotten into you?"

Weber looked like a man who had inspected his remaining store of fucks to give, and found it empty. He reached into the pocket of his parka and withdrew a handgun. He aimed it squarely at Malcolm and said, "I will not ask again, Doctor. You, Hamer, Cortez . . . leave *now*." Still Malcolm hesitated, but this time in shock. "I respect you, Ian. You have a fine mind, and it has been a pleasure and an honor to work with you. So, I shall tell you this much. I am sorry to inform you that the ZPE rig at Miskatonic University never worked. With the help of Dr. Giehl here, the results were falsified. We needed to be here. Specifically"—he nodded at the tall steel column dominating the center of the dome—"*that* needed to be here. We are conducting a scientific project, but not one to which you are privy. That is all I wish to tell you, and all that I have time to tell you. Go now or I shall kill all three of you."

It all still seemed too incredible. Malcolm was a great believer in the international brother-and sisterhood of science, that scientists were above political considerations, that scientists looked out for scientists. "You wouldn't," he said, and he believed it.

"He would, Ian." Lurline Giehl spoke up, her voice colorless, her expression defeated. "He would."

Dr. Malcolm looked at her, and suddenly he believed her instead. "Come on," he said to Cortez and Hamer, "he means it."

The Germans stood aside from the entrance as the Americans walked cautiously past them. As they came closer, they saw more of the Germans draw weapons.

"Kurt," Weber said to one of his junior colleagues in English for the benefit of the Americans, one who seemed to like handling a gun far too much, "accompany them out and see that they start walking down. If they refuse to go, or try to take an auto, shoot them."

"*Jawohl!*" replied Kurt. It was a small mercy that he didn't attempt to click his heels, but Weber winced all the same. Gesturing with his gun like a movie gangster, Kurt herded the Americans out.

Weber caught Giehl staring at Kurt's disappearing back with sullen loathing. "He wasn't my choice for the job, Lurline. The son of somebody with influence at Wewelsburg. Politics, even in

a matter such as this. It makes one's heart sink." She looked suddenly at him, her eyes widening. He smiled gently. "Yes. I'm afraid your orders haven't been coming from the Abwehr for some time."

Chapter 29

GOING HOT

Dr. Jessica Lo, tenured professor of high-energy physics at Miskatonic University, was finding much new to get used to in the current project. Firstly, that their partners from the Reich seemed to be so far ahead in the very esoteric field of zero point energy, so far ahead that they were close to unlocking it. The project at MU had been a very definite wake-up call for her and her colleagues, as the Germans unveiled new principles almost daily in the early part of it, while seeming amused in a patronizingly indulgent way that these were wonders to their American colleagues.

Now it seemed that ZPE was within their grasp, but to close their fingers around it meant shifting the entire project to—as he heard one of the technicians call it—"America's last ass hair." She wasn't keen on Attu, but the project was too glorious and potentially world changing to walk away from simply on the basis of a couple of months' discomfort. They seemed on the verge of securing a truly miraculous new source of clean energy. The American contingent's head, Dr. Malcolm, had coined the phrase "God's own Duracell," which Lo found fatuous, yet an undeniably striking image.

Still, there were the thousand day-to-day irritations to contend with. She hadn't expected simply getting to and from the experimental facility to be so time-consuming and, indeed, terrifying. She did not enjoy ascending and descending Mount Terrible in the slightest, and would generally spend her time during such journeys with her lips tightly set and her hands clasped in her lap, except for the moments when she would reflexively check her seat belt was secure. The food was, so far, acceptable, but she was very aware that soon their fresh supplies would be exhausted and everything would be coming out of the freezers and cans, or reconstituted from powders. The day that happened, and it could not be far away, she regarded with dread.

Even her ornithological ambitions had been thwarted by an inexplicable lack of birds. They just seemed to hate the eastern end of the island, and she didn't have time to get over to the west. Besides, after the horror story Dan Carter had told at dinner about how difficult it was to drive across the island once you were off the roads, she was beginning to think she wasn't that keen to go there after all, even if she had time.

Still, if there was one thing she really liked about Attu, it was the silence. She couldn't remember when she had last slept so well.

Thus, she was in deep sleep when somebody started pounding on her door and demanding she get right the fuck up *now*.

She opened the door, bleary and truly not even half-awake. She found the island's "deputy," Miss Lovecraft, standing fully dressed out in the corridor. "Get your shit together, Doctor," she said, showing—thought Lo in a slightly detached way—poor protocol. Then, remarkably, Lovecraft added, "You ever rebuilt an engine?"

Lo was now fairly confident that she was still asleep. She had never been asked that question in her life before, and it sounded like the sort of thing an unconscious mind might hash together to put in somebody's mouth. Still, she decided to play along; this dream sounded interesting.

"No," she said, slowly, "I've never rebuilt an engine. Why do you ask?"

"Because we need somebody with car-mechanic-type skills and we need them now."

"Have you asked Nick Bowles? He seems very *au fait* with—"

"Nick's dead. The Germans killed him. They've taken all the cars and we have to build a Ski-Doo fast if we're going to stand any chance of stopping them from doing whatever it is they're planning on doing up at the dome."

Ah, thought Lo, *clearly an anxiety dream based on my misgivings about the Reich contingent.* "Dr. Malcolm is up at the dome, I would expect. He won't let them."

Miss Lovecraft frowned at him. "Malcolm's likely dead by now. Didn't you hear me? I said they killed Nick Bowles. They shot him through the back of the head." Her eyes narrowed. "Shit. You think you're dreaming."

She slapped Lo with resounding force, snapping her head to one side. Lo looked at her in total astonishment, her hand on the reddening cheek.

"Get with the program, Doc. Nick's dead, Malcolm and the other Americans at the dome are probably dead, the Nazis are on the point of butt-fucking the whole human race with something truly esoteric and I need you to fucking *focus.* Do I have your attention?"

Lo blinked, the realization that maybe this entertaining dream was not such a dream after all becoming a full conviction. "The . . . we don't use the 'N' word," she said distractedly.

Lovecraft's expression of disgust was a thing to behold. "Oh, fuck you." She turned at the sound of another door opening, and Lo noticed for the first time that she had a viciously functional shotgun slung over her shoulder, the kind used for killing people, not game. Full consciousness came quickly on a wave of adrenaline and fear as she finally processed Lovecraft's words.

"You!" Lovecraft shouted down the corridor at one of the techs leaning out of his door in his skivvies to find out what the raised voices were about. "If you had a Ski-Doo in pieces, could you rebuild it quickly?"

The question caught him by surprise. "I . . . Well, I guess so."

"I could." Lovecraft looked the other way to see one of the postgraduate assistants pulling on a shirt as he spoke. "I used to work at my dad's garage in the summer. I reckon I could do it. What's wrong with Nick? Why can't he do it?"

"Nick's dead. You two get dressed ASAP and come with me to the vehicle shack." She turned to Lo. "Get everyone else up. Whatever those *Nazis* are doing up at the dome might kill everyone on the island. Everyone deserves to be awake for doomsday."

Lo was finding her center again. Under the circumstances, she was prepared to forgive Lovecraft for the slap. "If that's true, waking everyone might be an unkindness. Some might prefer to die asleep."

"Yeah, well, no. If I'm going to die with my boots on, ain't nobody going to sleep through it."

It was near miraculous. Carter took the radio from where he'd hidden it behind a panel in the "sheriff's office," switched it on, said, "This is Fleming. Come in, please," and immediately— *immediately*, as if waiting on cue—a voice replied, "Reading you, Fleming. Please go ahead."

The promptness of the reply caught Carter off guard. "Uh. Yeah. I . . . uh. Hi."

"Hello," said the voice on the radio.

"Sorry. There's a lot going on here. The Germans are doing something. They killed one of us . . . one of the Americans, and they've gone up to the dome. I don't know what they're doing, but they're doing it now."

"Please stay on the channel."

"Sure," said Carter, although he was pretty sure the radio operator at the other end had already gone. Almost two minutes passed, and then a familiar voice came onto the channel, the marine officer.

"Mr. Carter? Could you repeat to me what you told our CIS just now?"

Carter did so, adding, "They've taken all the cars, and it's a long walk up the mountain even in clear weather. We're trying to uncrate and construct a Ski-Doo to go after them, but, even then, it'll just be Emily and me. We know they have at least one gun—it's hard to believe they didn't smuggle in more."

There was a pause of several seconds. Then the channel re-opened with a new voice. "Mr. Carter? My name is Trescothick, I'm the captain of HMS *Alacrity*. Lieutenant Green and his party will be going ashore to assault the dome if need be, but it will be some time before they can reach it. We need eyes on the site as soon as is humanly possible. Would you go up there and reconnoiter for us?"

"You don't want us to engage?"

"Christ, no. It's bad enough we're sending foreign nationals to stick their necks out like this without asking you to get yourselves shot. No, just get up there and try to find out what they're doing."

"Captain, there's only one way into that dome. We can't get in unseen."

"Do what you can. Nobody is asking you to be a hero. At least, not the suicidal kind of hero."

Carter hesitated, thinking, then said, "The generators are outside the dome. Maybe we can wreck them and get clear before they come out to find out what the problem is."

"That would help, certainly, but don't get yourself shot over this."

"Captain, both Emily Lovecraft and I know how to handle guns. I'm an ex-cop."

"And Miss Lovecraft?"

"She trained as a librarian, and she terrifies me. We'll be fine. It's the Nazis who need to look out."

Carter joined Lovecraft in the maintenance shack where she was standing over Garner, one of the postgrad assistants, and Kelly, a tech, as they put the Ski-Doo together.

"How's it going?" he asked her.

"Fast. These boys know what they're doing." She raised her voice, "Do you have an ETA for when it's going to be ready to go?"

"Everything's here," said Garner. "Just a question of putting it all together. We *might* be done in twenty, thirty minutes."

"There's no guarantee she'll fire first time, though," added Kelly. "The battery's charging now, but she still might need a jump."

"Do the best you can, guys. Nobody's expecting miracles." She started to turn away, but leaned back to add, "Though a miracle'd be cool."

Carter stepped away and she followed him, asking in a low voice, "The British are coming?"

"Yep, but it won't be quick. Getting marines ashore from a sub must be a pretty tricky operation, when you think about it." He took a deep breath. "They want us to go up the mountain and scout it out for them."

Lovecraft took it philosophically. "We were going up there anyway. Hope they're not expecting us to go Rambo for them. We could always fuck up the generator, I guess."

"That's what I said. We'd have to run straight away, though. The Thule people will come boiling out of there if the power's interrupted and a firefight would be difficult."

"Would it?" Lovecraft looked at him with raised eyebrows. "There's one way out, and they're not soldiers. We could keep them bottled up, I reckon."

"Maybe so, but that counts as putting ourselves well into harm's way, and the sub's captain wasn't keen on that."

Lovecraft looked at the blue plastic sheet over Nick Bowles's body. "I liked Nick. I don't mind getting into harm's way if it gets him a little payback."

"What happened to not going Rambo?"

"I won't risk my neck for the Brits, but this ain't for the Brits."

Garner's estimate proved to be reasonable. Nineteen minutes later, he and Kelly were fueling the Ski-Doo. In the interim, Dr. Lo had been out to talk to Carter and Lovecraft, and to look at Bowles's corpse. Lo was famously even-tempered, but her face darkened as she looked at the dead man's face. She lowered the eyelids in a gesture from a thousand films and TV series, but then looked at her fingertips. Carter knew what she was thinking from personal experience; on a living body, it would be an intimate gesture, but with a corpse, it was simply lowering a couple of covers on a permanently broken machine. "A man, a good man, reduced to meat," Lo said. Then, addressing Carter, she asked, "Do you know who did it?"

Carter shook his head. "No. One of the Germans for certain, but there's no way to tell which."

Lo nodded, and drew the sheet back over Bowles's face. "If it comes to it, Daniel, Emily, give them the same chance they gave Nick."

There was an uncomfortable moment, which Lovecraft broke by asking, "Have you called this in yet, Doctor?"

Lo shook her head. "The satellite communicator has gone. We're marooned until Miskatonic starts to wonder why we don't get in touch tomorrow. They'll give it a day, assuming it's a temporary fault, and then they'll raise the alarm. Even if there's an aircraft available at Adak Island, it won't show up for thirty hours at the earliest. If the snow doesn't let up, God knows how it will land."

They were interrupted by the spluttering cough of the Ski-Doo's engine. It turned over a few times and died. Garner and Kelly, however, were ecstatic.

"D'ya hear that?" said Kelly as he finessed the air screw.

"Damn near first time! Damn near." He got clear and said to Garner, "Try her again."

Garner turned the key to the On position, and then, at a nod from Kelly, twisted it to run the starter. The engine roared, stumbled a little, but then picked up.

Kelly stood, grinning. "She's a new engine. We did the best we could with her, but try to be as gentle as you can."

"We can't really do that, man," said Carter, "we need to be on that mountain as soon as we can."

"She'll be fine, probably," said Garner. "Modern engines are pretty good right from the manufacturer. Ever ridden one?" Carter shook his head. "Oookay," said Garner. "Maybe you should take it gently for both of your sakes."

"You ever ride a motorcycle, Dan?" asked Lovecraft.

"Not since I was a teenager."

"I had a Suzuki up until a couple of years ago. I'll go up front, you hang on."

"A Suzuki?" said Garner. "Is that a motorcycle? Sounds Japanese."

Lovecraft looked at him as if he was joking before realizing her *faux pas*. "Long story, and we ain't got time. Let's get this thing outside and get started. I will try my best not to get us killed."

Chapter 30

WORLDS WAR THREE

Lieutenant Green's men had decided, independently and tacitly, that there was an excellent chance that they might not be alive in twenty-four hours, and that they would therefore consider themselves dead men until proven wrong. It was not a bad state of mind to be in, not so much fatalistic as pragmatic. They didn't want to die, and would do their damnedest to avoid that happening, but if it did happen despite their best efforts, well, that was the job.

The Thule—inevitably dubbed "Tools" by the men—were not the major threat in their equations. If they'd been up against Ahnenerbe troops, that would have been different, but both their own intelligence sources and the confirmation offered by the American contacts (research into the hitherto unknown detached service section of the OSS called the CIA was still ongoing) showed that the Thule in the dome were scientists first and fighters second. They were probably only lightly armed and had only basic firearms training.

No, the Thule agents were not the primary threat. That was the nuclear hunter killer, the HMS *Alacrity,* from whose Chalfont hangar they had deployed half an hour earlier. The hangar, a so-called dry dock shelter, was mounted behind the fin. A large can-like structure, it contained the minisub the SBS team used to travel to and from operations. Green and his seven subordinates had parked the minisub on the seabed some fifty meters from the beach and were swimming ashore. The *Alacrity,* meanwhile, had withdrawn to a range of about ten kilometers. Green knew that Captain Trescothick would have at least two Lancet missiles loaded into the *Alacrity*'s bow tubes. If the commando force hadn't gotten in, done their job, and gotten out again in four hours, both missiles would be fired at the dome. It would only take one of them to reduce it to fine rubble; the other was purely insurance. If Green and his team were still there in four hours or if the captain decided the mission was compromised and fired early, then that would just be too bad.

Lieutenant Green made a point of emphasizing to his team that he, for one, would prefer not to be a victim of friendly fire, and they should crack along with all dispatch, the sooner to scotch whatever the Thule were up to. The team agreed this was a good plan, and although, as commanding officer, he did not need their approval, he had it anyway.

They came ashore, slogging up the black sand toward where the snow marked a line of the falling tide, and took a moment to hide their underwater gear and prepare for the three-mile ascent of the mountainside. This time they'd emerged at the east side of Temnac Bay, and walked up the bed of the Ukudikak until they were clear of the beach. There was little they could do about leaving tracks in the snow, but at least the current steady fall would obscure them quickly enough.

"Sir?" Green looked up from checking his assault rifle to find Corporal Barnaby addressing him. "Sir, we're missing Cowley.

He was last out of the mini, but he should have made land by now."

Without a word, Green walked back down to the water's edge, flipping down his image-intensifier eye-set as he did and using his binoculars through them. Beside him, Barnaby did the same. It was unlikely an experienced diver like Cowley would get lost on the short trip from the minisub to the beach, but in dark waters even the best could sometimes lose their bearings. Green stood ready to use his torch to signal to Cowley if he'd surfaced somewhere out in the bay and needed a bearing, but he could see nothing. Then he heard Barnaby mutter, "Whoa," under his breath and then whisper, "Sir, hundred meters, south-southwest."

It irked Green that, despite repeatedly being told, Barnaby still insisted on giving compass bearings as if he were aboard a nineteenth-century whaler. Holding his irritation, he looked to about 200 degrees and studied the surface. At first it was difficult to make anything out through the steady snowfall, but then he saw something wallowing in the waves, black and slick as the water washed over it.

"He's facedown. I'll get him," said Barnaby and started for the water's edge.

"Wait!" Green's sharp command brought Barnaby to a dead halt. "Why's he floating at all with all the gear we're carrying?"

It was true. Cowley should have been carrying enough kit to hold him down; their own experience of coming ashore had been less swimming and more like walking into a high wind.

"He might have dumped his kit off to get to the surface?" said Barnaby, but even he didn't sound convinced.

"Including his rebreather? Back up the beach, Corporal."

"Sir?"

"Do it."

With evident reluctance to leave a comrade in trouble, Barnaby did so. Then he saw Green was readying his rifle. "Oh," he said, realization dawning, "fuck." He looked back to the sea in time to see Cowley's body—for he was surely dead—jerked below the surface as violently as if taken by a shark. He had been bait in a hastily conceived trap, and—now that it had failed—the trappers had angrily reclaimed him.

"Heads up, lads!" Barnaby's voice came through every headset. "The Foams had Cowley!"

"Form up," said Green. "Fighting retreat off the beach. We still have to get to the mountain no matter what."

Barnaby clicked off his microphone to speak directly to Green. "What about the mini, boss? The Foams'll have it on bricks by now."

"Worry about that when we get to it. Push comes to shove, we yomp to the north and *Alacrity* sends us an Avon. Right now, focus on the job in hand."

"Aye, sir."

They were almost at the mouth of the creek when the water rose in a dark mound, shockingly close to the water's edge. It sloughed off a black, glistening hide, and the first of the Fomorians came ashore.

It stood perhaps seven feet tall, and it was naked but for something like military webbing slung across its shoulders and secured at a belt. The material was uneven and looked organic, as if it had been extruded by some creature rather than manufactured. As for the rest of the Fomorian, it was just a dark shape in the snow when viewed by the naked eye, and a confused blur of shimmers and white flakes through the night-vision goggles. Behind it, the sea bloated and another thrust up into the air.

They'd never seen a Fomorian at close quarters. Yes, they'd seen pictures from other engagements and even pictures from postmortem dissections, but those had always seemed distant and academic, like pictures from a school biology textbook. It was impossible to believe such things existed and, if they did, that they were intelligent creatures, that they thought coherent, abstract thoughts that were not as the thoughts humans think, that they could create and use complex artifacts.

The first Fomorian reached for its belt and unhooked an object like an irregular, asymmetrical crescent made from bundles of fibers that looked like metallic nerves. It began to raise it and Green shot it through the head.

For a moment, it hesitated, as if it had just remembered a small chore that needed doing tomorrow, then it continued to raise the object. Green swore under his breath, toggled his rifle to burst fire, and turned the Fomorian's head to offal with three rounds. The creature continued to walk through the surf for another three steps before finally falling forward and lying still in the shallows. A wave that seemed to growl with anger swept into the bay and broke like a snarl over the carcass. When it fell back, the body was gone.

The commandos weren't there to see it, however. They were already heading inland in a determined jog that they knew they could keep up for miles. Behind them, shadowed figures rose from the waves all along Temnac Bay and walked forward through the swirling snow.

Carter knew he had some weirdness in his head. Lovecraft said he was a "dreamer," like it was a job description, and—in the rolling ball of extradimensional fuckery that was the Unfolded World—maybe she was right about that. If "dreaming" was a superpower, Carter felt shortchanged. Flying would have been nice, although he'd have settled for superstrength and, importantly, invulnerability.

It had never occurred to him that Lovecraft might have a superpower beyond being smart, and well read, and, worth repeating, really, *really* smart, but—now that she was concentrating on the snow-covered death trap it pleased some to call "the mountain road," concentrating to the exclusion of all else, including her passenger, and he realized that even if she wasn't, he wouldn't have been able to hear her over the wind and the engine—he saw her superpower was to be able to look into the maw of destruction and to tell it to fuck right off. He needed that right now, because without it, fear was eating him.

Since the Suydam case, well over a year and a half and a world and a universe away, he'd had to deal with things no one should, and he'd weathered it because of the dreaming and because of Lovecraft. Yet now, trapped in the little bubble of his isolation behind her, he found time to dwell on what they were getting into, and he felt a sick sense of fear that he hadn't felt since he was a cop facing situations that he knew were about to go real sour.

He wasn't afraid of Weber or his fellow Thule pals and what kind of fight they might put up. Yeah, they might get lucky, but none of them had ever struck him as especially combat-oriented. He'd seen one of the research fellows playing a first-person shooter after hours in Arkham, and he had sucked. It was just as well he'd been playing a player-versus-player game with a fast respawn, because it was painful watching him die pointlessly time after time. He'd charge into an enemy position, shoot at everything, hit nothing, and then spend the next five seconds swearing furiously under his breath—presumably at the injustice of his sudden and completely predictable death—while waiting to reenter the game. These might be people with paid-up membership for an actual, functioning secret occult society with its tentacles making the Third Reich dance, but they were not an impressive corporeal threat.

No, it was what they might do if not stopped that frightened him. Reality was a far more fragile thing than Carter could ever have believed or that they seemed to understand, and he didn't want this bunch of self-serving maniacs knocking it off the shelf with their elbows while trying to do whatever the fuck it was they thought they were doing.

To coalesce all the existential dread he felt into a single thought, Carter was not afraid of dying at the hands of the Thule nearly so much as living into a sinister reality they might create out of stupidity and hubris.

Sometimes he could feel the dreaming circling at the edge of his awareness like a wolf at the edge of the light cast by a campfire.

It was a positive thing, Lovecraft had assured him. The dreaming gave them an edge. An unusual edge, perhaps a unique one. It wasn't a threat. It wouldn't get him killed. It would not drag him into madness. He needed her to say that now, but she could not, because the storm made a ghost of the world and the engine roared, and all her concentration was on the snow-covered death trap it pleased some to call "the mountain road." Lovecraft was focused on it to the exclusion of all else, including the man behind her.

The great steel column at the center of the chamber was being opened section by section. Initially built in the Reich, the sections had been transported across the subjugated Greater Protectorate that was once Russia by rail to the naval base at Dönitzhafen (formerly Petropavlovsk), where it was picked up by the Kriegsmarine aircraft carrier the *Peter Strasser* and subsequently shipped to Attu Island, where the sections were airlifted by dual-rotor helicopters to the top of Mount Terrible.

The sections looked very much like larger versions of the ones that had gone to make up the column at the Miskatonic University, but that was the whole point. The interior of each section was profoundly different, however. Where the Arkham column had been a reasonable attempt at building a device to isolate and generate zero point energy, the Attu version was purely a mule by which some very different equipment could be imported. One of the sections, for example, had contained a case that looked like an instrumentation mounting, but was entirely empty of electronics, instead containing handguns and ammunition. This was the source of the Thule agents' seemingly miraculous supply of weapons. By and large, the cylinder sections contained the component parts of an entirely different device, a device whose principles would have confused the American scientists and whose function would have horrified them.

"What is it?" asked Dr. Giehl as the others cut open some parts of the cylinder and unscrewed other sections, removing pieces of equipment that meant nothing to her. "What are you building?"

Dr. Weber had assumed a supervisory role, but the team was well drilled and needed little oversight. Instead, he amused himself by talking to Giehl.

"Your field isn't nuclear physics, Doctor," he said, "but the root of all this is in the Moscow detonation that heralded Operation Barbarossa."

"I'm not a historian, either."

"Of course. Still, you must have heard all the conspiracy theories about how we managed to beat the Americans to the first deployable atomic weapon, despite them holding all the aces?"

Giehl thought about it for a moment before venturing, "The Abwehr stole atomic secrets from them?"

Weber laughed. Giehl had always liked the sound of his laughter, but she wished he would stop now. "Yes! That's the one. Usually mouthed by the Americans, because they have such trouble believing they might be beaten in anything, despite all the evidence to the contrary. It's nonsense, though. The Americans were still years from developing a viable weapon despite all their advantages. At best, stealing their secrets would only have given us the bomb in '44 or '45. But, you see, if you go into the ruins of Moscow with a Geiger counter, you will only get the sort of readings that you might almost get on the streets of Berlin. I know—I've done it myself. I have stood in the overgrown rubble that was once the Kremlin and listened to the slow clicks of a site that is now barely contaminated at all. I could hardly believe it. That's when it was all explained to me. The 'Sunset' device so famously detonated over Moscow by Hugo Trettner—may his sacrifice always be honored—was *not* an atomic weapon." He chuckled at Giehl's expression. "I know! I know! That was exactly how I felt."

"If not atomic, then what?" Giehl was trying to keep a tight rein on her emotions, but it was proving difficult. She wanted to say Weber was plainly insane, but the rest of her German colleagues were all with him in his insanity, as was her own country. They couldn't all be insane, but if that was true, what did that make her? "Antimatter?"

Weber cocked an eyebrow at the suggestion, considering it. "What an excellent idea. You know, I'd never considered that. But, no. It wasn't antimatter." He smiled again, like an uncle about to perform a famous conjuring trick at a children's party. "You will love the irony, Lurline. Moscow was destroyed using zero point energy."

She could not reply. She dared not reply. She could only look at him as he smiled about how history was a lie.

"Yes, we had access to ZPE all the way back in 1941, but there's a catch. It's extradimensional and uncontrollable. The ZPE we see manifesting routinely in this world filters through the membrane from elsewhere, if you will forgive the oversimplification. If we attempt to break that membrane, to access it, to exploit it, it pours through and then the membrane repairs itself. But we are talking of terajoules of energy, you understand. Perhaps petajoules—it's a chaotic release and well-nigh impossible to measure. More than enough to blow away a city and, alas, vaporize the device that created the breach in the first place."

Giehl looked at the machine the scientists and technicians were diligently building from the cannibalized column. A terrible, unacceptable idea had entered her mind. "What is that?"

"Well, said Weber indulgently, "I suppose you might also call that an irony. Our fake ZPE column was concealing a real ZPE device the whole time."

Chapter 31

A HIGHER AUTHORITY

The commandos were making good enough time across the rough terrain; being pursued by inhuman creatures from the ocean depths was providing excellent motivation. At first they'd tried to ignore the Fomorians, but then a tumbling stream of violet fire had sought them out in the darkness, searing the snow from the bedrock and sending clouds of steam up where it swept. The Foams couldn't shoot for shit, but their weapons maintained a beam for almost three seconds before cutting out, and in that time they could walk the beam onto a target just like a machine gunner might walk a stream of tracer-laden fire onto his mark. The first beam had failed to hit anything but the ground. The plumes of steam brought into the chill air seemed to have surprised the shooter as much as anyone else, and there was a pause of over a minute before the pursuers attempted the same trick.

Again their aim was poor and only snow was vaporized, and not flesh.

Aware that sooner or later a Fomorian was going to get lucky, Lieutenant Green ordered a halt, and the seven of them took cover in the snow-filled gullies, and returned fire. The Fomorians were not difficult to target, but they were horrifyingly resilient. A penetrating shot to the central body mass was a minor inconvenience for them. A burst from the L86A2 support weapon tore the gun arm off a target, but it simply reached down with its remaining hand, lifted its fallen weapon by what passed for its barrel, and shook it vigorously until the hand of the amputated arm lost its grip and fell to the snow. The creature juggled the device awkwardly until it was holding it correctly, and then continued toward the commandos.

"Head shots, boys. Head shots!" called Corporal Barnaby. More fire, and a Fomorian fell, its head pulped. A burst from the support weapon, and another collapsed, but only because its left leg had been blown off at the knee. It crawled onward, grunting in liquid hatred.

"Fucking hell, Migsy," said Barnaby, "how's that his head?"

Green had observed how effectively the steam had confused the Fomorians, and decided to act on it. "We don't have time for this bollocks, Corporal," he called to Barnaby. "Lay down smoke and chuck a couple of HEs in the middle of them."

It was impossible to call the Fomorian advance a "line"; they were each individually making the best speed they could up toward the commandos and were scattered across the Ukudikak bed and up both sides of the banks right to the shadow of the low cliff in the east. The leaders came to a cautious halt as the first smoke grenades landed just forward of the humans, and something like a Fomorian line formed by accident as the stragglers caught up. They were forming clumps about twenty-five meters away, which was bad news for them, as the commandos had at least three men who could hit the middle bail of a wicket at pretty much that range with total consistency. On this occasion, they didn't have to be nearly so accurate.

As the smoke swirled around in the falling snow, lowering poor visibility to almost nothing, two fragmentation grenades plopped with little fuss among the approaching rank. A third clipped a Fomorian on the shoulder and it looked around, trying to see what had struck it. All three grenades went off almost simultaneously. The commandos did not see the blasts, as they were very aware of just how far stray shrapnel from a grenade can fly and were facedown in the snow.

Through the smoke bank, they heard the muffled detonations, and they heard screams that no human throat would make without tearing itself raw, and strange ululating shouts that rose in crescendo before stopping abruptly, sounding more like the calls of birds in some alien jungle. Firing a few rounds into the murk where they thought they saw shapes flailing in agony, the commandos fell back. Mount Terrible stood before them, and time was short.

Toward the top, Green thought he saw the momentary sweep of a headlight flash across the falling snow at the last bend in the treacherous road, but it was impossible to be sure, and it was not repeated.

The note of triumphalism inside the dome suffered a major setback when it was abruptly pitched into total darkness. Somebody working on the ZPE weapon dropped a component and it clanged heavily on the concrete floor.

"For God's sake! Calm down, all of you!" bellowed Dr. Weber into the blackness. "If you're handling something large, put it down *carefully*. It's nothing. Just an outage. The cold may have affected the generators."

Now that they had a moment for their eyes to adjust, they realized the darkness was not quite absolute after all. Several pieces of equipment had independent power, and one—the radio set—drew current while it was available but had its own battery, too. It was one of the standard mobile units, the expedition having several, this one only being different in that it was immobilized on a workbench against one gracefully curving wall by being encased in a Faraday cage to prevent it from interfering with the experiment. Its usual aerial had been removed, however, and replaced by a shielded lead that terminated on a screw mounting in the wall above it. This, in turn, connected to an external aerial as—even without the Faraday cage—it was unlikely the steel-mesh-reinforced dome would allow a signal to travel in or out. In the sudden quiet of the electrical systems and ventilation falling silent, the insistent beep and flashing red light to indicate an incoming call were hard to miss.

A flashlight clicked on. "Give me that," demanded Weber, instantly commandeering it. As he made his way to the radio, more penlights and flashlights flicked into life. Almost everyone carried a light source on Attu; it was crazy not to. Weber had left his flashlight in his room in the panic that Giehl had dumped on him, and he was embarrassed by the oversight.

He approached the radio slowly, as if not quite sure what it was. He knew the set had a relatively good range as such things went, but it was still only thirty-five miles or so. Whoever was calling was somebody on the island, and there was nobody on the island yet outside the dome he really wanted to talk to. Despite a strong feeling that he shouldn't, he picked up the handset and toggled open the channel.

"Hello."

"Dr. Weber?" said the American voice through the speaker. Everyone in the dome heard it very clearly. "This is Daniel Carter. I just wanted to tell you that you don't have any power in there because we just cut it. In a minute, we're going to restart the generators. That won't help you, because we've physically disconnected the power cables. We've also run their exhaust pipes into the air-conditioning vents. You have one minute to throw out all your weapons and then come out as directed."

There was a sound of Carter's handset being jostled, and then Lovecraft's voice cut in. "Just in case you're having problems with the ramifications of that, he means disarm and surrender, or else we are going to gas you motherfuckers. And that's ironic in ways you really won't understand."

Weber toggled off the handset. "Block the vents! Now!"

Lovecraft returned the handset to Carter and laughed a little smugly as she did. "Think that did it?"

"Wouldn't you? They'll block the inlets and try to keep working by flashlights. I give them five minutes before somebody thinks they smell exhaust fumes and freaks out. Give it another five to get heated, then we call again and tell them we haven't turned the generators on yet, but we're going to. Chances are, if they haven't sent anyone out in those ten minutes to find out what we're doing, they will when they hear that."

"When did you get this sneaky?"

"Right from when I was a beat cop. You have to learn negotiating skills. Most of the job's one kind of negotiation or another." They walked out of the generator building to take positions in case the Thule tried a rush.

"On the street, usually talking people down, calming things down, like you'd expect. But sometimes you had to talk people up. Push people so they'd act without thinking it through. Our big advantage"—he drew his pistol—"is they don't know they're being played. In ten minutes, when they find out, they are going to be pissing vinegar. That's when they'll make mistakes, big brain scientists or not." They took positions in cover behind two of the hastily parked Kübelwagens, the four there of which already bore good coverings of snow. Where the fifth car had been, the void in the snow was softly filling in. Carter and Lovecraft had met Dr. Malcolm and his colleagues walking down the road already starting to freeze, their parkas insufficient to protect them from the environment. Carter and Lovecraft had continued to the summit, then Carter took a Kübelwagen and drove it back down the mountain shadowed by Lovecraft on the snow-mobile. They handed the car over to the grateful scientists and told them to get back to the settlement. The scientists had not been able to tell them much they didn't already know, although confirmation that the Thule agents had more than one gun among them was useful.

For several seconds they waited in silence crouched behind the cars, the snowflakes drifting down around them. Then Love-craft called, softly yet loud enough to be heard in that near soundless place, "Hey, Dan?"

"Yeah?"

"It's pretty here, isn't it?"

Carter considered the question.

"Yeah."

Kurt was doing what he did best, which was being an entitled asshole. It had become very clear to Weber early on in his asso-ciation with Kurt that somebody at Wewelsburg was looking to get rid of Kurt, and committing him to the Seidr project on Attu was a way of doing it while seeming to make a selfless sacrifice for the good of the Reich and Greater Germania. There had been few opportunities for speaking privately since they had arrived on Attu, and Kurt had been there since the *Peter Strasser* had dropped him off with most of the equipment, over a week be-fore the *Frederick Cook*'s arrival. In any case, Weber had assumed that everyone—with the exception of the Abwehr and Gestapo contingent—was fully aware of what the activation of the device would do. He had slowly come to realize, by Kurt's smug antici-pation of his heroic return to the Fatherland, that this was not true. Kurt honestly thought he was going to go home after Seidr was accomplished.

After considering the likely results of disabusing him of this fallacy, Weber had quietly told the others not to say anything to Kurt about what was actually coming. While they died in glory, Kurt would die in ignorance; his glory would be postdated.

Dr. Weber, however, had had neither the opportunity nor the motivation to ask Dr. Giehl to keep quiet on the subject. After all, he had never envisaged a situation where she would have the chance to tell him about it.

"They're all insane," whispered Giehl to herself, watching the device being built by torchlight. The Thule people were working more urgently now that they realized that perhaps they should have been more ruthless at the settlement. Maybe they should have shot the Americans while they slept. It certainly looked like they should have hunted down and dealt with the sheriff and his deputy. The assumption had been that, by the time a retaliatory force could reach the dome on foot, the job would be done and defending themselves would be moot. It was a mystery how Carter and Lovecraft had gotten to the dome so quickly, the snowmobile having been among the American supplies brought by ship and unknown to the Germans.

"No," said a voice near her, and she belatedly remembered how well sound traveled in that space even with the hum of electronics and the air-conditioning running. She looked up to see Kurt standing near her, watching the work proceed with a smile. It did not surprise her in the slightest that he was on the sidelines; she wouldn't have trusted him with a screwdriver either. He stood, arms crossed and a gun at his hip, the very model of a conquering hero. "We are making Germany great again."

"The Reich is already the most powerful country in the world," she scoffed. "When did it stop being 'great'?"

"We can't allow weakness. We must always seek strength." He looked down at her and she would have been delighted to slap that smug, pitying look from his face. "The Reich is vulnerable. Did you know, every month a procedure has to be carried out at Wewelsburg simply to maintain the stability of the state? What we're doing here today will ensure that is never necessary again."

She looked at him as if he were quite mad for a moment, then her expression softened, as she appreciated that, no, he was simply a fool. "You don't even know what you're talking about. How will detonating a bomb here change anything for the Reich? At best, we'll look like lunatics and, at worst, we'll start a war."

She looked up at him as she spoke, and was surprised and pleased to see the complacent smirk falter, and his brow lower. "Oh," she said, seeing she had the advantage here at least, "they didn't tell you that this is a suicide mission?" He didn't answer, so she pressed home her advantage. "What sort of *procedure*? How can anything that goes on in that nightmare of a castle maintain the state? What are you talking about?"

"You should help them move some of the newly freed components together, Kurt." Weber had appeared from nowhere. "They're quite heavy and a strong young man like you would be very helpful."

Kurt looked at him as if he'd just offered to sleep with Kurt's mother. "Doctor, this project, what exactly is going to happen?"

"Exactly what you have been told. A focused energy device will stabilize a problematical causal schism, thereby securing the future of the Fatherland."

"It's not a bomb?"

Weber laughed. "No. In a bomb, energy is released universally. In this case, it's focused into the causal membrane, to weld shut a door." He reconsidered. "No, that's a poor metaphor. More like taping down the corners of a piece of paper, so it cannot be folded again."

"Again?" said Giehl.

"At all," Weber corrected himself. "The mathematics of it are complicated, but we have reason to believe that a causal schism exists that would rewrite history from the late 1920s into the present. Ah . . ."—he raised a hand, seeing Giehl was about to argue—"I appreciate this sounds absurd, but we have empirical evidence. Stabilizing that schism can only be done in certain places, and politically and practically, here was the best one. We will doubtless have to grovel a little to the United States about our activities here, but they are sensible people and we shall be able to assuage their anger with a few concessions, I am sure. After all, there are as many in Washington, D.C., who will be delighted by what we do here as in Berlin."

"The Americans are complicit?" asked Giehl.

"Some of them. How do you think we were able to get permission to set up here so easily? It isn't simply because this is a cooperative effort with Miskatonic University, I assure you. There are sections of the U.S. government who know there is something unusual about the peak of Mount Terrible. Why do you think this structure was built here?"

"An early-warning station?" said Kurt.

Weber smiled at him. "Quite right, an early-warning station. But to provide early warning of *what*?" He nodded at the device. "Help the others, Kurt. We are working against the clock."

Confused but obedient to authority, Kurt went to do as he was told.

Weber continued smiling as he watched Kurt walk away, but when he spoke from the side of his mouth to Giehl, he was not amused. "Do not try to upset the boy again, Lurline. I don't have time to hold his hand." He drew up a chair and sat by her. "Why can't you just accept what is happening here? You're a patriot. You'd die for your country, wouldn't you?"

"Yes," she replied without hesitation. "I just doubt that's what I *will* be dying for. You've set yourself above the Party, above the state, above your homeland, Weber. Just who will you be dying for?"

He shook his head, amused by her naïveté. "Those are all petty temporal entities, Lurline. If you believe the Reich will exist for even a fraction of a thousand years, you're as deluded as poor old Adolf was. The Thule Society sees that. We are very good at looking at the long-term good."

"Whose good?"

Weber looked at her, head cocked, considering her like a challenging artwork. Then he leaned close and whispered in her ear, "There are higher authorities than the Führer."

* * *

"Dan?"

"Yes?"

"I changed my mind. I don't think it's so pretty out here anymore. Now I just think it's fucking freezing. They're not coming out, are they?"

Carter sighed with frustration, his breath pluming into the air. "No. I guess not."

"Plan B?"

"Plan B."

While Lovecraft continued to keep the door covered, Carter went around to the generator shack to restart the engines. It looked like they were going to have to gas out the scientists after all.

Chapter 32

A DANGEROUS INTELLECTUAL

The acoustics of the dome became more oppressive as every minute ticked by. Those working there had never entirely appreciated how much of what made the dome a bearable working environment was the humming equipment filling the structure with an ambient tone that did much to muffle its echoic qualities. Every sound seemed altered in some way and either too clear or not nearly as pure as it ought to be. There were mutterings among the Thule agents of whispering galleries and parabolic reflections, but none of them had dealt with acoustics beyond their school years and it was all conjecture. Those were not the only mutterings, however, for they seemed to continue even when all those present were silently absorbed in their work. There were whispers and other sounds that sounded like they might have been words, but the language was unfamiliar, as was the form of larynx that might create such syllables.

The scientists grew fretful and short-tempered. They knew more about the truth of the world, the universe, and the things that lay above and below and behind the universe, but knowledge is not the same as experience, and reading about "metasensory phenomena" was a very different thing than being exposed to them.

When a mechanical thrumming note began to resonate through the dome it was a relief, as—just for a moment—the Thule agents were in a happy second where they were spared both the torment of the whispers and the fear that came with the realization of exactly what the thrumming was.

"Oh, God," the first to understand said, "they're doing it. They're pumping carbon monoxide in!" None of them were chemists or biologists but they remembered enough from their school careers to know that carbon monoxide and a closed environment were a losing proposition for anything that had hemoglobin in its veins.

"Why aren't the vents sealed?" demanded Weber, "I asked that—"

"We don't have the materials to make full seals, so we just had to cover the lower vents and hope the gas wasn't under pressure when it came," said one of the assistants. "But there are vents higher in the dome that we can't even reach."

Weber shook his head in irritation. "Then we have little choice. There's a lot of air in here, but it will be unbreathable in half an hour or less. We have to go out and close down the generators." He looked at those around him, lit unevenly by a dozen flash-and work lights. "There are only two of them, but they have the advantage of being able to wait for us to come out. I shall require volunteers who aren't afraid to use guns."

He looked at Kurt, considered, then shook his head. "You stay here, Kurt. Help finish the device."

Carter and Lovecraft had decided that, if they had to wait while a bunch of scientists choked on carbon monoxide, they could do it in more comfort than crouching behind vehicles that had heating systems. Now they waited inside two of the Kübelwagens. Helpfully, the cars were ex-military stock, and it seemed the Wehrmacht feared not being able to get a vehicle going in a hurry more than it worried about theft. None of the vehicles had keys, none of the doors could be locked, and the ignition had a permanently mounted key bow that worked exactly like an ignition key, but that could not be removed. Both of them had cleared the exhausts from the snow, ran the engines long enough to warm the interiors, and then switched them off until needed again. Lovecraft had found the one she was in had some sort of music system, but after listening to about five seconds of heavily synthesized, light-industrial Europop, she turned it off, and it wasn't only the cold that caused her to shudder as she did so.

She was also the first to notice the dome's door opening. She slid out of the car and took up a firing position by the front edge of the Kübelwagen's driver's door, aiming the Mossberg over the hood. Taking his cue from her, Carter also left his vehicle quickly, and stood with his forearms braced in the snow on his Kübelwagen's roof.

The door creaked loudly, the hinges not having received nearly enough love during the site's refurbishment. From the gap a stick topped with a white handkerchief appeared and fluttered in the cold air. "Mr. Carter?" Weber's voice called. "Miss Lovecraft? Kindly do not shoot. I'm coming out."

They held their fire while Weber cautiously emerged, his hands up and the flag of truce gripped in one flapping dismally in the icy breeze.

"That's far enough, Doctor," called Carter once Weber was at the top of the short stoop of steps leading down to the entrance. "You can say your piece right there."

"Mr. Carter, first, I want you to understand that Nick's death was an . . . no, not an accident, but a misunderstanding. One of our number mistakenly thought Nick was armed and that he was intending to draw his gun. It is very regrettable."

"That's bullshit," said Lovecraft. "None of the techs have guns. Why think Nick did?"

"To be brutally honest, Miss Lovecraft . . . hello . . ."—Weber waved awkwardly at her with his free raised hand—"he was mistaken for Mr. Carter. Everyone looks alike in these parkas and, with the snow . . ." Weber shrugged.

"We'll leave that for a court of law to settle, Doctor. Right now, you need to tell your people to surrender."

"Oh, dear"—Weber shook his head—"no, I am afraid that is impossible. I didn't come out here to negotiate our surrender. I came out to negotiate *yours*."

Carter was about to say what he thought about that when he became aware of a subdued electronic bleeping. He'd left both the long-range walkie-talkie from the settlement and the British military radio on the passenger seat of his car and, glancing through the window, he saw it was the former signaling an incoming call.

"Hold that thought, Doctor. We can have a good laugh about it in a minute while your crew chokes to death in there. Got to take this call. Emily?"

"Yeah, yeah. Blow him in half if he tries anything. I'd be happy to." She nestled the butt into her shoulder and sighted directly at the doctor's torso. "Hi, Doc. Guess what a twelve-gauge cartridge will do to you at this range."

Dr. Weber smiled wanly.

Carter climbed into the car, closing the door behind him, and picked up the walkie-talkie. "Hello, Carter here. Go ahead." He was expecting to hear Lo's voice. Lurline Giehl's came as a surprise.

"Dan? Listen, I don't have long. First, the gas won't work quickly. They've found a vent that opens directly to the outside and, with the doors open, there's a Bernoulli effect drawing the bad air out. Don't depend on the gas doing your work."

"Shit," said Carter, and was about to expand on that, when she interrupted him.

308

"Just listen! They are going to try to rush you anyway. You've distracted them and Weber wants to get rid of you and take control of the generators."

Outside, Lovecraft's shotgun never wavered from its target. Carter half-laughed. "Yeah, he's out here now, and that's not really working out for him. I don't think he knew Emily is a BAMF with a boomstick. And a library degree."

"I don't know what a 'BAMF' is," said Giehl. "It doesn't matter. This is important. The device they're building is a bomb, I think. A ZPE weapon. If it detonates, it will kill everyone on the island. I don't really understand why they're doing it. Weber talked about stabilizing reality. It's like a shared delusion for them."

Carter sucked in a breath of shock. "The Fold . . ."

"Yes! He called it something like that. You understand what he means?"

"Yeah. Yeah, I do. They've got to be stopped. Do you have any weapons?"

"No. They all seem to have pistols except me. They only half-trust me. I'm Abwehr, but I'm not Thule. Their loyalties are skewed." Her tone was bitter. "They're fanatical. I wish I could blow them all to hell."

Carter glanced at Weber. He was looking cold and uncomfortable out there. Good. "Yeah. I'm beginning to wish we still had Jenner's bomb. That'd fuck up whatever they're building."

"Yes," she said, wistful for a bundle of explosives. "How did you get rid of it in the end?"

Carter frowned. "How did *I* get rid of it? That was your job, Lurline."

A pause. "I had—" The carrier wave light extinguished and he knew she was gone. He could only hope it was by choice.

Kurt stood over Giehl, his eyes flickering nervously from the radio set to her and then back again. "Who were you talking to, Doctor?" he demanded.

The snow was the devil's addition to the hell of Attu Island. The ground the commandos were covering between the bay and the mountain would be hard to traverse at speed in broad daylight and in dry conditions. In darkness during a heavy snowfall, it was a winter wonderland of traps and snares. So far they'd had several close calls as boots skidded into hidden cavities or tripped on covered rocks. Some hundred meters from the mountain road, their luck ran out. Marine Marshall's foot slid into a dip in the rock and his boot locked against the sides of the socket while his body tried to keep moving.

The sound of his ankle breaking was sickeningly audible to all of them, and if they were in any doubt as to the severity of the injury, Marshall's grunt of agony and muttered, "Oh, fuck!" served to dispel it.

"It's knackered, sir," he said as they laid him out, three of their number taking positions to provide cover. The Fomorians were well behind them, but they knew they wouldn't stop coming. "It's well fucked."

Corporal Barnaby carried out a cursory examination and came to much the same conclusion couched in similar terms. "We can strap his leg up, keep him moving."

"There's no time, Corp," said Marshall. "I'll get us all killed. Move on. I'll rear-guard."

Barnaby turned to Green. "Permission to stay with Marine Marshall, sir?"

"No." It was Marshall who spoke. "Don't be fucking stupid, Corp. You stay with me, we're both dead. Move on, complete the mission. Leave me the '86. I'll slow the buggers down."

With the fewest words possible, they swapped his assault rifle for the support gun, helped lay him down facing toward the enemy, deployed the weapon's bipod, and conducted themselves as in the offices of those at a deathbed. They left him there, wishing him good luck, and they meant it.

Two minutes after they left him, they heard the support weapon open fire. In the snow-streaked night behind them, they saw shadowed muzzle flashes. Then they saw the snow lit with electrical blue-and-violet fire. They kept moving as the hidden drama played out, as the whining crackle and muffled cracks of different weapons of different species warred. Presently, the low lightning stopped, but not one of the marines thought for a moment it was because Marshall had prevailed against their pursuers.

A change in the wind brought the distant sound of an automatic weapon firing from a mile or so away to the mountaintop. Lovecraft and Carter exchanged looks and, simultaneously coming to the wrong conclusion, crouched for fear of being flanked.

Weber couldn't hear the shooting from where he was, so far from the cliff edge leading down to the road's first meander and over the sound of the generators in their nearby shack. He was momentarily baffled by the Americans' disappearance behind cover, but got over his surprise quickly. He lowered his free hand and used it to signal in a series of wafting motions, as if driving away a wasp, that the three men and a woman crawling so low behind him that their faces brushed the freezing concrete should seize the moment. It wasn't acted upon quite instantly, but then one of them saw his signal, entirely misinterpreted it, leapt to his feet, and ran up the stoop past Weber, wearing what passed for a war-face in scientific circles.

"No!" shouted Weber after him, "the generators!"

The runner, Decker, a specialist in particle physics whose entire weapons training had consisted of a rainy half-hour on a Wehrmacht range at Bad Münstereifel, was too hyped on adrenaline to listen. He ran forward out into the open, exposed, snowy expanse in the middle of the area, painfully visible even in the weak light.

Carter and Lovecraft, crouched behind their Kübelwagens, exchanged glances and rose to see what was approaching. Seeing shapes move behind the cars, Decker fixated on the closer, and ran toward Lovecraft firing wildly. Lovecraft yelped with surprise as a bullet punched through her car's passenger-side window, then its counterpart on the driver's side. She ducked behind the hood while she decided what to do about this. Believing he'd hit her, Decker ran harder for the front of the car to flank it and shoot her again to be sure. Filled with triumph, he had forgotten all about Carter.

Carter had braced his arms and was setting Decker up for an embarrassingly easy shot. He took a breath, held it a beat, hesitated out of pity, then steeled himself and fired twice. Decker went boneless, then ran on a little farther as his legs failed, reminding Carter pathetically of the scarecrow from Oz. The dead man piled forward into the snow and lay still.

A shot plinked off his car's bodywork, the metallic reverberation absorbed by the layer of snow. He looked over to see Weber waving his arms around, gabbling unhappily in German at dark shapes that scurried behind the veil of white.

"Tell your people to get back inside, Doctor!" he shouted.

Weber turned slowly to face him and stood, his arms raised in an eloquent shrug, the false flag of truce still gripped in one hand. "Too late, Sheriff Dan. You should have cut us off at the pass while you had the chance." Then he ducked back quickly into the shadows of the doorway. A shotgun blast blew a cloud of chippings and dust out of the upper-right lintel of the door. Lovecraft racked in another cartridge, but he was gone.

"How many got into the shack?" she called to Carter.

He shook his head. "Hard to tell. Two, maybe three."

"We got to take it back, don't we?" she said. She didn't sound enthusiastic, and Carter was with her in that. In the same way they'd had the advantage while the Thule people were holed up in the dome, now the two or three in the generator shack would have an easy time picking off anyone who tried to enter. Carter bitterly repented letting Weber come so far out of the door now. The generator shack occupants would start shooting as soon as Carter or Lovecraft appeared at the doorway, white flag or not.

He'd wasted their advantage by not wanting to shoot a man under a flag of truce, and look where that had got them.

"I'm too softhearted," he said to himself as he started trying to devise a method of killing all the Thule agents in the generator shack without giving them a chance to defend themselves.

Lovecraft took a moment to head in a crouch to the cliff edge to see if their reinforcements were showing up yet; if the British would just make a triumphant entrance, they could take the shack in a New York minute and then she could talk to Marine Ryan about her etchings or some other shit.

It should have been hard to see anything in the gloom, but the sea to the south seemed to emit a dull glow, like the idea of light, that illuminated the snow-covered island like a dreamscape. It seemed she could look out across the little land like a child taking in an incredibly detailed illustration in a book. Every exposed rock was delineated, every flake of snow could be numbered. Lovecraft grimaced. Her mind was starting to hurt. Too much data. Too much everything. What the hell was happening to her? She remembered how Carter had tried to describe what "dreaming" in that very specific technical sense was like, and she hadn't been able to grasp it. Now, however, she was beginning to understand it all too well in principle if not the specifics. This was not what he had talked about, but the way he had spoken of the very inhuman . . . *unhuman* experience of it bore redolence of the sensory misalignment she was now feeling. She could feel waves of information from her surroundings, and things that lay above and below the current reality, and it made her giddy and vertiginous. The cliff looked less like a death trap and more like a minor geographical feature that part of her mind considered so trivial that she could safely step off it. The rest of her mind disagreed and she fell to her knees to make it more difficult for the suicidal urges masquerading as merely megalomaniacal conceit to take her over the edge. She could hear Carter calling to her, but it was just another datum in a galaxy of data. And amid the points of truth, she could discern figures down below on the approaches to the mountain, and on the road leading up.

"Emily!" Carter was suddenly at her side. He saw she was crying without sobbing, her eyes a long way away. "What's wrong?" She felt his hand take her arm and it was an anchor she clung to.

She looked at him, her gaze fierce and immediate. "I should never have read that book. I should never have read it. The *Necronomicon*'s fucked me up. I'm seeing things. I'm seeing everything." She gripped his hand. "They're coming."

"The British?"

She shook her head.

Chapter 33

CASE SEIDR

"Sir, there's somebody up on the road. Up on the rise, there." Marine Jones pointed into the gloom. The snow had abated slightly, but dawn was still some way away. Or, at least, it should have been. Things were easier to see than they should have been, but none of the men questioned it. They put it down to an effect of the snow-covered landscape, and never wondered why the light came from the south and not from the east.

There was somebody up on the second meander of the mountain road, and another two on the first. For one forlorn moment, Lieutenant Green hoped that they were merely humans, perhaps the Thule agents, although he could have put up with Ahnenerbe *hexensoldat* if need be. But he saw how they moved, slouching resentfully under a gravity unmoderated by water, and he knew the hope was in vain.

"Foamers!" he called. "Take cover, and kill them!"

He didn't say what they all knew. There was no possibility that their pursuers had somehow overtaken them. The creatures defending the mountain approach were a reserve that must have come ashore hours earlier. The commandos had been harried directly into their arms in a planned ambush.

Purple-blue and amaranthine fire arced out of the oppressive gloom from behind them and Jones died before he had a chance to obey the order to take cover. Maybe it was a lucky shot, but they felt in their guts it was not—the Fomorians were much better with their weapons than they had been pretending. They had not wanted to become mired in a firefight too far from their reserve force, so they had chased the commandos, pushing them forward the way beaters raise game birds. Now that their quarry was within range of the skirmish line ranged along the base of Mount Terrible, the trap closed, and the deception was discarded.

A fall of black ash that used to be a man scarred the virgin snow. Lieutenant Green went at full length into the snow and found a gully. The only option was to push forward, even though the enemy had had time to emplace themselves. To go back meant going into waves of their reinforcements. He made a quick head count: there were five of them against perhaps ten ahead although he could only see the three on the mountainside road and one by the road ahead, and God only knew how many more behind.

The commandos had entered the mission in the state of mind that they were already dead, and that tomorrow did not matter. Now they knew for certain that they would not see the next day. The only mark they could make on a world that did not even know they were there was not to go quietly. They aimed their weapons, conscious that these were among the last things they ever did, and they engaged the enemy.

SA-80 assault rifles cracked, Fomorian weapons crackled their response, and the snow hissed into steam.

Corporal Barnaby saw Marine Cox turn from flesh to soot in a great swathe from his shoulder to his waist, and he did not die, his guts and blood held into the remnant of his torso by the cauterizing fire. He looked into his comrade's staring eyes and saw the agony and fear there, a man unable to scream because he barely had one whole lung left to him. Without hesitation, Barnaby aimed and put a bullet through Cox's brain and thought it nothing more than what he would have craved if it had been him there, writhing in the snow.

Barnaby turned to report Cox's death to Lieutenant Green, but Green was gone with only a scar in the snow left to mark where he had been, the rock beneath glowing. Barnaby slid back into his protective gully as blue fire swept overhead. A Fomorian on the second meander of the mountain road dropped like an abandoned puppet and then the one by it was rocked back on its heels by a well-placed controlled burst to the head.

Did the Fomorians' lives matter even to them? wondered Barnaby. They barely used cover. They hardly seemed to care. Were they too stupid to preserves their lives, or did they really not think of their existence as something worth preserving? The commandos had been briefed any number of times on the known capabilities and mentality of these enemies, but they had always been represented as essentially humans that simply looked like monsters. Yes, the intelligence spooks had talked about the inhumanity of the Fomorians, but they barely touched upon their *un*humanity. To them, the Foams might as well have been ragheads or provos, just another bunch of terrorists who needed dissuading with bullets. For the first time, Barnaby wondered if they were not the whole be-all and end-all, that there wasn't some fish king of the fish men telling them what to do. What if they were all soldiers in somebody else's fight? And what if Barnaby was, too?

Corporal Stephen Barnaby realized nobody was firing anymore and that he wouldn't be getting answers to his questions. Around his tiny redoubt, the creatures slowly closed in.

"We need to set this up, right here." Kurt pointed at a space next to the ZPE device the remaining scientists were close to finishing.

"What?" One of the scientists, Huber, looked at him as if he was an idiot. Kurt had become used to looks like that. She shifted her attention to the unit he had wheeled over. "That thing's a fake. I don't even know why we brought it."

"It's not a fake," said Dr. Giehl, joining them with a length of telemetry cable she had gotten from the storeroom. "It just doesn't do what the Americans thought it was doing."

Nor, she knew, would it do what Kurt was expecting it to do. She had hoped that Kurt's discovery that the ZPE would blow the top off the mountain had been preying on his mind, and, yes, it had. A very great deal. When he had challenged her, he had been willing to believe almost anything she suggested as long as it led to a resolution in which he didn't die in the ass-end of nowhere, surrounded by people who treated him like an idiot. She had told him that she was an Ahnenerbe plant, sent to monitor the project, as it was believed it would be used to provoke a war with the U.S. and, in passing, eliminate some members of the Thule Society that a power group within the society wanted dead. Kurt's death, specifically, was intended to undermine his father within the Ahnenerbe.

It was all inspired lies, and Giehl was pleased with how well it meshed with current events without being in the slightest bit true, although now she did find herself wondering why Kurt had been assigned there. Perhaps she had inadvertently stumbled on a little bit of truth. In any event, Kurt gobbled up her lies and became almost pathetically eager to help her undo this villainy and, incidentally, save his life.

She had told him her ZPE detector unit was actually intended to disable the ZPE field when it was created, causing an attempt to trigger the device to fail and probably burning it out in the process. She'd muttered some nonsense about an "EMP hysteresis feedback effect" and he'd nodded eagerly as if he'd just been reading about them.

"But it has to be close by," she said. "I need to rewire the components to do its job properly. You make yourself useful with them, and I'll make the necessary alterations." By "rewire the components," she meant "arm a bomb," and by "do its job properly," she meant "blow the ZPE device to shit and shrapnel," but there was no need to burden him with the technicalities. Kurt had nodded, pathetically grateful, and done as she asked, while she unscrewed the detector's maintenance hatch and reattached Jenner's crude but effective bundle of dynamite to the power bus.

Huber was looking the box over now. "So what *does* it do?"

"It's a monitor and failsafe." Giehl's gift for impromptu bullshit had suddenly deserted her. The description didn't sound convincing even to her.

It didn't seem to be making much headway with Huber, either. She looked at Kurt, but he was making a great show of placing the detector just so, in an attempt to avoid being asked questions. He need not have troubled himself; she would have as soon consulted a Ouija board as ask him for technical details.

Huber turned her attention back to Giehl. "How are we even supposed to connect them? There's no provision, no ports, nothing."

A change of tack was required. Giehl shrugged. "How am I supposed to know? The thing just turned up at my laboratory a few days before I was due to go to Arkham. There was a sheaf of instructions and an order to burn them after reading." Huber showed no sign that this seemed extraordinary or even unusual to her. Giehl took a leap. "I have no idea how it works. Really, Gabi, do you know how that thing works?" She nodded at the ZPE device.

Huber's lips tightened and Giehl suddenly realized she had said exactly the right thing. "I just do as I'm told," said Huber.

"As do I. Let me just set the thing up and I will leave you in peace." She finished placing the detector as if there were specific rules to follow other than "as close as possible," and plugged in its power lead.

"It's useless without power, though. What about the device?"

Huber nodded and looked to the door to the entrance anteroom. There was still no sign of Weber or any of the others. "We need power. Unless they can get the generators up again to energize the device in the first place, we've wasted our time."

"You carry on," said Giehl, playing up the role of reliable colleague. "I'll find out what's happening outside."

Previously, hanging up parkas and changing out of boots in favor of soft work shoes in the entry room had been de rigueur. Tonight, however, nobody much cared. Giehl had dumped her own parka by her workplace and not bothered changing her footwear at all. Now she shrugged back into the coat and, telling Kurt to keep an eye on the detector and make sure it wasn't moved or interfered with, went out into the antechamber.

The first thing she saw was Dr. Weber stretched out on the floor groaning. His head was bloodied and, for a moment, she thought he'd been shot there. But no. The wound seemed to have been caused by him falling down the stoop, presumably while being shot at. There was no sign of the four others who had gone out with him, and she assumed they were either lying dead outside or had occupied the generator shack.

In the unhealthy yellow-green glow of emergency cold light stick racks that some wise head had decided should be fitted in the anteroom but not in the dome itself, she rolled him onto his back and looked at him. His parka was holed around the right shoulder and she realized he had been caught at the edge of a swarm of shotgun pellets. Giehl saw the hand of Emily Lovecraft at work there.

"Weber? Weber!" She slapped him as much because she wanted to as to make him focus on her. "Where are the others?"

"Others?" The idea confused him, then he settled on a meaning. "The others. They killed Decker. Decker's dead."

"And the other three?"

"In the generator shack. Have they repaired it yet?"

"No. Not yet. Weber, listen to me. All this, the ZPE device, stabilizing the world or whatever you meant. Who is it for?"

He looked at her curiously as if he'd never truly noticed her before. Then his gaze left her and looked past her shoulder. "Oh, Lurline. Such wonders. To be even spared crumbs is more than we deserve. It is humanity's only hope. If we resist, we die. If we submit, we live."

"You're talking about slavery. Slavery to whom?"

Weber shook his head and winced at the pain it brought him. "No. Service given willingly isn't slavery, and even if it was, better living slaves than dead heretics. No. No, better to be servants than slaves."

"Heretics? What are you talking about?"

Weber laughed a little, and said, "You're right to question that. Heresy means denying a faith. No need for faith when you have hard, scientific proof."

"Of what?"

He looked at her in that curious way once more, but now she saw he considered her a fool. "Why, of gods, of course."

Something was going on outside. She could hear raised voices and then the sound of an engine rev and speed away. Giehl searched Weber's pockets and found his pistol. "We make our own destiny, Weber."

Again that look, that pitying look. "No, Lurline. We have never made our own destinies. Do you even know what Seidr is?"

"The name of this project."

"The name of?" He laughed hoarsely again. "It is the old magic, Lurline. The magic of fate. We may pluck at a few of the threads of the tapestry, but we are not the weavers."

Giehl blanched at the mention of magic. "I believe in science."

A quiet laugh. "There's a difference?"

Giehl had had enough. "You're insane." For the first time in her life, she realized that she actually meant those words.

"To do other than I have done," he murmured, "*that* would be insane."

Giehl looked into his face—serene, calm, self-assured—and didn't know whether to fear him for his insanity, or envy him. She said, "You shouldn't have killed Nick," placed the gun barrel on his half-closed left eye, and shot him through it.

Then she went outside.

Chapter 34

BAMF WITH A BOOMSTICK

Lovecraft was adamant. "We have to help them. They're on our side. They're friends, right? We help friends."

Carter was trying to be reasonable, but Lovecraft's single-mindedness was almost maniacal in its intensity and she was worrying him badly. "Emily, the cavalry's supposed to ride to *our* rescue. If a squad of heavily armed professional soldiers can't handle the fish men, what are we supposed to do?"

She looked up from the field of muzzle flares and violet fire and glared at him. "I just said what we do, Dan. We help them."

She got to her feet, staggered momentarily as if on the deck of a pitching ship, and steadied herself. "We help them," she said to herself, and walked to the snowmobile.

"Wait, wait, wait." Conscious that they were both out of cover and with half an eye on the entrances to the dome and the generator shack, he went after her. "You can't seriously intend to go down there?"

"Fuckin' A," she said, sweeping the snow from the seat and straddling it. She unshouldered her shotgun and reversed the strap so the gun hung the right way up under her arm.

"Emily! C'mon, don't be crazy! You ride down there, you're dead. You know that?"

"Maybe." She started the engine. "We'll see."

She roared off in a flurry of white, almost clipping Decker's partially snow-covered body.

Carter watched her crest the drop onto the road and vanish from view with mixed emotions, none of them positive. He looked quickly to the dome and the generator shack in case any of the Thule bastards had come out to see what the fuss was about, but the shack's door remained closed, and the dome's door still ajar, but almost in its jamb.

As he was looking at the door, he heard a sound from within, a muffled crack he was confident was a shot. He raised his Colt to cover the door as shadows shifted in the unnatural light within the entry antechamber. Then the door opened and Dr. Giehl was standing there, a pistol in her lowered hand.

"Where's Weber?" said Carter, his gun aimed squarely at her chest.

She seemed disappointed, but answered, "He's dead. I shot him."

"Just now?"

"Just now."

Carter took this in and lowered his gun. "Good. Can you get me into the generator shack?"

She shook her head. "Weber's orders were specific. They're to hold the door until the generators are supplying electricity to the dome again. Even if I go in with you, they'll shoot us both."

"Into the dome, then?"

She glanced back. "That would be easier. Where's your friend?"

Carter didn't want to say the first thing that came into his head, which was, "She's probably dead by now." Instead he said, "She's gone to get reinforcements."

Giehl laughed without humor. "On this rock? Can you see Lo with a gun? Stay here, Daniel. They'll get suspicious if I'm gone too long. I'll find some way to get you in there."

For the first few hairpin corners of the descent, Lovecraft was muttering, "This is a stupid fucking idea," repeatedly to herself. By the time she turned the antepenultimate bend, she had put it to a little tune and was singing it in her mind. Anything to distract herself from what she was about to do.

As the second meander of road above the approach opened out before her, so did her sight once more, a wave of perception that rode out before her and told her everything she would ever need to know and far too much more about the upcoming encounter. There were two Deep Ones, Fomorians, fish men, bad guys on the road. One was dead, its head mulch, but the other was holed in the torso. She could detect its pain as a grumbling irritation more than a life-threatening wound, and if she hadn't been wary of their durability after reading a piece of marginalia in her copy of the *Necronomicon*, she surely was now.

She wondered when she'd started feeling so possessive of the *Necronomicon* that she considered it her property, but then the Fomorian was climbing to its feet and looked over to see her coming.

She hit it heavily in the side and sent it ricocheting off one of the roadside boulders and thence over the cliff edge and a steep drop down eighty feet of rock face. She had a sense of its irritation growing that felt like an ear at high altitude waiting to pop, and then the feeling blinked out and she knew it was dead. She figured that was probably her one easy kill of the night, and hunkered down behind the windshield to prepare for whatever came next.

The next bend came and with it, blue fire. A dark figure stood in the road a hundred yards away, and a fountain of angry fire hissed and crackled from its hand. But it was surprised, alerted by the falling body of its comrade and assuming the threat came from elsewhere. It also wasn't ready for a powerful full-beam halogen headlight blazing into its eyes, and so its aim was poor to start with, and over the few seconds the weapon vomited its burning torrent of blue, it only deteriorated.

The flame slid into the night and darkness. The shooter stumbled amidst the road edge boulders, its arm over its eyes. She would have loved to run this one down too—the meaty "thud" of amphibious bastard bouncing off the Ski-Doo had been the sort of thing that, if she ever had more evenings past that night, would surely keep her warm on cold ones. Trying to ram it while it was shielded by the boulders was too risky, though, so Lovecraft improvised. She drew up in front of the gap between the boulders and looked at the Fomorian, and it looked back at her. She could see now the weapon it had tried to kill her with gripped in its hand, a twisted, curved thing made from silver wires that seemed to have grown into an organic shape. Small blue flares of lights swarmed over the wires, slowly forming a pattern that, to Lovecraft's cold pleasure, she understood. He'd shot his bolt and now the weapon was—recharging was somehow the wrong word—*recovering*. She didn't read fear, or even an analog of fear from the creature, only a sense of fatalism. That seemed only right and proper to her.

"Morning, fuck face," she said, and shot it at point-blank range.

A fountain of viscera—or as Lovecraft named it in the heat of the moment, eviscera—rained off the road edge and onto the approach road and its verge below, momentarily followed by the dying Fomorian. Out on the relatively flat area on the other side of the road, a circle of the creatures was closing in on an area where the rock was rucked and furrowed. From it, steam and smoke rose. For a moment, that was the only movement she saw, and she feared she was too late. Then she saw a flicker in a

gully, and a burst of fire cut down one of the encircling creatures. The Fomorians responded immediately, hosing down
the area, but the shooter had already slid back into cover. She
counted twelve of them, and an idea that others who had been
approaching were returning to sea as they wouldn't be required.
That, she hoped, showed overconfidence on their part. None of
them were showing any interest at all on the light-and-guts show
she'd been participating in on the mountainside. Okay.

She looked down at the strange alien weapon lying on the
snow where the Fomorian had dropped it when it and its internal organs had parted company. There was no obvious trigger
or safety or any sort of mechanical interface on it at all. She
leaned down and lifted it. It felt awkward in her hand, more
awkward than its shape suggested. She drew off her glove and
gripped it again. Simply touching it with her bare skin was like
handling an entirely different object. Now it felt lighter, and fitted her hand easily. It wasn't so much that it was changing in
itself, as changing the spatial relationships between her skin and
the silver mesh. She could understand that. She had an art project cluttering up her study in Arkham that demonstrated several
similar principles if one knew how to look at it.

Blue motes fluttered under her fingers, and she knew the device was ready again. "Okay," she murmured to herself as she
took in where the Fomorians stood. "I got my Mossberg, my Webley, and my ray gun. Let's see how far they get me in fucking up
some frogboys."

As she turned onto the flat road, the snow glowed violet again
with another salvo. More steam, more molten rock, but no closer
to killing their tormentor in the gully. They seemed baffled more
than cautious, and did little to avoid being shot at unless a half-
squatting posture to reduce their profiles can be considered taking cover. The last couple of bursts from their prey had scored
no significant damage, but they had greeted each with a universal return of fire, and then half-squatted while their weapons

recovered. They would have won the battle a lot earlier if they would advance while firing, but this was apparently not doctrine for them. The man with the gun had perhaps realized this, and waited until they straightened up again and took a step closer before firing and forcing the cycle to repeat. It was a desperate tactic, and the endgame could only be the circle closed tightly enough that the gully no longer provided sufficient cover, or that he ran out of ammunition.

At least, those were the only resolutions discernible by the man and the monsters. In the larger context of entities from outside that closing circle, a third possibility was that it would give Lovecraft time to get her skimobile down the mountain, and out among the Fomorians.

She appeared amidst them like a cat among pigeons from hell. The first inkling they had that all was not well was when the spine of one, the skin and flesh above it, the cartilage-like bone around it, and some of the organs beneath it became a fall of burning ashes, pluming from its back like soot from an untended chimney. It made a piercing, ululating shriek, and fell forward.

Lovecraft was not entirely sure what she had done to trigger the device, but it had been as instinctive as squeezing a trigger, she knew that much. She also knew well enough not to expend the weapon's full charge in one shot, which meant she was aiming before firing as opposed to firing before aiming. She could only guess the Fomorians did it their way because it was tough setting up a firing range on the seabed. She'd turned the headlight off on her approach, but now she toggled it back on and the creature shied from its brilliance at least as much as from the armed and angry woman behind it. She fired again and again, and although the curling bolts of fire went wild thanks both to her unfamiliarity with shooting a weapon from a moving platform as much as the erratic terrain, they did serve to finally represent something the Deep Ones feared.

Corporal Barnaby looked up from charging his rifle to find a Valkyrie on a snowmobile come to a halt at the edge of the large circle around the gully where not only had all the snow been vaporized, but the rock itself was marred and molten.

"Where are the others?" shouted Lovecraft, bringing up her shotgun to bear and engaging the Fomorians ahead of her.

Sudden hope is a wonderful thing. Barnaby scrambled up out of the gully and across the dark powder that used to be his commanding officer. "They're dead, ma'am! They're all fucking dead!" His rifle was carried at the ready, and he head-shot a blade-wielding Fomorian as it ran at the rear of the snowmobile.

The Mossberg had run dry. She let it drop on its sling and drew the weird-ass ray gun from where she'd jammed it between the gas tank and the seat. It didn't look well, some of the filaments at the emitter end had become bent, and, she felt irrationally, wounded. The motes of blue light ran through the wires sometimes like cockroaches and sometimes like anxious blood, and she felt ruination within it.

"Well, this isn't good," she said as Barnaby climbed onto the snowmobile's pillion.

"Go! Go! Go!" he shouted right behind her.

"Yeah, I'm right here," she snapped at him, tossing the strange artifact over her head, and brought the snowmobile to bear on the road again.

"What was that?" said Barnaby as the weapon glittered over his head, the blueness of it beginning to tend toward white.

"Fire in the hole," said Lovecraft, and opened the throttle. Behind her, she felt Barnaby half-turn to look and maybe to fire. "Don't look back!" she shouted. She felt him look forward again. Perhaps he hadn't heard exactly what she had said and was going to ask her to repeat it. It didn't matter. All that was important was that he wasn't looking at the device when it . . .

Exploded.

The Fomorians understood their equipment well enough, although Lovecraft had real doubts they had made any of it themselves. They knew what the frantic vibration of the motes and the shift in color meant. They ran, but they were on land; gravity was cruel to them and their swiftest sprint was like the shamble of a drunk with his pants around his ankles.

The device failed in light and in heat and in something else that chewed away the bonds in molecules, the orbits of electrons, the affinity of quark to quark. A white wave of annihilation traveled out and obliterated each stumbling Fomorian where it stood, consuming it and, on finding another artifact, condemning it to a similar effect. Brilliant white spheres blossomed like fruiting bodies of fungus seen in time lapse. And then they flashed into nothing, and the battlefield was bare, but for perhaps a dozen large hemispheres melted from the rock, each about ten meters across, each smoothly walled. In the whole chain of destruction, the only sound was that of the snowmobile.

As the light flicked off in an instant, Lovecraft brought the vehicle around and they looked back into the darkness.

"Holy shit," said Corporal Barnaby. "That was one of their guns cooking off? Pretty fragile."

"Yeah. They are," said Lovecraft, but it was a lie. She recalled how, as she took the artifact from where she'd put it, she'd deliberately wedged the emitter tip into the gap and bent it, just so, to such a degree and no further. And when she'd held it, she'd done something to it just like she knew how to trigger it. Then and only then the motes had grown distressed and the energies had started to build. She didn't know quite what she'd done, or how she had known to do it.

She shook the feeling that she was no longer quite human away. She'd just read a book, that's all. Just reading a book doesn't make anyone into a monster, although the jury was still out on Dan Brown's.

"You still got any ammo left for that thing?" she said, nodding at Barnaby's assault rifle as she pulled cartridges from her bandoleer and loaded them into the Mossberg, consciously feeling like a real badass while she did so. It was a nice feeling, but then again she'd just saved a guy and she wasn't dead, so she felt she deserved some ego reinforcement.

"Most of a box in it, and another two in reserve, ma'am. How's the head wound?"

"Healing well, thanks. Now we got to go and wave guns at some Thule scumbags. You up for that?"

Barnaby looked at the patch of land where five of his mates had died. "I am, ma'am. I am very much in the mood to fuck up the people who are responsible for this."

Lovecraft nodded and drove back toward the road.

Chapter 35

BROTHER AND SISTER

Carter's options, which had not started as a broad panoply, were further hobbled by the precipitous departure of Lovecraft. Rushing the generator shack by himself was a losing proposition, so he was reduced to waiting to see if Giehl was able to get him into the dome.

The sound of a shotgun carried up the mountainside, and he looked down. The snow was a fraction of what it had been earlier, but over distance, layer upon layer, it still made visibility poor. He could see the beam of the snowmobile's headlight far below, almost at the end of the mountain road, but as they reached the last corner before descending onto the approach road, he lost them and the night grew darker, but for a fitful blue iridescence that throbbed beyond the snow like a dull headache.

He gave up—the Battle of Gettysburg could be being fought down there but he'd hardly know it—and was just beginning to turn when the night became white. He could see his shadow, hard-edged, utterly black, and long, drawn across the mountain spire behind the dome and onto the distant clouds. For a moment, it seemed the snow vanished from the very air, and he braced himself for the inevitable blast that must follow.

It did not come, the light only seeming to change direction in random jerks across a small arc, and then flicked into nothing, leaving Carter with his night vision utterly gone. He closed his eyes and reopened them slowly, trying to recover it. Great, there was the ground in front of him. Not much, but he would take what he could get. He carefully found the cliff edge and looked down again. It seemed much darker now, but he thought maybe he saw a light veiled by the snow, a solitary headlight. Either Lovecraft wasn't dead, or there was a Fomorian on a snowmobile coming; he concluded the former was the more likely scenario of those. He went back to his chosen Kübelwagen and settled in to warm up while he waited on Lovecraft and Giehl.

The lights came back on in the dome. One of the assistants started to cheer, but—seeing he was alone in this—allowed his voice to fade as if he were doing so ironically.

"Finally," said Huber. "Dr. Weber managed it. It's a shame we can't wait for him to get back."

"We should," said Giehl. "It is only right he should be here at the end."

Huber shook her head. "It sounds as if the Americans won't let him get back to the dome entrance alive." As far as she was concerned, Weber's plan had worked brilliantly; he and the others had triumphantly taken the generator shack in a hail of bullets, and he was leading efforts to restore power, and not, for example, dead and hastily concealed behind a packing crate in the antechamber with a tarpaulin thrown over him. Giehl had emphasized how willing the Americans were to fire, and how difficult it would be to reach the shack. This had seemed wise when she said it in order to discourage anyone else from going out there, but now it denied her an opportunity to play for more time.

Huber signaled to one of the others. "Check the power leads and stand by to trigger."

Lurline Giehl found she was standing by the detector, the lie in a box that had dragged her from Germany first to Arkham and now to an American island most Americans couldn't find on a map. It seemed fitting, somehow.

"Power is nominal, Doctor," called back the assistant. "Capacitors now charging."

Giehl ran her hands along the upper edge of the detector and down the upper sides, and then gripped it as if she were leaning on a lectern. "Before you activate that, I have a few words I would like to say."

The others looked at her with astonishment. "A speech, Doctor?" said Huber. "I'm not sure this is the time."

Giehl looked sideways across the dome at Kurt. He was sitting behind one of the desks, barely aware of what was unfolding, a spent force. As she watched, he laid his head upon the desktop as if falling asleep. He would be no use to her, but neither would he prove an impediment. This was good. She was in control here. She returned her attention to Gabrielle Huber.

"Not a speech so much as a declaration, and this is the ideal time." She looked at them and saw she would have their attention for a few seconds. That was all she needed.

"My whole life, I have been loyal. From the Hitlerjugend when I was old enough—the day I first wore my Jungmädel uniform was one of the proudest of my life—through my studies and my academic career, every waking moment has been dedicated to the Party, the state, and the Fatherland." She unconsciously touched her left bicep where once an insignia had been worn upon a uniform blouse. *Blood and Honor.* She lowered her hand, and allowed it to slip into the pocket of her jacket. "I thought I understood what that meant, but—until today—I was wrong. Blood. Human blood. Worrying about a scruple of melanin when that blood is threatened is foolish. What a luxury it is to despise the Semite when our true enemies wouldn't know an Aryan from a chimpanzee."

Huber's expression was curiosity mixed with an indeterminate but growing rage. "What are you saying, Dr. Giehl?" she demanded with an awful propriety.

"I am saying that the most barbarous black and the vilest Jew are brother and sister to me in the face of what you plan. I stand with them, shoulder to shoulder. I stand with them."

"Then you'll be exterminated with them."

An electronic tone sounded. "Capacitors fully charged," called the assistant.

Huber glanced at the detector and Giehl was sure that she now knew it was a threat. Huber shouted, "Activate it!"

Giehl drew her pistol and shot the assistant where he stood. The others scattered, crying out in surprise and sudden fear. Huber's rage wouldn't let her. She stood her ground, drew her own sidearm, and fired before Giehl could react.

Being shot hurt her more than she had thought being shot might. She wasn't entirely sure where she'd been hit, but there was pain down her left side that made breathing hurt, like a spidery cramp. She could see Huber coming toward her, and she heard another shot. The pain suddenly became distant, the dome darkened with it. She heard a clatter and realized she had dropped her gun. She hadn't even felt it leave her grasp.

Giehl knew she was dying. One last thing. She put her weight on the detector, and it rolled obediently on its wheels to come to rest by the ZPE device. Huber was trying to reach the device's activation board, but the fallen assistant was in the way and she had to step on him. Lurline Giehl watched her stumbling like an idiot on the injured man's body, slipping in his blood, and she laughed. She was still laughing when she pressed the detector's power switch.

Chapter 36

THE TROUBLE WITH EMILY

Lovecraft arrived with Barnaby and drove around the back of the Kübelwagens to give them a little cover. Carter looked at Barnaby with barely concealed curiosity, a look the corporal caught. "I'm it, mate. The fucking Foams ambushed us."

Carter had never been in the military, but a police force is, by nature, paramilitary, and he could understand a little of what the corporal had been through. He also knew he didn't need to go through it again right then. Instead he said, "Shit, man," and Barnaby nodded and they understood one another.

"What's happening in Thunderdome?" asked Lovecraft, making a reference that only made sense in a different iteration of the world.

"The shack's too dangerous, near as damn unassailable with what we've got. Even with the corp, we'd probably get shot to fuck. Lurline's going to try and get us into the dome, though. Still a firefight, but at least we'll have surp—"

The explosion blew out both the antechamber's inner door and the main door. All three of them threw themselves to the snow as a first reaction and lay there, hands over heads, for several seconds until it became clear there wasn't going to be a secondary blast.

Lovecraft raised her head and found Carter crawling forward on his belly to get a clear look at the dome. "Dan? I guess she . . . I'm sorry, Dan."

He looked at her, emotions shifting across his face. "She meant to do this. She wanted me to stay outside. The whole time, she meant to do this."

Barnaby was looking from one of them to the other. "Who's this we're talking about?"

"Lurline Giehl," said Lovecraft, "one of the Reich scientists."

"Giehl. I know that name from the briefing. Abwehr. No known Thule connections."

"Yeah. A good Nazi."

The main door to the dome lay down the slope of the stoop, its hinges shattered and even the concrete where it had been anchored torn out. Rusted steel showed at the fractures, the concrete rotted around it.

"I'd never noticed that before," said Carter, climbing to his feet. "The door opens inward. If it was supposed to protect against missiles, wouldn't it open outward?"

"Shit!" Barnaby checked his watch. "Sir, do you still have the radio Lieutenant Green gave you?"

"Sure." Carter fetched it from the car he'd been using. "Need it to get picked up?"

"Yeah," said Barnaby, "that and stopping us all from getting blown to shit if the *Alacrity* hasn't already launched missiles."

He opened a frequency and hailed his submarine. Lovecraft

looked at Carter. "Shouldn't we be, like, getting out of here? Just to be safe?"

Barnaby shook his head. "They must have seen the explosion and not launched. I can't raise the CIS, but it's past the time *Alacrity* was scheduled to fire and we're not dead. Captain must have thought better of it, thank fuck."

A disturbance near the dome made them bring their weapons to bear. The door to the generator shack opened and three figures emerged. They seemed stunned, and Carter wondered if some of the blast had caused an overpressure wave to travel down the cable conduit between the dome and the shack. Stunned or not, he was past feeling compassion for the Thule agents.

"Get your hands *up!*" he shouted at them, advancing with his gun aiming at the nearest and more than happy to fire if they gave him any trouble.

Then he looked at the dome and came to a sudden halt.

He heard Lovecraft breathe, "The fuck you say . . ." behind him.

The dome was melting.

The concrete was cracking and falling inward like melting polystyrene. It had no right to look organic, but there was a strange sense of an egg hatching, of something struggling to emerge. A roaring glow was growing in the gloom of the antechamber and its shattered doors.

"The ZPE bomb," she said, and Carter knew they were going to die right there and right then. The dynamite hadn't destroyed the device; it had triggered it.

For the last time, he felt that hollowing sense of dislocation that Lovecraft called dreaming and as it gripped him, he thought, *And a lot of fucking good it's going to do me.*

The Germans by the generator shack had turned to see what was happening, and as realization took them, one swore, one screamed, and one said nothing because what was there to say? Destruction hatched from the dome, and the all-consuming blast swept out to burn them to gas. The light was so intense, the whole world turned to white, and stayed white as . . .

Carter expected death by evaporation to be less drawn out than this. Or perhaps it had been instantaneous, he was dead, and there was an afterlife after all. Given what he knew about the reality behind reality, it wasn't going to be an afterlife he would enjoy.

"What have you done?"

The voice was not angelic or diabolical, just curious and very slightly pissed. Carter turned and looked around.

The world was turned to white, pure cheap eighties-promo-video white, but that was a simplification. There were stark black lines and, as he started to see them as lines of perspective, he realized they were still at the summit of Mount Terrible, and all the color in the world had been leached away. Everything was either stark white or stark black, there was nothing else. He could see the unmoving sea, the land of Attu, even a few flakes of snow, rimed in black outlines like a ray-traced animation.

No, there was color. His gloved hands held color: the gun gripped in one was not the total black of the environment, but the black a gunsmith brings to metal. And there was Emily Love-craft, looking astonished. Carter was reasonably sure he looked astonished too. And there was Henry Weston, and now Carter was positive he must be looking astonished.

"What have you done?" said Henry Weston. His tone remained difficult to read. He could have been offering congratulations for the creation of a wonderful piece of art, or discovering that someone had just shat on his grandmother. He was looking at the blast wave emanating from the dome, the convulsed air, the concrete shrapnel hanging in the air, all rendered in hard white delineated by hard black.

"I . . . don't know," said Carter.

Weston frowned at him. "Not you." He turned his attention to Lovecraft. "*Her.*"

Lovecraft considered the question carefully, and shrugged.

"Miss Lovecraft"—Weston's tone was now peevish—"you have stopped time. I fear no shrug, no matter how eloquent, shall furnish me with significant explanation."

"Ah," said Lovecraft, "I can't have stopped time. How could we be seeing anything? Photons would have stopped traveling and we wouldn't be able to see anything." She raised her forefinger and wagged it at Weston. "Ah." She was smiling, which was inappropriate, but Carter did not blame her for it. They were clearly all insane at that endless moment. He was mad, she was mad, they were all mad there.

"Do you honestly think you're seeing with *photons* right now, Miss Lovecraft?"

Carter looked past him, and saw Corporal Barnaby crouched by one of the Kübelwagens, as frozen as anything else. At least he'd had the sense to take cover when the dome had started to collapse, and not stood there looking at it like a rube.

"How are you here, Weston?"

"When time ceases to be a consideration, one may be very nearly anywhere. I probably walked here. It's unimportant." He looked at the sky, and Carter and Lovecraft followed his gaze.

The clouds had boiled back, clearing a column of clear air a couple of miles wide centered over the dome. Through this tunnel in the sky the stars were brilliantly visible. They did not twinkle, and they seemed so close.

"Do you see Algol?" said Weston, and pointed. There were as many stars as grains of sand on the beach of the nearby bay, yet they looked, and they saw. "There is a body near it, astronomical in size if not nature. Tonight it glows a little dimmer there, because it glows so brightly *here*." He lowered his hand and looked to the dome. He walked slowly toward it, the dripping concrete, the jets of destruction, the flying debris hanging, the shards of fire jutting.

He paused by the three hapless scientists who had emerged from the generator shack just in time to be consumed by the explosion. One stood, mouth open, a chunk of concrete just protruding from his upper back to the left, pieces of scapula pasted across the shrapnel's face. Another man had been standing a couple of paces closer and the fireball had partially consumed him. Weston paused by him and examined the man's outstretched arm where it entered the fire, the interface of burning cloth and flesh, the fine tracery of vaporization, the just-visible stump of the bone drowned in incandescence like a charred stick in aspic. The last, a woman, was currently untouched, but stood a couple yards before the wall of waiting energy, her parka hood back, her eyes still focused on the dome that had ceased to exist a tiny fraction of a second before. Her face was a mask of wonderment, a child seeing her first firework. If and when time began again, her life would not last a single heartbeat.

Weston examined them like waxworks in a museum as he spoke.

"Miss Lovecraft, when I advised you read the *Necronomicon*—"

"You didn't advise me to do anything but sell it to you."

"What would I want a copy of the Dee edition for? Very well, then, when I induced you to read the *Necronomicon*, it was on the understanding that it would be as a useful primer in matters pertaining to your current situation. Not . . ." For once, he seemed short of words. He turned to Lovecraft. "Miss Lovecraft, how did you *do* this?"

"It wasn't really deliberate. You sure I did it and not Dan?"

Weston spared Carter a withering look. "I would think not. Mr. Carter's talents lie elsewhere. This is your doing. The principles lie within your *Necronomicon*, but I never anticipated you would understand them."

This rankled Lovecraft. "You saying I'm too stupid to understand it?"

"Ms. Lovecraft, it is reasonable to say that your entire race—and to forestall a misapprehension I must emphasize I mean *Homo sapiens sapiens* in its entirety and not any particular racial grouping—is stupid. But then, stupidity is such a relative term.

I speak from experience when I say that any number of people have read one or other versions of the *Necronomicon*, a handful have understood it well enough to gain some knowledge, rather fewer well enough to see opportunities to power in that knowledge, and a grand total of none have stopped time with it. How did you?"

Lovecraft looked uncomfortable. "There was . . . maybe seventy pages in, there was a story about birds hiding in the grass. The way it was written, it got me thinking."

"And?"

"So I made a diagram."

"Wait," Carter said, "you got the idea to make that mess of string in your house from a story about birds?"

"It's not a story," said Weston. His eyes never left Lovecraft. "It's a metaphor."

Lovecraft scoffed. "Well, duh."

"Miss Lovecraft, I see I have sold you short. I never anticipated you being able to act upon some of the knowledge in that book, simply because nobody else ever has. That was an oversight. We now find ourselves in a unique situation."

"If Emily wasn't supposed to really understand what the book was about and just use it as some sort of monster-spotting guide, we'd be dead by now," said Carter.

Weston nodded. "Yes."

"You motherfucker, Weston. You sent us out here to die."

The insult entirely went by Weston, who had never had a mother. "That's not true, Mr. Carter. I expected you would probably die, but that's hardly the same thing. And, really, isn't ensuring that the Fold remains viable worth the sacrifice of a few lives?"

"I notice none of them were yours."

Weston raised his eyebrows. "Well, of course not. What would the point of that be? I am far too important, Mr. Carter. I thought I had intimated that previously, but repetition can be so important. There are, to use a vast simplification, politics involved. I am doing my best to keep the situation here under control. I am personally very opposed to the extermination of the human race."

"Gee," said Lovecraft. "Thanks."

"So, we're just pawns?" said Carter.

"No, no, no. They"—he indicated the Thule agents—"are pawns. He"—he walked over to the Kübelwagen behind which Barnaby sheltered and stood over him—"is a pawn. You two"—he considered for a moment—"are more in the nature of knights. Useful, if somewhat eccentric. Such an awkward situation. Still, a resolution is in the offing."

"A resolution?" Lovecraft glanced at Carter. "What sort of resolution?"

"A negotiated one."

"You're going to negotiate with somebody to stop us being blown to pieces by a ZPE explosion?"

"Miss Lovecraft, I am currently negotiating exactly that. You are laboring under many misconceptions. Firstly, the 'explosion' is anything but. The device must have malfunctioned. It is currently acting as a gate, and an entity is in the process of being drawn through. It does not essentially wish that, so I am discussing options with its representatives to put it back."

"It can't just . . . stop?" asked Carter.

"It lacks the intelligence to do such a thing. With great power often comes great irresponsibility, a principle one observes often enough among people. Secondly, I am not *going* to perform these negotiations, as I already *am* performing these negotiations. I appreciate that you are probably experiencing this conversation as a series of linear events, but we have always been talking and always shall, because time is at a halt. The negotiations to which I refer were concluded in the same instant they began. *This* instant. Presently, you will perceive me telling you that they were successful and you will be relieved, because it means this island will not cease to exist and you along with it." He paused as if listening. "There we are. The negotiations are successfully concluded."

Carter looked at Lovecraft. She rumpled her nose. "A spoiler alert would have been nice."

"Now all that remains is that Miss Lovecraft undo what she did and the universe shall move on again." He crossed his arms and looked expectantly at her.

"I have no idea how I did that."

"I know. And you will have no idea how you undo it, either. It might take you a while, but, as you've seen, having all the time in the world and having none at all can be very much the same thing."

The light flashed into darkness, and—in the closing funnel of open sky, Algol seemed to grow a little brighter.

Two of the Thule agents fell to the floor. Time was moving again.

The last Thule agent stood gasping. "What happened?" She stumbled over her words. "What—"

Henry Weston stepped up behind her and, with great economy of movement, snapped her neck. He turned to Carter and Lovecraft and raised his hands apologetically. "Part of the terms, I am afraid. No witnesses with the exception of yourselves. Bother."

Barnaby stood from where he had been crouched and leveled his rifle at the man in the staid yet expensive suit standing in the snow in his staid yet expensive Oxfords. "Who the fuck are you?"

"La," said Weston. "Kindly do not fire. I like this suit."

"Not him," said Carter. "He's with us."

"A deal is a deal, Mr. Carter. I cannot go chopping and changing as I wish. No witnesses to what has occurred here. The complications, the ramifications, hardly bear consideration. It is a necessity that Corporal Barnaby be collaterally damaged."

"No." Lovecraft stepped into Weston's path. "He helped me, I helped him. I didn't risk my life just to stand by and let you kill him. Not happening, Weston."

"Him?" Barnaby raised his weapon and sighted on Weston. "Like to see him try."

Carter raised his hands in a warning motion to the commando. "Don't man. Just don't."

Weston looked at her sadly. "I am truly regretting ever encouraging you to study that book, madam."

"Tough shit. I'm not moving on this. You decollateralize him or you're playing chess with a two-knight handicap."

"Be reasonable, Ms. Lovecraft. He is not even important."

"Importance is such a relative term."

Weston nodded, accepting the point. "As you wish, Miss Lovecraft, but he must come with me now. Now that we have time once more, it is short. The sun will rise soon and the site must look as if the ZPE device simply malfunctioned by then."

"What about the people at the settlement? They know the Thule people tried something."

"Well, yes, but that's hardly of great moment. There will be strongly worded intergovernmental communiques and the Reich will look more closely at Thule infiltration of the Ahnenerbe. Hardly before time. The theory will be that some overenthusiastic Thule agents tried to weaponize the ZPE device and blew themselves up in the process. The Reich knows more of the truth, but not what actually happened here. As far as their government knows, this was a legitimate experiment to make zero point energy a viable asset and not simply a weapon they're not supposed to have."

"I have to report in," said Barnaby.

"Of course you do, but let's get you off the island, hmmm?" Weston went to climb into one of the Kübelwagens. "If you're caught here, an unauthorized, armed British soldier on U.S. soil, think of the embarrassment to your country." Barnaby lowered his gun. Weston opened the passenger-side door and patted the passenger seat. "Good. Now let's hurry along, shall we? I'm not really meant to be here, either."

Lovecraft stepped forward. "You won't hurt him? You promise?"

"The corporal shall live, Miss Lovecraft. You have my guarantee. I have transportation already organized from the eastern bay. I shall leave the car parked by the old quay."

Before they could ask him what kind of transportation was waiting for him, Weston gave a wave and drove away. He took the first corner faster than Carter would have dared on snow, but the vehicle stuck to the surface as if glued to it, and was gone in a moment.

They went to the cliff edge to watch the headlights swing around the mountaintop, and then descend the switchback to the road below.

"We don't know what the fuck he is," said Carter.

"No. We don't. The only reason I can think of him kind of loosely as an ally is that he hasn't killed us."

"Yet."

"Yet." Lovecraft looked into the slowly brightening eastern horizon. "This was a weird night."

The world turned, and the new day began.

Chapter 37

THE BANALITY OF EVIL

Director Heinz Mühlan had spent a great deal of the telephone conversation saying, "Yes, Minister." He concluded it with, "I shall look into it immediately, although frankly . . . ," at which point he paused because the minister had already rung off. He put the receiver down slowly and looked across the room at his secretary. She ignored him entirely, continuing to type as she had done without pause during the slightly fraught conversation he had just endured.

"Irmgard," he said quietly.

The typing stopped instantly. "Yes, Director?"

"Ask Obersturmbannführer Voight to meet me in the chamber, please."

Irmgard—dear, sweet, terrifyingly efficient Irmgard—was already reaching for the telephone as she said, "At once, Director."

Voight was already waiting, key in hand, by the chamber door by the time Mühlan arrived. He greeted him with a nod, unlocked it, and entered first. As he reached for the light switches, Mühlan said, "No, don't bother, Axel. The windows and the flame will suffice."

He locked the door behind them as per routine, turned to take in the chamber, and sighed. "Take a seat. We have things to discuss."

Voight did as he was invited, sitting at one of the chamber's twelve stations, taking his cap off and dropping it to the floor by the stone bench as he did so. "Seidr?"

"Seidr." Mühlan took a seat at the station to Voight's right. "I have just had a very one-sided conversation with the minister of foreign affairs. It seems that the Americans are furious about the murder of one of their citizens on American soil by a member of the Reich's contingent on the zero point energy project." He said these last few words in a tone of high irony. "I gather they're most angry that the guilty party then went up the mountain and blew him- or herself up—the murderer's specific identity is unknown—along with most of the mountaintop."

"The device worked, then? Surely that's all that's important?"

"The device detonated, but the causal ambiguity has *not* been closed. I do not know why, but, given that two of the American agents were overheard using a British intelligence term, we may assume that either they or a British team caused this disaster. The site itself is compromised, both in terms of security and esoterically. It is utterly useless to us now. We shall just have to find another, somehow. We shall seek"—his eyes sought out the flame—"guidance."

"I must admit, I was looking forward to the end of the monthly procedure. It's very inconvenient." Voight sighed. "Very well; I shall maintain shipments from the east. What about the Americans?"

"Oh, they'll bluster for a while, be given a few sweet things to help them get over it. You know what children they are."

"No, I meant the American agents. What do we know of them?"

"Oh, them? Apparently detached assets of the OSS, but our OSS sources say they've never heard of them or this 'CIA' they claim to belong to."

"Really?" Voight frowned. "You accept that?"

Mühlan shrugged. "They've always been reliable before. They seemed bewildered even by the question. I would have assumed they were independent contractors, but if that's so, their covers are remarkably deep and detailed."

Voight looked at him with interest. "What alternative is there?"

Mühlan did not reply, but his troubled expression spoke of a forming conjecture. Voight understood then, and rested the back of his head against the wall, looking up into the middle distance. "Ah. Fuck. A war in heaven."

"Perhaps," said Mühlan, although he believed it to be true. He looked at the flame. If one were to look into the night sky with a very good telescope and seek out Algol, one might see near it a glowing body of exactly the same color. "Perhaps."

IN SHALLOW WATER

The scientific community on Attu Island was withdrawn at speed when the U.S. government was alerted to events there. There were no Germans left to evacuate, only the American contingent, one of whom left in a body bag. All German vessels were absolutely forbidden to enter into American territorial waters throughout the Pacific, a state of affairs that persisted for several weeks until matters were settled behind closed doors. The official story was that an argument had escalated until a member of the Reich's group suffered some form of breakdown, killed one of the Americans, and then sabotaged the experimental ZPE generator housed at the summit of Mount Terrible, resulting in an explosion that killed the murderer and all of his compatriots. Research on ZPE was halted for the time being, it now being regarded as difficult to control and potentially highly hazardous.

The settlement buildings were not removed, but used for a military presence while the island was scoured for clues. What they found was interesting if impenetrable. Of particular note was a series of deep, overlapping, hemispherical hollows in the rock not far from the mountain's approach road. They baffled the volcanologists and geologists to whom they were shown, who theorized about ancient exposed gas bubbles, but seemed unconvinced by their own conclusions. They also found what looked like marks on the rocks around the area that seemed to have been made by bullets, yet no bullets or shell casings could be found even after a painstaking forensic search of the area. All such researches and observations were rendered into a detailed report that was subsequently delivered by the director of the Military Intelligence Corps to the joint chiefs of staff, his counterparts in the OSS and FBI, and the senior advisor to the president. No specific executive action was sanctioned by that meeting, only increased vigilance. Between every line of the report was the ineffable sense of a narrowly dodged bullet. The brass returned to their assorted offices troubled, their awareness piqued. Presently, funds were released to special departments scattered throughout the military, intelligence, and security apparatus.

The report, and the research that led to it, had been painstaking, but it had missed a couple pieces of evidence. It could hardly be blamed for missing either, given where they were.

In the waters of the southern end of the eastern bay, some ten yards below the low-tide mark, lay an abandoned SA-80 assault rifle of British design and manufacture. Its magazine was almost full, and its cross-bolt safety engaged. Crabs scuttled across it and barnacles made it their home.

On precisely the same line of longitude, approximately four

hundred miles from the north pole, a frozen corpse lay on the ice. There was no way of knowing it by simple examination, but it was frozen long before it hit the ground and partially smashed upon impact. Despite the damage, it was still clearly that of a Caucasian male in his midtwenties who, antemortem, had been in good physical condition. The body had been stripped of all clothing, although, as no attempt had been made to remove fingerprints or teeth, whether this had been an attempt to conceal the dead man's identity was unclear, but seemed unlikely. It also seemed unlikely that the man had been alive even before being frozen and dropped from a considerable height into the white desert. The top of the skull had been removed flawlessly in a smoothly curved line that ran across the occipital ridge and around the brain pan to the nasofrontal suture and around again, totally excising the frontal, parietal, and occipital bones.

Of the brain and brain stem themselves, there was no evidence whatsoever.

LOVECRAFT'S ART PROJECT

There had been questioning. Dear Lord, but there had been questioning. When the remnants of the ZPE project were air-ferried out from Attu to Adak Island, there were several police officers and a federal marshal waiting for them. The marshal did some interagency voodoo that made the cops shy away and conducted all the interviews herself. Carter asked her why was she handling an investigation when that wasn't really a marshal's job, and she just smiled and said, "Special executive powers." It was at this moment that Carter realized she was a marshal in name only and that he and Lovecraft might be a very long way up Shit Creek indeed with only a cocktail stick for a paddle.

The questioning had taken a long time, but he and Lovecraft had come up with a story that was pretty much the truth except for skipping why the Germans had done what they did, and the

British, and the Fomorians. Now Lovecraft had never ridden the snowmobile down the mountain by herself, and they had no idea how that scientist's neck had come to be broken. Guess it was just a freak effect of the blast. It could hardly have been them, after all; they'd admitted straight up about Carter having shot Decker, so why lie about the dead woman? How do you break somebody's neck with your bare hands, anyway? You see it in films, but that's films. Wouldn't it take a lot of strength? I mean, her head was cranked around by maybe 150 degrees. How can a person do that? *Why* would anyone do that when they had a perfectly good gun in their hands and had solid grounds of self-defense to use it?

The marshal made some notes and moved on.

When they arrived in Anchorage, they went through the whole thing again. "We told all this to the marshal back on Adak," complained Lovecraft to the detective taking her statement. "Why can't you guys coordinate more?"

"What marshal on Adak?" said the detective.

Finally, they had been shipped back to Arkham on the university's dime. They got the impression that the university was long used to shipping staff back from disastrous expeditions. Certainly the procedures seemed to be well practiced.

Carter was offered his job in campus security back, but he regretfully declined, privately citing to the sarge bad associations with the place as his main reason. The sarge said he was sorry Carter wouldn't be returning, but he could understand that. They parted with a handshake and a promise to have a drink sometime that they both knew would never be honored.

Lovecraft returned to her house and didn't go into her study for three days. She kept thinking over what she could remember of her ancestor's stories. Keziah Mason, Asenath Waite (she recalled the occupants of Waite's Bill and knew the name was no coincidence), Wilbur Whateley: two witches and a wizard. What they had in common was forbidden knowledge. She had always pictured them poring over ancient manuscripts, fiddling about with dead frogs and alembics, doing all the wizard stuff, like they were at Hogwarts.

Lovecraft paused at this thought; the absence of the Harry Potter books in the Unfolded World had deprived her of any number of cultural references.

Like Hogwarts, then, whatever that was. But now she saw it wasn't true. Yes, there was a surface veneer of plain or only lightly coded information in the *Necronomicon*, but its true power was what swam beneath the textual surface. Ideas, connections, paradigms, all ticking away, hidden between the lines, between the words, between the letters, just waiting for somebody to be stupid enough to look at them in the right way or the wrong way and for the knowledge to squirt up from the page, in through the eyes, and fuck up the reader for all eternity. Lovecraft had thought she was sitting down to read the Unfolded World's *Monster Manual*, and instead turned herself into a witch. Nicely played, Emily. You're the champ.

The proof of it was inside her study and she feared those lengths of string crisscrossing the room more than she had ever feared anything else in her life. She had been blasé about the Fomorians. An intelligent species, entirely alien to humanity, and she had plowed into the middle of them like she'd been playing a first-person shooter. Even now, she could not think of them with anything other than a sense of pity. Stupid cannon-fodder in somebody else's war. Who that somebody or something or whatever might turn out to be was probably a bad thing. She'd find out eventually, though. Her options now consisted entirely of playing the game or killing herself. If the *Necronomicon* had done as big a job on her as its reputation suggested, she couldn't even be sure the latter course would be permanent. So, play the game, then. There, just on the other side of the Fold, was the promised land. She had promised it to herself, and she was going to get there somehow. Now she and Carter knew there were other players, probably lots of them, and this wasn't a game where the losers got a pat on the back and commiserations. This was to the death, or something like it, and in this game, knowledge was a weapon.

On the fourth day back, the news broke. The British Admiralty regretted to report that the hunter-killer submarine HMS *Alacrity* had been lost with all hands while on maneuvers in the Atlantic. They went into no further details, for "operational reasons."

For her sake, for Carter's, and for the Folded World, she could not afford to go unarmed. Emily Lovecraft opened the door to her study, and entered.

ANOTHER DAY, ANOTHER DOLLAR

Carter had invested in blinds for his office in Red Hook. Business was currently moribund, the case-related e-mails and mail he had found on his return consisting of the tying up of old work. There was an unexpected check from Miskatonic U, an *ex gratia* payment for his service and actions in the defense of the university staff in the Aleutians. He put it to one side. He would find a suitable charity to give the money to. He could never take it himself without the shade of Nick Bowles haunting his conscience.

What else, then? The casework cleared, he found an e-mail from Harrelson complaining that he had tried to write to Carter several times while he was on Attu, but the settlement's bandwidth restrictions had meant his e-mail had bounced thanks to the size of its hefty attachment. After the Jenner incident, Harrelson had looked into the background behind the removal of Dave Koznick from his job at the high-energy physics lab after he suffered some sort of breakdown, the incident that precipitated Jenner's little piece of domestic terrorism.

Harrelson had found nothing unusual in Koznick's record and Koznick himself was currently still in a mental health facility as he was considered a danger to himself. Harrelson concluded that, in his professional nonmedical opinion, Koznick was just a regular Joe who'd had a stress-related breakdown thanks to holding down multiple jobs. If Carter wanted to draw his own conclusions, Harrelson had helpfully if illegally scanned and attached the report to the e-mail.

Carter looked at the face of Dave Koznick and recognized him as the ghost he had seen in the lab.

Of course it was. He realized he'd suspected it right from the first. Some sort of bleed across the Fold, maybe? Over there, Koznick was having an easy time in his job. No Nazis to watch over, no weird science, no Arkham, no Miskatonic U. Just good old Clave College in good old Providence, and that one freaky night where he thought he saw—just for a second—the ghost of a security guard. Man, these empty buildings can get to you sometimes if you let them.

Carter went to the window and looked out across the parking lot and into the dull New York afternoon, overcast and drizzling steadily. He wondered, not for the first time, if he was truly insane by now. He was sure he knew truths that no one else knew. Wasn't that how some insane people thought? He sensed things others didn't, felt things others didn't, saw things . . .

He had no idea which sense warned him. His hackles did not rise in anything but the metaphorical sense, his ears did not keen, no prickling sixth sense troubled him, and yet he suddenly knew.

He turned to look at his desk.

"Hello, Mr. Carter," said Weston. He was sitting on the client's side of the desk, wearing an overcoat, his briefcase across his knee, and his hat on the desktop. He seemed to be bone-dry.

Carter took a breath through his mouth and exhaled it through his nose. He walked back to his desk, and sat.

Weston smiled, a sketch of an expression, and opened his briefcase. "I have a job for you."